Camden Corners
A Short Story Collection
by Jane O'Brien
Copyright 2011 Jane O'Brien

Dedicated to my sister-in-law and friend, Dorothy Taffner who encouraged me to try my hand at publishing these stories. My son, John O'Brien who started me on the path to self publishing. My daughter, Christine Wride who sings my praises and buys my books. My son, Tom O'Brien who thinks it's great his mother is an author and my husband, Dave O'Brien who wholeheartedly supports my efforts, reads my stories and shares his computer with me. I love you all.

Camden Corners

A New Beginning

Emma Patterson works for the Greensboro Weekly News and Record. Greensboro is a small Community located on the shores of Lake Greensboro. Emma's position with the paper is a jack of all trades with only herself and the editor, Mr. Harvey Wilson. Mr. Wilson is a crotchety old man and doesn't see any reason to update his equipment or expand the paper to include anything but the fishing report and his editorial which is often the combined opinion of his fishing and checker playing cronies as they while away the hours at their favorite fishing spot or playing checkers by the pot belly stove in Patterson's General Store. Emma is gathering advertising orders for this week's edition. One request is announcing the sale of the Looking Back Antique Shop in Camden Corners. Something in that ad makes Emma stare at it again and again. A feeling of deja vu comes over her. The strange thing is that Emma has never been to Camden Corners. Emma has always enjoyed shopping for antiques, As a little girl she often joined her grandfather on trips to the country when one of the old timer's belongings were put on the auction block for payment of back taxes or because the owner had passed on. Emma always felt a sadness as she walked through the old houses and barns knowing in her young heart that someone had been forced to give up their special things. Grandpa Amos sympathized but told her the treasures would give pleasure to someone new for many years to come. Grandpa owned the general store in Greensboro and the building it was in. The entire upstairs and most of the attic and basement were filled with treasures he had accumulated through the many years of his scavenger hunts. For several years he had a very active business going but as his health started to deteriorate and his mind wasn't quite as sharp as it once had been. Grandpa seemed to buy more items than he was able to sell. With Emma's keen eye, she was able to discern the valuable items from the junk. Grandpa refused to admit that he would ever buy something that held no value so everything stayed put and even the fine furniture, lamps and vases were hidden beneath a layer of dust and junk.

It was nearing the end of March during an early spring snowstorm when Grandpa took his last breath. Emma was sad but she knew Grandpa was in a better place and would be reunited with his beloved wife, Flora. After the memorial service, the townspeople met at the General Store with everyone bringing their favorite dishes. Music was playing in celebration of life that was fitting for the jolly fellow who loved a bargain.

Emma hadn't thought much about what was going to happen to the store or the building her grandfather had left behind much less the contents. Mr. Wilson pulled Emma aside and informed her that he held the deed on the property and he would be taking possession of the entire building the following Monday. Emma couldn't believe her ears. This was Grandpa's store, he had built it with his own hands from the ground up. He and Grandma had lived in the quarters above the store from the first day they had become husband and wife. Mr. Wilson, with a smirk on his face showed Emma the deed that was signed over to him just a week before. Emma knew Grandpa wasn't thinking clearly but didn't realize the extent of his deterioration. The document was signed and sealed and the witnesses included the names of Mr. Wilson's checker playing friends. Emma recalled overhearing Mr. Wilson ordering several new and very expensive fishing poles in the last few weeks. Now she knew who the recipients of those fishing poles were. Mr. Wilson also told Emma that the contents of the building must be moved out by 8:00 on Monday or everything would be destroyed and she would be paying the cost of the removal.

Emma's mind was racing. How would she be able to move everything from this building in just a few days and what would she do with it? Her dear friend Lily Kramer was helping clean up the last of the remains of the party and noticed Emma's ashen face. Emma told Lily what had happened and her friend was ready with a solution. Lily's Uncle Jonas lived on a farm just outside of Greensboro. He was in the process of selling off the farm animals before he and his wife Ethel retired from the farming business and moved to Camden Corners to be closer to their daughter Susanna and their grandchildren. There were several empty barns and Lily was certain her Uncle, a very generous fellow, would be happy to let her store the items in the barns.

Nettie Dawson happened to overhear the conversation. She knew what Mr. Wilson was capable of and wasn't surprised that he had taken advantage of Grandpa Amos and was now taking advantage of Emma.

Nettie gathered up the remaining townsfolk and came up with a plan. Tomorrow morning, as soon as the sun was up everyone would load up their wagons with everything in the store that wasn't nailed down and deliver it to the farm. Seth Greenfield was already on his way to the Fulbright farm to inform Jonas what was going to be taking place. Not surprisingly, the Fulbrights opened their barns and their arms to help Emma out of the mess she was in. Emma would also be without living quarters and Ethel Fulbright was busy dusting her daughter's old room so that Emma would have a place to sleep.

The next morning the town was a bustle of activity as the shelves of the store were cleared, the living quarters emptied and all the treasures Amos had stored were removed and placed carefully on one wagon after another. After each wagon made its delivery, they came full circle and reloaded. Nettie supervised the whole process and by late afternoon, everything was out of the building including a stray peanut that had fallen behind the counter.

Emma was very grateful to her friends for all of their help but felt a sadness when she walked around Grandpa Amos' store for the last time. It was time to move on though and on her way out of the store she noticed a copy of the Greensboro Weekly sitting on the bench just outside the door. Without thinking, she picked up the paper and realized she would now be out of a job because there was no way she would be able to work for that curmudgeon again.

Lily was waiting to drive Emma in her horse and buggy to her temporary home on the Fulbright farm. All of her friends from Greensboro were at the farm with tables of food set up in one corner of the only barn that wasn't filled with items from Grandpa's building. Mr. Warren was there to greet Emma and let her know that he would be buying all of the merchandise from Grandpa's store. He thought she might like to keep the old cash register as a memento. He paid her generously for his purchases. No one knew that Grandpa had helped him out of several jams through the years when things weren't going smoothly for him. Emma was learning more about her Grandfather's generosity every day and realizing what a truly remarkable man he had been. When she was afraid he was taking advantage of people who were losing their homes, he was actually paying more money for their belongings than they were worth. So many families had benefited from him buying their treasures and adding a bit extra to the purchase price enabling them to settle with their debtors. In helping out Emma, half the town was showing their gratitude to her Grandpa and the other half simply liked Emma and old Amos. Soon after most of the guests had departed for home, Emma walked Lily to her buggy in order to get the overnight bag she had packed. Lily picked up the forgotten newspaper, it slipped out of her hand and opened to the ad Emma had placed regarding the sale of the Antique Shop in Camden Corners. Emma and Lily looked at each other and knew at that moment that they would be on their way to Camden Corners in the morning.

It was a crisp day. Emma and Lily were on their way to Camden Corners to check out the Antique Store that was for sale. They were both full of anticipation and in their hearts they knew this venture would be a turning point in their lives. Emma was grieving for her grandfather and Lily was searching for adventure. Being Emma's friend for all of her 22 years she had tagged along on enough of Grandpa's treasure finds that she was able to spot a genuine antique when she saw one. She didn't realize this at the time, but she had seen some beautiful pieces of furniture being transported from the old general store in Greensboro to the Fulbright farm and instinctively knew that some of those items were valuable. Lily had a good head for business and was the head of new accounts at the Community Savings Bank. She wasn't unhappy in her job but she was looking for a little more excitement than she was finding in Greensboro. She found herself restless and dreaming of hopping a freight car and traveling out west to discover gold. She knew this wasn't going to happen but it was fun to dream. Young women her age didn't seek adventure, they were happy to settle down with a kind man and give her life to caring for him and raising his children. It wasn't that she was lacking male attention. She had several would be beaus but none of them were of interest to Lily. Emma on the other hand wasn't looking for adventure. She was happiest when she was scouring the vacated buildings and homes near the river. The spring floods and lack of work had driven most of the river dwellers from their sparse homes. Because they would leave in a hurry thanks to Mr. Harvey Wilson who was always at their door looking for his rent money, they would leave behind some of their most prized possessions. Emma would gather up all she could find and bring them home with her posting a note by the post office window in case one of the vagabonds happened to see it and wanted to claim their forgotten items.

The ladies finally arrived in Camden Corners and both were enchanted with the quaint village at first sight. Emma spotted the antique shop and knew this was her destiny. They hopped out of the buggy and gingerly approached the front door. Within a couple of minutes, a petite lovely woman who was obviously with child greeted them. She introduced herself as Edwina Van Dyke, sole proprietor of Looking Back Antique

Shop. She invited the girls into the shop. They were overjoyed at first sight. Miss Edwina Smythe had owned the shop for 15 years after her parents had passed on and she was beginning to feel as though she was one of the antiques she was always trying to sell. It was in early January of the previous year when Mr. Wallace Van Dyke entered her store to purchase a settee for his ailing mother. Edwina and Wallace were immediately smitten with each other. Wallace sought out Miss Edwina's only remaining male relative, her Uncle Clarence, and asked if he may be allowed to court the fair Miss Edwina. They were united in marriage on Valentine's Day and the following month Edwina was expecting their first child. Edwina's inventory was somewhat diminished as she had other things on her mind. She was willing to sell the building and all of it's contents for a price that was well within Emma and Lily's budget and before they left the store, they had reached an agreement. Emma and Lily were beside themselves with excitement. Both knew they had taken a risk but both felt it was a risk worth taking.

Everything happened quickly after that. Edwina was anxious to finalize the sale of the shop in order to be home to await the birth of her baby. Emma and Lily were anxious to start their business. They were delighted with the design of the store. The shop had a bay window with ample room for several small tables that would be perfect for serving dainty desserts and sweets with a cup of tea in the afternoon. The girls toiled all through the summer into the fall fixing up the shop just the way they wanted it with new wallpaper and sparkling woodwork, new fixtures and an intimate, cozy tea room. They had arranged with Diana of Warm Hearth Bakery and Maddie from Tempting Treats Candies, who were delighted the girls chose their establishments, to provide sweets for their customers. After the shop was just the way they wanted it, they started making daily trips to Greensboro to select pieces from Amos' collection. They were surprised to discover a beautiful mahogany Chippendale dining set, several Louis Phillipe fruit wood chairs and a Gothic revival tapestry settee. They cleaned and polished each piece lovingly and were rewarded with the beautiful results. There were full sets of Mason dishes in the Belvedere pattern, several sterling silver cigarette cards, an 18K Fusee pocket watch, every box and crate seemed to hold something unusual and valuable.

Uncle Jonas had been a farmer all his life but his hobby was repairing and refurbishing furniture. Ethel was an excellent seamstress and even with her eyesight not what it use to be, she could repair any piece of fabric to make it look like new. They were willing and more than anxious to lend a hand and their expertise as each piece was lovingly repaired and readied for display at the shop. Emma remembered the old cash register Mr. Warren had given her from Grandpa's store. Emma cleaned and polish the old relic and found that it was a beautiful addition to the counter in the new store. It made her happy to know that a little part of Patterson's General Store would now be with her in Camden Corners.

Open For Business

Finally, Looking Back Antiques opened for business under new management. Everyone in town was happy to see the shop taken over by Emma and Lily and couldn't wait to sit down with a cup of tea and enjoy the freshly baked brownies and delicious confections. The Antique store was a huge success. Word started spreading quickly and before long folks from the neighboring towns and eventually from nearby cities started frequenting the antique shop. The Fulbright farm was finally sold and Jonas and Ethel moved to Camden Corners. Jonas was happy to be on hand in the antique shop to greet customers and point out the beauty of each item in the store. Nobody realized how much old Amos had stored. There seemed to be a never ending supply of goods for Jonas to work on. Ethel loved being near her daughter and grandchildren. She was making friends quickly and enjoyed acting as hostess occasionally in the tea room. She wrote to Nettie Dawson excitedly telling her all about the shop and tea room. Nettie missed her dear friend and in a blink of an eye, she was on the train on her way to Camden Corners arriving just in time for tea. Nettie was a perfect match for the now bustling tea room. She was full of chatter and advice to all the patrons.

Emma, Lily and Jonas were working feverishly preparing the last of Amos' collection before the busy Christmas season began. They discovered there were very few pieces that couldn't be repaired or cleaned and sold as a valuable antique. Nettie and Ethel were delighted to find a huge crate filled with Tiffany lamps. They spent hours cleaning and shining each and every lamp while they talked about all of the Christmas celebrations they were looking forward to. Their first Christmas in Camden Corners was going to be a very happy one.

One afternoon, the Vicar Willard Duesenberry came into the shop to purchase a lace tea cozy for his faithful housekeeper, Mrs. Schrum. He saw her admiring it in the window one day last week and thought it would make a nice Christmas gift for her. Emma was having a difficult time opening Amos' old cash register and the vicar offered to take a look at it to see what the problem was. He discovered there was a tiny key that was lodged in the drawer. Emma couldn't understand why she didn't discover it when she so painstakingly cleaned and polished it. She took the key and set it aside wondering what the key fit and what it was doing inside the cash register. Another customer was inquiring about a Queen Anne sofa and Emma forgot about the key.

Harvey Wilson was sitting at his usual spot in the old general store cheating at checkers with his cronies. They knew he was cheating but also knew that if they called attention to it old Harvey would throw his considerable weight around and make trouble for his chums. The general store just wasn't the same now that Amos has passed on and it had been taken over by Harvey. The townspeople of Greensboro often traveled the distance to nearby Kendall to purchase their groceries and supplies at Silas Warren's store. Harvey did like to make a profit and didn't notice that he was losing customers one by one. George Whitfield had just returned from Camden Corners and was telling the group how busy the antique store was that Emma Patterson and Lily Kramer bought and how well they were doing selling Amos' things. Harvey's ears perked up.

"Excuse me gentlemen I have a little matter of thievery to check into. I do believe the junk Miss Emma stole out of this building was mine and I have the documents to prove it."

The small group was dumbfounded. This was low even for Harvey.

Emma and Lily were beginning to make a small profit in their antique business and finally had enough extra to bankroll them for their first scavenger hunt. They were anxious to start their journey before the heavy snows came. They took off leaving the shop in the capable hands of Jonas and the women. Susanna offered to pop in occasionally to check on things for them. The first time out they hit the jackpot. The hotel in Porterboro was going to be completely renovated and they were able to salvage almost a wagon full of treasures from there. They stopped at a farmhouse on the way to the next town and found many more items. With a few stops on their way back to Camden Corners they had filled their wagon to the brim and were giggling and laughing as they opened the door to their antique shop.

They were met with tearful eyes and worried faces and standing right smack in the middle of their store was Mr. Harvey Wilson with his smarmy lawyer, Caspar Dewitt standing next to him. Both were smirking as Caspar served the girls with a cease and desist letter demanding they lock the doors of the shop pending a lawsuit for ill gotten goods. Lily was fit to be tied and ready to flatten Mr. Caspar Dewitt but Emma's cooler head prevailed. She knew they would not be able to fight this fight in the middle of their store and accepted the papers asking them to leave and locking the door behind them.

"We need a lawyer and we need one quickly" Emma said.

Susanna, who happened to be in the shop when Harvey and Caspar walked in had already thought of that and had called Crowley law firm.

Mr. Oscar Crowley was a widower who owned the firm along with his very handsome sons, Robert and Richard. The elder Mr. Crowley was retired but lonely living in a big house by himself. He would find himself at loose ends and wander into the law office just to help out his boys. His office was always open to him and the boys enjoyed having their father around to help out with some of their more difficult clients. Oscar had a way about him that always calmed down the most frazzled and frustrated good folks of Camden Corners.

Susanna explained the situation to Mary, the firm's receptionist. Mary told Susanna to come right over and bring everyone with her. Mr. Oscar was in his office and would see them right away. Mary knew this was the sort of case Mr. Oscar would enjoy taking on. She knew from experience that Mr. Harvey Wilson didn't stand a chance against any one of the Crowley men.

The worried group walked into the law firm and Oscar stepped out of his office to greet them and introduce himself to everyone. Pausing for a moment when he looked into the tearful eyes of Miss Nettie Dawson. He invited them into his office as Mary was bringing in some extra chairs. Oscar knew they were upset and in his usual fashion was able to calm everyone's fears. He had dealt with Caspar Dewitt on a few occasions and knew him to be less than honest in his dealings and his choice of clientele. Oscar looked over the cease and desist letter and told them to feel free to open their doors again. He knew Caspar was using a scare tactic not necessarily a legal one.

Emma explained the situation and the threat made by Mr. Wilson that the contents of Amos' store would be destroyed at her expense if it was not removed. Emma was chastising herself for not getting a copy of the so called deed Mr. Wilson had shown her. Because of grief over losing her beloved grandfather and the shock of Mr. Wilson taking over the store, she wasn't thinking clearly.

Mr. Crowley was understanding of Emma's predicament and seething over the way she had been taken advantage of. He knew old Amos and knew what an honorable man he was. He assured her he would be securing a copy of the deed from the county court house and would get to the bottom of the matter. Emma and Lily were not in a financial position to pay for the services of an attorney. Their little shop was just beginning to turn a profit and they had spent that profit on their new purchases. Nettie spoke up saying she had a little money of her own and it would be her pleasure to pay the legal expenses to keep that snake, Harvey Wilson, out of their lives. Mr. Crowley had Mary draw up a retainer agreement with the amount of one half dollar as the retainer fee. He smiled at Miss Nettie and she blushed like a school girl finding herself wondering if there was a Mrs. Oscar Crowley in the picture.

It was too late in the afternoon for Oscar to make it to the county seat to check the deed to Amos' land but he thought he would check on precedents in one of his old heavy law books. Taking the book off the shelf, he happened to remember that he hadn't had a cup of tea this afternoon and wouldn't that hit the spot right about now? Lugging his oversized law book with him he donned his overcoat and top hat and walked around the corner to visit the Looking Back Antique Shop and the lovely Miss Nettie Dawson.

Nettie saw Oscar walk through the door and her heart skipped a beat. Oscar lost his beloved wife several years before and had not so much as glanced at another woman in all that time. There was something about Miss Nettie that the old gentleman found endearing. He felt like a schoolboy himself as he ordered a cup of tea with just a sliver of banana cake. He invited Miss Nettie to join him at the table.

He asked her what had brought her to Camden Corners and she explained that she had been a schoolmarm until she retired last year. She missed the children and having her very dear friend, Ethel move away was all she needed to make a change in her life. As a young girl she had loved Randolph Evans but three days before their wedding, he had been killed in a fire after heroically saving the lives of three small children and their mother. Her life had been full with so many students through the years. All of the children had loved Miss Nettie and she loved them as if they were her own. She'd had several suitors but none of them had measured up to Randolph. Until now, that is.

Oscar talked about his wife, Louise and what a happy life they had together. They had two active sons who followed in their father's footsteps and studied law. Robert and Richard were both unmarried and Oscar thought it was about time they settled down. Emma and Lily came to mind. What a pair of fine young ladies. Although he didn't need it, he may ask for both his son's assistance in girls' legal matter.

Nettie and Oscar sat and talked for well over an hour. Neither was aware of the time until the sun started to set.   Oscar wondered if Miss Nettie would be willing to join him for dinner at the Marino Trattoria. She, of course was delighted and happily accepted the invitation.   They had a lovely dinner and   Rosa, who could spot a romance blossoming, made sure they didn't lack for wine or delicious food.   She asked her her husband Eduardo to take a break from his kitchen duties to play a tune on his violin for the couple.   Eduardo was a very romantic fellow himself and enjoyed watching the couple as they gazed into each others eyes.

The following morning, the whole town of Camden Corners was abuzz with talk of the December romance between Oscar and Nettie.

Oscar visited the courthouse and secured a copy of the deed Harvey's lawyer had filed.   It was poorly written and it wouldn't be terribly difficult to disprove it's authenticity but it would take time to straighten the matter out and Oscar was hoping to spare the girls that frustration.   They had worked so hard and sacrificed so much to make a success of their shop. He would just have to get Robert and Richard involved.   They both happened to be in the office when Oscar returned from the county courthouse.   He spoke with them together explaining the situation. Richard left the office chuckling.

"That sly old fox, he obviously has something other than our legal expertise in mind for the Misses Patterson and Kramer."

"And I'm sure you will set the young ladies straight" replied his brother.

Robert was due in court shortly but Richard had some free time and decided to pay a visit to The Looking Back Antique Shop.   He was still amused at his father's obvious ploy as he entered the shop.   Emma was busy clearing off a shelf at the back of the store.   He spotted Jonas and laughingly told him he was here to check out the merchandise to see if they measured up to his usual standards.   His father was pushing him and Robert to find wenches and start producing grandchildren.   Suddenly a beautiful red haired girl popped her head up over the counter.   She was scowling and her face was getting redder by the minute.   Richard's face was as bright red as Lily's.   He didn't know what made him say something so crass.   He was about to apologize and beg forgiveness when a satin pillow came sailing through the air aimed directly for his head.   Emma heard the commotion and came running to the front of the store.   Lily was about to pick up a vase that was displayed on the counter when Emma caught her hand and rescued the vase and Richard's handsome face.   Jonas was speechless.   He had never heard a gentleman speak about a woman like that.   At least not in her presence.

Nettie and Ethel had been visiting with Maddie and Diana at one of the tea room tables. They told them that the rude young man was Richard Crowley. He sometimes puts his foot in his mouth but he is really quite a nice and genteel fellow. They explained that his father, Oscar was intent on getting his boys married off and that must have prompted him to speak in such a way. Emma's always cool head prevailed. She was able to calm Lily down somewhat and asked Richard if she could help him. Richard explained who he was and that he meant no disrespect towards either of the girls. He had a long complicated morning and his father was acting like a father and it had rubbed him the wrong way but that was no reason for him to have spoken as he did. Lily was enjoying his discomfort and decided to play the shrew for just a little bit longer. She couldn't help but notice that Richard had the most beautiful blue eyes she had ever seen. His shoulders were so broad, his teeth were so white, his nose was a perfect shape and his raven hair was full and thick. She didn't think she had ever seen a more handsome man.

Emma escorted Richard into the small office partly because she knew he would be talking about their legal trouble and partly to keep Lily away from the poor fellow for his own safety. She knew Lily would calm down but thought it best to give her a little longer to compose herself. Emma told Richard all that had transpired. His father had filled him in but he listened intently to Emma tell her side of the story once again. Like his father, Richard asked if Amos had written a Will or had put anything in writing before he became so ill. To Emma's knowledge, he hadn't. She knew Elmer Mayhew was an attorney and a good friend of Amos' but he had passed away 3 years ago. He had been semi-retired and Emma didn't know what had happened to all his files. He had never married and she didn't believe he had any living relatives. She called Jonas into the office and he couldn't give Richard any more information than that.

Richard was about to leave when he saw the beautiful girl he had insulted standing by the counter. He walked over to her to apologize. She picked up the vase again and he began to duck. Lily couldn't help herself, she started giggling. She told Richard she had never been referred to as a wench before but thought it sounded rather endearing coming from Oscar Crowley's son but she wouldn't recommend he use that term in her presence again. Richard couldn't help but notice that Lily not only had a beautiful face her figure was lovely although he didn't dare lower his eyes for fear of what she may do.

He said his goodbyes and turned to leave the shop when he realized suddenly that he had fallen in love for the first time in his life with the feisty redhead behind the counter.

He turned on his heel and said "I don't suppose you would be willing to go to lunch with an ill mannered lout like me?"

Lily wrapped her cape around her shoulders picked up her handbag and met him at the door. "Ill mannered you might be sir but a lout? Never!"

Emma knew her dear friend would never be the same. Nettie and Ethel, relieved that their young friend was in good hands bid goodbye to Maddie and Diana and went to the store room to carry a small crate to the front of the store. They expected to open it to find more beautiful Tiffany lamps but instead it held two identical mahogany boxes. They lifted one then the other out of the crate. They were both locked.

Key To The Future

After discovering two locked boxes, Nettie and Ethel looked for a key in the crate but there wasn't one there. They asked Jonas to take a look at the lock to see if he could open it. He did try but was afraid he would scratch or mar the boxes if he tried to force them open. Emma was nearby and wondered what they were doing. She wandered over and recognized one of the boxes. It held her grandmother's wedding dress.

When Emma was a little girl her Grandma Flora had promised she could wear the gown when she grew up and married. Emma felt tears welling in her eyes as she remembered the happy times she spent with Grandma Flora. Her parents had perished in a train accident when she was just a baby. Flora and Amos Patterson were the only parents she had ever known.

She wiped her eyes and suddenly remembered the key that she and the vicar found in the old cash register. She had put it in the drawer of the cash register and hurried to get it out. Jonas gingerly opened the first box. There was Grandma's wedding gown. Just as beautiful as she remembered it. Grandma had carefully folded it and wrapped it and it looked as lovely as it must have the day that Grandma wore it as she walked down the aisle. All the women were tearful at the sight of that dress. Emma thought of her dear Grandmother, Nettie thought of the love she had lost and Ethel remembered the day she became Mrs. Jonas Fulbright. Jonas cleared his throat and had to dab a bit at his eyes too. All in their own reverie, they suddenly remembered the other box. Again, being very careful, Jonas opened the second box. Inside was a stack of papers.

They began to look through the papers and discovered Amos had signed over all of his assets and worldly possessions to his wife Flora on their 50th wedding anniversary with a note saying, "All I am and all I have are because I was a smart enough fellow to marry the most wonderful woman God put on this earth."

Flora's Last Will and Testament was also in the box. She had bequeathed the general store and all her possessions to Emma.

Jonas called Oscar Crowley immediately. Oscar, never missing an opportunity, thought it best if Robert pay a visit to the antique shop with him. Oscar could detect a sparkle in his son's eye as he was introduced to Emma. The Crowley father and son read through the papers and both concluded that Patterson's General Store and building were not Amos' to sell when he was duped into signing the deed over to Harvey Wilson.

Both men immediately traveled to Greensboro to confront their learned colleague, Mr. Caspar Dewitt. As was expected, Harvey Wilson was furious, ranting and raving and threatening to take the matter to the Supreme Court.

Caspar found his courage and told the old goat to pipe down, face up to the situation and remove himself and his checkerboard from the premises. From that moment on, Caspar was a new man. His law practice began to flourish, he found himself representing the farmers and townspeople that Harvey had been swindling for years.

Harvey was a man without a friend. Even his old checkers pals were backing away. One morning he arrived at his newspaper office only to find four practically new, very expensive fishing poles resting at the front door.

Back in Camden Corners, Emma chose not to pursue any legal action against Harvey. She wanted the matter to be over and done with. Nothing could erase the wonderful memories she had of the General Store and she knew her grandfather would approve when she sold the store to Silas Warren at a very reasonable price.

Seth Greenfield was Silas' trusted assistant in his grocery store in Kendall and traveled six days a week back and forth from Greensboro to Kendall. He asked Seth how he would like to be the manager of the old Patterson's Grocery Store and building. Seth was overjoyed. He and Amy Marsh were planning a wedding in the spring. They would be able to live in the flat above the store and rent out the rest of the apartments. Silas planned to deduct a small amount of money from Seth's pay each week until he had enough to make a down payment on the property. Seth had become like a son to Silas and he would do his best to help the young couple along. Emma knew of the plan and wholeheartedly agreed with it.

Her heart was filled with happiness to know the walls of old Patterson's would be filled with love and laughter once again.

Lily and Richard had become inseparable. Helping Lily, Richard had even taken to sanding and staining the many finds that were to be sold in the antique shop. Lily, wanting to be close to Richard, helped search for precedents in the Crowley firm library. They were like two peas in a pod and ever since their first unfortunate encounter, there had never been an unkind word between them.

Emma was happy for her friend. Lily and Richard both thought Emma and Robert would be perfect together. Emma and Robert had become friends. Emma had been through so many changes in such a short time and Robert who had only passed the bar the previous June felt he needed to concentrate on his career. They would meet occasionally at O'Sullivan's Pub for lunch or dinner but simply as friends.

Emma learned of an auction that was being held in Kendall. Nettie had developed a fever and bad cough and Doc McMillan thought it best she stay in bed for a few days. Nettie argued that she was healthy as a horse and the girls needed her to watch the store while they went to the auction. Everyone agreed that Nettie was to follow doctor's orders.

Robert's schedule was rather light that week and Oscar offered to help with the cases that needed attention while Robert accompanied Emma to Kendall for the sale. They planned to leave at 8:00 sharp and be home with a wagon full of treasures before nightfall. Ethel packed thermoses of coffee, enough sandwiches to feed a troop of hungry scouts and bags full of cookies and candies. She made sure there were plenty of blankets to keep them warm. The sky looked a little menacing but the duo took off as planned. Jonas and Ethel stood arm in arm watching them travel down the road toward Kendall. Both were trying to hide their worry from the other.

Emma had the winning bids on almost every item she had chosen. Robert helped her load and cover the wagon securely. He found he was having a wonderful adventure and was impressed with Emma's know how and her professionalism.

They were laughing and joking with each other when snow started falling lightly and then heavier and heavier. Within the hour, the horses were having a difficult time making their way through the snow that was piling up. The wind started to howl. Robert had been in snowstorms like this before and knew it was going to be questionable whether they would be able to make it back to Camden Corners today.

They could see a small cabin less than a mile west of where they were and thought it might be best if they headed for the cabin instead of

18

following the road home. The cabin was abandoned and so was the barn next to it. The door to the barn was not locked and they guided the horses inside and patted them down as best they could with the blankets Ethel had insisted they take with them. There was enough room in the barn for the wagon so all of the purchases would be safe for the time being.

After the horses were settled, Robert and Emma made their way to the cabin. The door was locked but it didn't take Robert long to jimmy the lock. The cabin was cold but there was a fireplace and plenty of firewood. Robert started a fire and moved the big, over sized sofa in front of the fireplace. Before long, the cabin was warming up and the adventurers were famished.

"Bless Ethel for packing all these sandwiches." said Emma.

The wind was howling outside as Robert and Emma looked into the fire each with their own thoughts. Emma was feeling warm and it wasn't simply because of the blazing fire. Robert could smell a hint of lavender from Emma's golden hair as he was fighting the urge to take her in his arms. They looked at each other and as the flames from the fire shimmered on their faces, Robert lowered his lips to hers and the magic had begun.

They realized now what everyone in town already knew. Robert and Emma were in love. They agreed the timing wasn't right for either one of them but they knew they could never go back to being just friends.

The women folk in Camden Corners were beginning to worry. The snow was piling up and no sign of Robert and Emma. Oscar and Richard knew Robert would be able to handle any crisis. He had grown up in Camden Corners and heavy snow could often be the norm in this area. Because the ladies were concerned, the men decided to go out looking for the couple. The snow had let up somewhat when Oscar and Richard started their search. They were only a few miles out of town when they noticed smoke coming from a chimney at the old Whitehead cabin. They rode up to the cabin and heard the horses whinny in the barn. Oscar peeked through the window before knocking on the door and was delighted to see his son and Emma sitting together enjoying a nice warm fire and each other.

Emma and Robert were startled but happy to see their rescuers. Robert was surprised to learn they were so close to Camden Corners but not sorry they had found shelter at the old cabin.

The homecoming was a happy one. The couple was safe and their friends and family guessed they had finally admitted their true feelings for each other. Emma and Lily knew they had made the right decision to move to Camden Corners so many months ago.

GIRL

Joe and Diana Taylor had been married almost 5 years. They had not been blessed with children and were beginning to wonder if they would ever have the big family they both wanted. Joe was a fireman and Diana owned Warm Hearth Bakery in the village of Camden Corners They had known each other since they started kindergarten together at Camden Grammar School. Doc McMillan told them there was no need to worry that they would most definitely have their family one day. In the meantime, they had full and busy lives. Diana loved when the school children walked home each afternoon and set out a plate of cookies for them. Each child looked forward to passing by the bakery and choosing a delicious treat from the plate.

In the hills far above Camden Corners lived Earl Short and his daughter Iris. Iris had just turned 5 years old but nobody remembered the date of her birth.

Her mother Mavis was a bright young girl who found a package filled with books. They had accidentally dropped from a traveling salesman's wagon as he was making his way across the bumpy road near the shack she called home. Mavis hid the books and every chance she got she would pour over them until she taught herself to read. She lived in the world of Little Women and Jane Eyre and read them over and over again.

When Mavis turned 14, Maw told her it was time to marry and Earl Short had chosen her to be his wife and bear his children. Mavis knew she didn't have a choice and accepted her fate.

Mavis was calm during a very difficult labor and finally delivered a beautiful little girl she named Iris. Maw placed the baby in her arms and Mavis whispered a prayer that her daughter would be safe and grow up surrounded by love.

Earl arrived from tending his still just in time to see his wife close her eyes for the last time. He was furious that she hadn't given him a son and walked out of the shack without a backward glance at his daughter.

Maw did the best she could with the girl. Iris' name was never spoken. She was only referred to as "Girl". Paw rarely spoke to her at all and when he did he was issuing an order. Girl had taken after her mother in so many ways. She looked just like her and always was able to see the good in everyone and everything.

One day Maw started feeling poorly. She had always known about the books that Mavis kept hidden and showed Girl the hiding place. She wanted so much more for her granddaughter than she or her daughter had in life. Maw prayed Girl would find her way out of this place and discover whatever world there is beyond the hills. Maw passed away in her sleep several days later.

Earl was smoking his stogie next to his still one late autumn afternoon when a spark hit the still and it exploded and burned to the ground. He decided this was a sign to pack up his few belongings and leave the hills for the first time in his life. He'd heard talk of gold in the west and decided that was what he would do.

He would have to take Girl with him but she was getting old enough that she could start earning her keep. Early in the morning the pair started down the long road headed west. Girl was uncomfortable sitting in the back of the buckboard but she didn't complain.

After several hours they came upon the village of Camden Corners. Girl was enchanted. She had never seen anything like this before. Everything was so bright and clean unlike the drab and dusty cabin. The people were all talking and smiling at one another and looked so fancy. She looked down at her grimy little hands and hid them in her pockets. Paw got out of the buckboard and walked into a building called a P-U-B. Iris didn't know what a pub was but she knew better than to follow Paw. She looked across the street and saw a big white dog with black spots laying in the sun. She waited for Paw to return to the buckboard but he was gone an awfully long time. She couldn't help herself she just had to get out and pet the spotted dog. Iris sat down beside the puppy, she felt so warm to Iris's cold little body she cuddled up to her and fell asleep.

Paw didn't notice that Girl wasn't in the buckboard when he drove off down the street and out of town.

Two hours later, Sheriff Mendenhall came upon Paw's buckboard which had flipped over on a curve throwing Paw out and killing him on impact.

Girl woke up and saw that Paw and the buckboard were gone. She gave the loveable puppy a hug and started walking down the street.

She walked by Warm Hearth Bakery and there was a plate of the most wonderful looking treats on a plate. She knew she shouldn't steal but she was so hungry and those round things looked so good and smelled so wonderful. She took one off the plate and gingerly walked away.

She walked a little further down the street and came upon Nichol's General Store. Outside of the market she saw apples. There was an apple tree behind her home but they didn't smell as good as these. She helped herself to an apple.

She didn't feel so hungry anymore and wanted to visit with her new spotted friend again so she walked back to the big red building. The dalmatian saw her coming and came up to her licking her hand. Iris followed the dog into the building and saw she had her own pallet and was offering to share with her.

They sat together for a little while when someone called "Come here Girl".

Both the dog and Girl went running.

"Well, who have we here?" said Joe.

"My name is Girl, my Paw is taking us to find gold"

Joe asked where her Paw was and Girl told him she came over to say hello to the dog and Paw wasn't there anymore. Joe was just getting off duty at the fire station and was meeting Diana at the bakery.

He took hold of Girl's hand and walked the short distance to the bakery. Diana was just coming out of the store to pick up the empty plate the children had their snacks on. Girl's eyes were wide as she saw the empty plate.

"I didn't take all of them" she said. "I only took one and I'm sorry I stole it." Her little chin was quivering and Diana and Joe fell in love with this angel who called herself Girl.

Diana closed the shop and insisted they take the child home, clean her up and feed her a good meal before they visited the sheriff.

Under all the grime and dirt was a beautiful little face with curly auburn hair. She was way too thin but Diana knew she would be able change that in no time. Diana had some clothes she kept for the times her nieces visited and was able to find a pretty dress that fit the little girl perfectly.

Girl looked in the mirror and smiled. She thought she looked fancy like the people she saw on the streets of Camden Corners.

Girl had never had a meal as wonderful as the one Diana prepared that evening. Her tummy felt happy and so did her heart. She didn't want to think about riding in the buckboard again so she just didn't think about it.

Joe suggested it might be best if he went to talk to the sheriff alone while Diana stayed at home with Girl

"Diana," Joe whispered on his way out the door, "We can't just call her Girl, the child must have a name."

An hour later, Joe came home with Sheriff Mendenhall who was carrying a package of books he had found on the buckboard. Girl was excited to see her books and looked around gingerly for Paw since he didn't know she had them. They told Girl what had happened to her Paw.

She didn't cry, she didn't feel sad like she did when her grandmother didn't wake up. She climb up on Diana's lap and asked her if she could look at her books.

Sheriff Mendenhall was usually a pretty tough fellow but he could feel his eyes begin to sting. He thought it would be a great thing if the child could stay with the Taylor's for the night.

Tomorrow they would investigate to see if there were any next of kin. He hoped there weren't. Diana opened the first book. A well worn piece of paper slipped out of the book.

In a very weak handwriting it said "I love you my Iris." From that moment on, Iris had a name and she knew that her mother's spirit lived on in her. The next morning Diana felt a little queasy but she thought it was the excitement of the day before. It didn't take long before the courts determined Iris was without blood relatives and the adoption of Iris Taylor took place.

By the time the family of three was official, they were well on their way to becoming a family of four and Iris was about to become a big sister.

Beverly Sills

Camden Corners' Ladies Auxiliary is having their monthly meeting in the basement of Trinity Church. Martha Wharton has called the meeting to order.

"Before the reading of the minutes, Mary Agnes Brubaker has some exciting news for us. Mary Agnes , the chair recognizes you"

"Madam Chairwoman" the excited Miss Brubaker began. "My cousin, Elmer T. Brubaker of New York City, New York has been able to obtain the services of Miss Beverly Sills, the world renowned opera singer to perform in our very own Camden Corners Opera House. Miss Sills will only be available on Tuesday of next week. I am to let him know our decision by this evening."

The room was filled with enthusiastic chatter.

"What a coup this is for Camden Corners." exclaimed Hattie May Carlisle. The auxiliary voted unanimously in favor of having the famous opera singer entertain the good folks of Camden Corners .

They had just enough money in their bank account to cover the $24 for Miss Sills' concert and Elmer T. Brubaker's fee. Martha Wharton offered rooms in her boarding house at no cost to Miss Sills and her entourage.

Diana Taylor, who had been sitting quietly, raised her hand to speak. "I'm no expert on the subject, however that seems like a very small amount of money for a performance by someone of Miss Sills' stature."

Diana's words went unheeded and talk began of how to get the word out. Evelyn Keys, the principal of Camden Grammar School suggested the students make handbills to be distributed through the village and all of the surrounding towns. All of the shops in the village would place posters in their windows. This concert was going to be a huge success. The meeting was adjourned early because the ladies had so much to do if everything was to go off without a hitch the following Tuesday.

Mary Agnes was grinning from ear to ear as she made her way to the post office to send a telegram to her dear cousin, Elmer T. On her way down the street, a black cat crossed her path but she was so busy patting herself on the back she didn't notice.

Within hours, the whole town was busy preparing for the celebration of the arrival of Miss Beverly Sills. The High School Band was practicing in full dress uniform just to make sure their performance welcoming the special guest was flawless.

Mayor Horton had his best suit cleaned and polished the key to the city himself. He had written a short 40 minute speech and was practicing in front of his secretary as she was dozing off.

The vicar rode his bicycle from town to town delivering handbills as soon as the children colored in the last "S" on Miss Sills' name.

Finally the day of the concert was here. Miss Sills' train was due to arrive at any moment. The children had been let out of school early and all the shop owners had closed their stores for the day. The band started playing. Everyone was waving a handkerchief in the air. The train pulled in and the doors opened. Several passengers disembarked and the crowd waited in anticipation. Finally the conductor stepped off the train and said there were no more passengers inside.

"Miss Sills must have taken an earlier train," a disappointed Mary Agnes exclaimed. The crowd broke up and went home to dress and prepare for the concert.

In the meantime, a buxom blond was checking into Mrs. Wharton's boarding house for the night. Someone very special must be visiting Camden Corners by the looks of the reception they are getting, she thought to herself.

The concert was set to begin at 7:30. Elmer T peeked from behind the curtain.

"What a glorious crowd tonight. I wonder if I mentioned to Mary Agnes that my cut of the ticket sales would be 20%? I wonder why that orchestra is warming up. Beverly usually doesn't have such a fine accompaniment."

Martha Wharton stepped center stage to introduced the special guest for the evening. Elmer T had given her an introduction script. Martha welcomed everyone to the Camden Corners Opera House. "On behalf of the Camden Corners Ladies' Auxiliary, I now present Miss Beverly **MILLS**??? world famous **VAUDEVILLIAN** star. With that, Elmer T wheeled out a baby grand piano with Miss Beverly Mills perched on top.

Martha felt her knees go weak. In the audience Mary Agnes fainted into the lap of her escort, Milton Mellon. Mothers covered the eyes of their children. Gasps could be heard all around the room.

Beverly belted out *Bill Bailey Won't You Please Come Home.*

The children were trying to peek through their mother's fingers at the fancy lady on stage. The single men were whistling and carrying on while the married men were trying to hide their pleasure from their wives.

Diana and her good friend Maddie were giggling along with Emma and Lily. Even Nettie was getting a kick out of the spectacle.

Beverly realized there must have been a misunderstanding. She promptly buttoned a couple of buttons on her blouse, told Elmer T to cut the piano music, spoke to the orchestra leader and began singing family friendly songs in a beautiful, soft voice. She wasn't Beverly Sills by any means but she was a fine entertainer.

Martha's knees started feeling stronger, Mary Agnes came out of her stupor, mothers took their hands away from their children's eyes and everyone sat back and enjoyed the show.

The Pringles

Christopher and Priscilla Pringle were the proud owners of the Snowflake Christmas Shop in Camden Corners . Snowflakes was a favorite of all the folks in town and their many visitors from other villages in the area and even as far away as Chicago and New York City.

Chris was a jolly old guy with his white beard and round belly. Priscilla was a bit round herself. She always wore a bright red apron with red and white striped candy filling the pockets.

Whenever anyone opened the door of the Snowflake Christmas Shop, they would hear the sound of jingle bells and smell the aroma of fresh baked gingerbread and sugar cookies. The Pringles knew how to keep the

25

Christmas spirit going all year long.

They were never blessed with children of their own but they loved all the children in town and the children all loved them. They had a dog who answered to the name of Rudy. Rudy was a big old loveable dog who seemed happiest when he was laying in front of the cozy fireplace in the vestibule of the shop. Children would stop by on their way home from school just to pet Rudy and accept one of his sloppy kisses. Mrs. Pringle made sure each child in town had a special Christmas ornament to display on their Christmas tree each year. She molded and painted each and every ornament and made sure to personalize it with the child's name.

It was one warm summer day when she was relaxing on the shore of Lake Camden that she happened to see a small silk pouch wash ashore. Curiosity overcame her and she finally opened the pouch. There were a number of the most beautiful stones she had ever seen. Some looked like diamonds they were so sparkly and bright. Others were a deep red, some dark green and a few a golden yellow and even some very pale blue. Priscilla looked around and didn't see a soul. She took the sack back to the apartment above the store where she and Chris lived.

Chris suggested she put an ad in the local paper looking for the rightful owner. When no one answered the ad, they stopped in to see Sheriff Mendenhall. The sheriff thought the stones were very pretty but couldn't imagine they would be of any value and assured them they would not be committing any crime if they just kept them.

Priscilla had not begun her annual ornament making chore and thought the stones would be a fine addition to the children's ornaments this year. She made reindeer with lovely aqua blue eyes, Snowmen with emerald green eyes, Santas with ruby red noses, train engines with topaz yellow smoke billowing from their stacks and angels with sparkling diamonds in their hair. She wrote a child's name on every ornament holding out several for the many babies who were expected to arrive in Camden Corners before Christmas that year. Priscilla would never want to leave even the tiniest of them without an ornament.

Chris was walking Rudy down by the dock near Flanagan's fish market on a quiet Sunday afternoon. He spotted a stranger looking into the water near the shore.

"Hello my good fellow. Isn't this the finest looking lake you have ever seen. We townsfolk are very proud of our pristine waters here in Camden Corners . Are you looking to do some fishing here?"

The gentlemen barely looked up and mumbled something about just looking for something he may have dropped in the water. Chris offered to help him look for the object but the man declined and walked quickly away.

Ebeneezer Finch climbed on his horse. He was in big trouble. All he did was stop off at that pub called O'Sullivan's to wet his whistle a few weeks ago. He was really thirsty and it was such a hot day it wasn't his fault that he may have had one too many and dropped part of his loot from that jewelry store heist in Greensboro. Why had it taken his boss, Ronald Crump so long to discover part of the haul was missing? He remembered taking those jewels out of his satchel and admiring them as he was walking toward the lake. After all it was a very hot day and who could blame Eb for taking a little dip in the lake. Maybe he did fall asleep on the shore but he was very tired from the long ride. Just thinking about that nice cold draft he had at the pub made him thirsty. He should be looking for the gems but he was awfully thirsty and Eb needed a break from his search. That first cold beer went down so easily he found himself ordering a second, then third and after that he lost track.

Chris walked Rudy until they were both tired and thirsty. Maybe a little lager would taste good right now. Priscilla was filling in for the church organist and she and the choir members were practicing for the Wednesday Evening Summer concert. Chris didn't like going home to an empty apartment so he and Rudy stopped at O'Sullivan's Pub. Rudy was such a well behaved dog he was welcome in the pub. Chris didn't remember Rudy ever growling, especially at humans but he was certainly growling at the man sitting at the corner of the bar. Well, if it wasn't the stranger who had been walking by the water earlier. Chris nodded hello and tried to calm Rudy with a doggie treat he had in his pocket. Eb, obviously well into his cups, was keeping a close eye on Rudy. He didn't like dogs and this one was none too friendly.

It was time he was getting back to his search. Just as he walked in front of Rudy, he slipped on Rudy's doggie treat and fell forward catching his shirtsleeve on the edge of the bar stool. Chris felt terrible about the mishap and insisted the stranger come home with him. Priscilla would be home by now and she was a whiz with a needle and thread. Eb was none too steady on his feet and gave in letting Chris escort him from the bar. Rudy was still unsure of this stranger but stopped his growling.

Priscilla was indeed home and was happy to stitch the strangers shirt. Chris thought a cup of coffee might be in order for their guest. By the time the coffee was ready, Eb was sound to sleep in Chris' favorite chair. Afternoon turned into evening and Eb was still asleep. Priscilla covered him with a blanket and the Pringles called it a night.

In the morning Eb woke up not remembering where he was or how he got there. He slowly remembered that he was looking for the pouch with the jewels inside when he decided he needed a little liquid refreshment. He really needed to concentrate on finding those jewels. Seems like the jolly old goat had a jolly wife too. How Eb hated jolly people. Here they were offering him a breakfast of eggs, pancakes and sausages. He should just leave but the food smelled so good he couldn't get himself to walk out the door.

Eb was silent as he wolfed down three helpings of pancakes and a half dozen eggs. He happened to glance over towards the breakfront. He caught sight of what looked like Christmas ornaments. "What is this crazy woman doing with Christmas ornaments at this time of year?" Priscilla noticed Eb looking at the ornaments. He hadn't said more than two words since he had arrived yesterday. Priscilla told him what the ornaments were for, he glanced at them again and noticed sparkling red noses on the Santas.

He arose from his chair to get a better look and thought "Holy Smoke those are my jewels. What has Mrs. Jolly done with my jewels?"

Eb knew he had to calm down and figure out how he was going to get his jewels back even if it meant he would have to take those stupid ornaments with him. Suddenly, his whole demeanor changed. He admired the ornaments and enthused when Priscilla told him how she had found those pretty stones by the lake.

He was fit to be tied. Why didn't that old biddy just leave the pouch for him to find. He just had to get them back, clean them up and get them to his boss, Ronald Crump before Mr. Crump arranged for Eb to be buried in clay himself.

Eb listened patiently as Priscilla recited the names on each and every ornament and described each and every child in the town of Camden Corners. Priscilla knew Eb was a little hard around the edges but she suspected he was softening up hearing about the children and Christmas in Camden Corners .

Chris came up the stairs after taking Rudy out for a short walk and opening the shop. Eb watched as Priscilla packed up the ornaments for storage in the basement until it was time to present them to the children. Priscilla carried the container down the two flights of stairs. Eb started following but was stopped at the basement door by Rudy who was looking suspiciously at him. Eb wanted to kick the dumb mutt out of the way but his fear stopped him. He would find a way to get into that basement even if it meant he would have to hide in the bushes next to the shop.

Eb was out the door without so much as a fare thee well to the Pringles. What a strange man Priscilla thought but nothing, not even a grouchy old man could put a damper on such a glorious day.

Harry Plumb from Greensboro was the first customer of the day. Priscilla was finishing up the last of the delightful ornaments at her workbench in the shop. Harry was a good customer. He owned the Jewelry store in Greensboro and often stopped in to purchase a holiday memento for his best customers. Today he was ordering a wreath for his front door. He knew it was early, but he wanted to make sure he got his order in early and besides, it had been a while since he had paid the Pringles a visit. Harry noticed Priscilla's handiwork with the ornaments. Priscilla was truly an artist.

He noticed the jewels and thought they looked familiar. He mentioned that his store had been robbed a few months ago and the thief had made off with some jewels that he was storing for Mrs. Penelope Crane while she was traveling to Europe. Mrs. Crane had taken her authentic jewelry with her along with her body guard. Normally, the jewelry was kept in the safe at the jewelry store but they were exchanged for the paste ones the day before the heist. He had also stored a pouch with some beautiful, but imitation stones that looked a lot like the ones in the ornaments in front of him.

Priscilla felt terrible. These stones belonged to her friend Harry. "Why didn't she think to ask him about them? Who would have thought a pouch from Greensboro would end up on the shores of Lake Camden?" She explained about running the ad in the paper and visiting with sheriff Mendenhall. Priscilla wanted to pay Harry for the stones but he insisted they were his contribution to these beautiful keepsakes for the children.

Eb, who was hiding in the bushes heard every word of the conversation inside the store. His heart sank. He had stolen fake jewelry and had turned it over to his boss. Ronald Crump was not the type of man who would understand that Eb had made an honest mistake. He even had one of his henchmen pick up a Greensboro newspaper and that was where he read about the silk pouch that was stolen along with the jewelry. He was giving Eb fair warning that the pouch must be found and brought to him before the end of the week. The article in the paper didn't say anything about the jewels being paste. They probably didn't want to alert any other thieves that Mrs. Crane had the real stuff with her.

Eb decided he'd better take off on his horse riding west and just keep riding. When Mr. Crump caught up with him he would be toast anyway. That's exactly what he would do but not before he stopped into the Pub for one last beer.

Harry said goodbye to the Pringles. He had some other friends he wanted to visit while he was in Camden Corners . He stopped in O'Sullivan's Pub. Gus Reilly was working that Monday morning. While he and Gus were talking, Harry noticed a nervous looking man sitting at the end of the bar. He matched the description of the thief who had broken into his store a month ago.

Gus stepped out of the bar and flagged down Sheriff Mendenhall. He explained the situation and the sheriff approached Eb. Panic set in and Eb took off out the front door of O'Sullivan's leaving a full mug of beer on the bar.

He raced down the street to find his horse when Rudy who had been laying by the front door of the Snowflake Christmas Shop suddenly took off after Eb catching him by the seat of the pants.

Eb confessed his crime and many others that sunny Monday morning. A little nip on the backside and a few years in the state prison were nothing compared to the punishment Ronald Crump would have subjected him to. Rudy was the town hero and was allowed to ride next to his friend Spot on the front seat of the fire truck in the Christmas parade that year. The same year the children of Camden Corners all received their special Christmas ornaments lovingly made by Priscilla Pringle with the help of Mr. Ebeneezer Finch.

The Parker Family

Annie Spencer was just a little nervous as the train pulled into the station at Camden Corners . She still clung to the newspaper carrying the ad she had answered two weeks ago.

Wanted: A wife and a mother. Hope you can cook. Andy Parker P.O. Box 72, Camden Corners .

Annie was still recovering from a broken heart after Peter Stanford ran off with Eileen Becker last month. She couldn't believe she had actually gotten on that train yesterday morning and was here in Camden Corners today. What had she done? She had no money to get back home if Mr. Parker turned out to be an old reprobate and his children were monsters.

Annie had worked in the Stanford Emporium for two years before Peter left her at the alter and she needed to get away from the town where everyone knew of her humiliation.

Annie re-read the letter she had received back from Mr. Parker.

Please be here by Thanksgiving so you can cook our turkey dinner.

She knew she had lost her mind because nobody in their right one would have been on the next train to Camden Corners after reading that letter. What was she going to do now?

Andy Parker, who had just turned 9 and was much too clever for his own good, had just left the post office after closing the box he had opened two weeks before.

He had watched his Dad do many things as the Postmaster for Camden Corners and knew just how to fill out the paperwork so that he would be able to receive answers to his ad.

It didn't take much to place an ad in the classified section. Mrs. Willard was too busy at the newspaper office to notice what each ad said and he had broken into his piggy bank to pay for everything fair and square.

Andy ran toward the train station just as the passengers were leaving the train. Miss Annie Spencer was on that train and he would see her in just a few minutes. He was filled with excitement. She wrote that she would be wearing a yellow flower on the lapel of her navy blue winter coat. He waited what seemed to be an eternity and then he saw her. She was very pretty with dark brown hair tied back with a yellow ribbon. Her smile made him feel good all over. He was finding it harder and harder to remember his mama and what she looked like but he thought she looked a little like the lady who was standing by the door of the train looking right at him.

Jackson Parker and his beloved wife, Adele had been married for 10 years and had 3 children when she was stricken with influenza and died in his arms in the spring of the previous year. Jackson was beside himself with grief but he put up a brave front for his children. They were well cared for with the help of their housekeeper, Mrs. Bridges. The kind folks of Camden Corners were always on hand to offer their support.

Mrs. Bridges was a wonderful housekeeper and loved the children but she couldn't cook worth a darn. Jackson hadn't noticed during the first year she was there because he wasn't paying attention to much of anything then. Even though she couldn't cook, she was a big help to him and he was sorry when she told him she would be moving to Bloomfield to be with her daughter and her new baby. He would have to find someone to take her place but he didn't want to think about that right now.

He was worried about Andy. He knew something was going on with him, he had become very secretive the last couple of weeks. He was going to sit him down this evening and find out exactly what it was. Jackson worried about all of his children but Andy had been affected the most by his mother's death because he was 7 years old at the time and remembered her more than the other children. Carrie was only 3 and Allison was just a few months old.

Andy ran up to the kind lady and asked if she was Miss Annie Spencer.

"Yes, I am young man. I was to meet Mr. Parker here today. Do you know where I might find him?"

Andy smiled and introduced himself as Mr. Parker's son. He retrieved Annie's bag and started walking toward his home with his new mother. Annie thought it was odd that the elder Mr. Parker would send his young son to meet a stranger who would soon be his wife. They arrived at the Parker house just as Jackson was wending his way home from the Post Office.

Mary Nell Blanchard was looking after the children for him this afternoon. He would have to find a permanent arrangement for them. Mary Nell said Andrew never arrived after school today. She didn't know where he was but she knew the boys often played ball after school. Jackson had specifically told Andrew to meet him at the Post Office. It was definitely the night for a talk.

As Andrew turned at the corner, Jackson saw him walking with a lovely looking young woman. He knew he hadn't seen her around town before. If he had, he would have remembered her.

Andrew excitedly said "Dad, this is Miss Annie Spencer, your new wife and our new mother."

Jackson was flabbergasted and apologized profusely to Miss Spencer for his son's rude outburst. He didn't know what had gotten into that boy lately. Annie was embarrassed. It was obvious Mr. Parker was not aware of the arrangement she thought had been made between them.

Andrew looked sheepishly at both of them. "Dad, you need a wife and we need a mother and Miss Annie is going to cook our Thanksgiving dinner."

Jackson didn't know what to do. He invited Miss Spencer to step into their parlor and out of the frigid air. Andrew confessed to his father what he had done. Jackson told him to go to his room and take his sisters with him, he and Miss Spencer were going to have a talk. Jackson was having a difficult time controlling his temper. Miss Spencer was obviously up to no good because who in their right mind would answer an ad like that?

Annie admitted she had acted impulsively, she couldn't explain herself it just seemed it was a solution to an uncomfortable position she found herself in back home in Bakersville.

Jackson stood up and started pacing the room. He couldn't throw the poor girl out in the snow but she couldn't stay here either, it just wouldn't be appropriate. He looked at Annie with pity in his eyes and hit a nerve.

"Mr. Parker, I will not trouble you any longer. I'm sure I will be able to find a room for let. I'll see myself out."

With that she was out the door and halfway to the next block. She was trying desperately to hold back the tears. What a fool she was. No wonder Peter didn't want her. She didn't have a brain in her head or a nickel in her pocket to pay for a room. She would walk back to the train station and find a seat in the corner. Maybe she wouldn't be noticed and she would come up with a solution to her dilemma in the morning.

Jackson was still furious. He rarely raised his voice to any of his children so Andrew was very afraid when he heard his Dad shout his name. Jackson could see the fear in his son's eyes and realized Andrew had done what he thought would make the family happy. If it wasn't such a mess, he would think it was funny. Jackson gave his son a hug and then realized Miss Spencer had left the house.

He told Andrew to keep an eye on the girls while he left the house in search of his mail order bride. Annie didn't want Mr. Parker to know how upset she was. She tried to hide her face from him but he could see the glistening around her eyes. He had the feeling she was all alone in the world and he felt guilty for treating her like a criminal and an insane criminal at that. He begged her to come back to the house with him.

Mrs. Wharton had prepared a delicious lamb stew for their dinner and it would be ruined if they didn't get it off the warming stove very soon. Talk of the lamb stew was all Annie needed. She swallowed what little pride she had left and agreed to go with Mr. Parker. Just for supper and then she would be on her way again.

As Annie and Jackson checked the stew, she wondered if he would like her to make some biscuits to go with the stew. While she was making the biscuits, she notice there were the makings for a sponge cake. Before she knew it, she had cooked a meal fit for a king or at least a little prince and two pretty little princesses.

Jackson had been reading his evening paper and the children were playing by his feet. He didn't think he had felt this relaxed since before Adele got sick. The meal was wonderful and all the extras Annie had made were especially good.

After supper, she sat down on the floor and played games with the children Jackson joined them and they played until it was time for the children to go to bed. Annie read them each a story and tucked them into their beds. She was finding herself regretting that Mr. Jackson Parker was not the author of that ad.

While Annie was reading to his children, Jackson was knocking on the Wharton Boarding House door to see if Mrs. Wharton had a spare room. Jackson walked Annie to Mrs. Wharton's and thanked her for a fine evening.

Annie told Mrs. Wharton she would be on her way but thanked her for her offer. Annie didn't know that Jackson tried to pay Mrs. Wharton for the room but she wouldn't accept the money. Anyone that could brighten Jackson Parker's eyes like that was welcome in her home at any time. Mrs. Wharton insisted Annie stay. She could help her prepare breakfast and tidy up the rooms in the morning and they would call it even.

Annie was so tired she gratefully accepted the offer and slept dreaming of a handsome young prince and two beautiful little princesses. Maybe the King was in that dream somewhere too.

Mrs. Wharton encouraged Annie to stay in Camden Corners for a little while longer. Before long and much to the delight of Andy, Carrie and Allison, Jackson and Annie were married the Saturday before Thanksgiving and Annie prepared the most wonderful Thanksgiving dinner any of them ever remembered eating. Annie and Jackson were mostly thankful that Thanksgiving Day for a little boy who had placed an ad for a new wife and mother. Annie was just what the Parker Family needed.

The Bloom Sisters

Just north of Nichol's Corner Market and west of the Village Post Office in Camden Corners sits a quaint little shop called Bloom Quilts. The proud owners of the shop are twin sisters, Hyacinth and Dahlia Bloom. The sisters not only operate a quilt shop, their lives have revolved around quilts ever since they were toddlers sitting at their mother's knee watching her work her magic with a needle and thread.

Mother was a talented seamstress who was often hired as a dressmaker for the wealthy ladies of Fairville where the little family lived. Mrs. Genevieve Van Buren was one of those ladies and generously allowed Mother to take leftover fabric home where the scraps were combined and made into beautiful works of art.

The family moved to Camden Corners when the twins were just beginning their teen years. They were so busy making quilts in every shape and size, they didn't have time for any kind of social life and before they knew it, they were growing older and only had quilts to keep them warm on a cold winter's night.

The sisters purchased a lovely log cabin and with the help of some of the handymen of Camden Corners turned it into a quilt shop with a two bedroom apartment on the second floor. The walls of the shop and their home upstairs were covered with quilts. There were curtains made in a quilt pattern at the windows. They wore quilt skirts and jackets and even their flower beds resembled a quilt in the summertime. The ladies were happiest when they were teaching the young girls of Camden Corners how to quilt.

They may each have had thoughts of having their own family but they worked and lived as a pair and couldn't imagine life being any different than it had always been. It was difficult for anyone to tell the twin sisters apart. Both walked the same, talked the same and looked exactly alike. The twins didn't mind. They enjoyed the attention they received when strangers would enter their shop and think they were seeing double.

The sisters were not unattractive but rather plain. They wore their hair tied in a bun at the back of their necks. They didn't think it was proper for ladies to paint their faces and therefore never used any kind of powder or rouge to soften their complexion.

One autumn morning as the sisters were relaxing with a cup of tea on porch of their shop, along came Mr. Hennessy's covered wagon. Mr. Hennessy was a traveling salesman and the sisters bought most of their thread and quilting fabric from him. Instead of Mr. Hennessy, a younger man was sitting on the wagon. He was tall and very handsome.

"Good Morning ladies," the stranger called out "Harold Hightower at your service. Mr. Hennessy has taken a much deserved vacation and I am filling in for him for the next few weeks".

Hyacinth greeted the salesman cordially and walked to the wagon to see what treasures Mr. Hightower had with him today.

Dahlia couldn't catch her breath. Never had she seen a man as beautiful as the one that was standing near her porch on this lovely, glorious autumn morning. Her whole body seemed to float as she walked toward the wagon.

Hyacinth noticed Dahlia was acting rather strangely but didn't comment. Dahlia couldn't keep her eyes off of the salesman. She seemed to be in a trance. Hyacinth didn't know what to make of her sister's odd behavior.

Dahlia offered Mr. Hightower a cup of tea or a glass of cool lemonade. He was rather thirsty and gratefully accepted the spinster's offer.

"Please ladies, call me Harold. Mr. Hightower is so formal don't you think?"

Dahlia thought Harold was the most wonderful name she had ever heard. Harold was full of chatter and Dahlia hung on every word. Hyacinth thought Harold was a little too smooth and didn't trust him. It never occurred to her that her beloved sister had fallen head over heels in love with Mr. Harold Hightower.

The week progressed and Dahlia was still floating through the air. She and Hyacinth had never had a cross word between them even when Dahlia had mistakenly planted tulip bulbs in the daffodil planter on the front porch of the shop or when Hyacinth used some beautiful silk fabric on her quilted jacket that Dahlia was saving for a skirt. Hyacinth noticed that Dahlia was looking in the mirror much more often than she ever had before. She didn't know what had come over her sister but she didn't like it one bit. That kind of vanity was a sin and besides, Dahlia wasn't as pretty as Hyacinth. Everyone knew that!

The following day the ladies walked to Warm Hearth Bakery. Diana Taylor was at the shop with her new baby, Joey. The sisters oohed and aahed over the beautiful baby boy and inquired about little Iris who was happily attending school.

Hyacinth was looking over the array of cookies when Dahlia took Diana off to a corner of the store. Diana was so pretty and Dahlia was asking her advice about maybe changing her hairstyle and using just a touch of makeup. Diana thought Dahlia would look beautiful with her hair flowing and a bit of rouge on her lips and cheeks.

They excused themselves and went to the back room where Diana undid Dahlia's bun. Her hair flowed as though it was happy to be able to breathe. Diana took her scissors and trimmed just a little off the sides and gave Dahlia some wispy bangs. Then she brushed her cheeks with powder and a bit of red coloring. The final touch was pale pink lipstick. Diana handed Dahlia a small mirror. When she looked at herself, she couldn't believe it was her. She loved her new look but she dreaded facing Hyacinth.

Slowly she walked out of the back room and over to Hyacinth who was looking longingly at an apple pie. Hyacinth turned around and nodded to the young woman standing behind her. Dahlia spoke and Hyacinth nearly fainted when she realized the young woman was her sister.

"What have you done?" Hyacinth was grasping her chest. She thought her heart was going to burst it was beating so fast.

Diana tried to calm Hyacinth down but to no avail. Hyacinth marched out of the store forgetting all about the apple pie. Dahlia was fighting back tears. She loved her sister but she was tired of being known as one of the plain Bloom sisters. She was tired of always dressing in quilts. She wanted to be fashionable. She confided in Diana that she had taken a shine to Mr. Harold Hightower and wanted to look appealing when he came to town next week. Diana didn't want to burst Dahlia's bubble, but she didn't think a traveling salesman would be the type who would settle down in a small town like Camden Corners .

Dahlia settled in her room above the quilt shop, found some pretty fabrics and lace and proceeded to sew herself some new stylish dresses. Hyacinth was in the quilt shop rearranging all the quilts and materials. She couldn't believe her sister was acting like such a fool. The more she thought about the spectacle Dahlia was making of herself, the madder she got.

Several hours later Dahlia came down the stairs wearing one of her new dresses. Hyacinth couldn't believe how beautiful her sister looked. She felt like an old frump and was not too happy about that.

Dahlia tried to explain to her sister that she wanted to look pretty, wanted to have a life outside of the quilt shop. She was tired of having people look right through her and if a little make up and pretty clothes made her a bit more visible, she didn't see anything wrong with that.

Dahlia wasn't getting anywhere with Hyacinth so she decided to take a walk through town. Herman Smith was unloading a delivery truck in front of Nichol's General Store and almost dropped a 50 pound sack of flour when he looked up and saw Dahlia walk by. She greeted him and he realized it was Dahlia. He couldn't take his eyes off of her. He always liked the Bloom sisters but never thought of them as knockouts. Hyacinth was watching her sister from behind the window and noticed that all the men were tipping their hats and stopping to say hello to her. Hyacinth vowed she would never forgive Dahlia for her wretched behavior. The days passed by and the sisters barely spoke to one another.

Finally, the day approached when Mr. Harold Hightower would be riding by in Mr. Hennessy's covered wagon. Dahlia couldn't sleep the night before she was so excited about seeing him again. She had plans to buy several yards of the prettiest fabric in his wagon and she had no intention of using it to make quilts. She had made blueberry muffins that morning along with roasted coffee. Hyacinth would never approve of serving coffee but Dahlia didn't care. She knew most men preferred strong coffee to weak tea.

Harold pulled up in front of the shop and Dahlia greeted him with a big smile and her new look. Harold didn't recognize her as the shy twin sister he had met last week. He felt his heart skip a beat just looking at this pretty young girl. He told her he was there to see the Bloom sisters. Dahlia blushed and told him she was Dahlia Bloom. Harold sat on the porch drinking coffee and eating the best blueberry muffins he had ever tasted.

Hyacinth stepped out of the shop, quickly chose some fabric and thread and retreated back into the shop immediately. Harold explained to Dahlia that he was not cut out to be a traveling salesman. He would be happy when Mr. Hennessy returned from his vacation. He wanted to see Camden Corners and was thinking of buying a shop down the street. Mr. Hennessy had told him that the owner, Mr. Cromwell was planning to retire and was selling his store.

Harold asked if Dahlia would like to have supper with him that evening when his route was finished. Dahlia was beside herself with joy. She said yes right away but was concerned about Hyacinth. They had never had a meal apart.

Harold told her he understood about twins because he and his brother Howard are twins.

"Maybe, if Hyacinth would agree" said Harold "the four of us could have dinner at Marino's Trattoria."

Dahlia promised to try to convince Hyacinth to join them.

Hyacinth, who had been eavesdropping took a look at herself in the mirror. She had to admit, Dahlia did look very pretty. Not only that, she acted pretty. Maybe it wasn't such an awful thing to try to look your best. Besides, she had felt the same way about wanting a family of her own. She always thought it would be a betrayal of Dahlia but that seemed awfully foolish now.

Dahlia walked over to Hyacinth and said "We need to talk."

Hyacinth wrapped her arms around Dahlia and told her how sorry she was for the way she had been behaving. With that she pulled the pins out of her hair and begged Dahlia to make her look pretty too. The girls worked diligently sewing new dresses to wear that evening. Dahlia was excited about her date with Harold and Hyacinth was nervous about being seen in public as her new self.

The Hightower brothers called on the twins. Harold and Howard often fell for the same female and for once they each had one of their own.

They proudly escorted the ladies to the Trattoria. Along the way, the two sets of twins attracted a lot of attention. Diana Taylor saw the foursome from the bakery window and was so happy to see both sisters looking identical again. They had always been pretty but now they were striking looking especially walking beside two very handsome gentlemen.

They were married in a double ceremony three weeks later. The sisters wore white organza gowns without any sign of quilting. The fellows had dark gray suits with matching quilt vests. They wore their wives' handiwork with pride.

Welcome Home

Alexander Burke was one of the first settlers in the Town of Camden Corners . He had come to New York City from Ireland as a young man only to find himself missing the green meadows of his home in County Donegal. He worked diligently at what ever job he could find ending up at a brewery near Five Points. There he met Duncan Mackenzie who had left his home in Glasgow two years before. The two young men hit it off immediately. They both had their memories of a quieter life in their native lands.

They were roommates in a brownstone operated by Mrs. Geraldine O'Sullivan who told them stories of growing up in the town of Greensboro. Her memories included going to a place called Camden Corners for summer holidays. Geraldine was the only girl in a family of six boys and had learned how to rough it long before it was proper for a young lady to do so. She talked about the hills and lakes and how beautiful it was to see the sun come up over the water. Alexander and Duncan listened to Mrs. O'Sullivan tell stories of all the animals and birds in the area and the trout that she and her brothers caught for supper. They decided they needed to explore Camden Corners and worked hard and saved their money until they had enough to purchase a horse and buggy. They packed their few belongings, hugged Mrs. O'Sullivan goodbye and started their trek to their new home. They would miss some of the hustle and bustle of New York and a few of the pretty girls they had met while there but the excitement of seeing another part of the country kept them going on the long trip to their new home.

They were surprised when they arrived in Camden Corners. It wasn't quite the wilderness area Mrs. O'Sullivan had described from her times there. It wasn't a big city but it did have a general store, a post office, church, some homes and even a library. As the boys drove into town they noticed a railroad station was being built. This was going to be a fine place to settle down. They were lucky to find work around town helping the construction crews.

The railroad itself was almost completed and would go through Camden Corners from New York City to St. Louis. Alexander and Duncan were grateful to Mrs. O'Sullivan, without her they would never have known this lovely little town existed.

For the next few years, the town grew, the boys were busy with their construction jobs and had learned a great deal about the building business. They knew it was time for them to start their own business and what better business than a pub.

Miss Isabelle Simon was the town's librarian. Even with her hair tied securely in a bun at the nape of her neck and her prim and proper attire, Miss Isabelle was a beauty. Alexander took a shine to her the first time he saw her. Alexander and Isabelle were married in the Hilltop Chapel with Flora Marshall and Duncan Mackenzie as their witnesses. Three months later Flora and Duncan were married in the same chapel.

Between the two couples, they had twelve children.

The years went by swiftly and the two chums continued running the very popular pub they named O'Sullivan's after their good friend Geraldine O'Sullivan. Their children all married and kept their fathers happy presenting them with grandchildren on a continuing basis. Alexander and Duncan had a hard time remembering which grandchildren belonged to them and which belonged to the other. Even the grandchildren were confused since the two families were happiest when they were all together.

Alexander and Isabelle's oldest son, Liam married Nadine West. Nadine loved making candy even when she was a young girl. It was only natural she would open a candy shop. Liam and Nadine's oldest child was a girl named Maddie.

Duncan's son, Gordon married Fiona Rourke who made the best Irish stew Alexander had ever tasted. Fiona was delighted when her specialty became a very popular choice on the O'Sullivan's menu. Gordon and Fiona's first child was a son they named Gordon, Jr. but he was always called Mack.

Mack and Maddie were the best of friends for many years. Mack comforted Maddie and her broken heart when she saw her heartthrob Tommy Jones holding hands with Melinda Sue Reynolds. Maddie cheered Mack up when he broke his arm and couldn't pitch for the big game in his senior year in high school.

They were the best of friends until the summer after graduation when everything changed. Maddie had inherited her mother's love of candy making. She read about a candy making class in the Greensboro Weekly News. It was the only one of it's kind in the United States. Maddie showed her parents the article. They knew it was an opportunity for their daughter to learn a skill beyond what her mother would ever be able to teach her. Maddie's Aunt Grace lived in New York City and as luck would have it, she was very close to the culinary school where the classes were held. It seemed like such a perfect plan. She was excited and couldn't wait to break the news to Mack.

Mack was working at the pub when Maddie came in to tell him of her plans. Instead of being happy and excited for Maddie, Mack blew his top.

How could she do this to him? How did she find out he was going to the same culinary school to become a chef? Was she doing this just to keep an eye on him? He was looking forward to being on his own and not having to answer to anyone and now Maddie, his constant shadow was going to be following him to New York City. He could see the hurt in her eyes as he ranted and raved but he couldn't seem to stop himself. He was the oldest of 8 children. His aunts and uncles and all of Maddie's family had been around constantly while he was growing up. Even his job at the pub didn't bring the solitude he craved. He was tired of family, tired of friends and especially tired of Maddie.

Maddie left the pub trying desperately to hold back her tears. She knew if she told her parents what Mack said it would hurt them and she didn't want to do that.

She didn't see Mack again after his blow up. He didn't stop by her house to say goodbye when he left on the train for New York.

Her classes started the following month. She knew there was a possibility she would run into him but she would try to avoid him if she could.

Maddie did well in her classes. She learned so much about candy making and couldn't wait to get back home to show off her new skills.

Aunt Grace loved showing her niece all the sights of New York City. They took in a couple of Broadway plays and stopped in at O'Reilly's Irish Pub and met the proprietor Mr. Sean O'Reilly and his lovely wife Maeve.

Maddie never did run into Mack. Her mother asked her about him in her letters but Maddie kept saying their schedules were full and they couldn't find the time to get together. Nadine guessed the children had a falling out and didn't pursue the matter any longer.

Maddie's time in New York came to an end. As exciting as New York

City was, she was happy to be home in Camden Corners . She taught her mother all the tricks she had learned and Tempting Treats Candy Shop was even more popular than it had been before.

Mack was ashamed of himself for the way he had spoken to Maddie that day. He didn't know what had gotten into him. Maddie was the most honest person he had ever known. She didn't deserve what he had said to her. He'd had an argument with his father that evening. Gordon couldn't understand why a son of his would need to go to some dad gum school to learn how to throw a sandwich together.

Mack was determined to go and had saved his tip money all through high school. He paid for the train fare and tuition himself. Gordon couldn't stop him and after the shock wore off, he sent him off with his blessing. Gordon had to be honest with himself. He was afraid if his son spent any time in the big city he would never want to come back to Camden Corners .

Mack was enthralled with New York. He visited every museum he could find when he wasn't absorbed in his classes. He spent a bit of time in O'Reilly's and never tired of hearing Sean and Maeve O'Reilly tell the stories of growing up in Ireland. He got to know the whole O'Reilly clan and loved being with them. It reminded him of his family and his home in Camden Corners .

His studies took up some of his time but he found himself alone many nights in his room at the YMCA. He didn't even mind the noise on the streets that seemed to go on all night long. It was better than the deafening silence. He was missing his family and missing Maddie more than he thought possible. He knew she had been to O'Reilly's because he saw her through the window one evening. She was laughing and having a wonderful time singing Irish songs along with the patrons of the pub. Mack was embarrassed to see her and a little miffed that she was enjoying herself so much with all those other fellows. He walked back to his room and spent the evening alone.

It was a long hot summer in New York but by the first of September, Mack had graduated and was on the train heading home. The railroad station was overflowing with Mackenzies and Burkes. Mack looked through the crowd and was disappointed that Maddie wasn't among the welcomers. Everyone else looked wonderful to him and he knew from then on Camden Corners would always be his home.

Maddie was busy working in the the Candy Shop. She finally confided in her mother about the hurtful incident between Mack and her before he left for New York City.

Nadine and Fiona had suspected Mack and Maddie had feelings for each other and were both too stubborn to admit it. Fiona finally had a chance to talk with her son alone and encouraged him to pay a visit to Maddie.

Mack found himself strolling past the candy shop trying to catch a glimpse of Maddie. Maddie pretended she hadn't seen him the first five or six times he walked by.

"I must put an end to this." Maddie said aloud, "I can't spend the next 40 years not looking up when he walks by. "

She went to the doorway waiting for him to walk by again and called out. "Welcome Home, Mack".

Mack's face turned red as a beet. She looked wonderful to him. Was she always this pretty? He told her how sorry he was for the way he spoke to her months ago.

Maddie smiled and told him she knew he didn't mean it and what are friends for if you can't let off a little steam once in a while.

Mack gingerly walked towards her and gave her a hug. Did she always feel this good?

They talked about their experiences in New York and how foolish it was that they didn't get together the whole time they were there. They talked about O'Reilly's Pub and made plans to visit there again someday.

Maybe it was that day or maybe it happened years ago but Mack and Maddie finally realized they were no longer just friends.

They were married the following Sunday in the little Hilltop Chapel keeping up the tradition that their grandparents, the Burkes and the Mackenzies started many years ago.

The Reluctant Groom

The sun was shining through the window of Watson Bed and Breakfast as Grace Watson was adjusting her bonnet before Ted Evans came by to walk her to church one Sunday morning. Grace and her mother, Caroline owned and had their living quarters in the B&B. Grace loved running the B&B, she also helped out at the school three days a week and enjoyed a full and busy life.

Grace was feeling a little melancholy this morning. For the last ten years, her companion had been Ted Evans, proprietor of Ted's Hardware Store. Their romance had become routine and rather dull and ordinary.

Ted was head usher at St. Peter's Church, Grace handed out the Sunday programs. She served coffee to the parishioners after the service while Ted chatted with the men. After church he walked her back home where she and Caroline prepared dinner for him and any guests who were still enjoying their stay. She saw him on Wednesday and Saturday nights and occasionally in between, but normally they stayed with the same schedule week after week, year after year.

Grace couldn't remember the last time the subject of marriage was brought up. Ted said they would be married one day but here it was ten years later and she was still Miss Grace Watson.

Grace put a smile on her face and greeted Ted with a kiss on the cheek as they walked out the door on their way to church. The pair walked along Main Street waving hello to their friends and neighbors when suddenly there was an unfamiliar sound. They looked up and saw a horseless carriage coming down the middle of the road.

Grace had seen a picture of an automobile but this was the first time she had seen the real thing. Horses were being spooked all along the way, children were holding their mother's hands tightly as this strange contraption approached them. Men were running to catch up to the magnificent machine.

Chip Peabody, the driver, was in his glory with all this attention. He was about halfway to his destination and decided he would stay in Camden Corners for a few days. Honor the locals with his presence and let them admire his fancy automobile.

He stopped at the Watson House, knocked on the door but no one was there. They must have been with the group of church goers he had passed along the way. He happened to see a coffee shop on the next block and thought a cup of coffee would be nice while he waited. He parked his pride and joy in front of the window of the coffee shop where he could keep an eye on it.

On their way home, Grace and Ted were surprised to see the automobile parked on the street in front of the B&B. Caroline had come home right after the service and was registering Mr. Peabody as the couple walked through the door. Grace took a closer look at Mr. Chip Peabody. He certainly wasn't ordinary. He had a twinkle in his eye as he glanced in her direction.

Ted was oblivious to the sparks that were lighting up the room. For Grace, that Sunday had become anything but dull. Everyone sat down to Sunday dinner. After they had their apple pie and the ladies began to clear the table, Mr. Peabody offered to take Ted for a ride and drop him off at his home. Ted had planned to enjoy a nice long Sunday afternoon with Grace but he couldn't resist the opportunity to ride in an automobile for the first time. He gave Grace a peck on the cheek, thanked Caroline for the fabulous meal and was out the door ready for his joy ride. Chip drove him around the block one time then on to his house, dropped him off and returned to the Watson place within 5 minutes ready to give Grace a spin.

Grace was a little nervous but she took her place in the passenger side of the auto and off they went. Chip drove up into the hills and they stopped at the Camden Hill Ski Lodge. They sat by the cozy fire drinking hot buttered rum while Chip told her all about himself. At least what he wanted her to hear. Grace was enamored. Although she knew Ted loved her, Chip knew how to make a girl feel special. She hung on every word and didn't want the afternoon to end.

Caroline was worried when it started getting dark and the pair had not returned home yet. She knew her daughter had a good head on her shoulders but she also knew Grace was becoming impatient with Ted's reluctance in making a commitment. At that moment, there was a knock on the door. Ted was surprised to hear that Grace was not at home but out gallivanting with a stranger.

Chip and Grace arrived a little while later. Grace was just a tad giddy from the effects of the rum. Ted was surprised at Grace's behavior and just a little concerned that she might be succumbing to Chip Peabody's charm. There was tension in the air during supper but Grace was unaware of it. Ted left shortly after and fumed all the way home.

The next day Chip suggested they take another drive. Caroline told her daughter she could handle the B&B this morning and insisted she go along for the ride. She and Chip passed Ted's Hardware Store just as Ted was opening the doors. She didn't notice him standing in the doorway but he could see she was laughing and having a wonderful time with Mr. Big Shot with the automobile. Ted knew a long and worrisome day lay ahead for him.

As they drove to the edge of town, Grace was beginning to realize that the seats of the automobile weren't all that comfortable. She kept hitting her elbow on the door when they went over the ruts in the bumpy road. Chip wasn't quite as charming as he seemed yesterday. In fact, she was getting tired of hearing him talk about himself all the time. There were so many interesting things to discuss. She and Ted could talk for hours and she never tired of their conversations. She wondered why she was feeling so down in the dumps yesterday. Ted was a lot more fun to be with than this jerk.

Chip knew Grace was different from the girls he normally took for rides and it would take a little longer to persuade her to give into his charms but he was tired of waiting. He looked for a secluded spot and made a quick right turn. It was a little too quick because he ended up in a ditch.

His seduction plan was forgotten as Chip buried his head in his hands and cried. "What a revolting development this is!"

Grace, who was by this time anxious to be anywhere but with Chip Peabody, got out of the car and began to push back and forth until the wheel dislodge from the ditch. She told Chip it was time to turn around and get back to Camden Corners .

Chip was silent on the way back to the B&B. He couldn't believe this country girl hadn't fallen head over heels for him. Although he would have liked to work his charms on her, he was anxious to get out of this hick town with the dirt roads. He wasted no time packing his suitcase and left without as much as a nod in Grace's direction.

Grace marched herself into Ted's Hardware Store, locked the door behind her and told Mr. Theodore James Evans that he had 30 seconds to make up his mind. Did he or did he not want to marry her and if he did it was going to be before the month ended.

Ted shook his head and said "No, I don't want to wait that long. Let's get married this Saturday. I don't know why we have waited so long but I don't intend to let any city slicker take you for a ride ever again."

Mistaken Identity

It was a cold spring evening when Clarence Howell and his wife Miranda were coming home from a business dinner in Boston. The roads were wet with patches of ice. Clarence had plenty of staff to do the driving for him but he did like to get out occasionally and feel the reins in his hands. He was driving slowly when a clap of thunder spooked his horse who reared up and forced the carriage over on it's side with his passengers thrown into the creek by the road.

It wasn't until much later in the evening when a worried Hortense Hill persuaded her husband Julian to check the roads for their beloved employers. Julian came upon the wreckage and with grief in his heart carried them home knowing they would never see the light of day or be with their precious daughter Bethany again. Bethany awoke with a start. She knew something was not right but had never imagined when her mother and father kissed her goodbye earlier that evening it would be the last time she would ever see them alive.

Bethany was 11 years old and the only child of Clarence and Miranda

Howell. Bethany was a beautiful child who was turning into a beautiful young lady. She was loved by all the Howell household staff as were her mother and father. Her very best friend in the world was the daughter of one of the servants. Gertie had turned 9 on her last birthday and loved Bethany and her life in the Howell household. Her only nemesis was Eloise Hanover. Eloise was the caretaker's daughter and had a mean streak a mile long. Bethany was even able to find some good in Eloise and refused to say an unkind word about her. Gertie was afraid of Eloise and just stayed away from her as much as she could. Bethany was devastated by the death of her parents. Not even her dear friend Gertie could help her with her grief. Gertie just sat by her side and held her hand while she sobbed until there were no more tears to be shed.

Behind closed doors, the Howell lawyer was accessing the situation. "The household staff will be let go with a large stipend according to the Last Will and Testament of Clarence Howell and his wife Miranda. The estate and all assets will be sold with the proceeds going to their only daughter, Bethany making her a very wealthy young lady. Bethany will be sent to live with her Aunt Isabelle Howell."

Aunt Isabelle was a lovely elderly woman who had met Bethany only one time when she was 7 years old. She was happy to have the dear child come live with her although her heart ached for the circumstances.

Eloise kept a close eye and ear on everything going on in the household for the next few weeks. A plan was forming in her head. Not that her father would care, but she told him she was leaving Boston. She had found a position as a companion for an invalid 12 year old girl and would be living with her. Archie Hanover didn't know why anyone would want to have his daughter around their child but at least she would be out of his hair so she was welcome to move on.

Eloise hid out until the day Bethany was to leave. At the last minute, it was decided that Gertie would be joining her friend on the trip. Gertie seemed to be the only comfort Bethany had and she already had so much taken away from her everyone thought it best not to separate her from her best friend too. The train took off with the girls on it and hiding in between the mail pouches was none other than Eloise smiling her wicked smile.

Bethany was quiet on the trip but she was slowly coming around. Her grief was still with her but her better instincts were taking over and she knew she couldn't bring her parents back by wallowing in self pity. Besides, Gertie was looking so sad herself she decided she must make an effort to cheer her up. The train had been traveling for several hours when the conductor finally made it to the girls private car. Bethany was napping and Gertie assured the conductor that everything was satisfactory. Shortly after he left their car, Bethany woke up and looked into the evil eyes of one Miss Eloise Hanover. Eloise thought Bethany would be alone and was surprised when that sniveling little Gertie was gaping at her. Eloise was not happy and took it out on Gertie while she cowered in the corner. Eloise told her to be quiet and she wouldn't get hurt. With all the strength Gertie had in her frail little body, she picked up her umbrella and started striking Eloise on the head. In one move Eloise grabbed the umbrella and tossed it to the other side of the room with Gertie still clinging to it. Gertie's arm was terribly bruised but she didn't let the pain stop her from trying again to stop Eloise from harming her friend. Bethany grabbed Eloise by the arm and paid for the gesture by receiving a painful blow to the side of her head. Bethany passed out at that point while Eloise slipped off her fancy dress and put an old patched up garment on her. What did it matter what she wore, she would be dead anyway if someone found her before the buzzards did.

Gertie watched in horror as Eloise picked up Bethany's limp body and tossed her like a sack of potatoes from the train. The last thing Gertie saw before fainting dead away was a sign that said *Now Leaving Camden Corners.*

Eloise donned one of Bethany's beautiful dresses and fixed her hair with Bethany's combs. She was lucky that she and Bethany were the same size and had the same hair color. She looked in the mirror and was very pleased with her appearance. She knew that the new Bethany Howell was much more beautiful than the old Bethany Howell and she was out to impress the world with her new found money.

What Eloise didn't realize was that she would not have access to Bethany's wealth until Bethany turned 18. Could she keep up this charade for the next 7 years? Well, she was going to have to but at least she could enjoy all the things money can buy while she waited.

Gertie woke up from her stupor and cried uncontrollably at the fate of her dear friend. She had always known Eloise was evil but never realized how evil she was until that day. Gertie knew what Eloise had planned and she would not let her get away with it. She would tell the conductor what happened and he would stop the train and go back to find Bethany. Eloise would go to prison for what she did even though she was still a child herself.

Eloise could see the look of hate in Gertie's eyes and told her not to even think about reporting the accident or hers would be the next body to be found by the buzzards. Not only that, Eloise would find her way back to Boston and kill Gertie's little brother and sister.

Gertie knew she had to keep quiet for now but she willed herself to be strong. She would avenge Bethany's murder. It might take years but she would do it.

Aunt Isabelle welcomed Bethany and her friend Gertie into her home.

"Bethany is pretty," she thought, "but she looks so different than I remember her. Her lovely honey color hair is the same and although she seems to have a hard streak in her it is probably because she just lost her parents. Gertie, on the other hand, is very sweet and gentle although it seems she is a frightened little waif.

The years went on and Eloise was just as sour as she had been the day she walked into Aunt Isabelle's house. She was terse with the servants and treated Aunt Isabelle like a senile old lady. All she could talk about was the fact that all the money would be hers soon and she wouldn't need Aunt Isabelle any longer.

Gertie had grown taller and stronger. The day of Bethany's murder still haunted her. She was determined to find a way to outsmart Eloise before she got her hands on any more of Bethany's money. She had come to love Aunt Isabelle and took comfort in the fact that Bethany had inherited many of the older woman's good qualities.

Gertie had taken pleasure in reading the daily newspaper to Aunt Isabelle. Isabelle's eyesight wasn't what it use to be and she enjoyed this time with Gertie as much as Gertie enjoyed being with dear Aunt Isabelle. There was a small article on the second last page.

Mystery girl found near railroad tracks in Camden Corners, New York. Authorities determined she had been a stowaway on the train headed to St. Louis. She suffers from a head injury and cannot remember even her name although she was wearing a child's handmade bracelet with the letter B on it.

Aunt Isabelle had dozed off and didn't see the light come back into Gertie's eyes. She knew her dear friend was alive and being cared for. She wanted to shout it to the rooftops but knew Eloise would find a way to get to Bethany and finish the job so Gertie remained silent. Gertie had become friendly with Sheriff Dingle and his deputy Hal Lawson. She had come close to telling them the whole story before she stopped herself for fear Eloise would be true to her promise of hurting her brother and sister.

On that fateful day, Bethany lie in a soft patch of land. She awoke when a floppy eared dog started licking her face. There wasn't a spot on her body that didn't cry out in pain as she tried to lift her head but found she couldn't do it.

She heard a boy's voice calling "Grover, come here boy. What have you got there buddy?"

Rusty Burke had been out hunting rabbits when his dog suddenly took off barking and just as suddenly stopped in front of a bundle lying on the ground. Rusty couldn't believe his eyes when he saw it was a girl. He could tell she was still alive but just barely. He told Grover to stay with her while he rode into town to get Doc McMillan.

He called to his brother as he rode by their house to bring the buckboard and meet him at the old elm tree down by the railroad tracks.

By the time Doc arrived on the scene, Bethany had been able to open her eyes. She knew she had a friend for life in the attentive little mutt beside her.

Very carefully, Bethany's body was lifted onto the buckboard and slowly driven into town to Doc's office. Grover ran along beside not taking his eyes off Bethany for a second.

Doc didn't find anything other than bruises on the girl's body that indicated she fell or was pushed from the train. He noted her worn out dress but his nurse noticed her very expensive looking under garments. She was definitely a mystery. Everything except the dress spoke of wealth and yet she had very sad eyes. Something had gone very wrong in her life to warrant such a sorrowful look.

After several hours, Doc determined it was safe to move the girl, Rusty insisted she be moved to The Burke house where she was welcomed as one of the family.

Sheriff Mendenhall had checked with the railroad and everyone had been accounted for on the day Grover found the girl by the railroad tracks. There were no leads and the newspaper article placed in every paper from Camden Corners to St. Louis had not turned up any information.

Jennie Burke had just turned 11 and seemed the closest in age to this young girl. She began reading Little Women to Bethany and every time the youngest daughter Beth was mentioned, Bethany showed signs of recognition. Jennie began calling her Beth and the name stuck. She was known from that point on as Beth Burke. Grover sat by Bethany's side through her recovery. Her head injury seemed to healing with the exception of the loss of her memory.

The months spread into years and Beth was a real part of the family. She loved being in the kitchen and watched and learned as her adoptive mother prepared delicious meals and made delectable baked goods for her family. Rusty had a soft spot in his heart for Beth and he knew she would always be the woman for him. Beth had fallen in love with Rusty too but was afraid there might be something in her past that would be unforgivable.

The Burkes celebrated Beth's birthday on the anniversary of the day Grover found her all crumbled and broken out by the railroad tracks. The Burkes and the Mackenzies gathered for Beth's celebrated 18th birthday. Unknown to them, it was just a couple of weeks shy of her actual birthday. They all encouraged her to make a wish before she blew out the candles and her wish was that she would remember who she was. She needed to know that before she could marry Rusty. Rusty didn't feel the same way. He loved Beth and nothing in her past would change that.

Meanwhile in St. Louis, Gertie finally had the courage to tell Sheriff Dingle about the incident on the train and how Bethany was thrown in a heap near a place called Camden Corners. Sheriff Dingle thought nothing could surprise him but this took the cake. He and the rest of the town had never cared for the girl they thought was Bethany. They knew she had been unkind to Miss Isabelle. It all made sense to him now. He had heard for many years that Bethany Howell was a lovely young girl who would win the hearts of anyone who knew her. He and Deputy Hal made a call to Miss Eloise Hanover and arrested her for the attempted murder and impersonation of Bethany Howell.

Eloise shouted at Gertie on her way out the door "Your little brother and sister are dead thanks to your big mouth."

Gertie knew they were safe and the sheriff in Boston was aware of the threats. He told Gertie not to worry since her little brother had grown to be six foot four and he doubted any harm would come to either of them.

Aunt Isabelle was beside herself. How could she have believed for one minute that Eloise was the product of her dear nephew and his lovely wife. Everyone assured Isabelle that Eloise was a good actress and they all had been fooled by her.

The next morning, Gertie and Isabelle were on the train bound for Camden Corners. The sheriff sent Deputy Hal along with them to guide them on there way. Hal wasn't unhappy with his duty because he loved any excuse to be with Miss Gertie.

The sheriff sent a wire to Sheriff Mendenhall in Camden Corners telling him what had transpired. Sheriff Mendenhall was telling the Burkes and Beth the story Gertie had finally reported. Beth's wish had come true just a couple of days after she had made it.

Rusty and Beth waited for the train's arrival. Beth was nervous about meeting someone from her past and hoped to find some answers. As

Deputy Hal and a pretty young girl helped an older lady off the train, Bethany looked into her old friend Gertie's eyes and everything came back to her. She shouted Gertie's name and flew into the sobbing girls arms.

"Oh Gertie, Mama and Papa are dead" the memory of that awful night came back to her. Aunt Isabelle knew right away that this beautiful young girl was her niece from Boston. She could also see that the handsome young man standing next to her was head over heels in love with her darling Bethany.

The girls giggled and laughed all the way to the Burke home where Gertie and Aunt Isabelle were treated as royalty. Gertie was a little embarrassed by the attention and reminded them she was a servant.

"Not around here you aren't" said Rusty. "We will take care of you from now on. You brought our Beth's memories to life again and for that we will be forever grateful."

Several weeks later on Bethany's real 18th birthday, her solicitor from Boston arrived in Camden Corners. Bethany was an extremely wealthy woman. Bethany didn't want any of the money. She found her happily ever after with Rusty Burke right here in Camden Corners and couldn't imagine her life any different than it had been for all these years. The solicitor set up a foundation in Clarence and Miranda's name. Gertie was the first recipient of a full scholarship to a nursing school in St. Louis. Her brother and sister were the second and third. All of the children of the household staffs in Aunt Isabelle's home and those they could locate from Bethany's Boston home were given scholarships to the schools of their choice.

Several years later when the nurses cap was being placed on Gertie's head, Bethany, Rusty and baby Miranda Burke were there cheering her on along with Hal Lawson who was bursting with pride for his wife.

Eloise was sitting in her jail cell thinking about all the money that nitwit Bethany just threw away on her servant friends.

"What a waste!"

Doctor Julie McMillan

Julie McMillan had been a source of pride and exasperation to her father, Doctor Benjamin McMillan. Julie was the youngest of Mary and Doc McMillan's two daughters. Josephine was a quiet, well behaved young lady even at an early age. Julie was born during the worst

52

thunderstorm that anyone in Camden Corners could remember. With claps of thunder nearly breaking the sound barrier, the neighbors could still hear Julie's cries the moment she was born. She was a rough and tumble tomboy all through her childhood. Even the older boys in town didn't mess with Julie and if they did they had the bruises to show for it. Tommy Campbell was the only boy who wasn't afraid of Julie. He always treated her like a girl and Julie didn't like that one bit.

As the years went on, she noticed her heart beat a little faster when Tommy was close. It made Julie so mad she would punch him just because he was near her. Tommy just smiled at her and went about his business.

Tommy had known from a very young age that he wanted to be a doctor. When he was nearly 7 years old, his Momma had become very ill with a high fever that strained her heart. Doc McMillan had been by her bedside day after day until she showed signs of improvement. All of the neighbors that stopped by to see her left in tears. Although they didn't say anything to Tommy, he knew they all thought his precious Momma was going to die. Doc told him that he would not give up on her until she was well again and he was as good as his word. Doc believed in miracles as well as medicine and after his mother fully recovered, so did Tommy. From that point on, Tommy followed Doc around whenever he could. Eventually he applied to medical school and off he went with Doc's blessing.

Julie missed Tommy when he left town although she wouldn't admit that even to herself. Julie didn't know when her interest in medicine had begun. Maybe it was because she was following around after Tommy as he was following around after Doc. She announced one evening that she had decided to go to medical school herself and become a doctor.

Doc thought it was a noble profession, but not for a female. It was difficult enough for a man, but women had it so much harder. Julie, always up for a challenge, was not to be dissuaded. Mary told Ben he'd better just give in because Julie would do what she wanted anyway. Doc, Mary and Josephine saw Julie off at the train station. Mary knew Julie wouldn't appreciate tears from any of her family so they all remained stoic until the train left the station. If medical school had been difficult for Julie, she never let on. Dr. Julie McMillan graduated with honors and was ready to practice medicine alongside her father and Tom who had joined her Dad the previous year.

Doc McMillan was happy to have the extra help with his patients. He had been the only doctor in Camden Corners for many years. Mary began helping Doc with his office work when he started his practice on the first floor of the old McMillan family home. Together they decided it was high time they took a vacation and planned a trip to St. Louis to attend the World's Fair and maybe see some of the sights along the way.

Martha Wharton's niece, Louisa was coming to Camden Corners to stay with her aunt for an extended period of time. Martha suggested that Louisa would be available to help out with the office work while Mary was away. Louisa had worked for doctors before so Mary would be happy to have her fill in while she was gone. When Louisa arrived at the McMillan house, Mary invited her into the reception area. Since all the doctors were with patients, she began to show her the files and went over the routine of the office. Doc and Julie both finished with their patients and Mary introduced them to Louisa.

Before long Tom came out of the examining room after stitching up Willie Burke's split lip. He stopped in his tracks as Louisa Andrews threw her arms around him and gave him a big kiss on the lips. Tom had rented a room in his classmate Ted's house while he was in college. Louisa was Ted's sister. She was just a kid back then. He had to admit she wasn't a kid anymore. The fellows all teased him because Louisa would follow him around and moon over him. It was embarrassing then and he was really embarrassed now.

Tom had fallen in love with Julie McMillan when he first saw her pounding a bully on the playground because he was picking on a kid much younger and smaller than he was. Julie didn't seem to return the feelings then or all through high school.

Tom was determined to be a doctor and spent most of his time learning all he could from Doc. Since Julie had joined the practice, she was always pleasant but a bit aloof. Tom was mortified when he learned that Louisa would be living in Mrs. Wharton's boarding house just two doors down from his family home.

Louisa was very efficient in the office and Julie had no complaints about her work but she was none too happy with the way she acted with Tom. She had gotten in the habit of waiting for Tom to leave his house in the morning and stepping out of the boarding house at the same time so they could walk to work together. She arranged for Julie to take all the late appointments freeing Tom up to walk her home. Louisa made up her mind she was going to marry Tom Campbell when was 12 years old. She knew he was planning to return to Camden Corners after he graduated from medical school. She figured she would be just the right age for marriage at that time and was so happy her Aunt Martha just happened to live in Camden Corners. She knew it was fate when Aunt Martha told her Mary McMillan was looking for someone to take over for her while she was on vacation.

Louisa was getting very frustrated. She had done everything she could think of to make Tom fall in love with her. She knew she was very pretty and had a figure to match. She had her choice of any number of fellows back home. Tom was kind to her but there was no spark.

One day she noticed that Tom was looking at Julie with longing in his eyes and she immediately knew what the problem was and her name was Julie. Somehow, some way she would have to make sure he got over those silly feelings. Louisa began her vendetta that very afternoon. Julie had written a prescription for nausea medication for Joey Barber after he had eaten too many green apples. Louisa knew enough about medication to know that if she just changed one or two letters, Joey would be given something to make him just a little bit sicker. She would purposely write down the wrong messages for Julie or tell Julie she had time to go to lunch and then her next patient would show up and be left in the waiting room for an hour.

Tom was beginning to be suspicious of Louisa. Ever since she started working in the office mistakes were being made and the fault always seemed to point to Julie. Then the call came in from Mr. Flanagan. His son had fallen off a ladder and wasn't moving. Louisa said she would send Julie there right away but didn't even attempt to contact her. Tom happened to be taking a walk by the fish hatchery and noticed the commotion. He examined Terry Flanagan and determined he'd had the wind knocked out of him and would be just fine after a short rest. Mr. Flanagan said he had spoken to Louisa and she was sending Julie but Julie never arrived. Tom confronted Louisa. She tried to tell him she had given Julie the message. As it turned out, Julie was seeing the Henderson family at their home. Each one of their six children had come down with the chicken pox that morning. Julie had been there for several hours and wasn't upstairs sleeping as Louisa said she was. Tom wanted an explanation and Louisa admitted she wanted Julie out of the picture so Tom would notice her. Tom was normally a very calm and easy going man but his friends and neighbors were being jeopardized by Louisa's foolish behavior.

"You are fired and you are lucky I'm not calling the sheriff to have you arrested for for purposely endangering our patients. Julie McMillan is a fine doctor and the woman I love and have always loved now get out."

Julie walked into the office just at that moment and was speechless but not for long. She opened her purse and handed Louisa her pay and stood next to the man she had loved for as long as she could remember. Louisa made a quick exit and while Julie and Tom were kissing and laughing and kissing some more, she was on her way to pack her bags to get out of town.

Martha Wharton hated to admit it but she was glad to see her niece go. Louisa Andrews was a very annoying young lady.

A Mysterious Find

Sarah Lane, assistant librarian for Camden Corners Library was engrossed in the latest novel by her all time favorite author, J.K. Ellingsworth when she suddenly had the feeling someone was standing in front of her. Startled, she dropped the book and looked up into the most beautiful green eyes she had ever seen. Maxwell Harcourt smiled at the pretty young woman who happened to be reading his latest novel. Max was a tall muscular guy who didn't fit the mold of a romance writer although he never thought of his novels as romantic. It just made them a bit more interesting if there was a love affair going on while his hero was solving the latest murder or catching criminals. His agent told him with his good looks, he would sell even more of his works if he agreed to a book tour. Max enjoyed escaping with his pen and paper and letting his imagination spill out onto the pages. He had written 25 novels and no one except his trusted agent knew who J.K. Ellingsworth was. Max wanted to keep it that way.

He had just arrived in Camden Corners, rented a room in the Wharton House and set out immediately for the library to check out a reference book or two hoping inspiration would come for another novel.

Sarah composed herself and offered her assistance to this stranger with the green eyes. She was just reading about Gilmartin Trent and his latest escapade when she looked up and saw her hero standing before her. Of course he wasn't this fictional character but she was certain Gil would look just like this stranger. Sarah was pleased to learn Mr. Harcourt would be living in Camden Corners. There were a number of good looking men in town but most of them were already taken. She was happy to present him with a library card and guide him to the reference section. Sarah went back to her book but found it hard to concentrate while keeping one eye toward the back section of the library.

Max was contemplating his next novel. He had envisioned a village much like Camden Corners. A calm peaceful town where people knew and liked each other. A town where crime usually consisted of a young lad swiping a piece of taffy from the candy shop on Main, or a smitten teenager stealing a kiss behind the cottonwood tree in the park. Camden Corners would be the perfect location for a perfect crime.

Max spent the next two hours scanning books of history written about Camden Corners. One book had been placed behind other reference books on the uppermost shelf in the corner of the aisle. Max's arms were long enough to reach the large book and noticed it was covered with dust. It must have been hidden in this corner for a very long time. That being the case, Max was curious as to what was hidden and by whom. As he was leafing through the pages, he came upon an article that had been cut out of a newspaper and folded over several times.

The headline read: *"MYSTERY IN CAMDEN CORNERS. Aug. 11, 1801 – Long time residents of Camden Corners, Simon and Hannah Lane and Simon's brother, Caleb have disappeared from their home in the Camden Creek area. Friends and neighbors report the family had become reclusive the last few months. Simon and Hannah welcomed twin boys in early spring of last year. Friends calling on the Lanes claim a female caretaker was tending Mrs. Lane as she had contracted an undisclosed illness. Sheriff Martin from nearby Greensboro was summoned to investigate the property and found it to be vacated. Friends and neighbors are suspicious and fear for the safety of the family.*

Another article dated two days later reported three bodies had been discovered and quoted Sheriff Martin saying the deaths were accidental and he was doubtful foul play is involved and has closed the case.

Max glanced over towards Sarah. He remembered that her name plate said Sarah Lane.

"I wonder if she knows anything about this mystery and why the articles had been stashed in the book."

Max noted the time and realized the library had officially closed 15 minutes earlier. He apologized to Sarah for keeping her and checked out the reference book with the article inside.

"Would it be too presumptuous of me to ask you to join me for supper this evening" he asked an enamored Sarah.

"I would like that very much" replied Sarah.

The couple left the library after Sarah turned out the lights and locked the door. They stopped by Sarah's house. Sarah wanted to pick up her wrap as the air was turning cooler. Sarah introduced Max to her parents, Marian and Andrew Lane and her two little brothers who were playing a game of catch on the front lawn.

Marian could tell her daughter was taken with this handsome young man and worried about her. He seemed a bit too worldly for her sheltered daughter who lived in a fantasy world with her romance novels. Andrew, on the other hand was happy to see Sarah with a flesh and blood man for a change instead of having her nose buried in a book.

On the way to O'Sullivan's Pub, Sarah told him story after story of the little shops and the people who owned them. He was interested in the citizens of Camden Corners but wanted to learn more about the Lane family and if they had ever returned to Camden Corners.

By the time the corned beef and cabbage arrived at their table, Sarah and Max both felt they had known each other all their lives.

He asked about her family and how long the Lanes had been in Camden Corners. She told him her Dad was born and raised in Baltimore, Maryland. He had come to Camden Corners right after graduation from normal school and had been teaching at Camden High School ever since. Her mother had lived here all her life. Max wondered aloud what brought Andrew to Camden Corners and Sarah answered that he had relatives who had lived here.

"His great grandfather, Simon and his great great uncle, Caleb were members of the community. It seems, Simon was shot and killed protecting his brother from hoodlums who were passing through town. Caleb set out to capture the thugs and bring them to justice but was killed himself when he was trampled by a horse attempting to save a young lady from the raging waters of the Patapsco River. Simon's widow was so distraught over her husband's death, she died of a broken heart two months later leaving her toddler twin sons alone in the world. The twins were raised in an orphanage. One of those boys was my great grandfather Charles Lane."

"What a fascinating tale" thought Max. "I certainly can't ask Sarah about the articles now."

All too soon the evening ended. Max walked Sarah to her front door. He may have tried to kiss her cheek but Marian was standing in the doorway. Max thought he may have seen a rolling pin hidden behind her back. He hoped it was only his imagination. That night, Sarah fell asleep dreaming of her own happy ending with her very own Gilmartin Trent.

Max was enjoying a tasty breakfast served by Mrs. Wharton at the boarding house. He was the first tenant to arrive at the dining table. While Mrs. Wharton was serving him his eggs and bacon he nonchalantly mentioned the Lane Brothers.

Mrs. Wharton suddenly became very quiet.

Finally, she whispered "There is something very strange about that affair. Everyone has been led to believe that those brothers were the salt of the earth but when I was just a young lass, I heard my daddy and his friends talking about the murder. There was a newspaper article that told the story of the disappearance of the entire family, but it hasn't been found in over 70 years. Someone has tried to cover up something strange all these years. My daddy said Caleb Lane picked up a floozy named Sylvia from the pub, married her and took her back to his cabin. From that day on, sweet Miss Hannah had not been seen again. From what I have heard, Miss Sylvia was not a one man woman, if you know what I mean."

Mrs. Wharton paused to catch her breath and then went on. "You didn't hear that from me. I'm not one to speak ill of the dead, but there is something very strange about that whole thing. Why do you ask, Maxwell?"

"Oh, no reason, I just came upon the Lane name in one of the reference books at the library. I also spent a delightful evening with Miss Sarah Lane."

As soon as the words were out of his mouth, Max knew the very talkative Mrs. Wharton would be sharing this tidbit of information with the whole town.

Max had an appointment with Robert Crowley. He needed an attorney in Camden Corners if he was planing to stay here very long. His agent had recommended Mr. Crowley to handle his business affairs. Max wanted to keep his alter ego, J. K. Ellingsworth under wraps for the time being. Max was impressed with Robert and felt certain he would be trustworthy.

Max had carried the newspaper clippings with him in his brief case and asked Robert what he thought of it. He mentioned speaking to Mrs. Wharton and what she said about the missing articles. Robert thought it was very interesting. He had heard conflicting stories about the incident through the years but the man to speak with would be his dad, Oscar Crowley.

A Secret Revealed

Oscar Crowley liked to drop by the Crowley Law Office every day. He had total confidence in his sons, Robert and Richard to keep things going in the practice he began years before, but he missed being part of the action. He was as spry as anyone 30 years younger than he was and Miss Nettie Dawson might have been partly responsible for that.

Robert knew this mystery would delight his father and asked him to step into his office. Robert introduced the two men and showed Oscar the newspaper article Max had discovered in a book in the library. Oscar was amazed that it had been found and that it was so obviously hidden. Oscar's father was just a young boy when the Lane family vanished. Oscar remembered the adults always stopped their conversation about the incident whenever he was within earshot. He had heard enough to fear that one day he and his family might disappear in the middle of the night. To this day he liked to keep a small light burning near his bedroom door. Max thoroughly enjoyed being with the elder gentleman that morning as he told him everything he had heard about the mystery.

That afternoon Max stopped by the library. He saw Sarah in the children's section surrounded by preschoolers as she read them the story of The Ugly Duckling. Sarah was unlike any other female he had ever known. She was beautiful inside and out. Maybe he should drop the subject of the Lane brothers, after all it happened so long ago. He knew he wouldn't be able to do that. His instincts for a good story were too much a part of him. Sarah looked up from her book and grinned from ear to ear. She was very happy to see Mr. Maxwell Harcourt. She led the children back to their waiting mothers and nannies and greeted Max with a warm handshake.

It was almost lunchtime. Marian had packed Sarah a lunch that morning and as Sarah guessed, it was much more than she could eat alone. She asked if Max would like to share it with her out on the lawn where she liked to spread her blanket and watch people walk by. Today though, she wouldn't be alone as he readily agreed to join her. She picked up her lunch bucket and set aside her J. K. Ellingsworth novel. Max asked if she was enjoying the book.

"Oh yes, J. K. Ellingsworth is my favorite author and as much of a mystery as the novels he or she writes."

"He or She?" Max exclaimed just a little too loudly.

"I think J.K. is a man although he is very good about bringing romance into each story. Everyone else in my book club thinks she is a woman. Not that J.K. couldn't be a woman's name. Did you know that Louisa May Alcott wrote as A. M. Barnard enabling her to write darker and racier themes so that she could gain the financial freedom to write the way she really wanted in her later years? And do you know the name Mary Ann Evans? Most people know her by her pen name, George Eliot."

Max wondered if maybe he should have chosen a different pseudonym for himself. Ellingsworth was the name of his first grade teacher and J and K were two letters in the alphabet that had no special meaning except they happened to be side by side on his typewriter. It never occurred to him that anyone would think he was a woman. Maybe he was laying the romance on a little thick. He knew nothing about romance. He had never been in love and never found anyone he wanted to spend the rest of his life with. Not until now that is.

Sarah began extolling the virtues of Gilmartin Trent. The way she talked, old Gil was a real person. To Max he was a real person too but for crying out loud, he was a figment of **his** imagination not Sarah's. He couldn't believe he was thinking this way. Of course he wanted his character to seem real. That's what sold his books. Could he be jealous of this imaginary character? Max was feeling uncomfortable and finally, Sarah changed the subject. She wondered what brought Max to town. He told her he was doing some research on small towns in the area. He avoided telling her it was for his next novel.

Sarah and Max were enjoying relaxing under the big elm tree when Mrs. Wharton came scurrying across the lawn.

"Mr. Harcourt" she shouted. "Someone left this letter for you attached to your outside door. It is my duty as landlady to insure the safety of my tenants which meant I was forced to read the letter. It is a warning for you to leave town or harm will come to you. Mr. Harcourt, I must ask you to vacate your room immediately."

"Now Mrs. Wharton, calm down. I'm sure there is a logical explanation for this letter. Let me read it please."

The letter was exactly as Mrs. Wharton had stated but it gave Max some time to think what he would say to Sarah who was standing next to him with a very concerned look on her face.

"I understand your concern Mrs. Wharton, I am sure this is nothing but a prank but I will clear my belongings out of the room in your house."

Mrs. Wharton was relieved but Sarah had even more questions about this handsome stranger. Max decided it was time to reveal his identity to Sarah. He asked Sarah if he could meet with her when she finished her duties at the library. He had things to discuss with her and he didn't want to be interrupted. Sarah knew Max was a man of mystery and couldn't help comparing him with her fictional hero, Delmartin Trent. Could it be that Maxwell Harcourt was really J.K. Ellingsworth? Sarah thought that was impossible and discounted the possibility immediately, but she was wondering who her new friend really was.

Andrew Lane had heard folks buzzing about the stranger in town and the fact that he had been questioning people about the Lane family of years ago. Andrew didn't have anything to hide but he had made a promise to his grandfather that he would find out all he could about the Lane brothers and the woman who seemed to be so important in their lives. Andrew was happy being a history teacher in the local high school and was a content family man. He had never had the time or the desire to investigate the mysterious disappearance of his ancestors. Maybe it was time he paid a visit to J.K. Ellingsworth. Andrew had discovered several years ago that his favorite mystery author wrote under the pen name of J. K. Ellingsworth. As was typical of Andrew, he never did see any reason to reveal to anyone Mr. Harcourt's true identity. He had heard Mrs. Wharton's tale of finding a threatening note on Max' door that morning. Andrew decided it was time to confront Mr. Harcourt. He was beginning to worry that his beloved daughter might be falling for Max. He honestly didn't think that was such a bad idea but he did need to find out for himself whether Max was a charlatan or just an interested writer who was as smitten with his daughter as she was with him. Andrew arranged for Mrs. Green to oversee his classes for the remainder of the afternoon and set out to meet with Max.

Max wasn't totally surprised to see Andrew turning the corner and heading toward the park. The two men greeted each other cordially. Andrew confessed he knew about J.K. Ellingsworth. Max explained that he had submitted dozens of manuscripts under his own name before he became J.K. Ellingsworth. He decided since Maxwell Harcourt had worn out his welcome with every publishing company he would try another name and it worked. Andrew questioned Max about his interest in the Lane disappearances of long ago. Max explained finding the newspaper article hidden in the reference book. As a writer, he couldn't let the matter go without investigating. He did promise Andrew that he would do nothing to embarrass the Lane family and had already decided he was not going to make it the basis of his next novel. Andrew let Max know about his promise to his grandfather. He thought maybe now was the time to make good on that promise. They both went to see Oscar Crowley and let him know that Andrew's grandfather had asked him to find out what happened to his family and that Charles Lane had been left on the doorstep of an orphanage. Max left the law office to meet Sarah as she would be closing the library shortly. Andrew and Oscar were still deep in conversation.

Sarah was just walking down the steps of the library when she spotted Max walking toward her. Her heart skipped a beat as he took her hand. Although there was a chill in the night air, the couple found a bench by the lake where they didn't think they would be disturbed. Max explained that he didn't mean to deceive Sarah but he was the author, J.K. Ellingsworth. Sarah's heart skipped another beat. She was silently fearing she would call Max by her hero's name Delmartin. Max thought maybe he had lost any chance with Sarah because of his dishonesty.

Sarah then turned to him and exclaimed "I can't wait to tell my book club friends that J.K. really is a man."

Max filled Sarah in on all that was known about the Lane brothers. She remembered when she was young, she and her friends would go into the woods behind the Camden Hill Ski Lodge looking for the Lane cabins. Although the days were getting shorter, the couple thought they would have about an hour to explore the location before the sun set for the day. They borrowed Andrew's horse and buggy and were off into the woods to see what they could find.

Sarah could feel the excitement building inside her. She felt she was off to solve a mystery with her favorite fictional character, a living, breathing Delmartin Trent. It was a much shorter ride to the old cabins than Sarah recalled. Both cabins were barely standing. They walked to the first cabin, it was rather small with a fairly large area combining a cooking, eating and sitting area. Beyond was a room with a large bed and chest of drawers. The bed was covered in a handmade quilt that, although covered in dust, looked lovely on the hand carved bed. There were two very tiny beds in the corner of the room. Max wondered why after all these years, someone hadn't torn down the cabins or at least taken the furniture out of them. In spite of the dust and cobwebs, it appeared to be in the same condition as the former occupants left it so long ago. Max carefully examined every piece of furniture in the cabin. He discovered a journal secured to the underside of the chest in the bedroom. Carefully, he removed the journal from its hiding place. At the same time, Sarah was examining the quilt. There was a small tear on the left edge of the it and Sarah could tell something was inside.

She carefully felt around with her fingers and pulled out a piece of paper in shaky handwriting, it said "Something is happening to me. I am afraid Sylvia has been poisoning me with one of her potions. Simon will not believe me. I fear for my boys. With all the strength I have left in me, I have buried the treasure in the hollow of the old evergreen tree at the edge of the woods. I want my precious little boys, Charles and Seth to have the treasure. Please tell them how much their mother loves them."

It was signed Hannah Lane.

Hannah's Treasure

The journal Max found hidden in the chest of drawers was page after page of the life of Hannah and Simon Lane. They were childhood sweethearts. Simon and his brother, Caleb were only a year apart in age and were the best of friends as well as brothers. The first several pages of the journal were filled with what seemed to be the perfect life of a young couple. Eventually the twins were born and the happiness continued until a woman named Sylvia came into their lives.

Caleb had been to town enjoying a few beers with some other fellows when the very beautiful Sylvia Reynolds entered the pub. Caleb took one look at this dazzling young woman and fell madly in love. Sylvia sat down next to Caleb and ordered a beer. Caleb had never known a woman who drank beer before. His sister-in-law, Hannah made cranberry wine and apple brandy every fall but he never saw her indulge in a man's drink like beer. Sylvia was like no other woman Caleb had ever known. She wore a very low cut dress and Caleb had a hard time keeping his eyes away from the obvious endowments the good Lord gave her.

Back at his cabin, Simon began to be concerned about his brother. He hadn't heard Caleb return home as yet and he knew his brother couldn't hold his drink. Simon was afraid he might run into trouble. He kissed Hannah goodbye and started off to town to check on Caleb. Sure enough, Caleb was slumped over the bar. Simon threw him over his shoulder and started off for home.

The next morning, Caleb woke up with a terrible headache but knew he had to find Sylvia, the love of his life. He paid a visit to Simon and Hannah and told them that if all went well, he would be bringing home a wife very soon. Simon wondered where Caleb had found his intended and then remembered seeing a very striking young woman looking at him the night before as he was carrying his brother out the door. Caleb arrived in town and was disappointed to see Sylvia walking arm in arm with a nattily dressed gentleman. She spotted Caleb and introduced the gentleman as her brother, Horace Reynolds. Horace had just accepted a position as a reporter for the Greensboro News. The brother and sister were planning to settle down in this area and were looking for a place to live in Camden Corners. Caleb was overjoyed that Sylvia would be staying in town. He invited both Sylvia and Horace to supper that night. He shared his meals with Simon and Hannah and hoped Hannah wouldn't mind two extra mouths to feed. Horace thanked Caleb for the invitation. He had a meeting to attend that evening but he would appreciate it if Caleb would keep an eye on his sister for him.

Hannah was happy to have company that evening and took special pains to prepare a company meal. She thought she might even take out a little of her elderberry wine for the occasion. Hannah liked Sylvia upon meeting her. She was like no one Hannah had ever known. She laughed and joked and fussed over the twins. Hannah was happy for Caleb and when he announced his intention of marrying Sylvia a week later, Hannah was thrilled. Simon wasn't so sure but he congratulated his brother and kept his doubts to himself. The wedding was a quiet affair with a friend of the Reynolds family officiating. It took place in the woods behind the Lane cabins. None of the townsfolk were invited. Only Simon, Hannah and Horace Reynolds attended the ceremony.

Caleb was ecstatic for the next few weeks and then everything began to change. Sylvia was spending more time with her brother in Greensboro than she was with Caleb. When she wasn't with her brother, she was having tea with Hannah. Even Hannah seemed to be changing. She was tired all the time and not the happy go lucky girl he had known all his life. Simon didn't seem to notice. Although Simon initially wondered if Sylvia was right for his brother, he had become quite fond of her.

Marriage wasn't anything like Caleb had anticipated and he began to find solace in visiting Joel Mason's still for his moonshine more and more often. Hannah wrote in her journal that she was feeling poorly. She didn't seem to have energy anymore. She was beginning to wonder if Sylvia was really her friend. Maybe she shouldn't have told her about the treasure.

Hannah's great uncle, Reginald, had given her a satchel filled with money. He told her the day may come when she would need some extra cash and she should save it for a rainy day. She had put it away and hadn't mentioned it to Simon because she had been so happy with their lives and the money didn't matter to her. The entries in the journal were changing. Hannah's beautiful penmanship had become shaky and the content was difficult to understand until all the pages were blank except the very last page which said, "I must keep this journal away from Sylvia. She wants the treasure."

Max and Sarah were so engrossed in what they were reading they didn't hear the front door open or the man walk in with his gun pointed at Max's heart. He opened the bedroom door wider and didn't realize Sarah was behind it. For some reason she carried her book bag into the cabin with her. The bag contained 4 of her favorite J.K. Ellingsworth novels. She picked up the bag twirled it in the air around her head and with all her might let it fall onto the top of the intruder's head knocking him out cold. The bullet ended up in the foot of the bed.

Sarah was shaking like a leaf but managed to chuckle as she shouted "Delmartin Trent to the rescue."

She found some rope in the bottom cabinet in the kitchen and Max tied the stranger's hands and feet and still unconscious deposited him in the buggy to deliver him to the sheriff.

By the time the stranger woke up, Sheriff Mendenhall who had checked his identification was just receiving a telegram from the Baltimore Police Department. Mr. Errol Reynolds was wanted on fraud charges up and down the east coast. Errol's head hurt and his vision was blurry. He was afraid he was about to die and decided that the only chance for salvation was to tell the truth.

Errol confessed to being the great great grandson of Horace and Sylvia Reynolds. His grandfather, Horace Jr. was the only child born to Sylvia and Horace. Junior was brought up by his grandmother while his parents were going from town to town conning unsuspecting innocents like Caleb Lane. Normally, they only stayed in town a few weeks, that was usually all it took for their victims to succumb to Sylvia's charms and part with their money. Caleb Lane was just another chump but when Sylvia charmed her way into the Simon Lane home, her new friend Hannah was the answer to her prayers. She knew it wouldn't be difficult to get her hands on the treasure Hannah spoke of. Once they were through with Camden Corners and the Lanes, Sylvia and Horace would be able to take a vacation. Maybe spend some time with little Horace, Jr.

Horace had arranged for one of his old prison buddies to officiate at the wedding of Caleb and Sylvia. He knew he didn't have any competition in Caleb because Sylvia was slipping potion into Caleb's food and drink. She was doctoring Simon and Hannah's food too but she never went so far as to taint the twins' food. She wasn't a totally despicable person.

Hannah and Caleb died within a few days of each other. Simon was so distraught and suffering from the effects of the drugs he had been given it took all his strength to bury his brother and wife in the woods. As he was walking back to the cabins, Horace picked up Caleb's rifle and shot Simon letting his body drift down the river. He gathered up the twins piled them and a stunned Sylvia into his buggy and drove off. The foursome traveled to the county children's home near Baltimore and left the baby boys on the doorstep just before dawn. Horace and Sylvia headed back to their home and Horace, Jr. without the money from the treasure that Hannah had talked about.

Sylvia never recovered from the ordeal of seeing her husband kill a man in cold blood. In her mind it was worse than slowly poisoning someone. Horace, who had a penchant for gambling was shot and killed when he was caught cheating at poker. Sylvia rambled on day and night about the treasure in Camden Corners. Horace, Jr. promised his mother on her deathbed that he would find the treasure. Several years later he walked into the Camden Corners Library, found the newspaper article and buried it in a reference book and put the book as far back in the corner as he could. Junior thought he would be back to look for the treasure but went home to Baltimore and married Daphne Hill who gave birth to Errol's father.

When Errol was a youngster, his grandfather talked about the treasure. He never did go back to Camden Corners, Daphne called him a dreamer and wouldn't let him go off on a wild goose chase.

Errol heard the story of the treasure so many times he knew he had to find it. When he came into town a week ago, that nosy writer was already there and Errol thought he was snooping for his great grandmother Sylvia's treasure. He tried to scare him away but only managed to scare his landlady. He was going to make sure Mr. J.K. Ellingsworth never wrote another book. He thought he had him cornered when suddenly he felt a blow to the back of his head and now he was dying. After his confession and arrest, he was turned over to the Baltimore police department for prosecution in several crimes. Mr. Errol Reynolds would be incarcerated for many years.

Near the end of October Max finished his novel. It wasn't the story of the Lane family, but of the folks of a town similar to Camden Corners. The hero this time wasn't his old pal Delmartin Trent but a young writer who was looking for the perfect town and found it along with the perfect young lady. With encouragement from Max, Sarah wrote her own novel. She didn't want to let Max see it until it was finished and didn't tell him that she was writing a tragedy. Sarah felt Hannah's story deserved to be told. She asked Max to read it and give his honest opinion.

Max couldn't believe that Sarah had told her great great grandmother's story so beautifully. He didn't let on that he had read it. He told Sarah he needed to finish his novel before beginning hers because he would lose his concentration. She thought he was probably afraid he wouldn't like it and didn't want to hurt her feelings.

Max and Sarah were married soon after and moved into the small cabin in the woods where Hannah and Simon had been so happy for such a short time. They were able to buy the land and cabin from the county.

Neighbors all helped to make the cabin liveable for the honeymooners.

A few days before Christmas, Max and Sarah ventured into the woods behind their home looking for a pine tree to decorate for the holiday. Max found a tree that had been around for at least 100 years. It seemed to reach to the sky, as Max and Sarah stood back to admire the huge tree, Sarah happened to notice a bulge in the trunk. Max pulled away some of the bark and dollar bills began to flow. They knew they had found Hannah's treasure. They gathered up all the money and were astonished to find they were all $100 bills totaling over $100,000.

They took the money to Sheriff Mendenhall and called Oscar Crowley and Andrew to meet them at the sheriff's office. Since the money was found on Max and Sarah's land, the conclusion was that it rightfully belonged to them.

Without hesitation, the couple chose not to accept the money for themselves. The treasure had caused enough heartache for Hannah and her little family. They decided to donate it to the orphanage in Baltimore where the Lane twins had been left so long ago.

On Christmas Eve, in the quiet of their cabin home, Max presented Sarah with two beautifully wrapped gifts. Sarah was thrilled to receive the first edition of Max's new novel dedicated to her. The second was another book, she opened it up and there was her very first published work, Hannah's Treasure. Sarah was laughing and crying at the same time as Max took her in his arms.

Sarah suspected Hannah somehow knew that the real treasure was love. Just then Sarah glanced out the window and saw the stars twinkling brightly and reflecting on the old evergreen tree that had held Hannah's Treasure.

The Christmas Show

Maybelle Witherspoon was in a tizzy. Christmas was four months away but she just received a letter from her niece in Greensboro. Katrina was in the family way and Maybelle would be needed to tend to her during her infirmity and the birth of her child. Maybelle was happy about the baby but the timing couldn't have been worse. How in the world would she be able to plan for and present the annual Camden Corners Christmas Pageant from Greensboro?

Molly Edwards had been her assistant for the last few years. Molly was the second grade teacher. She dreaded the Christmas Program planning. Oh she loved everything about Christmas especially the excitement of the children but helping Maybelle Witherspoon was a challenge she wasn't looking forward to.

Maybelle fancied herself a talented singer. Not a soul in Camden Corners would ever want to hurt Maybelle's feelings with the truth that her singing was worse than a slew of caterwauling cats. Maybelle broke the news to the planning committee that she would not be involved in the Christmas program this year. The group feigned regret and congratulated Maybelle on the upcoming blessed event.

Molly saw Maybelle off at the train station as Maybelle boarded the train she was issuing orders concerning the program. Molly tried to hide her glee as she stopped for a cup of tea at Looking Back Antiques.

Nettie Dawson who had moved to Camden Corners just a few months ago wanted to know what the program was all about. Molly explained that it was the same year after year. The school children would gather on stage while Maybelle Witherspoon recited *The Night Before Christmas* and then sang several Christmas carols always ending with *Silent Night* when the children would join her in humming along.

Luke Shannon happened to be passing by the ladies on his way to chat with Jonas about a fishing date for that afternoon.

"Oh! The dreaded Christmas Program" Luke exclaimed. "Just when I was planning an enjoyable afternoon with a fishing pole in my hand, you have to remind me of that debacle."

Luke was the sole proprietor of the Village Toy Shop. He and Molly had been courting for quite a while but marriage didn't seem to be on the horizon. Molly loved Luke but couldn't imagine being married to a grown man who played with toys for a living. Luke loved Molly too but shied away from proposing since he wasn't sure he would be able to provide for her and the family they would have. He worked diligently in the toy shop trying to make ends meet. He had a bit of a cash flow problem because his generosity interfered with his profits.

Luke grew up in nearby Chesterton. His mother was widowed when Luke was only 7. He had three younger brothers and money was scarce. His mama had barely enough money to put food on the table for four hungry boys let alone buy toys for any of them. Luke didn't mind so much for himself but he wanted his brothers to have games and teddy bears and all the things little boys liked to play with.

Mr. Peabody, owner of the general store in town, taught Luke how to whittle and gave him leftover pieces of wood to carve toys for his brothers. Luke and his brothers all developed overactive imaginations playing with little wood carvings. Luke's mother eventually remarried and Luke's stepfather was able to provide well for the family. When Luke turned 10 years old, Mr. Peabody hired him to sweep the floor of the store and tidy up after school. Luke continued to work in the store even though extra money wasn't needed at home anymore. He graduated from high school and went to business school to learn the ins and outs of accounting. Mr. Peabody had heard that the Village Toy Store in Camden Corners was available for sale. He knew Luke would be a perfect match for the toy shop and he was right. Luke had saved enough money for a large down payment and was ready to fulfill his wish to provide toys for every boy and girl in Camden Corners.

Molly giggled at Luke in spite of herself. She had to agree with his assessment of the usual program. Luke was happy to hear that Maybelle would be out of town and unable to entertain this December. Molly informed him that she was now in charge and she was appointing him as producer of the program.

She thought he would balk at the suggestion, but he tilted his head and said, "You're on!".

Nettie, who was aware of Luke's quest to provide toys for every boy and girl, told Molly not to worry, Luke was a good man and would make her proud. Nettie wanted to shake Molly and make her see what a catch Luke Shannon was. She knew they were in love with each other and didn't want them to waste another day denying their love. Nettie knew first hand that the opportunity might not come again for a long time. She smiled as she thought of how love had come into her life again in the form of Mr. Oscar Crowley.

Later that afternoon, Luke stopped by Molly's house. He had an idea for the program. Molly listened as Luke reminded her of the fictional story of how the famous Christmas hymn, *Silent Night* was written. Luke's excitement was catching. Although there were only two main characters, with a little imagination they would be able to involve most of the children in the school in the skit and the others would be responsible for creating beautiful scenery that would lead to the inspiration for the song. Molly fretted about how Maybelle would react when she discovered the program would be entirely different than it had been under Maybelle's direction. Luke insisted it was time for a change and they could make this work. The children would be the stars of the show. Molly finally agreed with Luke and eagerly began jotting down notes.

The next day Molly called a meeting of the ladies auxiliary to discuss the plans for the program. All the ladies were overjoyed with the idea. They all offered their services in helping the children learn their lines and design the scenery. Molly made sure all the children would be participating. Some were anxious to be on stage and others were just as happy painting scenery.

Luke was busy writing the script with the help of Sarah and Max Harcourt. There were plenty of embellishments to the original story making it truly an original play.

Mr. Lane gathered the high school children asking if any of them would be willing to sing in the Christmas program that year. The moans were deafening as the students remembered the agony of sitting through Miss Merryweather's Christmas Programs of the past. Mr. Lane explained that unfortunately, Miss Merryweather would be out of town and a new and different program would be performed. Mr. Lane had no trouble recruiting after that announcement.

December was fast approaching and the Christmas program was the talk of the town. The children were busy learning their lines and painting the beautiful Christmas Eve scenery on backdrops. The skit was clever and funny, something the children and their parents could both enjoy. Mr. Lane's students were practicing *Silent Night* and some of them had beautiful voices. He knew the program would be a success.

Luke, however was worried that he wouldn't be able to provide every child with a toy for Christmas. His supply had been getting low and he wasn't sure how he was going to pay for the order he received that morning. Luke didn't think anyone should make a large profit on the sale of toys to children so the prices in his shop were much lower than most. He didn't have to be concerned with making a large profit because he wasn't making any profit at all.

Nettie Dawson stopped in his shop and saw Luke going over his books again. Nettie knew something had to be done to help Luke with his dilemma. She took it upon herself to go from shop to shop and business to business collecting money for a toy drive for the children. She explained Luke's problem and everyone generously contributed. Molly had stopped at Tempting Treats Candy Shop on her way home from school. She knew Luke liked Maddie's peppermint fudge and was picking up a pound to surprise him.

Nettie was there with her collection jar. Molly heard Nettie telling Maddie of Luke's plan and how he was coming up short on funds. She had no idea Luke was doing this. As it turned out, he did it every year but Molly didn't know. She suddenly realized she had underestimated Luke. He had taken over the Christmas Pageant and worked hard making sure every child had a part in the program. She remembered little Susie White was limping last week because her shoes hurt. That evening she saw Luke through the window of the shoe store and the next day Susie was wearing a brand new pair of Mary Janes. Molly looked at Nettie and her eyes filled with tears. How could she have thought so little of Luke when all along he had been a generous and loving man.

A few hours later, Nettie walked into Luke's store with a list she had gotten from the parents of the Camden Corners children. She handed the list to Luke and said if he would kindly gather up all the toys on the list she and the ladies auxiliary would be back in an hour with pretty paper and ribbons to wrap each gift.

Luke was overwhelmed with the generosity of the folks of Camden Corners. As he was about to pick a pretty little doll off the top shelf behind the counter, Molly walked in and offered to help. Together they collected each toy on the list just as the ladies were entering the shop laden with gift wrap and ribbon. When they were finished with their wrapping, Luke and Molly helped carry the beautiful packages to Len Branson's waiting buckboard.

The ladies left and Luke and Molly were alone. Luke's heart was full knowing all the children would have a Christmas present this year. He took Molly in his arms and asked her to make this his happiest Christmas ever by agreeing to be his wife. Molly didn't hesitate for an instant before saying yes.

Finally the day of the pageant arrived. The scenery was all in place in the Royal Theater. High school students escorted the patrons to their seats. April Hawthorne played the organ as the program began. Laughter filled the theater as the children performed their parts to perfection. The story written with the combined efforts of Luke, Max and Sarah was funny and tender at the same time. Everyone was so mesmerized by what was happening on stage no one noticed the door opening and a lone figure finding a seat at the back of the theater.

The finale was the singing of *Silent Night* as the high school children joined the younger ones on stage. The audience demanded an encore with their clapping and shouting *bravo*.

The children sang until a stout gentleman in a red fur trimmed suit came marching down the aisle shouting "Ho Ho Ho."

The children were too excited to continue singing as Santa Claus, who looked a lot like Mr. Christopher Pringle, called out the names of the children and handed each a package to take home and put under their Christmas tree.

When all the packages were handed out, Luke and Molly came on stage to thank everyone for their participation in the program.

From the back of the room came the unmistakeable voice of Maybelle Witherspoon. The room was silent as Maybelle made her way to the stage. Luke stood in front of Molly protecting her from Maybelle's wrath when Maybelle turned to the audience and exclaimed, "As you know, I was forced to leave Camden Corners to care for my niece a few months ago. As director of the annual Christmas show for the last 25 years, I left Miss Molly Edwards in charge of this year's program with explicit instructions to proceed with the established program. Now I say to you, citizens of Camden Corners, aren't you glad she and the toy shop fellow here didn't listen to me? Let's congratulate Molly and Luke on the wonderful presentation this evening and ask them to be in charge of next year's production too. My only request is that they allow me to take part. I would like to paint some of the scenery and I assure you, I am a much better artist than I am a singer."

The audience stood and clapped for Maybelle as she left the theater. She was in a hurry to board the train back to Greensboro to be with her niece who was due to give birth any day now.

As the train left the station, Maybelle recalled the words to *The Night Before Christmas*. She was sure her new little niece or nephew would enjoy hearing their Auntie Maybelle recite the poem to them for many years to come.

Timmy's Gift

It was three days before Christmas and four year old Timmy Hawthorne was eating his oatmeal at the kitchen table with his brothers and sisters. Papa had already left for the Hawthorne Garden Shop.

Lucas Hawthorne was a gardener. He loved plants and trees and anything that grew in the ground. The folks in Camden Corners often said he had a magic touch. Those who could afford his services were happy to have him take over their lawns and flower gardens in the summertime. He kept busy all year. He had a tree farm and grew poinsettias and holly bushes that he sold in his shop.

This was by far the busiest week in the year. Everyone wanted the perfect Christmas tree for their parlor. All of the shops along Main Street were decorated with holly and poinsettias from Lucas' shop. His wife, Laura was a big help to her husband with her skill at turning sprigs of holly into a beautiful wreath or garland.

Timmy was the youngest of the five Hawthorne children. Lucas, Jr.

and Abraham were talented skiers and had been hired by the Camden Hill Ski Lodge as instructors during the winter months. April, who wanted to be a nurse when she grew up, was filling in as receptionist in Doctor Julie McMillan's office during her winter break. Penny loved everything Christmas and was helping Mr. & Mrs. Pringle in their shop for the day.

Timmy was slowly eating his oatmeal. He had a question he wanted to ask his mama and brothers and sisters. They were all talking at once and nobody was paying any attention to him when he reached for the sugar bowl knocking over his full glass of milk. The milk spilled all over the table and floor and in April's lap.

"Oh Timmy, look what you have done. Now I have to change my dress and I will be late for Doc McMillan's."

Mama told April to hurry up and change and she would clean up the spilled milk. Lucas and Abe were on their way out the door when Timmy ran after them to ask them his question.

"Lucas wait up. Abe, I want to ask you something."

"Can't talk to you now little buddy, we have to go".

Penny was already on her way down the street.

"Hey Penny."

She was singing Christmas carols and didn't hear her little brother calling her.

April came downstairs in a clean dress. Gave him a pat on the head and was out the door on her way to the Doc's.

"I'll ask Mama," thought Timmy, "Mama isn't in a hurry." But she was.

After she cleaned up the milk she started washing April's dress and then she had all the breakfast dishes to clean before she started making wreaths from the holly branches Papa brought home last night.

"Mama, I have a question to ask you."

"What is it Timmy?"

"Well, I have a nickel and three pennies in my piggy bank and I want to buy a present for Jesus for His birthday but I don't know what He wants."

"That's nice Timmy but Mama is very busy this morning. Let's get your snowsuit and mittens and boots on you so you can play outside for a little while."

Timmy was all bundled up and went outside to play. He had his coins inside his mitten. He thought maybe he would walk to the Garden Shop to see Papa and ask him what he should buy for Jesus.

Papa was helping Mr. Greenly put a big tree in his truck.

"Hi Timmy what are you doing over here? Is Mama at Nichol's Market?"

Timmy said no but his Papa was busy with Mr. Greenly's tree and didn't hear him. Maybe he would come back later. He walked down the street to the bakery. Miss Diana was putting a plate of fresh baked cookies out on the porch.

"Hi Timmy, would you like a cookie? Is your Mama next door at the candy shop?"

"Thanks for the cookie Miss Diana. No, my Mama is not at Miss Maddie's. Can you tell me what to buy for Jesus for His birthday."

Diana laughed and bent down to talk to Timmy when baby Joey started to cry. She went in the other room to pick up Joey and when she got back Timmy had disappeared.

Timmy kept walking to every shop on Main Street. Miss Maddie gave him a gumdrop but then a customer came in before she could answer Timmy's question.

Andy Parker at the post office stamped his hand with his post marker but then had to give Doc McMillan his mail.

Doc walked him out of the Post Office and just when Timmy was going to ask him his very important question, Miss Nettie Dawson slipped on a patch of ice and Doc ran over to help her up.

Timmy stopped at the fire station and petted the fire house dalmatian.

He saw Miss Emma decorating a Christmas tree outside of the antique shop. She handed him a piece of fudge but Lily needed her help with a wreath she was hanging and Emma had to go back into the shop before Timmy could ask his question.

His next stop was to visit Mr. & Mrs. Pringle at the Christmas shop. Mrs. Pringle was helping Annie Parker who was buying a nativity set. She also bought a small fire engine ornament. Timmy was watching as Mrs. Pringle carefully wrapped the baby Jesus and the fire truck. Mr. Pringle called out to Timmy and handed him a peppermint stick. Timmy knew just what to buy the baby Jesus for His birthday and ran to the toy store, his eight cents still in his mitten.

Timmy searched and searched the store and finally found a bright shiny fire engine. He reached into his mitten and brought out his eight cents.

"Is that enough for the fire truck Mr. Luke?" Timmy asked.

With a twinkle in his eye, Luke told him it was just the right amount for the 25 cent truck. Timmy beamed as Luke handed him his purchase.

"Merry Christmas," Luke called out as Timmy walked out the door.

Timmy was getting a little tired but he was almost to his destination. He saw Carrie and Allison Parker outside of the Snowflake Christmas Shop waiting for their mother, Annie.

"Hi Timmy, where are you going?" asked Carrie.

"I'm on my way to see Jesus."

When Annie came out of the shop, Allison who was barely 2 told her, "Timmy wiff Jesus".

Annie had a funny feeling when she heard that but she was so busy that morning, she dismissed it.

Timmy was almost to St. Peter's Church. He had walked by the water because he liked the sound of the waves splashing on shore. He took off his mitten so he could eat his peppermint stick. He dropped the mitten on the shore but he didn't notice because he was happily eating the peppermint stick and admiring the fire truck.

He was almost to the church where Mary and Joseph were looking over baby Jesus in the manger. The three wise men were standing around them. They had gifts for Jesus but not as special as the gift Timmy was giving Him.

The peppermint stick was very good but his hands were getting awfully sticky. He climb up on the rocks and into the manger and put the fire truck in baby Jesus' hand. He thought he saw Jesus smile but he could barely keep his eyes open any longer and fell sound to sleep next to Jesus in the manger.

Laura was so busy with the wreath, she didn't realize how long Timmy had been outside. She went to the front door and called his name.

"Where could he be?"

She ran back in the house and called for him but still no answer. She put on her coat and started out the front door she went to the garden shop first. Lucas said he came there earlier but he was so busy he didn't know where he went. They both walked down Main Street.

Diana said, "Yes, Timmy was here but she was busy with Joey and he left."

Maddie said , "He was here but I was busy with a customer."

All of the shop owners said they had seen him but they were all so busy they didn't pay that much attention to where he was going.

Penny and April both heard that Timmy couldn't be found, they joined in the search. Word had spread up the hill to the ski lodge and Lucas and Abe came into town as fast as they could.

Timmy's brothers and sisters remembered that they didn't have time for him that morning and now he was gone.

Eric Flanagan from the fish market found Timmy's mitten by the water. Everyone was on the verge of panic when Annie remembered the words Allison had muttered earlier something about Timmy being with Jesus.

"Carrie, did you see Timmy earlier?" Annie asked her daughter.

"Yes Mommy, he was going to see Jesus."

Luke joined the concerned group and told them Timmy had been to his shop earlier and bought a fire truck.

The vicar remembered Timmy being very interested in the nativity scene that was being constructed at the church last week. Vicar was watching it being assembled when Timmy walked up with his sister Penny and looked on as the workers lay the baby Jesus in the manager. Vicar Will hopped on his bike and pedaled as fast as he could to the church.

Sure enough, there was Timmy sound to sleep in the manager. The vicar ran into the church and up the stairs to the tower and rang the bell until all the villagers came running. Everyone whooped and hollered that Timmy was alright.

He opened his eyes and looked around and saw that everyone was clapping and laughing. Mama had her arms around him and was crying.

"Why are you crying Mama? Jesus likes His birthday present. See He's holding it in His hand."

It was true. The truck had gotten sticky from the peppermint and was stuck on baby Jesus' hand.

Everyone in town had been too busy to listen to a little boy that morning. They all knew, from that moment on they would never be too busy for the really important things again. Decorations and customers and chores could wait but little boys shouldn't have to.

Best Laid Plans

Isaac Nichols was approaching 70. He had worked hard all his life. At the age of 20, he married his childhood sweetheart, Maude Jenkins and that same year, thanks to Maude's dowry, opened Nichols' Corner Market. For almost 50 years Nichols had been providing the residents of Camden Corners with the finest produce, dairy products, meats, poultry and advice thanks to Isaac and Maude.

The years were happy ones. The Nichols loved their market and took pride in their establishment. Lately though, Isaac noticed his back became sore by the end of the day and Maude didn't have that twinkle in her eye that used to make his heart sing. If only they had been blessed with children, it would be time to pass the torch to the next generation. Isaac's brother Ivan moved to Greensboro many years before. Ivan's son, Oliver just graduated that spring. Isaac and Maude attended his graduation and were so very proud of their nephew. Maude remarked that if they'd had a son she would have wanted him to be just like Oliver. Isaac thought it was worth a try to persuade Oliver to take over the store until they were able to find a buyer for it. Isaac knew he would never sell to just anyone and maybe, just maybe, Oliver would become the new proprietor of Nichols.

Isaac and Maude had never had a vacation. The market was only closed on Sundays and holidays. Isaac liked to stay close by in case any of the townsfolk needed a loaf of bread or a bottle of milk during the evening or on Sunday afternoon. If Oliver was willing to take over the store within the next few weeks he could be there to guide him and after a reasonable time he would surprise Maude with a trip to New York City. Maude always wanted to visit New York and loved to listen to Maddie Mackenzie regale her with tales of her time in the big city with all the Broadway shows and beautiful shops. Yes, he would send Oliver a wire today inviting him to come for a visit.

Oliver loved his Uncle Isaac but could see right through his invitation. Maybe he would help the old folks for a little while but he wasn't in the market for a job, especially one that would keep him tied down for the rest of his life. No, Oliver had plans. He was going to do some traveling. He had made up his mind that he would go to California where the winters were warm and people grew oranges on trees in their back yards. He packed a few of his belongings and was on the next train to Camden Corners. The sooner he got started at the market, the sooner Uncle Isaac would find a buyer and Oliver would be off to California. He didn't bother to pack a winter coat or hat or gloves. He wouldn't need them come December because he would be basking in the sunshine and enjoying a fresh picked orange or maybe a little wine made with California grapes.

"Yes, life was going to be good."

Cassie Lambert was toiling in the kitchen of the small house on Fern Street where she and her three younger brothers had been born. Three years earlier Cassie and the boys had lost their parents in a tragic accident. Cassie had just turned 18 and the last words she heard her mother utter were to take care of the boys. Cassie promised she would and kept that promise. After some failed attempts at cooking and with the help of the ladies of Camden Corners she had become an excellent cook. The boys were all well fed and content even though each of the children missed their Mama and Papa every day of their young lives. Cassie never complained that she had given up her dreams of becoming a fashion designer. Before the accident, Cassie had applied and been accepted for an internship at the House of Clarice in New York City.

Cassie was determined her three teenaged brothers would grow into fine men that both Mama and Papa would be proud of. She worked with them every night on their school work, made sure they were clean and presentable every day and loved them all very much. Cassie's devotion paid off, Raymond, Eddy and Fredrick were three of the nicest young men in Camden Corners.

Cassie was willing to wait until her brothers were settled in their lives and then she would find a way to fulfill her dream. Her ultimate goal was to go to Paris, France and join one of the famous fashion houses there. She never even considered the possibility of marrying and having children. She did love taking care of her brothers but she wanted to explore the world and experience life away from Camden Corners. Cassie did enjoy designing and creating children's clothes. With all of the children of various sizes in Camden Corners, she was kept busy with her sewing. Maude Nichols loved Cassie's work and offered to give her some space in the market to display her clothing. The Nichols were very fond of Cassie and admired how she had taken charge after the Lamberts passed away. Cassie never charged very much for the beautiful outfits she sold but it was enough to build a savings for her *someday* trip to Paris.

Oliver arrived in Camden Corners and Isaac began showing him all the ins and outs of running a general store. Isaac noticed Oliver seemed to be a natural for taking over for him. He had no idea Oliver was counting the days until he would be boarding the train for his trip out west.

Cassie stopped in the shop with an armload of children's outfits. Isaac introduced her to Oliver. They both felt an attraction to the other but neither wanted any kind of a relationship so they ignored those feelings. Oliver thought it was strange that there would be a section in the store to display children's clothing. He didn't voice his doubts since someone else would be taking over proprietorship of the market and it would be their problem.

No sooner had Cassie placed her latest creations on the display table when three women walked in the store and started oohing and aahing over them. Oliver couldn't believe they purchased several outfits each and were tempted to buy more but felt they should leave something for the other women. Oliver knew nothing about fashion and especially children's fashion but upon looking over the tiny outfits, he knew they were beautifully made. He was impressed with Cassie's skill. She blushed at his praise. Isaac and Maude smiled at each other. Those two young people were a perfect match for each other. It would just take some time for them to discover it themselves.

Oliver was in his second month in Camden Corners. He was happy to be able to help Uncle Isaac out but he was anxious to start his adventure. He sat at Isaac's kitchen table and told him he would be leaving soon.

Isaac was afraid this day would come and had to accept the fact that Oliver wouldn't be taking over Nichols Market. He did have a backup plan. He knew the Lambert boys were very responsible and Cassie had often helped them in the store as payment for displaying her goods. He wondered if the Lamberts would be agreeable to running the store while he and Maude were away. After the vacation, he would begin looking for someone to take over permanently.

The Lamberts were more than willing to work in the store. The extra money would be a big help with their college savings fund.

Cassie was delighted that the Nichols would be taking a vacation and was excited that Maude would finally see New York City. Cassie wished she could go along with them, but her day would come and maybe sooner than she'd planned with all the boys working in the store.

Just as the leaves were beginning to turn in early autumn, Isaac and Maude boarded the train for New York City. Cassie designed several outfits for Maude and surprised her with them on the day Isaac told her where she was going. The twinkle was back in her eyes and Isaac was as proud to be with her as he was that day 50 years ago when she was his new bride.

Oliver didn't want to admit it but he was touched by Cassie's generosity. He wondered silently if she would be willing to consider a move to California one day.

A few days later, Oliver was on the train headed west. He had planned for this day for as long as he could remember but he wasn't filled with happy anticipation. He and Cassie had spent more time together than he realized and he was missing her smiling face.

California was even more beautiful than Oliver imagined. He found a small room to rent just outside of Los Angeles. The room was clean and the neighborhood was quiet but there weren't any oranges growing in the backyard. There wasn't even a backyard. He was miles away from any vineyards and the only wine he found to sip was at the local tavern where it was dark and gloomy. He thought of O'Sullivan's in Camden Corners where he could always find someone to talk to and the light was always bright even on a cloudy day.

Oliver found that his college degree wasn't doing him much good without experience anyplace except his uncle's store. He was used to being able to walk anywhere in town but Los Angeles was much bigger and everything was much farther away. He was offered a job at Sherman's Market just a block from where he lived and thought he'd accept it until he found something else. Oliver's attempts to have friendly conversations with customers went nowhere. He missed the friendly people in Camden Corners and he found himself missing Cassie more than he thought possible. He had to admit that he had made a big mistake in coming to California. He was just a small town fellow at heart. It didn't take long before he was on the train headed east to Camden Corners.

Cassie was deep in conversation with Diana Taylor when she looked up and saw Oliver walking through the door. Her eyes lit up and she smiled so broadly she thought her cheeks would crack. Oliver held his breath. He had forgotten how lovely Cassie was. Diana greeted Oliver and left the store anxious to spread the word that Oliver was home again and by the smile on his and Cassie's faces, it looked like he was home to stay.

Oliver could no longer keep his feelings to himself. He loved Cassie and wanted to spend the rest of his life with her right here in Camden Corners. He drew her into his arms and from that moment on Cassie and Oliver knew they would always be together.

Two smiling faces peeked around the corner. Isaac had the papers all ready for Oliver to sign. He and Maude had a lovely time in New York but they were home to stay now. They purchased a small cabin by the lake and pictured many happy weekends with Oliver, Cassie, the Lambert boys and a bunch of grandnieces and nephews that would surely come along.

Cassie still held on to her dream of Paris but life had taken a different turn and she found she enjoyed being her own designer. They were married before the last autumn leaf fell off the maple tree in the front yard of the Lambert home.

Oliver had a Christmas surprise for Cassie. A trip to Paris, France in the spring where they would celebrate their belated honeymoon. Cassie had a surprise of her own. Paris would have to wait at least 18 years. There was much to celebrate that Christmas for the Nichols and Lamberts. Isaac built a cradle for the new baby and Maude lovingly made a little quilt. The Lambert boys were already planning to teach their little niece or nephew how to fish.

Oliver's parents visited from Greensboro and loved Cassie and her brothers as much as Oliver did. The snow was falling in Camden Corners.

Oliver and Cassie stepped outside to watch the flakes spill from the sky. Oliver loved the feel of winter with his arms around his wife and couldn't remember why he thought he would be happy living in a place without snow.

A Wife for The Vicar

The fine ladies of Camden Corners were assembled once again in the basement of Saint Peter's Church. Mary Ellen Brubaker was still recovering from her embarrassment over the Beverly Sills fiasco. She had yet to forgive her cousin Elmer for his deception. The ladies assured Mary Ellen that there were no hard feelings. The evening had turned out to be a success and everyone had a good time.

Vicar Willard Duesenberry stopped in to wish everyone a good day. Everyone loved the friendly man of the cloth. Alma Schrum, the vicar's loyal housekeeper sighed as her boss left the meeting room.

"Vicar Will is such a wonderful man and deserves to have a fine woman by his side." exclaimed Alma.

Millicent Merryweather Stout spoke up "Our next project should be finding a wife for the vicar."

Everyone chuckled at the suggestion but several of the ladies were pondering that suggestion. Millicent mentioned her niece Melanie Merryweather.

"Oh, she is a fine lass. She lives in Greensboro with her family but I'm sure she would be happy spending some time with her Auntie Millicent over the Thanksgiving holiday."

What Millicent had failed to mention was that the day before she had received a letter from Melanie's father. Melanie was associating with a boy of questionable lineage. His family had recently moved to Greensboro from Chicago, Illinois. Chicago was practically the wild west. Melanie's mother was beside herself with worry. Millicent made up her mind, she would send a wire today to her brother suggesting Melanie come to stay with her until she was over this silly infatuation.

Agatha Carson thought her cousin Arlene's daughter might be a good choice for the vicar.

Catherine White's good friend's daughter was another suggestion.

Almost every one of the ladies thought they had the perfect match for the vicar but they all knew if Millicent Merryweather Stout set her mind to something, it was sure to happen so they all accepted the fact that Millicent's niece would be the new Mrs. Willard Duesenberry.

After the meeting, Evelyn Keys pulled Alma aside to tell her how happy she was that her granddaughter, Kate had accepted a teaching position at Camden Grammar School. Alma hadn't had a chance to mention it to the ladies but Kate would be staying with her through the school year.

Alma's daughter and her family had moved to Larkspur a couple of years ago and Kate was homesick for Camden Corners. She had received her teaching certificate in the spring and was anxious to begin a new chapter in her life. Alma was happy caring for Vicar Will and had many friends in Camden Corners but she was beside herself with joy that her granddaughter would be living with her. Kate was a quiet and very serious young lady. She loved being around children and they loved her.

Within the week, Melanie Merryweather arrived in Camden Corners. As she stepped off the train Millicent knew this was not going to be a pleasant visit. Melanie was pale and drawn. Her eyes were as red as could be and it was obvious she had cried all the way from Greensboro. Millicent thought it best if she didn't bring up the subject of the boy she left behind. Melanie hardly spoke on the ride to her aunt's house. Millicent's maid had cooked a very special meal but Melanie only took a few bites and asked to be excused to her room.

"I'll let the girl have one more night of feeling sorry for herself but tomorrow we are visiting the vicar. If she will only smile, I'm sure the vicar will fall in love with her at first sight."

Millicent retired at her usual 8:00 that evening and didn't hear the sound of pebbles hitting the bedroom window or hear the squeal of delight when Melanie looked out the window and saw Michael Cassidy smiling up at her from the ground below. Melanie opened her bedroom door as quietly as she could and heard Auntie Millicent's snores coming from the room down the hall. She tiptoed all the way down the stairs, opened the front door and flew into Michael's waiting arms.

Melanie couldn't understand her parent's dislike of Michael. Maybe his ancestors didn't come over on the Mayflower but what difference did that make? Most of the Merryweather's friends were insufferable bores. Michael's family and friends were all fun and loving and enjoyed being together. Melanie's mother had packed her bags and her father practically carried her to the train station and off to Camden Corners. Her little sister Melinda found the telegram Auntie Millicent had sent. While her parents were otherwise occupied, Melinda ran down the street to find Michael and tell him what was happening with Melanie and where she was going.

Michael had a plan. His uncle was the vicar of the First United Church in Greensboro. He had gone to school with Vicar Will and they had remained friends. Michael wondered if Uncle Jason would write a letter of introduction to Vicar Will. He would find a job in Camden Corners. Maybe he and Melanie would be able to figure out a way to be together. Michael caught the next train to Camden Corners and was on his way to find the love of his life.

Vicar Will wasn't born yesterday and knew there had to be more to Michael's story than he was telling. He sensed Michael was a fine young man and his friendship with his Uncle Jason was all the assurance he needed to offer Michael use of the spare room above the rectory.

At breakfast the next morning, Millicent was happy to see that Melanie's cheeks were pink and she was her old self, full of chatter. Millicent was surprised when Melanie seemed almost anxious to visit the church and meet Vicar Will. As they arrived in Millicent's fancy carriage, Michael and the vicar were clearing the walkway of the fallen leaves. Introductions were made and the wise vicar knew instantly what, or rather who had brought his old friend's nephew to Camden Corners. Millicent could see the young people's smiling eyes and began wondering if Vicar Will was really the right person for her niece. The days passed by and Millicent mentioned to her friends that she thought the vicar was not quite right for her niece. Millicent could see that Melanie and Michael had fallen in love. She knew her brother would like Michael. He was a fine young man who's uncle was a clergyman and a friend of Vicar Will. Millicent wrote to her brother and told him Melanie hadn't so much as mentioned her old beau since coming to Camden Corners.

Interestingly enough, the ladies of Camden Corners began inviting their nieces, granddaughters and daughters of friends to join them for a day or two. One by one, they were paraded to the church. Pretty ones, plain ones, slender and chubby ladies were all introduced to Vicar Will. The vicar was flattered at first but he was finding it difficult to care for his flock properly when he was so busy having tea nearly every afternoon. The vicar hadn't thought much about marrying. He was happy with his life the way it was. Alma was a wonderful housekeeper and made sure he ate three square meals a day. He didn't see any need to change. He was happy for Alma that her granddaughter would be living with her. He knew how much she missed her family.

He was walking home from yet another afternoon tea with another giggling prospective bride when he came upon Alma walking with a lovely young lady. Alma introduced her granddaughter Kate. He noticed

Kate didn't giggle when he grasped her hand. With the sunlight shining in her hair, she was a vision. The vicar wondered what was happening. Had the ladies of Camden Corners put the notion of marriage in his head? He reached out and took hold of Kate's traveling bag and offered to walk them home. Alma had prepared a special dinner for her granddaughter's arrival and was pleased when the vicar accepted her invitation to stay.

Also on the train that afternoon was Neville Merryweather. He was marching toward his sister Millicent's house as red as a beet. He banged on the door and demanded he be allowed to enter. The housekeeper hid behind the couch as he stomped his feet by the door. Millicent was astonished at her brother's behavior.

"Where is my daughter?" he demanded.

Millicent told him calmly that she was perfectly safe and had taken a walk with the vicar's ward who was a very respectable young man.

"She is with that lowlife Michael Cassidy and don't you deny it."

Millicent rang for the butler to bring her brother a brandy to help him calm down.

Just then Melanie and Michael walked through the door. Neville ranted and raved and Melanie was in tears. Michael told Mr. Merryweather that he and Melanie were in love and that he was going to marry her with or without his permission. Neville's mouth flew open.

"How dare you speak to a Merryweather in such a fashion."

Millicent finally had enough of this arrogance.

"Neville, there is something I must tell you. Our great grandfather came over on the Mayflower all right. He was a stowaway who gambled his way across the ocean. He made his money playing poker and cheating good folks out of their money. He married our wealthy great grandmother and left her with young children to go out west where he was shot and killed running from the local sheriff. Our dear father confessed this tale to me on his deathbed and swore me to secrecy. I have never told a living soul until now. Neville, my late husband Mr. Stout, was a good and kind man who gave me everything in life I ever wanted except children. What I wouldn't give to have a son like Michael. He is an exceptional young man and if you and that twit wife of yours don't welcome him with open arms, he and Melanie are invited to make their home with me in Camden Corners."

Neville was dumbstruck. His sister had never spoken to him like this before. He knew she didn't praise others easily and it made him wonder if maybe he should give Melanie's young man a chance. Neville remembered a young lady from his youth. He had fallen head over heels for her but she was from the wrong side of town and their relationship just couldn't be. He had run into his former sweetheart a few years ago when he was on a business trip. She was just a lovely as she had been 20 years before. After that brief meeting, Neville wondered what his life would have been like if they had married. He couldn't let that happen to his precious daughter. He grasped Michael's hand and welcomed him into the family.

As the Merryweathers were rejoicing, just outside walking arm and arm were the vicar and Kate. Alma Schrum was watching from her window as were several of the ladies of Camden Corners. They had all hoped their friends or relatives had been the one to capture Vicar Will's heart but they were happy he found the perfect match without any help from them. Alma, however, was thanking God for answering her prayers and already thinking ahead to the arrival of her first great grandchild.

The Farmhand

Just a few days before the official start of autumn, the handsome stranger arrived in Camden Corners on the 10:40. He didn't really pick Camden Corners, it picked him since his funds were limited and he didn't want to spend what little money he had on a ticket that would take him any farther west.

As he hopped off the train, he wondered what he had gotten himself into. This was really a small town. The first thing he had to do was choose a name for himself. He didn't want anyone to know his identity. Charlie had a friendly ring to it. The fellow he met on the train told him he was traveling to Brentwood. Charlie Brent. That would be his new name. Sounds like an honest type guy.

Charlie spotted O'Sullivan's Pub and made that his first stop. Mack Mackenzie introduced himself to the stranger.

"Will you be settling down in Camden Corners or just passing through?" he asked.

Charlie liked this friendly bartender immediately.

"Looking for work for a few months and then I'll be on my way" replied Charlie. "Know anybody who is hiring"

Not that he had any skills, but it was worth a try.

"I heard, just this morning that Grandpa Wally Wallace is looking for someone to help him clear some land. You might want to pay him a visit. His house is just over the river and through the woods."

Grandpa Wally wasn't Mack's grandfather. Everyone in town called him Grandpa Wally and his wife was Grandma Bess. Charlie finished his corned beef sandwich and draft. He thanked Mack and was on his way to cross the bridge and find his way through the woods to Grandpa's house.

Mack's mother, Fiona was setting tables getting ready for the lunch crowd when she overheard Mack and the stranger's conversation.

"Maybe you shouldn't have told that fellow where Grandpa Wally lives, Mack. You don't know anything about him. He seemed a little hesitant when he gave you his name, like it was something he had just thought up."

"Oh, Ma, he had an honest face. He's from New York City and I don't mean from the seedy part of town. He has class."

"Did he tell you this son?"

"No, I just know it from living there for a while. I'm sure it will be OK."

Fiona could see the flicker of doubt in her son's eye and wasn't surprised when he called his father in to help with the lunch crowd. Mack decided to take a little walk to Grandpa Wally's just to make sure Charlie found his way without a hitch.

Wally and Bess were delighted to meet this charming stranger. Wally was getting up in years and the farm was taking more and more out of him. Wally knew there had to be more to Charlie than he was telling but he had a good feeling about him. Duke, his old bloodhound, took a liking to him too and Wally had faith in Duke's judgment.

Charlie was a muscular fellow but it was apparent he had never done much physical labor. He was soft but that wouldn't last too long with the work he would be doing in the fields. The two shook hands and Charlie was ready to go to work right then and there. At that moment, Mack appeared saying he wanted to make sure Charlie didn't have any trouble finding Grandpa Wally's farm. Charlie saw through the excuse but was touched that Mack was concerned enough about the old man to leave the pub during such a busy time of day just to make sure everything was as it should be.

Camden Corners might be a hick town but he was beginning to like it very much. Grandma Bess was happy Wally would have some much needed help and was busy washing blankets for the bunk in the barn. Charlie wouldn't have to worry about sleeping arrangements and he could already smell a ham baking in the oven. Yes, he was going to like Camden Corners that was for sure. By the end of the first day Charlie was so sore he could barely move his legs enough to climb into the comfortable bunk. Wally chuckled at the way Charlie tried to hide his pain. He was curious about the boy but knew he wasn't going to learn his story until Charlie was ready to tell it.

Charlie had been working for almost three days when he noticed Grandma Bess had company as the men walked toward the house for lunch. Grandma Bess introduced Charlie to their granddaughter, Betsy. Betsy was a beauty with fiery red hair and the greenest eyes Charlie had ever seen. Wally and Bess smiled broadly as the two youngsters nodded hello.

Betsy worried about her grandparents. They worked way too hard and now she wondered if maybe they trusted too much. Who was this good looking stranger? He didn't look like a farmhand to her. More like a man of the world. She asked Charlie how long he was planning to be in town but Wally stopped her questioning.

"Leave the young fellow alone, Betsy. He's been working up an appetite all morning and he doesn't need you prying into his business."

Betsy, would let it go for now but she was not going to let Charlie off the hook that easily. Look at those hands, they were a little scratched up and sunburned but they certainly hadn't had a lifetime of hard work like any farmhand she had ever seen.

Charlie was enjoying every meal he had with Wally and Bess. Bess made the most wonderful tasting dishes. Charlie was afraid he was eating them out of house and home but Bess kept piling food on his plate. They laughed and joked and all had a good time.

Betsy was certainly a beauty. Charlie knew he shouldn't be interested in her but he was in spite of himself. Betsy, still curious about Charlie found him to be a fascinating conversationalist and very easy on the eyes. Yes, there was more to this fellow than he was letting on and she would get to the bottom of it. Charlie mentioned meeting Mack Mackenzie.

Betsy stopped by the pub on her way home to find out what Mack knew about the stranger who seemed to be an important part of her grandparent's life now. Mack told Betsy he was sure Charlie was from an upscale part of New York City. He was a bit leery of him too and worried about Wally and Bess. Betsy's next stop was the library where she searched the New York papers for the last few months. Betsy's heart sank when she saw a picture of Charlie and a very sophisticated beauty. The caption read:

Mr. & Mrs. Charleton Granholm Wentworth, III announce the engagement of their son, Charleton Granholm Wentworth, IV to Miss Phoebe Evandale Samuelson, daughter of the Honorable Herbert Jamison Samuelson and Mrs Carolyn Clement Samuelson of Washington, D.C.

Charlie wasn't smiling in the picture. He looked stiff and totally miserable. Miss Phoebe looked as though she was whiffing a very unpleasant odor. Betsy chuckled to herself when she wondered if Miss Phoebe's nose filled with water when it rained since it was pointed so far upward toward the sky.

Betsy was sorry she went snooping. She didn't like to think of Charlie being with that horrible snob. She had to admit to herself that she was jealous of this girl. Before Betsy left the library she confided in her friend Sarah Harcourt.

Sarah had heard the Wallaces had a stranger working for them and decided it was high time she and Max introduced themselves to the newcomer. Max was an author and could size people up in a hurry. He also had many contacts in New York and Washington and maybe he could find out some information about this mysterious stranger who looked just like the rich, spoiled New Yorker whose photo was in the newspaper.

Betsy and Sarah made plans to meet when school let out that day and Annie Mackenzie could take over Sarah's duties in the library for the afternoon. They stopped by Sarah's home on the way to the farm and Max joined their little adventure. Max loved a mystery and was working on a new one of his own.

Grandma Bess was delighted to see Betsy again and gave Sarah and Max big hugs. Nobody could fool the old woman, she knew exactly why they were here.

"Did you find any information at the library Betsy?" she asked with a sly smile on her face.

"Grandma, how did you know I went to the library" said Betsy as her face began turning a pretty shade of red.

"I know my granddaughter and you weren't going to let the Charlie matter go. Besides, if you hadn't found something in the New York papers, you and Sarah wouldn't be here now and you certainly wouldn't have torn Max away from his writing just for a friendly visit."

Max laughed. He loved this old woman. Her body might be giving out a bit each year but her mind was as sharp as it had ever been. He never knew anyone who could pull the wool over her eyes or Wally's for that matter. He wasn't worried about the stranger because he trusted their instincts but he was curious and was determined to see if Charlie was really Mr. Charleton Granholm Wentworth, IV. Max had met Chip Wentworth as he was called. He didn't know him well but did remember talking to him at a gathering one time. He was very interested in Max's writing and wondered how he had gotten started in the business.

The foursome walked out into the backyard. They could see Wally and Charlie in the distance. They were using a two man saw on one of the dying birch trees out by the woods. Suddenly a gust of wind came up. Bess saw the tree start to sway and yelled Wally's name. Charlie heard her at that moment and pushed Wally down on the ground shielding his body with his own. Max and the girls ran as fast as they could to the pair. Bess was on her knees in prayer. Wally had the wind knocked out of him but was able to stand up and wave to Bess. Charlie was trapped under the tree and lay unconscious.

The four of them were able to lift the tree off Charlie but didn't dare move him. Betsy sat with him while Sarah walked Wally back to the house and Max ran to get one of Wally's horses to ride into town for the doctor. Doc Tom grabbed his medical bag and rode back to the farm with Max while Doc McMillan gathered the back brace and readied his buckboard for the trip. Doc Julie stayed behind to tend to a waiting room full of patients.

Doc Tom could tell right away that the stranger was seriously injured. He didn't appear to have any broken bones but there was deep gash on his forehead and no signs of consciousness. Doc did his best to patch up the head wound while he waited for his father-in-law to arrive with the back brace and buckboard. They knew it was dangerous to move the patient but they needed to get him away from the woods. The three men very carefully lifted Charlie and slowly carried him into the farmhouse where Grandma Bess had just placed fresh sheets and blankets on the bed just across from the kitchen. The doctors knew Charlie's condition was serious. They told his anxious friends that he may come out of the coma within a day or two or he could remain unconscious indefinitely.

Max couldn't be certain but he did believe Charlie Brent was same fellow he knew as Chip Wentworth. They shared their information with Wally and Bess. Wally was not pleased that Sarah went snooping into Charlie's personal business but even he had to agree it would be best to contact Charlie's parents.

Max rode into town that evening and sent a telegram to Mr. Wentworth. Betsy stayed by Charlie's bedside for the next three days. Wally and Bess watched over him hoping and praying he would open his eyes.

The 10:40 pulled into the train station on schedule. Mr. and Mrs. Charleton Granholm Wentworth, III exited the train with Miss Phoebe trailing behind.

"Why did that little twit have to come along?" Charleton grumbled to his wife.

Phoebe was covering her nose and mouth as though she was afraid to breathe in the fumes of fresh air. Max met them at the station and gave them a ride to the farmhouse to visit their son.

Charleton entered the small bedroom and was shocked to see the condition of his son. To his surprise, his eyes filled and his hand shook as he touched his son's cheek. He remembered that horrible day when the two quarreled. He had said some terrible things to Chip. He told him he was ashamed to call him his son. A son he had trained to take over in the financial world and all the boy wanted to do was write stories and live in a fantasy world. What kind of a man was that? Chip was furious with his father because he had announced his son's engagement to that driveling half-wit Phoebe Samuelson. Marry the girl? He couldn't stand to be in the same room with her. Her father was extremely influential and Charlton wanted the connection. He couldn't understand why his son wouldn't jump at the chance. He didn't have to love her, just have a couple of children with her and then he could bed whomever he wanted for the rest of his days. Chip turned on his heel and walked out the door. That was the last Charlton had seen his son until this moment when he looked to be on death's door.

Phoebe burst into the room and swooned as Max caught her before she hit the ground. She cried uncontrollably until Bess guided her out of the room and sat her on the sofa telling her to get a hold of herself. The tears stopped immediately once her audience had disappeared.

Charleton looked around and saw so many kind faces of those who cared about his son. Doc McMillan explained the situation to him. His first instinct was to call in every specialist in New York and Washington but he sensed that everything was being done for his son right here in the small town of Camden Corners.

Charlie's mother, Daphne, was sitting quietly next to her son's bedside. She was observing the young girl named Betsy. Her instincts told her Betsy's feelings were stronger than a simple friendship with her son. She knew he would never marry Phoebe and she didn't blame him. Unlike his father, Chip was not a shallow man. Charleton had married Daphne so many years ago, not because he loved her but because her father was an influential man. Daphne wasn't unhappy with the arrangement but she wanted more than a marriage of convenience for her son.

Charleton could take Miss Phoebe no longer and arranged for her transportation to the train station and sent her on her way. This was the least he could do for his son. He didn't want that insipid girl's face to be the first thing Chip saw when he woke up. Charlie was aware of voices in the background. His head was very sore and it was difficult to open his eyes but he wanted to know what all the commotion was about. He slowly opened his eyes and looked into the smiling face of Betsy Wallace. Doc McMillan was also smiling and hovering over him welcoming him back from his long rest. He suddenly remembered the tree falling down on Wally. He called Wally's name and when he saw the old man who's cheeks were wet with tears, he knew everything would be alright. It didn't take long before Charlie was feeling as good as new. His head was healing nicely and he was thankful for the new friends he had in Camden Corners.

Charlie and his father had a long talk. Charleton came to the realization with the help of Daphne that his son was his own man. Writing was a noble profession. Just look at William Shakespeare. Charlton also realized that Daphne was a pretty special woman and maybe his marriage meant more to him than just convenience. Charlton and Daphne bid goodbye to the good folks of Camden Corners with the promise of a return trip very soon. How about a Thanksgiving wedding Charleton shouted as he hopped on the train. Charlie and Betsy just smiled as Charlie squeezed Betsy's hand.

Made for Each Other

Nettie Dawson stopped by the Post Office on her way to the antique shop one sunny morning. Awaiting her was a letter from her dear friend, Edna Best. Nettie and Edna grew up next door to each other in Greensboro. Edna's family moved to Springville when the girls were just beginning 7th grade. They remained close all these years through letters and occasional visits.

Edna wrote that it had been way too long since Nettie had come to visit and wouldn't it be wonderful if they could share a cup of tea together. Nettie agreed and made arrangements to visit the following week.

Oscar Crowley admitted to himself that he didn't want his best friend to leave Camden Corners if even for a few days. He had grown accustomed to being with her every possible moment of every day. It still amazed him that at his age he had fallen in love again.

Nettie was packed and ready to go when Oscar came calling for her on the day of her trip. He made sure she was on the train and waited until the train was rolling down the tracks before he turned to walk away.

He noticed Lionel Cotton as he walked off the train with a glum look on his face. Lionel was a rather timid fellow whose life revolved around the train station and every train that arrived and departed from Camden Corners. He had been the railroad station manager for 15 years. He was very diligent in his job and took a special interest in all the passengers boarding the train on any given day. After issuing the last ticket he would board the train himself to be sure every rider was comfortable and in the proper seat.

Every Wednesday for the last 10 years, sitting in coach class was Miss Millie Newman. She never missed a week and always sat in the same seat. Ten years earlier Lionel was doing his routine stroll through the train when he spotted Millie sitting demurely by the window in seat 3B. She looked up at him just as he was looking down at her. He tipped his cap and she smiled softly. Lionel didn't know what to make of the flutter he felt in his heart at that moment.

"If only I weren't quite so cowardly, I would engage this young woman in conversation." he thought to himself.

Millie was having the same strange feeling in her heart but was much too bashful to even say hello to this handsome gentleman. Lionel determined that Millie traveled from Covington to Springville on Wednesday and returned to Covington on Saturday each and every week. He wondered who she was meeting in Springville but was not bold enough to ask.

Nettie sat by the window in seat 3D in order to wave goodbye to Oscar as the train pulled away from the station. Lionel greeted her as he walked by her seat and she noticed he barely looked in her direction but across the aisle at the pretty young woman seated there. The young people nodded to each other and Lionel continued through the passenger car and on to the next. Nettie noticed a tear falling down the young woman's cheek. Just then the train started pulling away from the station and she waved and blew kisses to Oscar as he waved and blew kisses back to her. She was going to miss that man even though she was only going to be away from him for a few days.

Nettie knew she should probably mind her own business but another look at the young woman next to her made her determined to attempt to comfort her. It was Nettie's nature so there was no use in fighting it.

Meanwhile, Oscar was concerned about Lionel. The young man, although rather shy had always been smiling and cheerful.

"Is something the matter, Lionel?"

"No, Oscar. Everything is fine except I am just a spineless fool."

Lionel replied.

Oscar encouraged Lionel to take a break and join him in the station's coffee shop. Oscar had a way of making people open up and Lionel was no exception. Lionel confessed he had been in love with Miss Millie Newman since he first saw her on the train ten years before and he never had the nerve to even speak to her in all this time. He didn't know who she was seeing each week but it was probably a beau. He had imagined all different kinds of scenarios and none of them were to his liking. Oscar couldn't believe Lionel had kept his feelings to himself for all these years and decided then and there he was going to find out who Miss Millie Newman was. If she wasn't the sweet, beautiful woman Lionel had imagined, it was best he find out and the sooner the better.

Nettie moved to the seat next to Millie and asked if there was anything she could do to help. With that Millie burst into tears. Nettie wrapped her arm around the girl and let her cry it out. Millie told Nettie she was on her way to visit her aunt in Springville. Her Aunt Thelma was very special to her and she visited her once a week to help with the household chores. Nettie mentioned that she knew a Thelma Newman in Springville. She had met her a time or two when she visited her friend Edna.

Nettie recalled Edna telling her about Thelma's young niece. Thelma was worried about the girl because she had a secret crush on a fellow she saw twice a week in Camden Corners but had never even spoken to. Thelma wondered why this young man was leading her niece on. He must be a scoundrel to inflict such pain on poor Millie.

Remembering the way Lionel and Millie looked at each other, she wondered if Lionel was the scoundrel Thelma had been talking about. Nettie could think of many words to describe young Lionel but scoundrel wasn't one of them. Nettie asked Millie if she by any chance knew Lionel Cotton. With that Millie burst into tears again.

"Oh Miss Nettie, every week I plan that I will say something to him when he comes through the passenger car and every time he does I can't even speak. He is so handsome and worldly I can never get up the courage to even say hello."

Nettie wanted to chuckle at the thought of Lionel Cotton being worldly but she controlled the urge. Nettie had a plan.

"How would you like to visit with me on your way back to Covington? I have an extra bedroom in my apartment and since I am acquainted with your aunt, I'm sure it would be proper for you to spend a few days with me in Camden Corners. I will formally introduce you to

Lionel and maybe that will make it easier for you to speak to him."

Millie was filled with anticipation and trepidation with the prospect of meeting the man she had dreamed of all these years, but she was determined to go through with it and if she didn't, she had a feeling Miss Nettie would see to it that she did.

Nettie thoroughly enjoyed her visit with her old friend Edna and they spent a good bit of their time with Thelma and Millie Newman. Thelma was happy to hear Lionel Cotton was a fine upstanding young man and trusted Nettie's instincts that he felt the same way about her niece as she did about him.

Saturday arrived and the ladies were on their way to Camden Corners. Millie was as nervous as a cat and Nettie was tempted to order some sherry to calm the girl down. The ride was a smooth one and they arrived in Camden Corners in no time at all. Millie put a big smile on her face and held onto Nettie's arm more for her support than Nettie's. They walked off the train and Lionel was the first one to greet them.

"Lionel Cotton, I would like you to meet Miss Millie Newman. Millie will be my house guest for a few days and I would appreciate it very much if you would help me to acquaint her with our fair town."

Lionel's mouth flew open and then he grinned.

"How do you do Miss Millie? It is a pleasure to meet you."

Millie replied "Thank you Mr. Cotton, it is my pleasure to meet you also."

The first words spoken between them in ten years were just the beginning. Lionel and Millie both came out of their shells. The people of Camden Corners were astonished to see the change in Lionel. He was no longer the shy young man who seldom spoke more than a few words. The town welcomed Millie with open arms. She rented a room in Mrs. Wharton's boarding house until her marriage to Lionel. They didn't waste any time getting married. After all, they had known each other for ten years.

The Photographer

The Marino Family was happily preparing the Trattoria for a big party honoring Rosa's baby brother, Luigi Rossi. Luigi graduated that morning from college and was arriving in Camden Corners on the 4:15 that very afternoon. Rosa was bursting with pride. Her baby brother a college graduate.

95

Luigi came to the United States just as he was about to enter high school. Luigi showed no interest in the family business. For generations the Rossi families had produced high quality wines. As heartbroken as Mama and Papa Rossi were to watch the ship carry another child to the United States of America, they knew Luigi would be well taken care of by his older sister, Rosa.

Rosa and Eduardo Marino opened the Marino Trattoria in Camden Corners three weeks after they arrived in the United States. Eduardo was a master chef and Rosa was just a very good cook. Eduardo's great aunt Antonia didn't want someone else to reap the benefits of Eduardo's excellent cooking skills and sent him along with enough money to buy his own restaurant.

Eduardo and Rosa arrived in New York and found an advertisement in the paper for a quaint sounding restaurant in a village called Camden Corners. They bought the restaurant sight unseen and were off to Camden Corners the next morning. The restaurant had possibilities but it was nothing like what they had read in the advertisement. They were newlyweds and maybe just too naive to realize they had been duped.

They started scrubbing and fixing and decorating and before too long the Trattoria looked just like they dreamed it would. The people of Camden Corners had never tasted Italian cooking before and were a bit hesitant to try it but after having a meal prepared by Eduardo and served by Rosa, they came back again and again. The restaurant was a success and in just a few short years they were able to expand their establishment along with their family. Eduardo, Jr. was the oldest followed by Antonio, Giorgio, Daniella and Maria. Eduardo began helping his father when he was just a young boy and it was a foregone conclusion that he was a natural in the kitchen. Antonio tried but he had to settle for clearing tables and washing dishes.

The 4:15 arrived right on time and the whole town came out to welcome their friend and neighbor. The party was in full swing when Luigi announced he had a meeting with Mr. George Weston of the Weston Camera Company in Wilmington. Mr. Weston was interested in graduates with degrees in engineering and his professor recommended Luigi. Antonio, who liked to be called Tony, wasn't sure what a camera was. His uncle saw the look of confusion on Tony's face and explained that a camera was used to take photographs and promised he would bring one home the next time he came for a visit.

Mrs. Granville who lived on the corner of Phillip Avenue was very concerned about Luigi going to Wilmington. She had heard it was very close to Niagara Falls and maybe he would have too much of the devil's brew and try to go over the falls in a barrel. Maybe he should just stay here in Camden Corners where it is safe. He could be an engineer on the train. Luigi laughed and gave Mrs. Granville a hug. He loved this little town and all the people who lived here.

Tears were shed as Luigi boarded the train again, this time to take him to Wilmington. He was sad but also anticipating the opportunities waiting for him there. He met with Mr. Weston and was hired on the spot.

Several days later, Jackson Parker received a special delivery package at the post office for Master Antonio Marino from the Weston Camera Company. It wasn't often the folks of Camden Corners received special delivery packages and Jackson rushed out the door to personally deliver the package. Tony was sweeping the floor getting ready for the lunch crowd when Jackson came in with the package. The entire Marino family came out to see what the commotion was. Tony opened the package. There was a note from Luigi.

My Dear Nephew Tony, I spoke to Mr. Weston regarding your curiosity involving cameras. He was glad you showed interest in photography and wanted you to have your very own camera. Instructions are enclosed along with film for picture taking. When you have completed a roll of film, mail it to me and I will develop and print your pictures. Mr. Weston and I hope this will be the beginning of a lifetime of photographic pleasure. Fondest regards, Your Uncle Luigi.

Everyone was excited for Tony and Papa Marino told him to take the rest of the day off to try out his new camera. Tony had no trouble loading his camera. He began immediately using one roll of film and then another. Before Jackson had closed the Post Office for the day, Tony was there with three packages of film ready to be mailed to Uncle Luigi. Jackson was as excited as Tony wondering what the photographs would look like and he put in a rush order and delivered the package to the mail car at the train station himself.

In no time, Luigi received the film and developed it. He was astonished at the quality of the photographs. He expected some silly pictures of the brothers with goofy faces or the sisters with exaggerated smiles but these weren't anything like that. One was of his nieces standing on footstools glancing down with wonder at a mother robin feeding her baby birds. Another of Giorgio holding Mrs. Penrose's arm as he guided her down the front stairs of the restaurant. Another of Eduardo nuzzling Rosa's neck as he helped her tie her apron.   Mr. Crowley and Miss Dawson sitting on a park bench feeding the pigeons and looking into each others eyes. Every photograph seemed to tell a story. Luigi knew Mr. Weston would be pleased that his gift had been so well received. Mr. Weston was indeed pleased and insisted Luigi take all the equipment and products necessary to Camden Corners and help young Antonio set up a darkroom of his own. Luigi was concerned that this would be a monumental task but wasn't about to argue with his new boss.

Luigi arrived with all the equipment necessary for the darkroom. The restaurant had a large closet with a sink that would be perfect for Tony to use. With the help of Eduardo and Ted Evans from the hardware store, the room was completed in record time. Tony was a quick learner and it didn't take long before he was developing his own photographs.

Rosa proudly displayed his work in the entry of the restaurant. Before long people were offering to buy the photos. Tony enjoyed his new hobby too much to take money for them and gladly gave the photos to whoever wanted them.

At the edge of town that summer Mr. Rufus Melville was setting up camp. He was chuckling as he hid his stash of gold nuggets. Rufus' motto was *there's a sucker born every minute* and he knew there were a lot of minutes in a day. His plan was foolproof. Maybe not foolproof but the fools were certain to fall for his scheme. He followed the river to a small town called Camden Corners. He had a few of his precious gold nuggets and carefully dropped them into low points of the river.

He meandered into town and stopped at a friendly looking establishment called O'Sullivan's Pub. He knew he had to keep his wits about him and ordered a beer that he planned to savor for an hour or so. He found the local watering holes were the best place to plant the seeds for his latest schemes. Rufus congratulated himself on his good luck at arriving at the tavern just as the railroad workers were ending their shift. He wasted no time in displaying a handful of gold nuggets to the bartender. Within just a few minutes, every man in the room was hovering over his shoulders trying to get a glimpse of the sparkling gold pieces.

Rufus put on his best smile and started his scheme in motion. All eyes and ears were on Rufus as he whispered about his find in the river just outside of town.

"One hundred years ago, an old miser lived on the top of that there mountain just west of Camden Corners. He spent his youth in South America in a place called Columbia. The story goes he fell in love with a beautiful senorita but her heart belonged to another. He packed up all his gold and sailed the ocean to the new land. He found his way to this part of the country and buried his treasure in the mountain's peak. Through the years, the mountain has been wearing away and gold pieces have been falling down the mountain along with the melting snow. My employer has authorized me to collect those pieces and bring them to him. I found these just an hour ago."

He held out his hand with several shiny gold nuggets.

"There will be too much gold for me to find it all myself so I am willing to rent a portion of the river to anyone who is interested in becoming rich for a measly $3 a day. My employer will pay you 50 cents for each gold nugget you find. I'm holding 8 nuggets in my hand which would be a profit of $1 for 15 minutes of work."

The men, who had been working for 12 hours that day couldn't wait to hand over their hard earned money to Rufus to rent a portion of the river. They all followed Rufus out the door and to the camp he had set up just out of town. Each man stood in line and handed over their rent money to Rufus who would then give them a torn piece of a map marking off their individual spaces. Earlier Rufus had placed 5 nuggets throughout a small stretch of the river. As Rufus was counting his money, $45 in all, word was spreading through town about the *huge buckets of gold* being lifted from the river that very afternoon.

Rufus had a hard time keeping up with the demands for river rentals. By nightfall, all five pieces of gold had been found and each prospector had received 50 cents as promised. By the third day Rufus thought maybe he had better drop a few more pieces into the river. He could afford the expense since he was now bringing in close to $200 in rent fees each day.

Tony was still taking pictures of everything and everyone he could find. His younger brother Giorgio had caught the photography bug too and wherever Tony and his camera were, Giorgio was right there with them.

Just after dark one night, the boys thought about experimenting with nighttime photography. Up until that point all of Tony's photos were taken during the day. The moon was exceptionally bright that night and was shining brightly on the river. Tony and Giorgio rode their bicycles to the river with Tony's trusted camera and he started snapping pictures. They spotted a figure walking along the river. He appeared to be throwing something in the water. Maybe a stone or pebble. They walked behind and stayed back far enough so the stranger couldn't see them. He was whistling and singing about how he had duped a whole town of fools. Tony's instinct made him start photographing the man as he tossed another nugget in the river. The boys followed him to the camp he'd set up and took more pictures. They went back to the restaurant and developed the photos. They weren't as clear as daytime ones but they were clear enough.

Eduardo was relaxing after a busy night with some cronies at one of the dining tables. Most of the crowd had gone home but a few of the older men in town lingered since they didn't have anyone to go home to. The boys showed the pictures to the men.

Alvin Sweeney recognized the stranger. He had heard tell that gold was being found in the river. Alvin knew the mountains like the back of his hand and had explored every inch of them.

"There is no gold in those hills" he laughed.

Darnell Webb told of his neighbor who had given this fellow twelve of his hard earned dollars and had found one piece of gold that he was paid 50 cents for. His wife was about ready to wring his neck along with her chickens if he didn't stop throwing their money away. Eduardo thought it might be a good idea to ask Sheriff Mendenhall to investigate this stranger.

The next morning, Eduardo, Tony and Giorgio went to see the sheriff with the photos in hand. Sheriff Mendenhall as it turned out was visiting his sister and her family in Greensboro for the week and Deputy Arnie Pfeiff was in charge. Arnie was a pretty nice guy but not much of a lawman so Eduardo decided he would ask the Crowley boys what they could do legally to check this fellow out.

Robert was in his office and was very interested to hear about this scam.

"Dad would love to be involved." he said and he was right.

Oscar went straight home to put on some old clothes and met Eduardo, Wally Wallace, Chris Pringle and Isaac Nichols at the Trattoria. They wended their way to Rufus's camp and found him counting his money with a big, happy smile on his face. After each of the men paid their $3 rental fee, they were given a map of their space to search. Deputy Pfeiff who had been standing out of sight appeared with a set of handcuffs and the photos Tony had taken. Oscar informed Mr. Melville that it was quite illegal to rent portions of property that was owned by the State of New York. Rufus was kicking himself. He had planned to leave town two days ago but he was enjoying the fall weather and relaxing by the river as he counted his money.

He agreed to give back all of the money to all of the people who fell for his get rich scheme. Everyone who had invested in the gold scheme was invited to come back and claim their money. All of the prospectors were honest and only took what they had given Rufus. They were too embarrassed about being duped to exaggerate how much they had surrendered to him. Anyone who had found the gold nuggets and sold them back to Rufus was invited to keep their 50 cents.

The gold nuggets as it turned out, were nothing more than jagged stones painted bright gold. Rufus sat in jail until Sheriff Mendenhall returned. He was given a stern warning about taking advantage of people. The sheriff asked young Tony to take some photos of Mr. Rufus Melville so that he could send his picture to every county in the state.

Tony continued taking photographs throughout town. He was especially busy that Christmas. Everyone wanted photos of their families around the Christmas tree. Tony wouldn't accept payment for any of the photos as he had been so grateful to Mr. Weston and his gift. The whole town got together and presented Tony with genuine gold nuggets. Mr. Travers at the bank put them in the vault for safe keeping until Tony was old enough to go to journalism school and become an investigative reporter and photographer which is exactly what he did.

The Second Time Around

Nettie Dawson made her way through the snow to the Hilltop Chapel. Nettie loved the peace she felt when she entered the quaint little chapel with its beautiful stained glass windows. She could almost hear the angels singing as she sat in the pew near the altar.

Nettie was happy she had made the decision to follow her dear friend Ethel Fulbright to Camden Corners. She had made many friends in the short time she had been here and had lost her heart to Mr. Oscar Crowley. Nettie never married after the tragic death of her fiance just days before their wedding was to take place. Oscar lost his wife a few years ago and neither imagined they would ever find love again in their twilight years but here they were, two senior citizens acting like lovestruck teenagers. Nettie hadn't had this much fun in over 30 years.

Nettie was deep in thought and prayer when she became aware of muffled crying near the back of the chapel. She walked towards the sound and found a young girl holding a baby close to her heart with tears running down her cheeks. The girl looked up and Nettie recognized her as one of her former students from Greensboro, Polly Cooper. Polly was one of her better students who showed an interest in becoming a teacher. Nettie wrapped her arms around the young girl and waited patiently while Polly cried herself out.

"Miss Nettie" she exclaimed. "I have made a terrible mess of my life and my Pa has disowned me. I had just enough money for the train ride to Camden Corners and I knew you had moved here. Oh, Miss Nettie, I have nowhere else to go.."

Nettie's heart broke for the girl. She knew Marlin Cooper well and knew he was a very strict man who ruled his household with an iron fist. Nettie liked almost everyone she ever met but she didn't hold Mr. Cooper in high regard at all. Nettie guided Polly and her precious baby out the door and towards her home where she made tea and placed homemade cinnamon muffins on a plate.

It was obvious Polly hadn't eaten in a while as she gobbled up two of the large muffins. Nettie made a pallet for baby Faith who was soundly sleeping. Polly began her story.

A fellow named James Philpot found his way into Greensboro. He was a handsome young man who won the heart of Polly at first sight. Polly was enrolled in Normal School and studying to be a teacher as she had always planned. James knew right away that Polly was his for the taking but she would be the type who would insist on marriage before she would give into his many charms. The Coopers had a farm on the outskirts of town and owned acres of land near the river. James was a swindler who thought he would be able to ingratiate himself into the family. Mr. Cooper was not to be fooled though and refused to allow Polly to associate with this scoundrel. Polly could not understand why Pa couldn't see how charming and delightful James was. James suggested they go to a Justice of the Peace in a neighboring town. They would be married and Mr. Cooper wouldn't have any choice but to accept James into the family. Polly's head was telling her not to do this but her heart won out and she went off to become Mrs. James Philpot. James had no intention of actually marrying this country bumpkin.

He arranged for his cousin to pose as a Justice of the Peace and perform the bogus ceremony. It didn't take Polly long to discover James' true colors but by the time she did, she was expecting a baby. Her father would not welcome James into the family and told Polly she was no longer his daughter. When James discovered there would be no dowry or land given to him, he fled Greensboro with only a note telling Polly to find a way to get rid of the brat and informed her they were never legally married.

Polly's heart was broken but more than that she didn't know what she was going to do. Her Aunt Bertha was willing to put her up in her boarding house until the baby was born and sent off to an orphanage in Pennsylvania. Polly was expected to earn her keep by cleaning and cooking. She didn't complain, just tried to stay out of Aunt Bertha's way. Polly cried herself to sleep at night thinking of her baby. She had grown to love the unborn child and was determined to find a way to keep it.

One evening in October, Polly began to feel pains and knew her child was about to be born. Polly had never felt such agony in her life and kept praying that her baby would make it through the birth. She heard a voice telling her to *have faith.* Polly who had been present at her younger brothers and sisters births had some experience with babies being born. Pa refused to pay a doctor to attend to his wife and Polly was the only help she had. She knew it was truly a miracle when her baby girl was born healthy.

Just before dawn that morning while Aunt Bertha was still sleeping, Polly bundled up her newborn daughter, took her money out of its hiding place and walked away from Aunt Bertha's house and the prospect of giving her daughter away. Polly and Faith were well on their way to Camden Corners before Aunt Bertha discovered Polly was gone. She was glad to be rid of that ungrateful little tart. Aunt Bertha never knew Polly had given birth that evening or that her great niece had come into the world. When she told her brother about Polly's departure, the only thing he said was "Good riddance."

Nettie was appalled that Polly was treated so shabbily. She immediately opened her home to the young mother and her sweet little baby. Polly assured Nettie she would not overstay her welcome and would be on her way very soon. Nettie wouldn't hear any talk of her leaving. She was already planning a baby shower for the new arrival and couldn't wait to show off the little girl. Nettie felt like a first time grandmother and enjoyed the feeling very much.

Oscar arrived for afternoon tea at that very moment. He was captivated with Faith and was looking forward to the day when she would have a cousin or two to play with. Oscar loved his two sons but wouldn't it be fun to have a frilly little girl to make a fuss over?

Polly felt truly loved for the first time in her life. She knew she had made the right decision when she remembered hearing Miss Nettie had moved to Camden Corners.

The weeks ahead were filled with happy times. Nettie couldn't wait to decorate a little alcove of her apartment for baby Faith. It became clear that her cozy apartment was just not big enough. Polly was apologetic that she and Faith had caused Nettie any inconvenience but Nettie was happier than she had been in a very long time.

Oscar had a solution, the women could move into his large home.

There was way too much room for just one person. Polly and Faith would each have a room of their own. Nettie blushed knowing there were only three bedrooms in the house but Oscar sat her down on the sofa, tried his best to get down on one knee and slipped a beautiful diamond ring on her finger. Nettie said yes and they were married in the chapel that very weekend. The reception was in full swing when the door of O'Sullivan's Pub swung open and James Philpot appeared with a smirk on his face.

"Where is my daughter?" he shouted staring directly at Polly.

Diana Taylor was holding the baby at the time and stepped into the background. Oscar approached the cocky fellow and was pushed aside. Robert and Richard were on their feet immediately. Oscar, always the negotiator, tried talking quietly to James. James walked directly to Polly and demanded she present him with his baby.

"You mean the baby you wanted me to get rid of, James?"

He was surprised by the strength in her voice but continued "My child is somewhere in this room and I will find it, take it and you will never see it again."

That was all Sheriff Mendenhall needed. He slapped cuffs on James and with the help of several of the men dragged him to the jailhouse to sober up and cool down.

Polly was mortified. Because of her, James had ruined Oscar and Nettie's wedding reception. "No, no," said Nettie, "The party has just begun."

The festivities went on but Polly found herself wondering if James really did have any claim to Faith. Randy Burke was watching Polly from across the room. He had been attracted to her the moment he first laid eyes on her. He could tell she was a loving mother just the way she cared for little Faith. Maddie Mackenzie saw the glint in her brother's eye when he looked at Polly. Maddie, always the romantic, knew this was a match made in heaven and encouraged Randy to court her. Randy knew Polly wasn't ready for a relationship with anyone. He was willing to wait a while before he let her know his feelings. Even though Polly was smiling, he knew instinctively that she was afraid of James Philpot and what he might do.

Randy pulled Oscar aside and the two of them went out the back door and into the law office down the street. Oscar put some papers together and sent Randy on his way to the jailhouse. Randy was a big, husky fellow and looked extremely mature for his age. He walked through the jailhouse doors and confronted James in his cell. James had sobered up just enough to be aware of Randy's presence.

"Hey guy," called Randy "I knew I couldn't be the father of Polly's brat. I've got here some papers for you to sign telling the world that you are the kid's father. Old man Crowley says I'm responsible for that kid until she is 18 but I don't want any part of it. Polly's kinda cute but who needs to be dragged down by a dame and a kid. Sign these and I'll be outta here."

"Hey, wait a minute, that's your kid? Hey Sheriff, let me out and I'll be out of town before the street lights go on."

"Not so fast," came a voice from behind. "my client here is willing to give up custody of his kid to you." drawled Richard Crowley. "I've got some papers for you to sign, Pops."

"Hey, wait just one minute," chimed Robert Crowley. "You shouldn't have to be saddled with a kid now when you are such a young fellow. I have some papers here saying you are not the father of the little troll. Sign these and for a small fee of $100, I will file them in court for you tomorrow and just let that Polly try to collect any child support from you."

James reached in his pocket and gave Richard all the money he had, grabbed the papers, signed them and was gone before the cell door closed behind him. The four men shook hands and delivered the papers and the $100 to Polly who was noticing Randy Burke for the first time. Everyone joined in the celebration as Oscar exclaimed, "Love is lovelier, the second time around."

Polly looked into Randy's eyes and whispered, "Falling in love for the first time is quite lovely too."

Finding Iris

Cody Hill was only 9 years old when he first saw Mavis Short in the woods behind the shack the Hill family called home. Mavis was Mavis Cooley at that time. It would be two years until she married old Earl Short. Mavis was the prettiest thing Cody had ever seen. She was reading a book. Cody had never seen a book before let alone ever read one. Mavis called him over and showed him her secret stash of books that had fallen from a traveling salesman's wagon a few years back. Cody sat down next to her in the small patch of grass while she read him the story of Little Women. She made Cody promise not to tell anyone about the books. Learning, especially for womenfolk, was frowned upon in the backwoods. Cody was able to sneak out every day to visit with Mavis and listen to her reading her precious books. Mavis learned to read when she was just barcly 7 ycars old with thc hclp of old Mrs. Crenshaw.

Agnes Crenshaw had lived in Greensboro until she was 16 years old when she was married off to Gideon Crenshaw who had been a mountain man all his life. Mrs. Crenshaw hoped that Mavis would be able to leave the mountain someday but she knew that it was almost impossible to escape this backwoods country.

Mavis read her books out loud to Cody and eventually taught him to read also. Cody didn't mind that the stories were about girls, he was happy to have stories to read over and over again. The two friends met every day when weather permitted. Mavis was like a big sister to Cody. He knew she was resigned to marrying Earl Short. Mavis never complained about the mean, unpleasant man she called Sir. Earl was out of sight most days and Mavis was happy to have her time with Cody reading and dreaming of a better life.

Cody guessed Mavis was going to have a baby even before she discovered it herself. Cody had been around his aunts and cousins enough to know the signs. Mavis knew in her heart that the baby was a girl. She told Cody she would name her Iris after the beautiful irises that bloomed every year by the river. Her joy was contagious and Cody anxiously awaited the time when little Iris would be born and he could be a big brother to her.

An early winter storm hit the mountain on a day that had started out very calm. Cody's Paw was felling trees when the winds started blowing. He was knocked unconscious by a falling tree and died shortly after. Maw took to her bed after Paw's death and eventually died of what Agnes Crenshaw said was a broken heart. Cody's aunts and uncles would have taken him in but Agnes saw something different in Cody. She knew that Mavis had taught him to read . He was just a boy, not quite 12 years old.

Agnes wrote a letter to her brother in Greensboro and explained the situation to him. Melvin Tanner agreed to give the boy a home. Melvin was a kindly old gentleman who lost his beloved wife several years before. His only son lived in New York City. Melvin never understood why their parents married off Agnes to Gideon Crenshaw so many years ago. Agnes did seem to be happy with Gideon through the years but her life was very difficult in the mountains.

Cody was heartbroken to have lost both of his parents and Mavis comforted him as best she could. He told Mavis about Professor Tanner's offer to take him in. He didn't want to leave Mavis but she insisted he go to Greensboro where he would be able to go to school.

"One day you will come back to get me and Iris and we will all find a way to a better life."

With tears in his eyes, Cody left the mountain. He tried to fight the feeling that he would never see Mavis again. Mavis died later that winter giving birth to baby Iris.

Cody's life had changed dramatically. Professor Tanner introduced him to so many new things. They visited museums and art galleries. The following summer they took a train ride to New York City to visit the professor's son. Cody had never imagined how much the world had to offer. He didn't miss the mountain but he did miss Mavis. The professor broke the news to him about Mavis. Cody wanted to go back to be with Iris but he knew he was too young to care for her. He made a vow to Mavis that he would get an education and save little Iris from Earl Short.

Cody was true to his promise and excelled in school. Any time he missed while growing up on the mountain was made up when he set his mind to learning as much as possible. Professor Tanner grew to love the boy as another son and Cody felt the same way. Mrs. Crenshaw passed away two years after Cody left the mountain. Mrs. Crenshaw was his only source of information about little Iris Short since there wasn't another soul on the mountain who could read or write.

Time passed quickly and Cody graduated with honors from Greensboro High School the day after his 18th birthday. Professor Tanner knew he would be going back to the mountain to look for Iris before he started college in the fall and sent him on his way with his blessing and a little something extra to tide him over until he returned to Greensboro.

It took two days of hiking and climbing to reach the midpoint of the mountain where he had lived the first part of his life. He came upon the bungalow he called home. Another family was living in his old home. He decided not to bother them and went directly to Mavis' old cottage. This time he found no sign of life. It was obvious the hovel had been abandoned. He noticed two graves further down the lane. The graves had crosses made of rocks on the top of them. Mavis' name was scratched on one rock. Cody assumed the other was that of Mavis' maw. Cody couldn't help the flow of tears as he remembered the many happy times he and Mavis shared so long ago.

He walked slowly along the path that led to his aunt Ellie Sue's place. Cody didn't recognize his aunt. She had aged considerably in the few years since he left the mountain. Ellie Sue was happy to see her nephew. She gave him a weak hug and stood back to look at the handsome young man standing before her. Ellie Sue scolded Cody for leaving the mountain.

"Mountain men stay where the good lord intends for them to be and this is where you belong."

Cody knew it wouldn't do any good to argue with the woman and ignored her remark. He asked if she knew what had happened to Iris. Ellie Sue's memory had lapsed but after several minutes of prodding, she did recall a young thing Earl called Girl. Her maw died when she was born and nobody ever thought to give her a name. Earl took off down the mountain one day with Girl in his buckboard. The authorities came shortly after that asking about Girl's kinfolk. We told the man she had nobody.

"You understand, don't you, Cody? We have to struggle to feed our own and there isn't enough for anybody else."

Cody didn't understand but he needed more information if he was going to find Iris. Ellie Sue couldn't remember where the man was from. All he could get out of her was that it was some town down the mountain. Cody bid farewell to Ellie Sue and headed back down the mountain. He was so thankful to be leaving the place where the only good memories were of Mavis. He knew he would never come back. He also knew it would be useless to try to persuade his kin to move out too. He looked upwards to heaven and thanked Mrs. Crenshaw for sending him to live with the professor.

Cody wasn't sure what to do next. He tried to think like Earl Short would have thought. Maybe he had heard about the gold rush and would head west to California. That is probably just what the nasty old man would do. As he found his way down the mountain he turned west. He walked for several miles when he came upon a sign that said *Welcome to Camden Corners.* Cody was happy to see civilization again and vowed the first thing he was going to do was buy himself a horse. He wasn't accustomed to walking and climbing.

Camden Corners was a pretty little town. It was much smaller than Greensboro but had a very friendly look to it. He spotted a shop called Warm Hearth Bakery. Diana Taylor, Owner. His food supplies were enough to sustain him but the thought of a something sweet made his mouth water. He walked into the bakery where he was greeted by a nice lady who he assumed was Diana. He picked out 3 cookies and Diana poured him a glass of cold milk. He sat at a small table and began to devour the cookies when he heard a young girl's voice calling, "Mama, may Joey and I have a cookie?"

Diana turned toward the backroom and said, "Yes, Iris. Bring Joey out here and you may each pick out the one you would like."

Cody's mouth flew open when he saw the little girl who looked so much like his dear friend Mavis. It must just be a coincidence, he thought. This little girl has a Mama. Cody finished his cookies and milk trying not to stare at the little girl. Diana noticed that the color had disappeared in the young boy's face. She asked if he was feeling alright.

"Yes, ma'am, I'm fine but I would like ask you about a little girl I am trying to find." Cody began telling her about his friend Mavis when Diana seemed to hurry the children into the back room.

"What do you want?" she asked. "Who sent you here?"

Just at that moment Joe Taylor walked through the door. He knew immediately that something was upsetting his wife.

"This boy is asking about Iris. We adopted her a year ago and nobody is going to take her away from us."

Joe put his arm around his wife's shoulder to try to calm her down.

"Let's all sit down and find out what the lad wants with us."

Cody apologized for upsetting Diana. He wasn't here to make trouble. He explained his friendship with Mavis and how he was sent to live with Professor Tanner after his parents passed on. He told of the promise he made to Mavis that he would be back one day to save her and her baby girl from the mountain life. He told them how Mavis had named her daughter before she was even born and that she loved her with all her heart. Cody's eyes filled with tears as he talked about what a special person Mavis was and how happy she would be to know Iris was obviously loved and living in a beautiful town like Camden Corners.

Diana wrapped her arms around the boy and this time she apologized for jumping to the wrong conclusion.

"Iris means so much to us and I think I have always feared someone would try to take her away. I can see you loved her mother and I think it would be good for you to get to know your friend's daughter. She is a special little girl and just from the little you have told us about Mavis, I think I know where her wonderful qualities came from."

Joe thought the boy was being sincere but didn't want to take any chances. He suggested they wait until tomorrow to introduce Cody to Iris. Joe was afraid she wouldn't be able to sleep that night because of the excitement of meeting a friend of her mother's. Cody agreed, the men shook hands and Joe pointed toward Watson's B&B where he was sure Mrs. Watson had an open room. A real bed sounded like heaven to Cody who had been sleeping on the ground the last several days.

Cody's A Hero

Joe Taylor wanted to believe Cody Hill was on the up and up but knew he couldn't take any chances with his precious daughter, Iris. He immediately left the bakery to pay a visit to the Crowley Law firm. Oscar Crowley was just leaving as Joe walked up the stairs to the office.

Oscar began the law firm when he first passed the bar exam. He was retired but often dropped in to see what was going on. His sons, Robert and Richard had taken over the day to day running of the office but enjoyed having the old man around. Oscar, a widower, was recently remarried to newcomer to town, the former Nettie Dawson. They were married in the little chapel in the woods with their friends and family in attendance. Nettie had never married after the tragic death of her fiance just days before their wedding years ago. She was a school teacher in Greensboro before coming to Camden Corners. One of her former students, Polly Cooper and her new baby daughter unexpectedly came into Nettie's life and she opened her heart and home to both of them before she married Oscar. Oscar was also taken with Polly and little Faith and decided it was high time he popped the question to Nettie. All four of them are now living together in the Crowley home.

Oscar knew immediately that Joe was troubled about something and asked if he would like to walk with him to the Looking Back Antique Shop where Nettie was finishing up her shift. Joe told Oscar about the visit from Cody Hill and his concern that the boy might not be on the up and up. Since Nettie had lived in Greensboro and taught school there for many years, Oscar thought she would be the person to ask.

As they entered the shop, Nettie was just putting her coat on and greeted her new husband with a wink and a tender hug. Joe was happy to see the always cheerful Nettie. The threesome sat down at a vacant table near the window. Joe mentioned the name Cody Hill and Nettie responded with delighted surprise that Melvin Tanner's ward had arrived in Camden Corners. She listened as Joe explained the situation. Nettie was beside herself when she realized that she had information that would have helped the Taylors in their search for Iris' kin. She had never put two and two together. She had been aware that Cody lived in the mountains and Melvin's sister had suggested the guardianship arrangement. She also knew that little Iris had lived her first few years in the mountains herself.

Nettie assured Joe that Cody was an honorable young man. She

110

remembered the first day he arrived at school. He was very awkward and she had all she could do to keep him in the classroom with the snickering that was going on with the other students. He quickly learned to fit in and became one of the most popular and promising students she ever had.

Joe left the shop relieved that Cody wasn't there to make trouble. Nettie suggested she and Oscar pay a visit to Cody at the B&B. She would verify that Cody was who he said he was and she was also anxious to see the young man and inquire about the other citizens of Greensboro.

Cody had just settled into his room when there was a knock on his door. Mrs. Watson told him he had visitors waiting for him in the parlor. Cody was surprised and pleased to see Miss Dawson waiting for him. It had slipped his mind that his favorite teacher had moved to Camden Corners over a year ago.

"Miss Dawson, how wonderful to see you."

"It's wonderful to see you too Cody but my name is Mrs. Crowley now and this is my husband Mr. Oscar Crowley."

Oscar suggested since Polly and Faith were having dinner at the Burke house they dine at the Marino Trattoria where the two old friends would have a chance to catch up. After an enjoyable evening, Oscar was assured that Cody's intentions where Iris was concerned were honorable. Cody was sorry to hear of Earl's fate but glad Iris was living in a home filled with love. He looked forward to telling her all about the woman who gave birth to her and how much she loved her little girl long before she was born.

After saying goodnight to Cody, Nettie and Oscar stopped by the Taylor house to let them know that Cody was only interested in Iris' well being. Joe and Diana would tell Iris about her mother's friend in the morning and arrange for the two to get together.

Iris knew that her mother died when she was born and also knew that her father had died in an accident. She had no real feelings for her father but hoped he was in heaven now. She was sure her mother was in heaven because an angel had sent her to her new mama and papa and she knew in her heart that angel was her mama Mavis. Iris was excited to meet Cody and hear all about Mavis. Joe stopped by the Watson house and asked Cody to join the family for breakfast. Iris' eyes grew wide when she saw Cody. She wondered if she had disappointed him because his eyes were filled with tears when Papa introduced them. Cody tried to wipe the tears away and his voice quivered when he tried to talk. He was finally able to speak and told Iris she looked just like her mother. Cody told Iris how special her mama Mavis was and how much she loved her. That she named her for the pretty wild irises that grew by the river. Irises were her favorite flower and she would pick one to put in her hair. Iris was happy to hear about her mother. No one, not even her grandmother talked about her before. After breakfast while Iris was helping Diana carry dishes to the kitchen, she stopped Diana in mid-step.

"I love you mama."

Diana heart swelled with pride. She knew this precious little girl was assuring her that no matter how much she loved listening to Cody talk about her other mother she would always love Diana.

Cody's mission was complete and he still had the whole summer ahead of him before it was time to go to the University in the fall. He sent a telegram to the professor telling him he had found Iris and he liked Camden Corners and thought he might stay a few more weeks. He had heard the fish were biting in the lake this time of year. Wasn't it time Professor Tanner took a vacation for himself? Melvin read the telegram and thought that sounded like a swell idea. He messaged back that he was getting his fishing gear in order and would bring Cody's too when he arrived at the end of the week.

Cody was not use to being idle. He held a job every summer and after school since the first year he came to live with Professor Tanner. He noticed Nichols' Market and headed on over to see if they happened to be looking for any extra help. Cody introduced himself to Oliver Nichols. Oliver was happy to meet him but didn't need any extra help. His three brothers-in-law all worked in the store and his Uncle Isaac, although retired, was always there to help when needed. Cody couldn't resist the penny candy in the big, inviting jars by the counter and was picking out some favorites when he heard someone giggling over toward the pickle barrel. He looked around and saw two smiling faces looking at him. The giggler was the younger one. He noticed the older girl was very pretty. He hadn't paid too much attention to girls in high school. He had usually gone to the school dances with his pals and maybe shared a dance with one of the girls while he was there. He felt awkward and shy around girls his age in spite of the fact that he always felt comfortable with Mavis. Mavis was like an older sister to him and not like any of the silly girls at Greensboro High.

Isaac Nichols was sitting at the checker table with Chris Pringle and Duncan Mackenzie. It was early June but the day felt more like a fall one. There was a storm brewing in the north and the chilly air had already arrived. Isaac had gotten up to stoke the fire in the pot belly stove when suddenly a spark flew out and landed directly on the back of April

Hawthorne's shawl. Her little sister, Penny screamed as Cody grabbed the hooked rug that was lying in front of the counter, rushed to the girl and gently but firmly wrapped her in the rug and rolled her on the floor.

April tried to catch her breath as all the men and customers ran to Cody's side and while patting him on the back and shaking his hand congratulated him on a job well done. April was appalled. That hooligan just knocked her down on the floor and everyone was making a fuss over him. She slowly got up and was about to give him a swift kick in the shin when Penny grabbed hold of her and shouted. "April, that boy just saved your life."

Everyone turned to April and asked if she was all right.

"It's about time someone paid attention to me. I was the one who was manhandled and thrown to the ground like a sack of potatoes."

She let the rug fall and only then did she notice her shawl had been burned along with the skirt of her dress.

Joe Taylor walked through the door as everyone was congratulating Cody and told the boy he did just the right thing. Joe was impressed with Cody's quick response in what could have resulted in serious injury to April Hawthorne. Oliver voiced his regret that he couldn't use Cody in the store. He knew he would be a fine addition. Joe was interested to learn that Cody was planning to stay the summer in Camden Corners and was looking for a short term job to help with his expenses.

"We can always use help at the fire station, Cody. It wouldn't pay much but your meals would be covered and fire fighters are known to be excellent cooks. How about it?"

It was settled. Cody would start in the morning. April finally approached Cody and thanked him for saving her. Cody's face turned red with all the attention.

"It was nothing that anyone else wouldn't have done. I just happened to be the one who saw that spark hit your shawl."

Penny spoke up and invited Cody to the Hawthorne home for supper. She knew her mother would be grateful to him and would want to thank him for his heroics. Cody found himself wanting very much to see more of April and agreed to accompany the girls home.

Laura Hawthorne was busy preparing dinner when her daughters appeared in the doorway with a young man who Laura had not seen before. She set down her mixing bowl and greeted Cody warmly. Penny could hardly get the words out fast enough telling her mother about the fire ball and how April was almost burned to a crisp. April and Cody laughed at Penny's exaggeration but when Laura saw the condition of

April's clothing, she embraced Cody thanking him for saving her daughter.

One by one the Hawthorne boys, Lucas, Jr., Abraham and Timmy heard the story and each time it was embellished a little more by Penny. By the time Lucas, Sr arrived home from work, April had been saved from an inferno. Lucas was grateful to Cody for his quick thinking realizing the situation though not dire could have been much worse for his daughter.

Cody sat down to enjoy a wonderful meal with the Hawthornes. Little Timmy told the story of last Christmas when he was looking for a present for the baby Jesus and the whole town was searching for him.

"They even thought I drowned in the lake" he said proudly.

Cody could see the flash of fear still in the family's eyes and he knew they must have been very worried.

Cody told them of his life in the back country and talked about Mavis. Timmy was curious about Iris having two mothers and thought she was lucky 'cause he only had one. He felt very comfortable with this close knit family and was happy he made the decision to stay in Camden Corners for a while.

The rain that had been threatening all day finally started coming down. April and Cody sat on the swing on the front porch as the lightning was brightening the sky. Penny headed out to the porch to sit with them but Laura guided her into the kitchen to help with the dishes. Laura could see the signs of puppy love in her older daughter's eyes and she was not unhappy that the object of her affection was a lad named Cody Hill.

The Crystal Ball

Professor Tanner arrived as scheduled checking into Watson's B&B. He had missed his ward. It was quiet in his house without the presence of Cody and his friends. In all his travels he had never visited Camden Corners but could see why Cody wanted to stay for the summer. It was quaint and charming he could only imagine what it looked like in the winter covered with snow.

Cody was anxious to show the professor around town and thought he might like to visit Miss Dawson who was now Mrs. Crowley. The professor was happy to hear that his good friend had found happiness in her later years. The pair dropped by the antique shop and was greeted by owners Emily Patterson and Lily Kramer who had left Greensboro almost two years ago to open their own antique shop.

Professor Tanner was impressed with the shop and happy for two of his favorite students. They were both glowing and the reason, he later

114

realized, were the two Crowley fellows who were just as smitten with them.

Nettie entered the room with her arms outstretched. The old friends embraced and Melvin could see Camden Corners and those Crowley men brought out the best in all three of them. Nettie invited her friends to dinner that evening and said Ethel and Jonas Fulbright, more Greensboro natives, would be returning this afternoon from Pleasantville where they were attending an auction.

The Fulbrights had come to Camden Corners shortly after Emma and Lily bought the antique shop and were becoming very serious scavengers.

Cody and the professor continued on their tour of Camden Corners. The professor couldn't believe how many people Cody had met and become friends with since his arrival just days before. They stopped by Doc McMillan's office to meet April Hawthorne. April's face lit up when Cody walked through the door. The professor suspected his ward may have more of an attachment to Camden Corners than just the scenery. The last stop before heading back to Mrs. Watson's was a visit to Tempting Treats Bakery where Professor Tanner was introduced to Iris. He had only met Mavis Short one time but this beautiful little girl was the spitting image of her mother.

Nettie outdid herself with a special company meal. Polly was learning to be a wonderful cook too. She loved helping Nettie with the cooking and cleaning to show her gratitude for giving Faith and her such a lovely home to live in.

Polly was starting courses at Middleton Normal school in September. She was looking forward to becoming a school teacher and only hoped she would be as gifted at teaching as Nettie had been. Polly and Randy Burke had become close friends. Randy was instrumental in saving Faith from her birth father, James Philpot. James had taken advantage of Polly by arranging a phony wedding ceremony thinking her father would give the couple his land as a wedding present. Polly was in the family way when James informed her that they were not legally married and never would be.

Marlin Cooper sent his daughter off to be with an aunt until the baby was born and deposited in an orphanage. Polly escaped her aunt's house with newborn Faith and found her way to Camden Corners and her dear friend Nettie. Randy had fallen in love with Polly and Faith shortly after he met them but he knew Polly needed time before she would be ready for another relationship. Randy was a patient man and it was paying off. Just the other evening, Polly put her hand on his and told him how grateful she was for his friendship. She then kissed him on the cheek. It wasn't much but it was a good first step from a young woman who had been betrayed by someone she thought loved her.

The dinner party was progressing well. The guests were all chattering and laughing. Iris who had come with her parents was playing with little Joey and Faith on the floor by the grownups.

Ethel told of the Fulbright's adventure in Pleasantville. The estate sale they had gone to was in an old Victorian mansion. They were able to bid on several beautiful pieces including a chandelier that they almost couldn't fit into the wagon for the ride home. As they were about to leave, a fortune teller's crystal ball came up for bid. Jonas wanted to leave but Ethel was intrigued by the lights shining on the ball. She bid a few dollars on it and won the bid. Jonas told her she had wasted her money but she thought it would be a good conversation piece for the antique shop. The wagon hadn't been emptied yet and Ethel insisted on bringing it in so everyone could see it.

Jonas walked into the house with the ball in hand and placed it in front of Nettie. The sun suddenly went under a cloud and the dining room became dark with only a light from the crystal ball shining. The light lit up Nettie's face just like a fortune teller.

"I am Madam Crowley," chuckled Nettie, "I see a future of many marriages in Camden Corners starting with several at this table."

Oscar Crowley glanced at his sons lifting his eyebrow as if to say it was about time for both of them to pop the question.

"I see a number of babies being born before the first snow of winter."

Emma Patterson glanced over at Diana Taylor just in time to see Joe smile at her and squeeze her hand.

Nettie looked down into the crystal ball again, the ball suddenly turned dark and just then the sun came out again and brightened the room. Nettie had an uneasy feeling. She was not a superstitious person but there was something about that crystal ball that sent a chill up her spine. She placed it on the coffee table and proceeded to pour more coffee and brandy for those who wanted it.

Joe looked at Diana and she nodded. He then announced that at least one of the crystal ball's predictions would come true. He and Diana were expecting a baby in the fall. Everyone at the table was happy for the couple. They thought at one time they were not going to be blessed with children. Just about the time Iris came into their lives, Diana discovered little Joey was on the way. Iris was happy to hear she was going to be a big sister again.

The group started talking about the Founder's Day picnic that would be held the following Sunday. April was excitedly telling Cody all about the celebration.

"Each year on the Sunday following the summer solstice the whole town gets together to welcome the season. Everyone brings a picnic lunch, we make ice cream and have a pie and cake auction, a three legged race, we play croquet. Oh Cody, it is so much fun. I hope you will still be visiting in Camden Corners then."

"I will if you will be making a pie so I can bid on it. My favorite is blueberry."

"Oh yes Cody, I will make a blueberry pie. I hope you will be my partner in the three legged race."

April had never made a blueberry pie in her life but she was determined to make one for the picnic.

Nettie said she hoped Melvin would be staying for the picnic too. He told her he was enjoying his stay in this lovely town and thought he might think about staying for a while. The table was abuzz with talk of the picnic. It was obvious to the newcomers that the people of Camden Corners enjoyed spending time with their neighbors and were looking forward to getting to know more of the townspeople.

The party came to an end and everyone was getting ready to leave.

"Don't forget your crystal ball, Ethel."

Nettie went to pick it up and it slipped out of her hands crashing to the floor and breaking into pieces.

"Oh Ethel, I'm so sorry. How clumsy of me."

"Don't worry Nettie. I think Jonas was right. It is a rather strange item. I don't know why I bought it in the first place."

Nettie picked up the pieces to put them in the trash and she was filled with fear and trepidation.

"What's wrong dear? You look as though you have seen a ghost." exclaimed Oscar.

"I'm just being silly, I know, but that thing gives me the creeps."

"Let me take it out to the trash now and it won't bother you anymore."

As Oscar lowered it into the trash barrel, the thing lit up with a flash and then darkness. Oscar thought his imagination was working overtime but decided not to mention his experience to Nettie. He did feel the need for another nightcap when he came back into the house and wasn't surprised when Nettie joined him.

The Miracle

Melvin Tanner was walking down Main Street enjoying the beautiful early summer weather. He strolled by St. Peter's Church where he came upon the vicar and a young man planting petunias in the flower bed in front of the church. He greeted the two and introduced himself. The planting was almost completed and Vicar Willard Duesenberry left his handyman to finish the job while he and Melvin entered the church office for a cup of Alma Shrum's tasty coffee.

Alma had been the church housekeeper and cook for as long as she could remember. She loved the vicar like a son and was very protective of him. She was thrilled that her granddaughter, Kate and the vicar were a couple although their courtship was going terribly slow. Alma brought out a pot of freshly brewed coffee and a plate of oatmeal cookies that she had just taken out of the oven. One bite into the warm cookie and Melvin's heart melted. It had been 25 years since Melvin's wife passed away. He had never even considered becoming involved with another woman until now.

The vicar was interested in how the professor happened to become Cody Hill's guardian. He believed in miracles and saw the professor's tale as proof that they are possible. Melvin checked his pocket watch and realized he had taken up well over an hour of the vicar's time.

"No bother at all, Professor. I have enjoyed our chat very much and I hope you will join me for dinner very soon. Mrs. Schrum is a superb cook as you can tell by my expanding waistline."

Mrs. Schrum entered the room just then and poo pooed the idea that the vicar was fat.

"You are too skinny, vicar. You need to put some more meat on your bones."

Melvin chuckled at Mrs. Schrum's gentle teasing. He would like to have asked if there was a Mr. Schrum but he couldn't think of a way to say it without seeming forward. Before he knew it he had blurted out, "Mrs. Schrum, I would like very much to get to know you better and wonder if I may have another of those wonderful cookies. Oatmeal are my favorite."

Melvin's face turned red and he was mortified at what just came out of his mouth. The vicar had never known Alma Schrum to be speechless but she just stared at the professor with her mouth open.

"Alma, why don't you show the professor around the church grounds, the roses are beautiful now."

Alma took hold of the professor's arm and guided him out the back door to the garden. She finally found her voice and the two talked so long it was almost dinnertime and she hadn't even begun preparations.

The vicar told Alma to take the night off. He was going to ask Kate to stop over after school and together they would be able to find something to sustain them for the evening.

"Professor, the Marino Trattoria has a wonderful menu in case you and Alma are hungry a little later."

Kate found it incredible that her grandmother had a beau. She couldn't wait to write to her mother to give her the news. The letter could wait. Tonight she was going to cook up a storm to show Will she was almost as good at cooking as her grandmother.

The vicar was standing in the doorway smiling at this beautiful girl. He had a ring burning a hole in his pocket just waiting for the right time to pop the question. Maybe tonight would be the night. Every time he planned to ask Kate to be his wife, one of his parishioners knocked on the door in need of his help. The meal was wonderful. Every bit as good as Alma's. The mashed potatoes were heavenly and the gravy was sinful. Just the way Will liked it. As he was taking the last bite of his peach pie, there was a knock on the door.

Will was called away and Kate stayed behind to clean up the kitchen and said to the cat, "I'd better get use to these interruptions if I am to be a clergyman's wife. I just wish Will would give me that ring he has been carrying around with him all this time."

Alma and Melvin had been inseparable since the day they met in the vicar's office. Melvin stopped by to escort her to the Founder's Day picnic. Excitement spread through the whole town. Other than Independence Day and Christmas, the Founder's Day Picnic was the biggest event in Camden Corners. Alma's picnic lunch consisted of fried chicken, potato salad, cucumbers and tomatoes from the garden and two pieces of chocolate cake with fudge frosting. She also carried along her entry for the pie bidding contest, a strawberry pie brimming over with strawberries picked just this morning. Melvin's mouth was watering. He loved sweets of any kind and Alma was very good at making his favorites. He wondered why it took him so long to find a companion and then realized he was just waiting for Alma to come into his life. Alma was proud walking arm in arm with Melvin. Her dear Harlan passed away just before Vicar Will became pastor of St. Peter's Church. Harlan was the head caretaker of the church and planted many of the trees that were towering over the grounds now. It never occurred to Alma that anyone would be taking Harlan's place in her life and in her heart. Somehow she knew he would approve of her choice in Melvin. Harlan had a sweet tooth too and Alma loved baking. The vicar was much too conscious of his waistline and never had seconds of Alma's delicious treats.

As promised, everyone was having a wonderful time at the picnic. Cody and April came in a close second in the three legged race. They were beaten by Joe and Diana as Iris watched them rolling over with laughter.

Oscar, Chris Pringle, Doc McMillan and Isaac Nichols strolled through the picnickers in their Barber Shop Quartet garb singing in beautiful harmony.

Croquet and horseshoe games were being played all over the park. Some of the older fellows found a nice big tree and set up their checkers game. Kate and the vicar organized relay races for every age group. Sounds of laughter could be heard throughout the park. April Hawthorne's blueberry pie turned out very nicely and Cody bid a whole day's pay on it.

The sky began to turn a little dark and everyone started packing up after a long and happy day. Iris, Timmy Hawthorne and some of the Burke and Mackenzie children were playing tag down by the lake. Nettie found Cody and asked him to run quickly to the lake to bring Iris to her mother. He started toward the lake and April followed along with him. Just as they approached Iris and the rest of the youngsters, the sky turned very dark.

Nettie, who was watching from the picnic area had a terrible sinking feeling. She remembered looking into the crystal ball a few days ago and it looked just like the dark sky above. Oscar felt it too and wrapped his arms around Nettie. Within the next few seconds a bolt of lightning shot through the sky to where Iris was standing and struck her. Nettie screamed as Iris fell to the ground. Cody ran to her and very calmly got down on his knees and pressed gently on her chest stopping and starting and covering her mouth with his began breathing air into her little lifeless body. Diana and Joe came running.

"What are you doing to my baby?" she yelled at Cody who was continuing with this strange procedure.

She and Joe both tried to reach their daughter but their legs seemed to be glued to the ground. Doc McMillan looked on in amazement. He didn't know what Cody was doing but he could see the little girl start to move and then cry out. Cody leaned back and Iris looked over at Diana.

"Mama went back home." she said in a weak little voice.

"I'm right here, sweetheart." said Diana as she took Iris in her arms.

"No, my other Mama. She said I would be alright and that I needed to stay here with my new Mama and Papa."

Doc McMillan examined Iris immediately and determined that she was in excellent health. He suggested the Taylors take her home and bring her by his office in the morning. He was shaking Cody's hand and told the crowd that what Cody had done saved Iris' life. Everyone was congratulating Cody and calling him a hero.

He turned to April, "I'm not a hero. Something or someone made me do what I did and I'm not even sure what that was."

Nettie and Oscar were both relieved that Iris was going to be fine. Nettie was still shaking at the sight of the lightning bolt hitting the little girl. Ethel and Jonas were visibly upset too.

"There was something about that crystal ball that predicted what just happened." said Ethel.

"That is impossible, my dear" said her husband.

The vicar joined the foursome, he had overheard something about a crystal ball. Jonas explained that they had bought it at an estate sale.

"Something strange came over me and I had to bring that thing home. Jonas tried to tell me to leave it there, but I insisted and look at what happened." Tears were welling in her eyes.

"Now dear, I'm just as much to blame. I could have been more forceful but the truth was, I didn't really want to stop you from buying it. There was something about that thing that seemed to take over."

"I know what you mean, Jonas. That was how it affected me too."

Nettie agreed with both of them. She told them about what she saw in the ball and how it made her feel. She was happy it dropped and broke. Oscar then told how it appeared to almost be alive when he disposed of it in the trash.

The vicar was listening intently. "You know I am in a business where miracles are promised. Do you think maybe the crystal ball was just warning all of you of that lightning bolt?"

"Nettie, I remember you telling Cody to hurry to get Iris. You didn't mention the other children and they were all together. Is it possible you knew something was going to happen to Iris even though your conscious mind didn't know what it was?"

Cody had joined the group by this time. "Cody, you said you didn't know what or why you were doing what you did to Iris but according to Doc McMillan, you saved the little girl's life. Diana and Joe both said they were going to stop you but they couldn't get their feet to move. Little Iris seems to think her mother was with her when she was unconscious. Maybe her mother was protecting her from what she knew was going to happen. We will never know, but don't fault yourselves because you were tempted by the crystal ball. We members of the clergy don't normally advocate anything resembling predictions of the future but in this case, I think we should make an exception."

Everyone agreed that they would not talk about the crystal ball anymore or tell the other townspeople about the strange happenings around it.

The park cleared out just as the clouds disappeared and the moon shone brightly along with several stars including one that was twinkling especially bright that night. The friends all smiled at one another as they wiped away a tear from their eyes.

After Oscar and Nettie arrived home, Oscar looked in the trash and saw that the crystal ball had shattered into little pieces. The glass was as clear and bright as could be and had lost its menacing appearance. He called to Nettie pointing out what had happened to the three broken pieces. There was no darkness or bright light shining from the remains. It looked just like what it was, a broken glass ball with no magical powers.

Uncle Shane's Surprise

In the small drawing room of the apartment above The Bloom Quilt Shop, Dahlia and Hyacinth Bloom Hightower were each bubbling over with excitement, they both had strong suspicions that they were expecting. It seemed reasonable that the identical twins would have babies at the same time since they did everything together. Dahlia and Hyacinth had only one falling out in all their days.

The sister's lives revolved around quilts and quilting. If they weren't running their quilt shop or teaching quilting, they were quilting anything from blankets and jackets right down to tea cozies and sachets. They hadn't much time left for themselves and although they were well thought of and admired, the townspeople often referred to them as dowdy spinsters.

That ended the day Mr. Harold Hightower, filling in for Mr. Hennessy with his wagon full of dry goods, stopped by the quilt shop that also served as the residence of the Sisters Bloom. Dahlia took an instant shine to the handsome young Mr. Hightower and with the help of Diana Taylor, a little make up, a pretty hairdo and stylish clothing she borrowed from Diana, she had turned into a swan. Hyacinth was appalled that her sister was flaunting herself and the girls didn't speak for several days. Mr. Hightower, again filling in for his friend, stopped by the quilt shop and this time he did notice Dahlia and was instantly smitten. Hyacinth finally acquiesced and asked Dahlia to help transform her into a beauty too. The twins new found pride in the way they looked on the outside gave them each a boost of self confidence and they were no longer referred to as dowdy spinsters. Harold just happened to have a twin brother himself and it wasn't long before the Bloom twins and the Hightower twins were a family.

The previous year had been the best either of the girls could remember. Howard Hightower adored his new bride, Hyacinth, and she was beside herself with love for her husband. Howard and Harold had been doing odd jobs around town but hadn't found anything they liked. They struck up a friendship with Nicola Rossi.

Nicola or Nick as he preferred being called was Rosa Rossi Marino's brother. In Italy, the Rossi family owned and operated a large vineyard. Nick had been the only Rossi boy who had taken an interest in growing and producing wine. He loved the feel of dirt between his fingers, the aroma of the growing grapes and especially the process of fermentation. Papa Rossi wanted his son to have the best education possible and sent him to live with his sister so that he could enroll in college as his brother Luigi did several years before. Nick was a smart young man but had little interest in book learning. He loved being in the open air and working the fields. The closest he came to farming was the small garden behind the Marino Trattoria where he planted vegetables and herbs his sister and brother-in-law used in their cooking. He also planted and cared for grapevines that were growing over trellis on either side of the restaurant. Howard and Harold were examining the grapes and Nick explained these were wine grapes. Not especially good for snacking. He commented that the soil in Camden Corners was almost perfect for some varieties of wine grapes. Harold and Howard who had never even considered wine coming from anything but a bottle were impressed with Nick's knowledge and wondered how they would go about acquiring some land and going into the wine business. They laughed at themselves knowing they would never be able to afford such a thing.

Two days later, both Harold and Howard received registered letters from a law firm in New York City. They had been requested to attend the reading of the Last Will and Testament of Mr. Shane Howard. The brothers had received word a month before that their Uncle Shane had passed away. Uncle Shane was a recluse, if that was possible, in the big city of New York. When their mother was alive she would dress the boys in their Sunday best, pile them on the train to make the long journey to

123

visit their Uncle. He was kind to the boys but he never acted especially happy to see them. As the years went by, they visited Uncle Shane a couple of times a year.

Harold laughed at the thought that the man who lived in a one room flat and appeared to own nothing but a moth eaten sofa and a rickety old table would have wasted the paper it would take to write a will. Howard, who was christened Howard Shane Hightower after his uncle was skeptical too. After talking it over with their wives, they all decided the men would make the trip to New York City. They were sure their uncle had left them a remembrance he had saved from his beloved sister and their dear mother.

The law firm of Brown, Hammer, Brown and Pike sent word a representative of the firm would be meeting the brothers at the train station and escorting them to the law office where the will was to be read. The men were surprised when none other than Seymour L. Brown, Sr. and his assistant were waiting for them at the station.

Upon arriving at the impressive law office, they were ushered into a huge conference room, seated in the front row and were offered beverages of their choice and plates of hors d'oeuvers.

Harold whispered in his brother's ear, "You better close your mouth, you look like the country bumpkin you are."

Howard noticed his brother's eyes were as big as saucers and commented, "That makes two of us."

Mr. Brown proceeded with the reading. If Harold's mouth was open before, it was cavernous now. It seems Uncle Shane was a poor man only because he never spent any of his money. He had holdings in numerous companies, land in several states and bank accounts in amounts the Hightower brothers had never imagined. The last statement was directly to Harold and Howard.

To my only remaining relatives, Howard Hightower and Harold Hightower, I leave the land I purchased on the advice of my good friend, Mr. Herbert Hennessy. The land is located on the west side of the small village of Camden Corners. Herbert drove his dry goods wagon by that land once a week for 32 years and felt it would be a good investment. The only condition is that they use the land wisely. I also leave them a sum of money that will be disclosed only to them. I hope this money will bring happiness to them and their wives.

On a personal note, I know you boys thought your old uncle was a crackpot but you always treated me with respect and yes, I believe you loved me. After your sainted mother died you continued to come to visit me. I have visited you too.

I watched as you both graduated with honors from the University. As a favor to me the director allowed me to sit in the orchestra pit. I saw you marry the lovely Bloom sisters in a double ceremony. I was disguised as a florist on that day. I have passed through Camden Corners many times. It is a charming town with good people who think the world of the two of you.

I never revealed who I was although I think Oscar Crowley may have been suspicious but he never let on. You may ask why I didn't come forward. Remember, I'm an eccentric old man. I'm set in my ways and have been since I was 18 years old. I have never taken pleasure in spending money, only making it. Now that I am at the end of my journey I realize what a mistake that has been.

I do have one request. The Widow McCoy who lives in the flat next to mine has been extremely kind to me. Her husband was shot and killed on his way home from work two years ago. Mrs. McCoy is raising their young daughter by herself while taking in laundry and cleaning apartments in the building. She was always so kind and took a special interest in this old man. I would like you to invite Mrs. McCoy and her daughter, Cassandra to move to Camden Corners. It may be inappropriate of me to leave her money directly and therefore I am asking that you help them to relocate out of the dangerous apartment they are living in now. Seymour has the address and will be sure you have safe passage. He has already delivered my personal note to Mrs. McCoy and has requested that she be packed and ready to go. I trust you both will follow my directions.

God be with you and your families. Signed: Shane Howard

Howard and Harold were in a state of shock. The money left to them was well into the millions. Mr. Brown arranged for most of the money to be put into a trust for them and their families. They were still in a state of shock when they arrived at the apartment of the Widow McCoy. Lucinda McCoy slowly opened the door after the brothers announced who they were. Even though she was very thin and pale, she was a very pretty woman. The little girl, Cassandra came running from the small alcove that was the kitchen. She was grinning from ear to ear.

"Mama said we might move to the country. I want to see cows and pigs. Are you going to take us there?"

Cassandra was looking at Harold and then glanced behind him at Howard and couldn't believe her eyes. Two men who looked just like each other. Lucinda asked the brothers to sit down on the clean but rather worn

125

sofa.

Lucinda said, "Cassandra was in the room when Mr. Brown stopped by with the letter from Mr. Howard. Mr. Brown was the one who mentioned moving to the country and Cassandra hasn't stopped talking about it since. Mr. Brown assured me that Mr. Howard was an honest man and he was doing what he thought best for my daughter. I just don't know. As tempting as it is, I can't just pack up and leave."

With that there were sounds of commotion and a gun shot out the window. Cassandra didn't even flinch. Harold asked if that happened often.

"Yes. Cassandra doesn't remember when her father was killed from one of those bullets but I do. It makes me shudder whenever I hear it and I hear it often."

Harold came up with a solution. "Why don't you come back to Camden Corners with us for a visit. Mrs. Watson has a lovely home with very nice rooms to let. We will prepay the rent on this apartment and you can stay in Camden Corners as long as you would like. If you decide to move back to the city you will have a place to come home to."

Howard knew his brother would never let them move back into this place but he knew Lucinda wouldn't just pack up and leave permanently.

Cassandra was jumping up and down. "Can we Mama? can we go with Mr. Howard and Mr. Harold, please?"

Lucinda couldn't resist her precious daughter's request. "Yes, we will have ourselves a little vacation. Let's pack up all the things we want to take with us. When were you planning to leave Mr. Hightower?"

"We will be leaving by train in the morning but why don't my brother and I help you pack up and you can stay in the hotel we are staying in tonight. It will be much more convenient for getting to the train station in the morning."

Lucinda was about to decline the offer of a hotel room when gunshots rang out again. She quickly packed their few clothes and some mementos, Cassandra had her doll and a necklace her papa had given her with a little pink heart. She only wore it for special occasions and this was a special occasion so she put it around her neck and Harold helped her with the clasp. He thought to himself how nice it would be to have a little girl to care for.

Back home, Dahlia and Hyacinth were just leaving Doctor Julie Mcmillan's office where she had confirmed what they both knew. They were both in the family way. They walked cheerfully to the train station.

"Wait until the boys find out our news, they will be so excited" said

Dahlia.

Hyacinth piped in "I wonder what Uncle Shane left them. I certainly hope it isn't that dirty old spittoon he had in his living quarters. The poor old man had nothing worthwhile to leave the boys."

The train pulled into the station Howard and Harold were smiling at their wives as they walked with a pretty young woman and a little girl. Both looked like they were scared to death.

Cassandra saw the twin sisters and started giggling "Does everybody in Camden Corners look like somebody else?"

The sisters laughed as they were being introduced to Cassandra and her mother. Their husbands were full of chatter about the money and land that was left to them. The baby news would have to wait. Dahlia and Hyacinth didn't think their husband's hearts would be able to take another shock just yet.

A New Home For Cassandra

Dahlia and Hyacinth are happy to welcome Lucinda McCoy and her adorable daughter, Cassandra to Camden Corners. The sisters, once again thinking identical thoughts, insist the two come to their home for a cup of cocoa and some freshly baked cookies. The twins ask Cassandra if she would like to visit the Quilt Shop downstairs while her mother and Mr. Howard and Mr. Harold discuss business. Cassandra has never seen so many soft warm blankets as she looks around the Quilt Shop. Dahlia and Hyacinth ask her to pick one out that she would like to keep for her very own and to pick one she thinks her mother would like. Cassandra has a very difficult time deciding but she chooses a pink one with bunnies on it for herself and a lavender one with white roses for her mother. Meanwhile, Howard and Harold reassure Lucinda that she is doing the right thing by accepting Uncle Shane's money. Lucinda insists that she will keep track of the money that they give her and pay back every penny if it takes until she is 93 years old. It is decided that they will visit the Crowley brothers in the morning to set up a trust fund.

Cassandra bounces into the room with her new quilt wrapped around her. Lucinda tries to tell the sisters that they can't accept these beautiful quilts but to no avail. She loves the quilts and hugs her new friends. Dahlia can feel her ribs when she hugs back and insists they take cookies with them to Mrs. Watson's.

Mrs. Watson welcomes the McCoys with open arms. She has the perfect room for this lovely young woman and her darling little girl.

Cassandra's eyes are as big as saucers when she sees two canopy beds covered with fluffy down comforters and soft pillows. She puts her new quilt on one of the beds before her mother has a chance to even enter the room. Harold deposits their little traveling bag on the bench by the window and bids them farewell for the evening. Mrs. Watson says she will let them get settled and be back to see what they may need in a little while. Howard tells Mrs. Watson what he knows of their situation and the way they were living.

Cassandra happily splashes in the bathtub next to their room, brushes her teeth, puts her thin little nightgown on and climbs into the big bed holding her doll and pulling her new quilt up to her chin.

"Mommy, I like Camden Corners. I hope we can stay here forever." with that her little eyes close and she falls sound to sleep.

There is a soft knock on the door as Mrs. Watson arrives carrying a tea pot and two cups. She thought Cassandra might be asleep and wanted to get to know Lucinda better. They talk as they sipped their tea. Lucinda tells her she doesn't know how she is going to repay the kindnesses. Mrs. Watson assures her that she would find a way to help someone else out some day and that she had already befriended old Shane Howard and was being paid back for her own kindness.

The Hightowers walked back home still unable to believe all that had happened in just a couple of days. They worried that Lucinda McCoy's pride would get in the way of her finding a life in Camden Corners.

"We will just have to make sure that doesn't happen." said Harold.

"We'll have the girls check around to see if anyone needs help in their shops. She is so good with Cassandra it's too bad we don't have any children for her to look after while Dahlia and Hyacinth are tending the shop."

"It will be nice to be home again, brother. Do you realize this is the longest we have been away from our wives since the day we said I do?"

They arrived home to big hugs and kisses for what they were doing for their new friend and her daughter.

"We have something we would like to discuss with you." said Hyacinth.

"We have decided that since we do everything together, we should tell you our news together"

In unison, the sisters excitedly announced "We are going to have a baby."

Lucinda slept through the night without the sounds of the city disturbing the quiet. She dreamed of a lovely meadow and Cassandra running through the grass chasing butterflies. She woke up well rested and really hungry. It must have been the smell of bacon wafting through the house. She would have to get dressed quickly to help Mrs. Watson with the cooking. She had to start paying her way. Cassandra was busy showing her doll all the lovely things in the room.

"Don't you just love it here Dolly?" She then put her little fingers on Dolly's forehead making the doll nod in agreement.

"See, Mama, Dolly likes it here too."

"Let's get you dressed and we will go downstairs to help Mrs. Watson in anything we can. Cassandra, I know you like it here. I hope we will be able to stay too."

Harold was ecstatic with the news that he would be a father soon. He was unable to sleep all night and woke to the sound of the door knocker. He didn't want anyone else to be disturbed and rushed to the door to find a special delivery letter secured to the door. The letter was from the law firm of Brown, Hammer, Brown and Pike.

This letter is to inform you that we have discovered new information concerning your deceased uncle Mr. Shane Howard.

Your uncle secured the services of a private detective to investigate his deceased son and any possible descendents he may have had. There is a record of your uncle marrying a Miss Maria May Alcott on December 13th, 1832 at St. Cecelia's Cathedral in Baron's Point, New York. Maria died giving birth to Roland P. Howard the following year. According to Mr. Shane's journals, found under a loose floorboard in his apartment, Shane fell into a deep depression when his wife died and would not acknowledge his young son. The boy grew up in the care of servants who did their best to care and love the lad. Roland was given every financial advantage but never the love of his father which was the only thing he really wanted. The private detective completed his investigation after your uncle's death. He delivered his report to our office. You will find the complete report in a separate envelope accompanying this letter.

The summary of the report is as follows: Roland met a young girl named Marguerite Blake. Marguerite was the only child of Harrison Blake of Oklahoma. Harrison was the owner of the largest cattle ranch in the state. Although he loved his daughter, it was a crushing blow to him when he discovered she would be his only child. He only came to this conclusion after his 6th marriage and no other children had been born.

Marguerite had been provided with anything her heart desired and she desired Roland P. Howard. Harrison agreed to the marriage only if Roland would legally change his last name to Blake so that any children would bear the proud name of Blake. Roland agreed since the name Howard had never been especially important to him. They were married in the spring and Marguerite gave birth to their son naming him Peter. Two months after Peter's birth, the couple boarded a ship bound for London, England. The ship ran into trouble in the choppy waters and several people jumped overboard hoping to be the first ones to reach the rescue boats. Roland panicked and was one of the first to jump overboard to his death. A distraught Marguerite followed him into the water leaving her sleeping baby on board.

In the confusion that followed, the baby was mistaken for the child of a young peasant girl who suffered a head injury and died without regaining consciousness. The ship returned to the New York dock and all the passengers were transferred to another ship to complete their journey.

The baby was deposited in the closest orphanage. Mr. Blake was informed that his daughter and son-in-law were missing and presumed dead in the waters of the Atlantic Ocean. Upon hearing the news, Harrison Blake suffered a massive heart attack and died the following morning. The authorities attempted to locate the next of kin of Mr. Roland Blake but to no avail. A couple of the servants wondered about the little baby but it wasn't their place to question the happenings of the household and they never voiced their concerns. The extensive report goes on to say that while in the orphanage, Peter Blake was given the name Paul McCoy.

When he was 7 years old, a girl his age came to live at the home. She was a sad eyed little girl as she had lost her parents and had no one to take her in. Her name was Lucinda and Paul took her under his wing. They were the best of friends until their teen years when they fell in love. On Paul's 18th birthday he left the orphanage vowing to work as hard as he could to save money for the couple to marry. Paul kept to his word. He worked two jobs during the week and was able to find another for the weekend. Three months later when Lucinda reached the age of 18 she joined him and they were married by a Justice of the Peace.

They lived frugally but happily for the next 5 years. Paul loved his wife with all his heart and was beside himself with joy when his beautiful little girl was born. When she was only two years old he was fatally shot on the way home from his job leaving a devastated Lucinda to care for their daughter alone.

The detective believes Mr. Howard had his suspicions about Cassandra being his great granddaughter although he took his reasons to the grave. I leave you gentlemen to do what you will with this information. The firm of Brown, Hammer, Brown and Pike was retained *by your Uncle and has no obligation to inform Mrs. McCoy of this discovery.*

The brothers were fascinated by this story. They had no idea their Uncle had been involved with a woman let alone married one and had a child. They had been wanted and loved by both their parents and it was hard to believe a brother of their dear mother would be so callous as to abandon his only son through all of his life. They, of course, would give the report to Lucinda. She had a right to know about her daughter's family. Knowing this information might also make it more palatable for her to accept Uncle Shane's money.

Lucinda is astonished and sadden while reading the report. She wonders aloud what made Shane Howard suspect that his grandson was the same man Lucinda had loved and married. Dahlia and Hyacinth looked at each other.

"Are you thinking what I am, sister?"

Dahlia nodded and both women went directly to the cupboard in the hallway and brought out a box they had covered in quilted material and labeled *Hightower Family Mementos*. The gentlemen had brought the box with them when they moved into the apartment above the quilt shop. Dahlia held up a photo that she remembered seeing when they first went through the contents. The photo was the spitting image of little Cassandra right down to the dimple in her chin. A note on the back read *Louisa May Howard – age 5*. The question of why Shane Howard began his investigation was answered.

Everyone hugged each other and welcomed Lucinda into the family. Lucinda was thrilled that she and Cassandra would be part of a loving family. Soon Cassandra would have two new cousins to play with.

The brothers had a map of the land left to them. It was decided the whole family would ride to the area and see exactly what they were dealing with. Their new property extended far beyond what they had imagined. There was a small stream running alongside and trees swaying in the breezes at the back. It was a beautiful spot that would be perfect for a vineyard.

Harold had mentioned that possibility to Howard and they both agreed to ask Nick for his advice. At that moment, Nick came riding up on horseback. Dahlia and Hyacinth thought they detected a little sparkle in Nick and Lucinda's eyes as they were introduced. Nick picked Cassandra up so she could pet the horse. She giggled as he whinnied. Nick surveyed the land and checked the soil. He agreed with the brothers that this would be a perfect spot to grow grapes. Everyone agreed that this would be a wonderful use for the land. Nick was hired on the spot to oversee the project. As soon as they were able they would set up a meeting with Richard Crowley and see about getting permits and licenses. Nick told them winter was the best time to start grape plants and they had a lot of work to do preparing the land before that. Dahlia and Hyacinth were gazing over the land and imagining what their new home would look like. It had been decided earlier that with the babies coming, the apartment would be much too small for all of them. It never occurred to them to build separate houses. The Hightowers and Blooms would always be a package deal.

Loving Again

Lucinda and Cassandra were walking hand in hand on a beautiful Sunday morning. The birds were chirping in the trees as they passed by on their way to services at Saint Peter's Church. Lucinda was thinking back to just a few weeks ago. She didn't know where she would find the money to pay the rent on their tiny apartment in the big city. Now she and Cassandra were living in a beautiful room in the loveliest town she had ever seen. She had friends and was making new ones each day. They entered the church and sat down in the pew. Both mother and daughter were kneeling in prayer and thanksgiving for the home and family they had found in Camden Corners.

Seated behind them and to the right was Nicola Rossi and the entire Marino family. Nick's heart skipped a beat when he looked up and noticed Lucinda and Cassandra sitting so close. He had only met Lucinda one time but the attraction to her was almost overwhelming.

After services, Lucinda thought it would be fun to take a walk by the beach. Cassandra was squealing with delight when they came upon a traveling carnival with a carousel, fortune tellers and games of chance. Nick, who had been waylaid by several of his friends finally caught up with them. Lucinda was happy to see a familiar face.

The three of them rode the carousel several times. Nick won a stuffed bear for Cassandra that was almost as big as she was.

As they strolled by the fortune teller, she asked if "The little family would like to know how many more children they would have? Madame DuPont will tell you for only five cents."

Nick laughed while Lucinda's face turned bright red.

"It is almost time for dinner at my sister Rosa's house. Would you and Cassandra like to join us today?" asked Nick.

"Oh my goodness, we couldn't impose on your family without warning."

"Are you kidding? Rosa would be insulted if you didn't come. Besides, I saw you in church and promised her I would bring you and Cassandra back before the bread finished baking."

"I'm hungry, Mama. May we eat with Mr. Nick today?"

"Hey, you two are ganging up on me. I'll give in if you are sure it's alright with your sister."

Lucinda was finding out what it was like to be a part of a big happy family. She was welcomed with open arms by every one of the Marinos. Nick's nieces took Cassandra by the hand directly to the playroom where there were more dolls and doll houses than Cassandra had ever seen. His nephew Tony brought out his camera that was never very far away and started taking photos of everyone.

"Nicola, show Lucinda your garden and the grapevines. She can see what a wonderful farmer you are and what a superb vintner you will be."

"You'll have to forgive my sister. She exaggerates when it comes to her family. According to her we are all the best at anything we do, the smartest of people and the best looking specimens that have ever been created."

Lucinda laughed. She loved this family already. Now she felt close to two families in Camden Corners and she liked that feeling. Lucinda was impressed with what Nick had planted. The grapevines were growing nicely. Not that she knew anything about grapevines or grapes. She tasted one and it was sweet and tangy at the same time. Nick told her the vines on the left were ready to be harvested and he would be beginning the process of making them into wine. His father was a vintner in Tuscany and he had been working the fields since he was a young boy. Ernesto came outside with a glasses filled with wine made from the grapes. Lucinda thought it tasted good but had nothing to compare it to. She had never tasted wine before since she and Paul never had enough money to buy any kind of spirits.

It was well into the evening when Lucinda was able to tear Cassandra away from her new friends and all the wonderful toys. Rosa and all the family hugged their visitors goodnight.

Nick walked them back to the boarding house. Mrs. Watson was sitting on the porch and offered to take Cassandra up to bed while Lucinda chatted with Nick. They sat on the porch swing. Nick took her hand in his and Lucinda pulled it away. She apologized and said she felt a disloyalty to her husband. She knew that was absurd but she couldn't help

133

herself. Nick apologized himself for being so forward. He admitted he was very attracted to Lucinda but he was willing to accept friendship only if that was all she was able to give. He hoped it wouldn't be too long before she felt comfortable enough to open her heart to him. They said goodnight and Lucinda walked up the stairs to her room.

Mrs. Watson was just dimming the light as Lucinda walked in to see her daughter sleeping soundly. Mrs. Watson could tell by the worried look on Lucinda's face that something was not right.

"Oh Mrs. Watson, I don't know what I am going to do. I do like Nick and I think he likes me but I feel so guilty for all the wonderful things that have happened lately. Paul worked so hard and struggled through his life and now I am finding happiness without him."

"My dear child" replied Mrs. Watson "Allow me to tell you my story of how my guilt drove me away from a man I truly loved."

My mother and father were married for several years before I was born. They thought they would remain childless but my birth proved them wrong. Mother was rather fragile and my birth was difficult for her. From what I remember of her she was a very tender and loving woman. I was only 9 years old when she contracted pneumonia and passed away. My father was devastated by her death but did his best to raise his little girl.

When I was barely 16, he passed too. His best friend, Mr. George Watson had never married. He took me into his home as I had no other relatives. It was considered scandalous that a young girl was living in the home of a man without benefit of marriage and therefore, at the age of 16 I was married to a much older man. He had taken me in when I had no one else. He was kind and loving and although I wasn't in love with him, I loved him very much.

Grace was born two years later and on her third birthday, George was taken from us. Money was not a concern since we had been well taken care of for the rest of our lives. The two of us lived in this big old house all by ourselves. I loved being a mother to Grace but I felt something was missing in my life. I had the idea of turning our home into a boarding house and renting rooms out to travelers and as a temporary home for newcomers to Camden Corners.

Oscar Crowley arranged a meeting with a young architect friend of his from Gilford. I remember the day Jamison Bentley came into my life. He was young and very good looking. I felt myself blush when he tipped his hat to me. He seemed to know exactly what I had in mind for this house. He took notes and drew sketches and had a plan the next day. It

134

was exactly what I had dreamed of and work was started the following week.

Jamison arranged for all the workers that were needed and the transformation had begun. He was here every day supervising and I knew in my heart that I was falling in love for the first time in my life. The work was finally finished and I was happy but also sad because I knew Jamison would be leaving to return to his home in Gilford. The day the house was completed he showed me all the rooms and we walked out into the garden where he had built the gazebo.

The sun was setting and there was a soft breeze blowing the sycamore tree when he took me in his arms and kissed me as I have never been kissed before. Or since, I might add. I found myself kissing him back and feeling that kiss down to my toes. He told me he loved me and had from the beginning. He said we would be married as soon as possible and he would adopt Grace and we would give her plenty of brothers and sisters. It all sounded so wonderful to me but then I remembered George. The guilt took over and I told Jamison that would not be possible. I didn't love him and he should go back to Gilford and forget we ever met. I ran into the house locking the door behind me and sobbed for what seemed to be an eternity.

Jamison wrote to me several times but I returned his letters unopened. Finally, the letters stopped but my memories of him and that kiss were still with me as they are to this day. One of my roomers left a copy of the Gilford paper in his room and there was a notice of the impending nuptials of Mr. Jamison Bentley and Miss Hillary Carson. This time I only sobbed for half of an eternity.

"Oh, Mrs. Watson. What a heartbreaking story."

"You now know my deep, dark secret that even my daughter doesn't know. Please call me Caroline."

"I'd like that, Caroline. I think the next time I see Mr. Nicola Rossi, I may be brazen and reach for his hand this time and hope he doesn't yank it away."

"I don't think he will" Caroline said with a wink.

"Have you ever heard anything about Jamison Bentley through these years?"

"Only that he has two sons. His wife passed away a couple of years ago. I almost wrote to him when Oscar Crowley told me that but it seemed too soon and besides, I'm sure he has forgotten all about me by now."

Lucinda doubted that but didn't say anything. She hugged Caroline

135

and thanked her for confiding in her. The two women bid each other good night.

The next morning, Lucinda joined Hyacinth and Dahlia. The twins were planning the house that would be built on the property.

"What you need is an architect and I think I know where to find one" said a smiling Lucinda.

"Let's check with Oscar Crowley. He will know where to find Mr. Jamison Bentley of Gilford."

Second Chances

Looking out the window of his high rise office, Jamison Bentley was tempted to tear up the letter he had received from his old friend, Oscar Crowley. He didn't see much of Oscar anymore. His father had been a college friend of Oscars. He knew Hillary had corresponded with him until her death a couple of years ago. Jamison always admired the old guy but any thoughts of Camden Corners brought sadness to him even after all these years. He loved Hillary and the life they built together with their two sons but Caroline Watson remained on his mind and in his heart since the first time he laid eyes on her. He knew her daughter, Grace, would be grown now probably with children of her own. He often wondered if he had pursued Caroline just a little longer if she would finally open her heart to the love he was offering her.

Seemed two young marrieds were looking for an architect to build their dream house on property left to them by an uncle. Eventually they wanted to build a winery and looking further down the road, a hospital in Camden Corners. Such ambition for these young people. Jamison hadn't drawn up plans for a residential dwelling since he started in the business over 20 years ago. His sons had followed in their dad's footsteps and had become architects too. Maybe he should just hand this project over to them. Something stopped him from doing that and before he knew it, he was on the train leaving for Camden Corners.

The Hightower boys had left the designing of the new home to their wives. They knew they wanted to build a house big enough for several children. They would have a joint living area and kitchen and two separate wings. Their plan was to have four bedrooms in each wing. They could always build on if they needed more in the future. The Bloom twins weren't getting any younger but they would welcome any future children with open arms.

Jamison was surprised to see how much the town had grown since he had been here. The Opera House had been one of his first architectural creations. He recognized it immediately. He had to admit, it was still a fine looking structure. Jamison rented a horse and carriage and was given directions to the Hightower property. He avoided passing by the Watson House on his way. He needed to brace himself to see Caroline again. He wondered if she ever married, if she ever thought about him. Probably not. She never answered his letters which would indicate that she wasn't interested back then and she certainly wouldn't be interested now.

Jamison arrived at the site and introduced himself to the Hightowers. He remembered the Bloom twins from years ago and couldn't help but marvel at how wonderful they both looked. They were still identical but each had an air of loveliness about them. A far cry from the dowdy young girls he remembered. He was introduced to Lucinda McCoy. He thought he detected a twinkle in her eye as she shook his hand. The girls knew exactly what they wanted and Jamison knew it would be a simple task to draw up plans for them this evening and present them the following day.

Lucinda spoke up "Mr. Bentley, I'm sure you will be requiring lodging for the duration of your visit. I happen to be residing in a lovely room at Watson's B & B and I am quite sure Mrs. Caroline Watson has a vacant room in her home. I would be more than happy to escort you to her establishment."

Jamison felt his heart beat a little faster. Oscar had generously offered to shelter him while he was in Camden Corners but he couldn't seem to say anything but, "I would appreciate your assistance, Miss McCoy."

Lucinda was full of chatter on the way to the Watson house. Jamison barely heard her voice over the beating of his heart. They stopped in front of the home and Lucinda suddenly remembered she needed to pick up her daughter at her friend Iris' house. She could see Caroline in the garden and she was sure Mr. Bentley would be able to find his way to her.

Jamison walked slowly to the garden gate. He could see her tending the rosebushes. She was as lovely as the day he kissed her so many years ago. He stood where he was and watched her for several minutes. Caroline had the feeling someone was there and turned her head. She thought she was imagining seeing Jamison Bentley standing at the entrance to the garden. Her heart skipped a beat and she was afraid to speak. Jamison walked toward her and took her hand. They looked into each others eyes and the years disappeared. He bent his head to kiss her and she didn't resist. They stood in the garden for the longest time, neither daring to speak for fear they were in a dream that could end at any moment.

"Mother, are you back here?" called Grace.

She stopped in her tracks when she saw her mother in a gentleman's arms.

"Mother!"

Caroline stepped back and tried to regain her composure.

"Hello Grace dear. You remember Mr. Bentley don't you? Of course, you don't. You were much too young. Jamison, this is my daughter Grace. She's married to the Evans boy." Caroline knew she was babbling and couldn't stop herself.

Jamison said "I remember Grace. You were very little when I was in Camden Corners. You have become a lovely young woman. You look very much like your mother, don't you?"

Grace wanted to chuckle. Her mother and this handsome stranger were acting like school children who had been caught stealing kisses. She had never seen her mother in the arms of a man before. Grace and her new husband Ted had been a couple for ten years. They knew they would be married one day but that day didn't seem to be happening. A stranger came to town one weekend and caught Grace's attention. Grace saw through the randy young man and knew Ted was the one for her. Ted realized his love for Grace was all he needed. He didn't know why they had put off being married but decided the time was right and they became husband and wife. Grace had a suspicion that she was going to be making her mother a grandmother but this did not seem the time to make that announcement.

"Mother, I came by to see if you were available to have dinner with Ted and me this evening but I can see you are busy. We will make it another day. Mr. Bentley, it was nice to meet you again. I'm sure you will enjoy your visit to our town."

Grace bid farewell to the couple, turned and walked down the street to visit with Emma Patterson. She knew her mother had tea quite often in Emma's Antique shop and wondered if she knew anything about her mother's gentleman caller.

Caroline finally felt her composure return. She suggested Jamison join her in the parlor for a cup of tea. He held her hand as they walked into the house. He wasn't about to let her change her mind again. That kiss told him all he needed to know. Caroline still loved him, he was sure of that. Caroline didn't let go of his hand until she needed to free it to pour the tea. She was sorry she didn't have anything stronger to offer Jamison. She thought he could probably stand something and she wouldn't mind a drop of whiskey herself.

Jamison told her about his life with Hillary and the boys. He had given up on their love and Hillary happened along. He did his best to make a good life for his family but Caroline was always in the back of his mind. Caroline admitted she felt as though she was betraying George's memory.

"It took several years before I realized that George loved me more like a daughter than a wife and he would have wanted me to find happiness with someone else after his death. By then, I knew you were married and that was a closed book. There has never been anyone else in my life."

They were talking and laughing when Lucinda and Cassandra came in the front door. Lucinda was grinning and Jamison realized now why he had seen a twinkle in the young woman's eye when they first met.

He said aloud "I wonder what prompted Oscar Crowley to contact me about designing the Hightower house. Oscar knows I haven't specialized in houses in many years."

"And to think," replied Caroline, "I never told a soul about my feelings for Jamison until I told my young renter here."

"I think you picked the right person to tell, Lucinda seems to be able to get right to the heart of the matter."

"Yes, she does and now we must encourage her to follow her heart too."

"I'm working on it" Lucinda said with a wink.

Just then there was a knock on the front door.

"Well, if it isn't Mr. Nick Rossi." Caroline said as she introduced the two men.

Nick apologized for barging in but he just happened to be taking a walk and wondered if Lucinda and Cassandra would like to join him for dinner at his sister's house. He knew it sounded lame when he said it but he just knew he wanted to spend the evening with Lucinda.

"I have dinner on the stove and it will be just me tonight if you take Lucinda and Cassandra away. Jamison," she said softly, "I hope you will join us tonight too."

"I would be delighted, but only if you will allow me to help. I'm not a gourmet cook like my friend Nick here, but I am a whiz at boiling water."

Cassandra wanted to help too, so all of them walked to the kitchen where the men were given aprons. Nick plopped Cassandra on the counter next to a big pot of vegetable soup. He showed her the art of adding just a pinch of this and a dash of that. She giggled as he kissed his fingertips exclaiming "magnifico" and waving his hand in the air. She did the same thing several times until her mother told her that was quite enough with the magnifico. Everyone was talking and laughing and enjoying their little adventure in cooking. It continued as they all sat down. Cassandra said grace and thanked God for her new family in Camden Corners. They all were sorry to have the evening come to an end. Jamison was retiring to his basement room. The room had its own entrance and was not accessible through the main house so there would not be any talk of impropriety when a single man stayed in the boarding house. He held Caroline's hand and told her twenty five years was long enough to wait to make her his wife. They planned to make wedding arrangements in the morning after he dropped off the plans for the Hightower house. As he passed by the hydrangea bushes, he heard a rustling sound.

"You'd best secure the trash barrel, I do believe the raccoons are hungry tonight."

Nick said good night to Lucinda and Cassandra. He turned and started walking away when he heard a little voice

"Good Night Mr. Nick, I love you."

This little girl could pull on his heartstrings more than any child he had ever known. He turned around, bent to his knees and said

"I love you too, Miss Cassandra."

Lucinda thought she detected a little tear in his eye. The three were standing on the porch steps when they heard a sneeze.

"I don't think that's a raccoon in those bushes" said Caroline as she pulled back the branches and saw four little eyes staring at her.

Two and Two Make a Family

After a delightful evening filled with good food and good company, Caroline and Lucinda are about to retire for the night when they hear a sneeze in the hydrangea bushes under the porch railing. They discover two children hiding there.

"We mean no harm ma'am. We were just looking for any scraps of food you might be throwing away" said the little boy who couldn't have been much more than 9 years old.

"Come out of there children. Where did you come from and what are you doing hiding in the bushes?"

Along with the boy, a little girl around 6 stepped out. They were both filthy dirty and shivering although it was a warm summer evening. Caroline and Lucinda hustled them into the house. They didn't wait for an explanation but started filling the bathtubs with warm soapy water.

Caroline guided the boy to one room and took the girl by the hand into the other. She had a stack of clothing that tenants had left behind. Caroline always laundered the items and placed them in a safe place in case their owners ever came back for them. She was able to find a pair of pajamas that she thought would fit the boy and Lucinda found a nightgown of Cassandras that should fit the girl just fine for the night.

The little girl was all but falling asleep in the warm water. Caroline washed her grimy hair, rinsed her off and wrapped her in a towel before putting on Cassandra's nightgown.

"What is your name, sweetheart?"

There was no reply. Only the two big eyes staring at her. By that time the boy had emerged from the tub, clean from head to toe. Caroline wasn't accustomed to little boys but she imagined that they usually didn't get themselves this clean.

"She doesn't talk" said the boy.

The women took the children into the kitchen and started warming up the leftovers from the evening meal. They both devoured the plates of food. Caroline shivered at the thought of how long it had been since they had eaten. After they had finished eating, the little girl was barely able to keep her eyes open. Lucinda carried her up the stairs to one of the guest rooms.

"No, I have to stay with my sister. She will wake up and be afraid if I'm not there."

Lucinda said she would sit in the room with her until he came upstairs but he would need to stay and talk to Miss Caroline before he came up to bed. Cassandra brought her favorite doll into the room to help comfort the little girl. Lucinda was proud of her daughter. That doll was the last thing given to her by her Papa and it was very special to her. The little girl woke up and looked around for her brother.

"Your brother is downstairs and will be here soon. Cassandra and I will keep you company until he comes."

Cassandra was amazed that the little girl didn't speak.

"My Mama and I lived in New York City in a big building next to my grandfather. But, I didn't know he was my grandfather. But, he died. But, we came to Camden Corners. Camden Corners is a magic place. You will see. If you stay here you will be able to talk again. I just know it. Do you like the park? There is a big park by the water. Mr. Nick took Mama and me there. Maybe he can take you too. We will have fun."

Cassandra went on and on. Lucinda would have stopped the little chatterbox but the girl seemed to be hanging on every word. She thought

141

she saw a little glimmer in the child's eyes. She couldn't help but wonder what had gone on in this little girl's life that caused her to be unable to speak. Meanwhile the boy was sitting at the kitchen table with Caroline.

He said "My name is Kenny and my sister's name is Rebecca but I call her Becky."

Caroline fixed him a tall glass of milk and a plate of cookies as he told her how he and his sister ended up hiding beneath her hydrangea bushes.

"We lived in Portersville with our mama and papa. Mama always sang songs to Becky and me but one day she stopped singing. Papa said she was very sick and it was hard for her to talk. She would smile at us and give us hugs but she didn't talk to us anymore and finally she went to sleep and didn't wake up.

Papa was so sad that he went to see Mr. Benson to get some medicine. He would bring the medicine home in a big jug and drink from the jug until he fell asleep. Papa cried a lot and didn't talk to us anymore except to tell us to be quiet. Becky liked to sing the songs that Mama sang to us but Papa told her to stop that singing or she would end up dead like our mama. Becky stopped singing and stopped talking too. The doctor said Papa had too much medicine and he went to heaven to be with our mama.

The sheriff told us to gather our clothes that he was taking us to live with our Uncle Sven. Uncle Sven didn't have any children and told the sheriff to take us to the orphanage. He didn't want his brother's brats around him. He said his brother was a drunken fool who married a frail, sickly young thing and his offspring would turn out to be the same. The sheriff took us home with him that night and let us sleep in a big bed. He thought I was asleep but I heard him tell his wife that he was going to have to deliver us to the orphanage the next day. She said it was too bad we wouldn't be able to stay together.

I couldn't let Becky be alone without me. She would be so scared. After the sheriff and his wife went to sleep, I woke Becky up and we started walking toward town. Becky was very tired and we stopped near Mr. Poulson's dairy farm. We slept in the barn and then the next morning we climbed into the wagon Mr. Poulson was filling with milk bottles to deliver to the general stores in all the nearby towns. His last stop was Camden Corners and we got off the wagon here and hid in the bushes.

"We won't bother you anymore after tonight, Miss Caroline. I can't let my sister go to the orphanage by herself. We will be on our way tomorrow, I promise."

Caroline's heart was breaking that this sweet child was going to take care of his sister.

"You and Becky will not be going to an orphanage. You can stay here in this house until we figure out what to do."

Caroline knew what she was going to do but didn't want to make any promises until she talked it over with Oscar Crowley. Kenny started yawning. Caroline walked him upstairs and tucked him in next to his sister.

"He said his sister would be afraid if she woke up and he wasn't there." Caroline said tearfully.

She was determined that these children would never know fear again. She and Lucinda said goodnight to Kenny and the sleeping Becky. Cassandra had fallen asleep at the foot of the bed and Lucinda carried her into her own bed.

The next morning, Jamison was surprised to find two little faces staring at him as he entered the kitchen.

"Who have we here?"

"My name is Kenny sir and this is my sister, Becky."

Caroline pulled Jamison aside and told him what Kenny had told her the night before. Jamison had a worried look on his face and Caroline was afraid for a second that he was going to tell her she had to turn the children over to the authorities.

She was happy when he said "They can't be sent to an orphanage. How do you feel about a ready made family?"

Lucinda stayed with the children while Jamison drove the carriage to Portersville. They picked up Oscar Crowley on the way and because it was such a pretty day, Nettie came along for the ride. Oscar had known Judge Herman Blake for a long time. He knew he was an honest man and recommended they stop to see him as soon as they arrived in Portersville. The judge was interested in the matter. He mentioned that he knew there was a small house on the outskirts of town but had no idea two children lived in that house. Sheriff Billings is a fine old gentleman but his memory has been failing him recently. He sent his assistant to fetch the sheriff. When he arrived in the office, Judge Blake asked him about the children.

"I seem to remember a couple of small children coming to the house the other day. Yes, I don't know where they went though. They weren't there yesterday when the wife went to fetch them for breakfast. Maybe their uncle changed his mind and decided to take them in after all."

The judge and his visitors rode out to talk with the children's Uncle Sven. He refused to open the door for them and told them if they bothered

143

him again about those two rotten kids he'd greet them with his shotgun. Jamison had to hold Caroline back. He knew she was about to bop the old man on his head for saying such terrible things about those precious children.

The judge was having temporary custody papers drawn up. The adoption would be final in a couple of months. Caroline and Jamison were grateful to the judge for his help and would he mind doing them one more favor? Would he marry them that afternoon. Judge Blake said he would be delighted and with Oscar and Nettie as their witnesses, he pronounced them husband and wife.

The ride back home to Camden Corners was a joyous one. Oscar had packed a bottle of champagne in a satchel and they drank a toast to the happy couple.

"This has all happened so quickly I haven't even had a chance to tell Grace about finding Jamison again and now we are married with a brother and sister for her."

"We will stop by the hardware store and pick her up on the way home."

"This calls for a celebration!" said Nettie.

Grace was thrilled for her mother and had some news for her also. Not only was Caroline a new bride and a new mother, she was going to be a grandmother in just a few months.

Jamison and Caroline sat Kenny and Becky down on the sofa in the parlor while everyone was enjoying Caroline's lovely garden. Kenny couldn't believe his ears when he learned that he and Becky would be living with Mr. Jamison and Miss Caroline. He held Becky close and whispered that they would always be together now. Becky smiled and wrapped her arms around Caroline. Caroline wondered if life could get any better than this.

Reggie's True Love

Hyacinth and Dahlia couldn't have been more pleased with the design Jamison Bentley prepared for their new home. It was just exactly what they had envisioned. Their husbands were busy working along side Nick Rossi and the crew preparing the earth for the vines to be planted and left the house design and building to their wives. The foundation was being laid as the girls looked on. The Hightower brothers insisted that no corners be cut in anything they did and those instructions were being followed. Reggie Blackburn was a perfectionist himself and as head contractor, he was watching over the crew like a hawk.

Reggie was very polite and respectful to the sisters but they suspected something in his life had made him terribly sad. Reggie came highly recommended by Jamison and the girls trusted him enough to hire the man sight unseen. Jamison stopped by the site a couple of times a day. He was always smiling and the girls suspected his happiness was the result of his marriage to Caroline Watson.

Dahlia knew she was prying but decided to ask Jamison what was troubling Reggie. Jamison had known Reggie since he was born. He had grown up with Jamison's two boys. Reggie had fallen for a young lady by the name of Elena Malone. Jamison had never seen a young boy so devoted to a member of the opposite sex. His boys were more interested in teasing the girls in town than carrying their books home from school. Elena was a very pretty young girl and as she grew she became a real beauty. Jamison thought she was a rather spoiled and selfish little girl who was even more so as she grew older. Reggie was a popular fellow through his high school years. The boys liked him and most of the girls had a crush on him but he only had eyes for Elena. Reggie worked his way though college and asked Elena to be his wife. She accepted his proposal and a big wedding was planned for the second Saturday in September.

Reggie's friends all tried to dissuade him from marrying Elena so quickly.

"Reggie, you have been going to school non stop for years. Give yourself some time to enjoy your carefree days before settling down"

What they really meant was *give yourself some time to get over Elena*. Reggie wouldn't hear of it. He was going to marry Elena and that was final. Just three days before the wedding, Elena was sipping a soda at the drugstore when a handsome young fellow entered the store. He was drawn to the beauty sitting at the counter and came to sit next to her. He flashed a big bright smile at the girl and told her she was pretty enough to be on Broadway and he should know because his boss was none other than Nelson Grant, the famous producer. It didn't take Elena much time at all to rush home and pack her clothes and join this young man at the train station. She planned to send a telegram to Reggie when she arrived in New York but somehow never got around to it. Reggie was devastated. The soda jerk at the ice cream counter heard every word that transpired between the stranger and Elena and repeated it to Reggie. Reggie just knew Elena would be returning to him after she realized everything she ever wanted was right here in Gilford.

145

Jamison realized it had been close to a year since Reggie was jilted.

"That young man should be getting over his crush on that ungrateful girl by now." he said to Dahlia.

Dahlia and Hyacinth felt sad for Reggie. There were plenty of nice girls in Camden Corners but if he was still pining away for this Elena person, he probably wouldn't be interested in any of them.

Just as Jamison was leaving, Josie McMillan drove up in Doc's buckboard. She waved to Nick and the Hightowers as they were doing their last check of the plots before they began planting the first of the grapevines. Josie was Julie McMillan's sister. She wasn't married and had just purchased a small cottage by the lake. Like Julie, who became a doctor in spite of the fact that there were very few female doctors, Josie ventured out on her own. Most girls her age who were not married lived with their parents in the houses they grew up in. Josie was not like other girls. Thanks to a mother and father who had raised their daughters to be their own person and not what society told them they should be. Josie knew construction had begun on the new house and was anxious to see how they were coming along. She loved her little cottage but it needed some repair and she was determined to learn all she could about construction and make the repairs herself if at all possible.

She couldn't help but notice the tall good looking fellow who seemed to be in control of the project. The twins gave Julie a hug and she commented on how much their tummies had grown since she saw them just a couple of weeks ago. She was introduced to Reggie and he was quite impressed with the fact that she was interested in the construction business. He offered to let her observe and possibly lend a hand.

"Keep in mind though, I don't allow any shoddy workmanship on my jobs."

"Keep in mind" Josie replied "I don't allow any shoddy workmanship on my jobs either".

He apologized immediately for his insensitive remark and decided it would be nice to have a female on the job to keep him in line. Besides, she wasn't that bad to look at.

After what seemed an eternity, the day the first planting of the grape plants had arrived. The precious cuttings Nick's father had sent from Italy had also arrived. Nick had received cuttings from various established vineyards in the state and as far away as California. He had treated them with tender loving care and gingerly handed a cutting to each of the Hightowers as well as to Lucinda and even little Cassandra. They each lovingly planted their cuttings as the Marino family, all of Reggie's crew and half the town looked on and cheered. Nick had hired some of the best workers he could find and the planting began in earnest. Harold and Howard worked alongside the men as well as Lucinda who was able to keep up with the best of the them. Dahlia and Hyacinth wanted to help but their husbands insisted they stay off their feet as much as possible. Everyone couldn't help but notice the Bloom sisters had really begun to blossom out.

The planting was finally done. There wasn't much to do in the vineyards except wait and watch until spring when the vines began to grow. Nick lent a hand to Reggie and the Hightower house was coming along nicely. Josie was learning more than she had anticipated and after working all day would return home to her little cottage and put in another full day of work. One Saturday afternoon Reggie let the crew leave early. They had been working non stop for many weeks. By the looks of the growing Hightower wives, the sooner the house was livable the better.

Reggie asked Josie how her place was coming and she admitted she had run into a snag or two but she was working out the problems. Reggie offered to accompany her home to look over her work and possibly offer some suggestions. Josie was grateful for the assistance and happily accepted the offer. Reggie was impressed with the work Josie had done. The cottage suited her perfectly. Reggie felt right at home in this little house by the lake. They sat on the back porch watching the water and talking like old friends. Before long the sun was going down and although the days were beginning to shorten, they realized it was getting late and they hadn't had any dinner. Josie insisted Reggie stay while she heated up the stew she had made that morning. They sipped wine and ate the stew with a loaf of bread her mother had baked and delivered earlier. Josie finally had to admit what she had been denying these last couple of months, she had fallen in love with Reggie Blackburn.

The next morning during services at St. Peter's Church, Vicar Will announced that the ladies auxiliary was auctioning off tickets to the play Saturday night at the Opera House.

"The name of the play is *The Taming of the Shrew* starring one of our neighbors from Gilford, Elena Malone. This play will be performed on Broadway soon. It says here Miss Malone is a rising Broadway star." Jamison Bentley's ears perked up. Elena Malone, was the name of the girl who left Reggie at the altar. I wonder if he knows she will be in town.

He turned to Carolyn and whispered "She will be able to play the part of the shrew without even acting".

Carolyn chuckled. Jamison had told her Reggie's sad story. Just at

147

that moment, Reggie was walking down main street and noticed a playbill in the window of Nichol's General Store. *Taming of the Shrew starring Elena Malone.*

The theater's production company arrived in Camden Corners the following Tuesday. Josie had heard the story of Reggie and his broken heart and felt the need to torture herself by getting a look at the love of his life. She and a few of the ladies in town were a part of the welcoming committee for the troupe as they disembarked the train.

Miss Elena Malone paused on the top step and glanced through the crowd. She had heard Reggie was in Camden Corners and was sure he would be at the station to greet her. Josie looked up and held back a gasp. She had never seen a lovelier looking woman in her life. With her long dark hair and flashing blue eyes, she was a true beauty.

Reggie had forced himself to stay away from the train station. He wanted to see Elena when she wasn't surrounded by other people. The pain of her leaving was still in his heart. He planned to plead his case to her. He would never interfere with her desire for stardom and his love for her was strong enough for the two of them. He went about his business and looked around for Josie. He missed her when she wasn't there. She was a good kid and his men thought the world of her. She had a cute way of smiling at him when she finished a project he had given her. He would miss her when he moved to New York with Elena. He would miss Camden Corners too as the little town and its people had begun to grow on him. Just a touch of sadness came over him but that was ridiculous, in less than an hour he would be seeing his true love again and they would be together forever. Maybe, Vicar Will would be able to marry them this afternoon.

The troupe was staying at the Ritz and had taken over the entire hotel. Reggie announced his arrival exactly one hour later. The hotel clerk rang Elena's suite.

"Have him come up, Jasper, and direct him to the sitting room." ordered Elena. "He should have been at the station to greet me so he can just sit and wait."

Reggie sat on a very uncomfortable Louis XV upholstered chair which was not designed for anyone over 4 feet tall.

Jasper poked his head around the corner. "Miss Malone is powdering her nose and will be with you shortly Mr. Bluebeard."

"It's Blackburn" Reggie called out as the little man disappeared around the corner again. Reggie could hear Elena's voice inside the other room. She was issuing orders left and right. One of the hotel maids who

Reggie recognized from town ran out of the room in tears.

"I've been fired because there was a feather on the floor but that feather came from Miss Malone's boa. The room was sparkling clean when she arrived."

Reggie assured the girl that he would talk to Miss Malone and she wouldn't lose her job. Next came the busboy shaking his head. His face was red as a beet.

"Miss Malone didn't like the way I opened her trunk. She is telling the hotel to withhold my pay for the day."

Reggie could hear commotion going on inside the other room. Every few minutes another person would exit either crying or grumbling about Miss Elena Malone. She must be tired from her trip, I'm sure after she rests, she will be fine again.

Thirty minutes later, Jasper appeared again "Miss Malone will see you now."

He ushered him into the room. There she was, the love of his life, sitting at the mirror. She glanced in his direction and turned around. If possible, she was more beautiful than he'd remembered. She stood and walked toward him.

"Reggie, darling, so good to see you. Fetch me my robe dear boy."

Reggie looked around. All he saw was a flimsy gown with feathers all around the neck.

"Is this a robe?"

"Don't be a fool, Reggie. Of course it is."

Elena grabbed the robe out of his hands in disgust. "Whatever brought you to this dingy little town, Reggie? You must have been more distraught over my leaving than I ever imagined."

Reggie couldn't believe his ears. Was this shrew really the girl he had been pining away for? He looked into her eyes and saw nothing but coldness. Suddenly he had a vision of another face. A smiling face with sparkling eyes. A cute little laugh and bouncing blond hair. What a fool he had been.

"Elena, it has been good to see you again. Good luck with the play."

He was out the door and running down the street as Elena looked out her window watching him vanish out of sight.

"He'll be back" she whispered to Jasper.

Somehow Jasper didn't think so.

Summer's End

Reggie ran the entire mile to the cottage on the lake stopping only to buy a bouquet of daisies at the flower cart outside Nichols General Store. He knew Josie's favorite flowers were daisies. How did he know that, he wasn't sure. He knew her favorite color was yellow, her favorite season was spring, she loved children and wanted a dozen at least. He felt as though he had known her forever and it had only been a few months.

He had wasted so much time longing for Elena Malone. What a fool he had been. He hoped Josie would be home. He had so much to tell her. He loved her and he hoped she felt the same about him. It would serve him right if she didn't. He treated her like one of the fellows instead of the beautiful girl she was.

She opened the door and saw him standing there with a smile on his face and a beautiful bouquet of daisies in his hand. Those must be for Elena she thought to herself. Daisies are my favorite flower. Reggie must be on his way to see her and decided to stop by to tell me he's moving to New York City with her.

"Hi Reggie. How was your reunion with Elena?"

"My reunion? Oh, it was good. I came by to tell you that I am in love with the most beautiful girl in the world. I have loved her since the first day I laid eyes on her but I was too blinded by my foolish infatuation to realize it."

Josie could no longer hide her tears. "I wish you a long and happy life with Elena but I'm busy now so I will just say goodbye"

She put her hand on the door to close it and Reggie pushed it open again.

"Long and happy life with Elena? What gave you that idea? I'm here because I finally realized it is you I love, you I want to be with for the rest of my life and I'm praying I might have a chance with you. You are the girl I want to wake up with every morning and go to sleep with every night. I want to call my crew over right now and start building bedroom additions on this cottage so that we can fill them with the dozen children we both would like to have someday. Now, will you invite me in so I can hold you and kiss you and ask you to be my wife?"

"But Reggie, you have loved Elena for so long, I do love you but I won't be anyone's second choice."

"You aren't my second choice, I was with Elena this afternoon and I saw her for what she is, a selfish, spoiled beauty who doesn't know how to love anyone but herself. When I was looking at her all I could see was

150

your face smiling back at me. It was then I knew I didn't want this superficial woman and I don't think I ever really did. She was a childhood crush and I have finally grown up."

With tears streaming down her cheeks, Josie kicked the door closed with her foot and said "Let's see what kind of a kisser you are before I agree to marry you."

It didn't take too long before the whole town was buzzing about Josie and Reggie. The two of them were incapable of hiding their feelings even if they tried. Josie was one of the town's favorites and now that Reggie wasn't pining away for unrequited love, he was becoming a favorite too. Doc and Mary McMillan were happy with their daughter's choice and even happier when Reggie informed them he and Josie planned to make their home in Camden Corners. Reggie loved the friendly little town almost as much as he loved Josie. Jamison Bentley was glad Reggie had come to his senses about Elena Malone. She and the theater troupe left shortly after their last performance the week before. No one would call the production a smashing success. It needed more work and Jamison suspected the producers might start by finding a new leading lady.

The Hightower house was completed and none too soon. The sisters were almost to full bloom. Because of their conditions, the girls accepted any help they were offered in preparing their new home. Emma Patterson and Lily Kramer practically furnished the entire house with treasures they had found in their hunts. They were able to fill every one of the eighteen rooms with beautiful heirloom furniture. The two nurseries, one in yellows in the left wing and one in pale greens in the right wing. Quilts were displayed throughout the house. Curtains and draperies were pulled back to allow the late summer sunshine in. Each window had its own unique view. Some overlooking the lake others the freshly planted vineyards. In the spring work would begin on the winery allowing it to be ready for the first grape picking next summer. The Hightowers were so grateful for all the help they had received and the interest everyone had taken in their new home they thought a summer picnic on Labor Day would be fitting. Most of the town arrived just after noon on that Monday. All the women brought along their favorite picnic specialty. The children had plenty of places to run and play. The young people took advantage of the nearby lake and set up makeshift rafts to escape the prying noses of their parents.

The food was all eaten, the dishes cleaned and put away and the ladies were all relaxing around the fire pit near the front porch. The men were having horseshoe tournaments one after the other with small wagers on the side. Nick Rossi had just made a ringer and was collecting his winnings from Reggie who was determined to get his money back in the next game.

Lucinda McCoy caught herself staring at Nick. His shoulders were so broad, almost as broad as his smile. She knew in her heart she had fallen in love with this wonderful man but couldn't get past the guilt of betraying her deceased husband Paul by giving into her feelings.

Josie whispered in her ear "I think it's time for a walk in the trees over there and I'm going to put an end to this game and drag my soon to be husband away from it and into the woods. Come with me, I know you'd like nothing better than being in the shadows with Nick".

Lucinda's face turned red. She had been sipping a little too much of Caroline's blueberry brandy and it was going to her head. Caroline overheard Josie and encouraged Lucinda to do just that.

"I'll watch out for Cassandra. Paul would want you to find happiness again."

Josie downed the remainder of her glass and walked over to Reggie.

"That's enough with the horseshoes, it's time for a walk in the woods."

Reggie winked at Nick and off he went hand in hand with Josie. Nick asked Lucinda if she would like to take a walk by the lake. She thought that was safer than the woods and agreed. They walked without speaking for a little while and then without warning, Lucinda threw her arms around Nick's neck and kissed him firmly on the lips. He was so stunned he started losing his balance and Lucinda, being unsteady on her feet after a little too much brandy pulled him down the rest of the way. They landed in the water laughing and kissing and making up for lost time. When they finally arrived back with the group, all eyes were staring at them. Everyone was smiling including Cassandra who was hoping Nick would be her new daddy very soon.

Nettie Crowley asked what names had been chosen for the babies. Hyacinth said they wanted to keep flowers in the family as their mother did and if either one had a girl, she would be named after a flower.

Howard spoke up and said "If it's a girl, we are naming her Daffodil and call her Daffy for short."

Everyone laughed except Hyacinth who shook her head at her husband.

"No, if it's a girl, she will be called Daisy Bloom Hightower and if it's a boy he will be Henry Shane Hightower."

Dahlia spoke up. "Violet Bloom Hightower for a girl and Harry Shane Hightower for a boy."

She had barely gotten the words out when she doubled over in pain.

"Sister," cried Hyacinth "Is it time?" as she too, grabbed her round tummy.

The babies weren't due for another two weeks but it didn't look like they had been told when to arrive. Luckily there were three doctors available. Harold and Howard carried their wives into the house and to their bedrooms. The girls hadn't planned on giving birth at the same time and wanted to be there for each other so the men moved the two beds into the big living room and were then shooed away to wait outside with the other men.

Less than an hour later, Josie opened the window and shouted "Harold, you have a son."

Five minutes passed "Howard you have a daughter and Harold you have a daughter too" then

"Howard, you have a son."

Lily came running out of the house.

"Richard!"

"I know" cried Richard "Go get two more cradles."

"This has been the perfect ending to a perfect Labor Day" said Caroline Bentley. She hadn't been a witness to the births, she and a few of the other women had watched over the children. Earlier she had been sitting next to Doc McMillan. Doc said those women didn't need him up there. Julie could handle it and he'd only get in the way. The womenfolk don't like stuffy old doctors around when babies are coming into the world.

"How are you feeling Caroline? You look a bit pale." he asked his friend.

"Well Doc. To be honest I haven't been myself lately. A bit tired but I blame it on all the changes in my life these last few months."

"Come into the office tomorrow morning. We'll run some tests and maybe get you some vitamins."

Jamison overheard the conversation and didn't like it one bit. He had been worried about Caroline himself lately. She hadn't wanted him to hire a housekeeper but he was going to insist. After all, she wasn't a young girl anymore and she had two youngsters to keep track of. His sons were coming to Camden Corners tomorrow. It would be the first time they met Caroline. He was happy about that but worried if Caroline was sick how much of a burden it would be to have his sons added to the mix. Doc could see the worry on Jamison's face and patted his back telling him not to worry. He didn't think anything was really wrong with Caroline. He had his suspicions but thought it best to wait until he was sure.

All the guests were invited into the house to meet the new additions to the Hightower family. All four babies had the same faces.

"Is there such a thing as identical cousins?" asked April Hawthorne.

Caroline congratulated the happy couples and said how lucky they were to have two babies to care for. "It's so nice having a baby in the house."

Unexpected Company

The morning after the Labor Day celebration, Jamison went with Caroline to see Doc. He examined her and called them both into his office. Jamison was on the edge of his seat. Doc told him to relax. What he had to say was going to come as a shock to him and he didn't want him having a heart attack before Caroline gave birth to his child. The two faces looking back at him were white.

"That can't be Doc. I'm too old to have babies. I'm going to be a grandmother in just a few months."

"That's it! Jamison said sternly "You will have a housekeeper, a maid and a butler if it will assure that you are healthy."

By the time they left Doc's office the news was just beginning to sink in. The shock was wearing off and suddenly the two of them were dancing down the street.

"Jamison, do you have any idea how often I dreamed of having your baby? I didn't think it would be possible and here I am, expecting our own child. The family will be all together tonight and we will tell them the news. Becky and Cassandra will be excited about a baby. You saw how they were mesmerized by the Hightower cousins."

Lucinda knew something was going on with her friends. It was natural they would be excited about Jamison's boys, Todd and Alex coming for a visit but there was something else that was making them giggle and smile at each other while they were preparing for the big celebration tonight. Lucinda knew Caroline would tell her in time but she was still very curious.

The boys arrived shortly before 4 o'clock. Jamison picked them up from the train station and brought them back to the now busy household. The boys gave Caroline big hugs and thanked her for putting that smile on their dad's face. Jamison announced that Caroline was expecting a baby and everyone started hugging and kissing. Cassandra wanted to know when she and Becky could play with the baby. Kenny said he hoped it was a boy because they already had enough girls in the family. He liked having two big brothers though so if it was another girl it would be OK with him. Grace couldn't hold back the tears. She was so excited that she and her mother would be having babies the same age.

Lucinda was crying too just thinking about Caroline and Jamison's love story. Nick put his arm around Lucinda and hoped the day would come when they would have an announcement to make too. The ring he bought this morning was in his pocket. Lucinda said she loved him and he wasn't going to waste any more time.

Caroline looked around the room at all these wonderful faces and marveled at how her life had changed in such a short time. She had Lucinda to thank because without her intervention Jamison wouldn't have come to Camden Corners and she wouldn't be happier than she had ever been in her life. The tears were streaming down her cheeks too as she looked around at her home brimming with people and love. Caroline felt a tug on her sleeve. She looked down and saw Becky staring up at her.

"Mama" Becky said quietly. "Cassandra said I wouldn't die if I told you I love you"

Caroline only thought she couldn't be happier. These were the first words she had ever heard her new daughter speak.

"No Becky, you won't die."

The tears were flowing as everyone rushed to Becky to listen to her sweet little voice. Cassandra was smiling in the background. She was getting tired of doing all the talking for both of them. Soon after, the girls went out to swing on the swings Jamison had hung from the oak tree in the back yard. Through the window, Caroline and Jamison could hear the two little voices singing happy tunes as they were swinging through the air.

Vicar Will and Kate were strolling leisurely passed the busy Bentley home. Will was the first to hear the little girls singing. He stopped to marvel at Becky singing her heart out. Kate's eyes filled with tears. She had worried about Becky since the first day Caroline brought her to school. Kate tried her best to coax the little girl into speaking. Kenny had told her how their father in his grief over the death of their mother let Becky believe she would be the next one to die if she continued speaking. Kate suspected Becky had been a chatterbox and her father was trying to quiet her as he drank himself into an early grave. Kate marveled at Becky's singing voice.

"Will, she sounds like an angel. Now is not the time to call attention to her singing ability but I will mention it to Principal Key."

Will wasn't paying too much attention to Kate. He had something else on his mind. He was determined tonight would be the night he asked

155

Kate to be his wife. He bought the ring two months ago and never had the opportunity or the nerve to slip it on her finger. Even now he was afraid she would turn him down. He didn't want to face the heartbreak he knew he would suffer. As they strolled toward the beach, Kate was having her own thoughts. She had known for quite some time that Will purchased an engagement ring. She understood that he was shy with women and he was a busy man but this was getting ridiculous. Kate knew he loved her and she loved him. They weren't getting any younger and Kate wanted children. If he didn't propose tonight she would do the unthinkable and propose to him. What a scandal that would cause. She chuckled to herself as Will nervously walked beside her.

Without warning, a tree branch fell from a sycamore tree along the path barely missing the couple. Will gasped and wrapped his arms around Kate protecting her from the other branches that might be ready to fall. Will kept his arms around Kate. He looked up to the heavens and Kate heard him whisper

"Alright, I'll do it."

His eyes wide, he looked at her lovely face gasping for breath he said "Kate, will ah you ah be my ah wife?"

She replied "Yes, Will, I would be most happy to be your wife."

He slipped the ring on her finger, took her in his arms and kissed her until she was the one gasping for breath. Will's shyness disappeared he was back to his old confident self and he told Kate how he had been afraid she would turn him.

"For a man of faith, you didn't have much faith in me Willard Duesenberry!"

He led her to a bench by the railroad tracks.

"How much time do you need to plan the wedding?" he asked.

"How about Saturday morning?" she replied. "I will wire my family tomorrow morning and I'm sure they will be on the next train. Grandmother has been preparing for this day since I was 12 years old. I noticed she had her old wedding gown unpacked and was sprucing it up just the other day. I have always wanted to wear the gown she and my mother were both married in."

Will was surprised and happy to find that Kate didn't want to wait before they were husband and wife. He was dreaming of the life they would share together when the 6:29 from Harrisburg was slowing down as it approached the train station. Kate and Will were stunned when they saw what appeared to be two young boys jump from between the cars. The conductor was shaking his fist as they struggled to stand up and run. Will was too quick for the boys and he stopped them in their tracks.

"Well, well, what have we here? A couple of hardened criminals stowing away on the train?"

Kate rushed over to the boys afraid they had been hurt.

"What a foolish thing to do!" she scolded them. "You both could have been seriously hurt or even killed jumping from the train like that."

The older boy looked defiantly at Kate.

"Mind your own business lady."

Will was ready to pop him on the head for speaking so disrespectfully to his intended but he controlled himself and continued to hold the two by their collars.

"What are your names and why were you on that train? Did you run away from home? Your parents will be worried about you."

"My name is Billy and this is my friend Butch. We always ride the train but this is the first time that stupid conductor caught us. We don't have parents and we don't need them. We're old enough to take care of ourselves."

Kate had never heard such a thing. Everyone had parents. Maybe not the best parents but parents just the same.

"How old are you Billy?"

"I'm 18 and old enough to be on my own and so is Butch."

"You look more like 12" Will replied.

"We're small for our age. Now let us go or I'll have you arrested."

"I don't think you really want to call the sheriff now do you? He might wonder why the conductor chased you off the train."

Kate spoke up "Listen boys, why don't you come to Will's house with us. My grandmother is there and she was cooking up a storm when we left an hour ago. She has two chickens in the oven, potatoes and corn and a big pumpkin pie for dessert. You can clean up and have supper with us before anybody calls the sheriff."

Butch, who hadn't said anything until that moment piped in. "Come on Billy. Lets go eat. I'm hungry."

Billy's mouth was watering at the mention of such a tempting meal. "Okay, but we leave right after we eat."

The foursome walked towards the church and Will's house. The boys had forgotten about the small satchel Billy lost beside the tracks as he was jumping off the train.

Alma Schrum was happy to have extra mouths to feed but insisted these two ragamuffins clean themselves up before sitting down at her table. Alma filled the tub and told them they had better use a lot of soap because if they had a speck of dirt on them she would be in to scrub them down herself. Melvin Tanner, who was a frequent guest at the Duesenberry household, chuckled as he watched the boys scramble to the waiting tub and close the curtain tightly.

Meanwhile, the vicar deposited their filthy clothes in a pile outside the back door and rode his bicycle to the Burke home to borrow some clothes in the boys sizes. Between the Burkes and Mackenzies, every size of children's clothing was available. He brought home everything from outerwear to underwear and even nice warm pajamas. He had the feeling these would be the first clean clothes those two young boys had ever worn.

With all the commotion going on, Alma hadn't noticed the sparkling ring on Kate's finger. Kate nonchalantly held her hand out while setting the table. Alma almost dropped the bowl of freshly mashed potatoes as she hugged her granddaughter tightly. She had known Will's intentions for quite some time and was almost ready to get down on one knee herself if he didn't pop the question. Will came through the door and she wrapped her ample arms around him welcoming him to the family. Her eyes were filled with happy tears as the boys entered the dining room shiny clean from head to toe with their hair slicked back and wearing fresh, clean clothes. Alma was impressed that even the dirt under their fingernails was gone. Will was sure they had scrapped off a couple of layers of skin. Everyone sat around the big table and two little hands stretched out to grab a piece of chicken.

"Whoa boys, in this house we thank God for His many blessings." Will said as he folded his hands in front of him and bowed his head.

The boys followed his lead and Billy wondered who this God person was and where was He? He'd just have to wonder about that later because now it was time to eat and he didn't think he could wait another minute.

Melvin was reminded of the first time he and Cody shared a meal. He watched as the boys ate until they could eat no more. They didn't know where their next meal would be coming from and they weren't about to stop while they still had room in their bellies for another bite.

While the women were cleaning up after dinner, the men and boys took a seat in the parlor. Will picked up his old family bible and started reading aloud from it. "In the beginning...." Billy's eyes were as wide as saucers as he heard the words Will was reading. Accustomed to reading these passages to a young audience, Will added his own twists to the scripture to make it more easily understood. Butch was attentive but Billy seemed to hang on every word. He was very curious about God and couldn't understand how He could be all around him and Billy couldn't see

Him. Will knew he wouldn't be able to teach Billy what faith was, he would have to discover it by himself.

The boys were getting very sleepy and Will and Melvin helped them upstairs with Kate and Alma following to tuck them in. Neither boy had any recollection of being in such a soft comfortable bed or of having anyone cover them up with fresh smelling quilts and give them little hugs as they told them to sleep well. As they lay there in the darkness, Butch sleepily said "Billy, I like it here, don't you?"

"Yeah Butch, I like it here too." Billy was thinking about God. If He could create heaven and earth, maybe talking Will and Kate into letting them stay here one more day wouldn't be too hard a task for Him.

Meanwhile in the parlor, Will was asking Kate how she felt about a ready made family. Kate was thinking the same thing.

"Will, we can't let those boys go back to roaming the streets. Let's talk to the Crowleys first thing tomorrow. We have to find a way to keep them here with us."

Alma was beaming, she was going to be a great grandmother. Melvin squeezed her hand as he thought of what fun it would be to take the boys fishing just like he had done with Cody and his own son so many times.

The Silver Chalice

Will, Kate, Alma and Melvin were enjoying one of the few remaining summer nights on the porch of the vicarage. It had been an eventful day. Will and Kate had become engaged and were going to be married this coming Saturday. Two orphaned boys were sleeping soundly in the bedroom upstairs. Will was sure it was the first real bed they'd ever slept in.

Kate spoke aloud "I can't help but wonder if somewhere the boys' mothers aren't frantically looking for their children."

Melvin spoke up "From what little Billy said tonight, I don't believe anyone is looking for them. I am under the impression that the boys are from New York City. New York is a fascinating and exciting city but the poverty is overwhelming. The wealthy have a tendency to believe that if someone can't take care of themselves they deserve the life they live. There are more children like Butch and Billy than we can imagine. Some whose parents have died from industrial accidents, illnesses or the bottle. Some who simply have too many children at home and abandon the older ones because there isn't enough food to feed them all. Many of these children's mothers are mere children themselves. Butch and Billy are both

159

intelligent boys. Most of these youngsters are not as well spoken as either of them. I would guess it is Billy who is the observer and recognizes the proper way of speaking and conducting himself. I believe, in spite of his questionable beginning, he has the promise of a brighter future. Of course, that would be more easily attained if he were to be adopted by the two of you."

Kate's heart was breaking for all the lost children. She knew she couldn't solve all of their troubles but she was determined to make a difference with the two boys upstairs. She and Will walked to the bedroom and watched them sleeping soundly. Kate pulled the covers up over Butch. She knew Billy considered himself too old for tucking in but she gently patted his head. She thought she saw him smile and hoped he was having a nice dream. A tear rolled down her cheek as Will gave her a hug. He knew he had found his very own angel and she would soon be his wife.

While Butch and Billy were sleeping peacefully, Angus Keefe was frantically searching the passenger car he had been riding in since he left New York City. The train pulled into the station in St. Louis an hour ago. Angus couldn't believe he had lost the chalice. His chalice. After years of hearing about the Mount Keefe Silver Chalice he was finally bringing it to its rightful home. His home, Angus Liam Keefe, direct descendent of Liam Shamus Keefe. The chalice was given to Liam by the artist in the late sixteenth century. His brother, Cain persuaded Liam to donate it to St. Patrick's Church in Dublin and there it had been all these years. Angus firmly believed the chalice should be his and traveled to Dublin several months ago. He spotted the chalice and at just the right moment, grabbed it out of the Father O'Connor's hands as he was celebrating holy communion. He ran from the church to his rented room, placed the chalice in the satchel he carried with him and was on the boat headed for New York before nightfall!

When the ship arrived in New York, he boarded the train for his home in St. Louis. Everything had gone so smoothly he was celebrating his success with a bit of port. The satchel was strapped to his arm but he found it difficult to eat his meal without the use of his right hand. He removed the strap intending to place it back on his wrist after dinner but was so enjoying his port, he fell asleep with the satchel unsecured.

"I've been robbed" Angus shouted.

Early the next morning Alma was in the kitchen stirring pancake batter. Ham and bacon were frying on the stove. The vicar, still sleepy from a late night, wondered how Alma did what she did. She wasn't a

160

young woman anymore and here she was bright eyed and busy as a bee.

"Good morning Will. Did you sleep well? Kate was up with the birds this morning, she has gone to the telegraph office to wire her parents about the wedding. I hope you aren't disappointed that it won't be a big, glamorous affair?"

"As long as your granddaughter becomes my wife, I don't care what kind of wedding it is. I just hope it isn't a disappointment to Kate."

With that Kate entered the kitchen. "I would think the mother of two would have more things on her mind than a big fancy wedding. I just want to marry my sons' father."

They all laughed including Oscar Crowley who Kate happened to run into on her way home.

"I've told Oscar all about the boys and he wants to talk with them. He thinks, if the boys agree, there shouldn't be a problem adopting them. He knows the judge who would hear our case and thinks it would go smoothly. Oh Will, I hope you haven't changed your mind. I have already spoken to Nettie and she has offered to tutor the boys so they will be able to attend school in just a few months."

"You have been busy this morning, haven't you? No, I haven't changed my mind. In fact, I haven't thought of anything else all night. Now, let's go wake up our sons so we can all sit down to this wonderful meal Great Grandmother Alma has prepared."

Upstairs, two boys were waking up

"Hey Butch, what did you do with that satchel you swiped from that guy on the train?"

"Golly Billy, I forgot about that. I think I dropped it when we jumped off the train. It was just some dumb old cup anyway. I thought it was the man's lunch and I was really hungry. Billy, I think I smell bacon."

Will tapped on the door telling the boys it was time to get up and come down for breakfast. They arrived in the dining room and saw Oscar Crowley. He greeted them in a deep voice. For an instant Billy was afraid Will really did call the sheriff on them but he saw the smile on the old gentleman's face and sat down folding his hands and bowing his head waiting for grace to be said. After breakfast, Oscar, Will and Kate called the boys into the parlor. Oscar wanted to know how they would feel about staying with Will for the next few days and Kate after the ceremony on Saturday.

"On Monday morning we will go to visit with a judge to see about Will and Kate being your new mother and father. Do you think you would like that?"

161

Butch was beaming. "You would be our ma and pa? Billy, did you hear that? It's even better than what you asked God for."

Billy, didn't say a word for a few seconds. He glanced around the room and then said "You know what Pa? You were right about God, you can't see Him but you know He is there." Everybody hugged and cried and laughed.

Oscar was beaming as he entered the Antique Shop.

"Sometimes things just work out as they should" he told Nettie.

Nettie was beaming herself. "Richard and Robert stopped by this morning. They asked us to join them and Emma and Lily tonight at the Trattoria for an early supper. The girls have been giggling all morning. I hope it's what I think it is and they have announcements to make."

"It's about time" grumbled Oscar. "If I dragged my feet with their mother as they are doing, they never would have been born."

Everyone was right on time that evening. Rosa had a bottle of champagne waiting for them as they sat at the table. Richard began the conversation by saying they would like Oscar and Nettie's help in planning a double wedding ceremony for them. After congratulations, handshakes and hugs, Lily said they thought a Christmas wedding would be nice.

"Christmas!" cried Oscar. "That's three months away. Haven't you kept me waiting for grandchildren long enough and you want to wait another three months?"

Nettie put her hand over his trying to calm him down.

Emma thought for a moment and then said "Would the first day of autumn suit you any better Father?"

"Now, here's a girl who makes sense. I'd rather the wedding were tomorrow but I suppose I can wait one more week."

Everyone laughed at Oscar's impatience but they all agreed the sooner they were married the happier they would be.

After dinner, Oscar and Nettie excused themselves. They thought they'd head home to check on Polly and Faith. It was only a matter of time before Polly and Faith started a new life with Randy Burke. That was what Nettie wanted for the girl who had become like a daughter to her but she would miss them terribly.

The young people decided to take a walk along the beach before heading home. Richard and Robert were reminiscing about their dad while they were growing up. Although he was an extremely busy attorney and the only one within 50 miles back then, he always found time to be with his family. Both boys looked up to him and were very happy when some of Oscar's old clients compared them to father.

"The least we can do for the old man is give him a houseful of grandchildren." Robert said with a twinkle in his eye.

"I'm all for that" replied Lily, her eyes flashing back at him.

Richard noted that Emma looked a little sad. "What's wrong, dear? You aren't having second thoughts about marrying me are you?"

"Don't be silly Richard. I can't wait to marry you. It's just that I don't have any family anymore. I was thinking of how happy my grandfather would have been to have a great grandchild."

Lily spoke up. "Emma, there are so many people in Camden Corners who think of you as family. Nettie would be so hurt if she heard you talk that way. You know she thinks of both of us as daughters."

Emma shook her head in agreement and was a little ashamed to be sounding so selfish. Richard squeezed her hand. At that moment, she began to fall. Richard grabbed her arm to catch her. She had stumbled on something half buried in the sand. She picked it up.

"This looks like a silver chalice and by the feel of it, I suspect it's quite old. There is some kind of writing on the bottom but it's too dark to make it out. Let's take it back to the shop, I'm curious as to what it says."

When they entered the shop and turned on the light Emma realized the writing was in Latin.

"Nice to have an attorney around when you need one. Let's see how much of your Latin you remember."

Richard read the words *COK.ME.FIERI.FECIT.ANNO.DOMINI. 1590*. Together the Crowleys translated the words into English *COK had me made in the year of the Lord 1590.*

Emma and Lily knew they had found a very valuable work of art. It would be a busy day tomorrow what with planning a wedding in just a couple of weeks and researching this silver chalice that they stumbled upon.

Still ranting and raving over his missing satchel, Angus was close to strangling the conductor if he didn't tell him who could have stolen his property. The conductor did remember chasing two boys off the train and he may have seen a satchel flying through the air when they jumped. Finally he remembered it was just as they were coming into Camden Corners. He warned the Camden Corners station master, Lionel Cotton that the boys might try hopping on the next train and to keep an eye out for them.

Angus was at the ticket counter within minutes. He would track down those ruffians if it was the last thing he did. After all his hard work getting the chalice back to its rightful owner, he was not about to lose it now.

The Rightful Owner

Angus Keefe was determined to retrieve his family's silver chalice. After receiving information from the conductor on the train from New York City to his home in St. Louis, he was returning to the small town of Camden Corners where the conductor believed the ruffian had jumped from the train with Angus' satchel and chalice still in his grubby little hand.

The passenger car was empty and since there was no one around to be bothered by the music Angus took out his clarinet and started playing. Angus was a music teacher.   He loved music and could play any instrument but his favorite was the clarinet.   He had dreamed of performing on stage in all the great music halls in the world. The truth was, he just wasn't good enough but he loved music and it soothed him.

He had just turned 27 that spring. He would like to settle down and marry his sweetheart, Abigail Wentworth but she told him she couldn't marry him until he got over his obsession with the Mount Keefe silver chalice. For as long as he could remember, his father and grandfather spoke of the chalice as though it were a living, breathing thing. On his deathbed, his father made Angus promise he would make the journey to Ireland, find the chalice and return it to the Keefe family where it belonged. Angus was fulfilling that promise until he foolishly sipped a bit too much port and allowed that urchin to steal the heirloom right from under his nose.

Emma and Lily were busy making plans for their double wedding ceremony and hadn't thought too much about the silver chalice Emma stumbled over in the sand. Emma ran into Sheriff Mendenhall on her way to Tempting Treats Bakery to pick up some confections to serve with tea at the antique shop and mentioned her find to him.

"I haven't had the time to do the research on the cup, but I do believe it may be very old and valuable to someone." she told the sheriff.

"Couldn't be too important to anyone if it was just dumped in the sand but I'll nose around to see if I can locate it's owner."

The sheriff had heard about the upcoming marriages of the Crowley boys. He knew old Oscar would be beaming. Those boys were his pride and joy and it was obvious to everyone in town that they had found their perfect mates.

"Goin' to be a lot of celebrating in the next couple of weeks." The sheriff winked at Emma.

She knew he was a tough old bird but he did have a soft spot for romance.

The sheriff noticed a stranger over by the train station.

"Can I help you find your way mister?" he asked a nervous looking Angus. Angus noticed the gentleman walking toward him and was almost blinded by the bright shiny sheriff's badge he wore on his chest.

"No thank you sir. I'm headed to the boarding house down the road, but thank you just the same."

The sheriff noted the stranger's odd behavior and made a mental note to check on the fellow while he was in town.

After Angus checked into the boarding house, he clutched his clarinet and began to walk around town to see what he could find. It was a quiet and comfortable town. He could picture himself sitting under that big old maple tree with its colors beginning to turn with Abigail at his side. He was beginning to wonder if he had done the right thing by taking the chalice from Father O'Connor's hands in the middle of communion. Maybe the guilt was what made him drink too much port on the train. He wasn't a violent man and wasn't even much of a drinker. He had to be honest with himself, having that chalice didn't give him the satisfaction he thought it would. In fact, he was wishing he had never gone to Ireland and never taken the chalice in the first place. All he wanted was to go back to St. Louis and marry Abigail. He knew what he had to do. He had to find the chalice and return it to the church where it was meant to be. Angus always thought best when he was playing one of his beloved instruments and began playing his clarinet.

Billy and Butch were going from shop to shop in Camden Corners. Kate and Will were outfitting each boy in their very own clothes. It was the first time either boy had ever had shirts and pants that didn't belong to someone else first. Their last stop was Floyd's Barber Shop where Butch went first.

"What handsome boys they are" Kate whispered to Will who was thinking the same thing.

When Butch was done he asked Kate if he could go out and walk around the park.

"Don't go too far dear, we don't want to lose you."

Butch's heart skipped a beat. Nobody had ever cared where he went or whether they would ever see him again before.

Butch walked across the street to the park and heard the most wonderful sound. He had heard music before, there was always some kind of music coming out of the taverns on the streets of New York but this was different. He walked over to the man playing. It was quite some time before Angus noticed he had an audience.

"Hello, young man" he said "Do you play the clarinet?"

"No, sir" replied Butch "I don't know how but I sure do like to hear you play. How do you know how to do that."

"It takes a lot of practice but here, you try it."

Angus gave the boy some basic instructions. He had never seen anyone pick up on it so quickly and he'd taught many students.

"I think you are a natural son. Would your parents mind if I bought you a clarinet of your own? I saw one in the window over there in that antique shop that I think would be good for you to practice with."

Strangers never frightened Butch because he had lived on the streets for as long as he could remember and everyone was a stranger. He followed Angus to the antique shop.

Lily thought it was odd that this man was buying young Butch an instrument, but Butch seemed to be comfortable with him. She had seen the family enter the barber shop a little while ago and thought it best if she went to find Will and make sure it was alright with him. Emma was standing close by and had the same fear as her friend. Emma knew what Lily was thinking and said "Lily dear, let me take over this sale, you don't want to be late for your appointment with Floyd". Lily rushed out the door. Angus was paying for the clarinet when he happened to glance up on the shelf above Emma's head and saw the chalice. He knew in an instant that it was the Mount Keefe Chalice. He said in a much harsher manner than he intended "Where did you get that chalice?"

Emma with a bit of fear in her voice said she had found it in the sand on the beach.

"It isn't for sale sir, until we do some searching for it's rightful owner."

"I'm its rightful owner" Angus said excitedly "It was stolen from me while I was sleeping on the train to St. Louis. The thief was just a young kid who was chased off the train in Camden Corners."

Butch's eyes were as big as saucers as he realized who this man was and that he was thief he was talking about. He bolted from the shop and ran smack into Will who still had the barber's towel wrapped around his neck.

"Who are you and what do you want with my son?" Will shouted.

Butch was crying as Kate came around Will to hold him tightly. Between sobs, Butch told them he had taken the man's satchel. He

166

thought maybe he had food in there but it was just a dumb old cup. He would have given it back but the conductor came after them and he forgot to let go of the satchel until he jumped off the train. He said he was sorry and he would go back to New York but please keep Billy with them. He's not a bad boy like I am.

Kate, Emma and Lily were all in tears as they heard Butch's plea for his friend.

Will said "Butch, stealing is never the right thing to do but we are your family now and families stick together."

"But you haven't adopted me yet and you don't have to" he whimpered.

"Son, adoption is only a matter of signing some papers our hearts have already adopted you and Billy. We love you and you will be our son forever."

Angus could not imagine what transpired over just the last few days to make this little ragamuffin a part of such a loving family. He would like to know the story but first he had to make it clear that he meant Butch no harm. He could tell Will was a reasonable man but he was protecting his child from a stranger whose intentions he wasn't sure of.

Angus explained that he was a music teacher and he suspected Butch had a natural musical talent that should be tapped. He had noticed the clarinet in the window earlier and thought it would be a good place to start. He then called Butch over because he wanted to clear the air with him regarding the chalice. He told the story of his promise to his father on his deathbed, his obsession with getting the chalice and the wrong he had done in stealing it. He realized the obsession that was passed down from generation to generation would have to stop with him. He thanked Butch for making him see what a real family is and he was going to sail back to Ireland to return the chalice to the church.

Will realized Angus was a good and decent man who never intended to hurt Butch. He and Kate invited him to supper that evening.

After the meal, they all gathered in the parlor. Kate played the piano, Will strummed his guitar, Angus helped the quick learning Butch with his clarinet and Billy sang his heart out even though it was just a little off key. Alma looked on through the kitchen doorway. Her heart burst with joy at the sight of this little family before her.

Angus wrote often to Butch and he and his wife, Abigail visited Camden Corners once a year after they were married. Each year they brought another little Keefe with them until they had 8 children in all. Angus returned the chalice to Father O'Connor and St. Patrick's Church.

Father refused to press charges against Angus. He thought putting an end to the chalice obsession was the best solution. He also thought the chalice should be on display rather than being used for communion. Besides, the bishop made sure he had a more modern chalice to use and it was much lighter and easier to handle than the old one. Angus and Abigail visited St. Patrick's on their 25th wedding anniversary and there in the vestibule was the chalice on its pedestal with the inscription:

MOUNT KEEFE SILVER CHALICE
Donated by: Liam Shamus Keefe 1590
Donated by: Angus Liam Keefe 1896

Hidden Assets

Nick Rossi was busy working the vineyards. It would be several years before the Hightower Vineyards would be producing the quality of grapes necessary for the truly exceptional wines he envisioned. The same wines as his father's vineyards in Tuscany were known for. Nick had saved some money and was being well paid by the Hightower brothers for his work in their vineyards. The brothers had inherited millions from their uncle who had been a recluse for most of his life. He knew Lucinda McCoy was also a beneficiary of Mr. Howard's estate. He assumed she had received a pittance because her daughter, Cassandra was the great granddaughter of Shane Howard. He was happy for her since Lucinda and her late husband had struggled to make ends meet since the day they left the orphanage where they both grew up.

Nick had fallen in love with Lucinda and her daughter. He was holding onto the ring his father sent with him when he came to America several years before. The ring belonged to his father's beloved Aunt Nicoletta and as the second born son, it was given to Nick for his future bride. He had no doubts that Lucinda was the woman for him but he wanted to be able to provide for her financially so she would never have to worry about money or the lack of it again.

Nick had been investing in the vineyard since its inception. The project wouldn't make a profit for a few years and the expenses were enormous. Work had begun on the winery. The Hightowers spared no expense in the building but the the brothers had enough money to cover any costs and still come out ahead. Nick's knowledge of the business was invaluable and he oversaw every detail.

Lucinda was working at the vineyard too. She acted as bookkeeper and general office manager. Cassandra had started school and since they lived in Caroline Watson Bentley's boarding house where her new husband, Jamison had hired both a maid and housekeeper, there wasn't enough to keep Lucinda busy. Not only that, she enjoyed being so close to Nick all day. She loved watching him work in the fields. He loved the work and it showed. Lucinda knew he would be popping the question any day now and was getting anxious to start their life together. She thought it was high time Cassandra had a houseful of brothers and sisters. One of the reasons she still lived in the boarding house was because of Kenny and Becky Bentley, the newly adopted children of Caroline and Jamison.

Lucinda had been shocked when she was notified that Mr. Shane Howard had remembered her in his will. She and Cassandra were millionaires. It didn't seem possible that less than a year ago she and her precious daughter had been living in poverty in New York City. Lucinda turned over her finances to Leland Harvey, the local banker. He kept close tabs on the investments he made for her and her money kept growing. Mr. Harvey encouraged her to spend more on herself but all her life she had been frugal and found it very difficult to change.

It was a rather warm fall day and Lucinda had made pitchers of lemonade that she carried out to the fields for the workers. One of those workers, Marco French added whiskey to his canteen and it was starting to show. He flirted openly with Lucinda. Lucinda brushed off his advances but Nick didn't like it one bit. Marco lifted weights when he wasn't working and it showed in his oversized muscles. The men all helped themselves to the lemonade and Lucinda left to go back to the office.

"That sure is one fine looking woman" Marco said rather loudly.

The other men tried to quiet him but to no avail.

"Not only is she a knock out, she's loaded too."

Nick walked over to Marco and in no uncertain terms told him to shut his mouth.

"Hey I didn't see a ring on that little filly's finger so I'd say she was up for grabs. Who knows what she did for that old man, Shane Howard to get put in his will. He left her millions and I wouldn't mind taking some of that dough along with her."

The other men knew that Nick was ready to strike a blow to Marco and they also knew Marco was capable of killing a man with his fists. They all grabbed Marco and forced him away from Nick.

"I don't need this hick town anyway" shouted Marco as he mounted his horse and rode towards the village.

Nick was furious. He didn't like anyone talking about a woman that way and especially Lucinda. Harold Hightower came over to see what all the commotion was about. Harold knew Marco French was a troublemaker. He would have Lucinda make out a final check with an additional bonus check. Harold was certain Marco would be at O'Sullivan's Pub and would deliver them personally to him. The bonus would be given only if Marco agreed to leave town and not return.

Nick was trying to calm down. He didn't realize how protective he felt toward Lucinda. He would gladly have faced the beating he would surely have received from Marco had they fought.

"Harold, what's this about Lucinda being a millionaire? I know Marco was just shooting his mouth off but why would he say a thing like that?"

"It's true Nick. My Uncle Shane was a strange man. He never acknowledged that Cassandra was his grandson's daughter. In fact he never acknowledged his grandson or even his son. Lucinda is worth a fortune although she hasn't spent much on herself or Cassandra."

Nick was shocked and knew he had to confront Lucinda right away. She was busy cleaning up the pitchers from the lemonade when she saw Nick walk through the door. She knew something was wrong the minute she looked into his eyes.

"Why didn't you tell me you were rich?" he said frowning at her. Before she could answer he said "You know I can't marry you now. I would never be able to give you what you couldn't buy for yourself. Why weren't you honest with me Lucinda? Never a mention of the millions of dollars you have in your bank account. If there is one thing I can't abide, it's dishonesty. What other lies have you told me?"

Without waiting for an answer, Nick turned on his heel and walked out leaving Lucinda with her mouth open in disbelief.

Harold saw Nick stomping out of the office and knew there was trouble. He quickly ran to Lucinda. She was shaking and seemed to be in shock. He helped her close up the office and took her to the main house where he knew Dahlia and Hyacinth would be able to comfort her. He didn't understand Nick but would catch up with him and find out what transpired between the two of them. He had his suspicion that Nick was overreacting to the fact that Lucinda hadn't shared her financial circumstances with him.

Leaving Lucinda in the sisters capable hands, he left the house to find Nick and try to calm him down. Lucinda was still in shock.

"He accused me of being dishonest. The subject of the money never came up and you know I don't think of that money as being mine. I have been waiting for a good use for it and planned all along to give it away. I have never seen Nick like that and I'm not sure I ever want to see him again."

Hyacinth wanted to wring Nick's neck.

"How could he do this to our dear Lucinda? I hope Harold finds him and gives him a good talking to."

Nick climbed on his horse and rode to town. He was tempted to go to O'Sullivan's Pub but knew he didn't need to be imbibing when he was angry. He was sorry that he had spoken so harshly to Lucinda but how could she have kept quiet about having all that money. Rosa was surprised to see her brother in the middle of the day. It was just after the lunch crowd left and it was the quiet time of day for her before the early evening diners started arriving.

"What in the world is wrong with you Nicola? You look like you are ready for a fight."

Nick told her about Lucinda and her money.

Rosa replied "How could you not have known about the inheritance? Everyone in town knew that. Lucinda doesn't talk about it because she doesn't think she is deserving of the money but it's a known fact. You are a darned fool if you have accused her of being dishonest. Oh Nicola, how could you?"

"Maybe I did overreact but the fact remains that I cannot and will not marry someone who isn't completely honest with me."

Rosa knew her brother and knew there was more to his anger than Lucinda's money.

"What else happened today Nicola?"

Nick couldn't keep anything from his sister. "One of the workers was openly flirting with Lucinda and she did nothing to stop him. I couldn't help thinking of Marietta, she acted the same way when anyone flirted with her and and look what happened to our relationship."

"Nicola, that was so long ago and there is no comparison between Marietta Keene and Lucinda McCoy. Do you remember that Lucinda spent most of her childhood in an orphanage? She told me once that the only way to avoid being bullied was to ignore the bullies. I'm sure that is what she was doing with that degenerate today. Have you ever seen her flirt or carry on with anyone before? Nicola, what has gotten into you. I haven't seen you act like this since you were 16 years old and had your heart broken by that insipid creature, Marietta Keene. I hope you haven't ruined the best thing that has ever happened to you. Now, go find Lucinda and beg her forgiveness before it's too late."

Nick gave his sister a hug. She was right. He had been a real jerk. He only hoped Lucinda would be in a forgiving mood. He made his way back to the vineyard and passed Harold on his way to O'Sullivan's Pub to settle the account with Marco French.

"I don't know if she will see you Nick but I hope you can straighten out this mess."

Nick gingerly knocked on the Hightower's front door. Hyacinth showed him in. He could tell Lucinda had been crying but was doing her best to hide it.

"Can we talk Lucinda?"

"I don't know what there is to say Nick, you said enough this afternoon."

"I don't know why I spoke to you that way. I was frustrated because I want to be able to build a big beautiful house for you and Cassandra and I simply don't have the money to do it. Just when I was feeling like a failure, Marco started making remarks. I guess I thought you should slap his face or something and you had no reaction at all. I was jealous. Marco is a good looking man, the type any woman would be able to fall for and then he said that about you having so much money. I didn't believe it but Harold confirmed it and everything blew up in my head. I know that isn't any excuse for the way I spoke to you but I hope you will forgive me."

Lucinda was quiet for a moment and then she said "Nick, I understand that sometimes frustration can be overwhelming. I have felt it too. When Cassandra and I lived in New York and I didn't know where I would get the money to put food on the table or whether her tiny feet would grow out of her only pair of shoes. I don't think you have ever missed a hearty meal or limped because your shoes were too small. I'm not judging you Nick, but I don't understand why you lashed out at me. I never tried to hide the fact that Mr. Howard left us money. It's money I don't feel deserving of. I don't want Cassandra growing up thinking that money is the only important thing in the world. I don't need a big sprawling house. I'm perfectly happy in one room of Carolyn Bentley's home although I know we can't live there forever. As far as Marco French goes, I couldn't tell you what that man looked like let alone whether he was good looking or not. I knew he was saying inappropriate things to me but I didn't find it important enough to respond to. Nick, I think we shouldn't see each other, at least for a while. It will give you time to think about your true feelings. Maybe your blowing up today was a sign that you are not ready to start a life with me and Cassandra. Now, if you will excuse me, school will be letting out soon and I must leave to meet Cassandra."

She thanked Hyacinth for her hospitality and was out the door before Nick could think of any response at all. Hyacinth and Dahlia didn't hide the fact that they had been standing in the doorway listening to everything that was said.

Nick looked at them sheepishly "You ladies don't have to tell me what a heel I am, I'm well aware of it."

He, too, was out the door.

"Don't worry about those two Hyacinth, this is just a little bump in the road. I think we should start planning a wedding"

The sisters giggled as they walked up the stairs to the nursery where four babies were not so quietly awaiting their arrival.

A Worthy Cause

It had only been three days since Lucinda McCoy and Nick Rossi had parted ways. Nick didn't need his sister, Rosa, telling him what an utter fool he had been to ruin everything with the only woman he had ever loved. He had been a jealous fool and there was no reason for it. One of the vineyard workers had spoken improperly to Lucinda and Nick didn't like her reaction or more appropriately her lack of reaction. When he thought of the way he had blown up at her because of that and because he had just found out she inherited millions from Shane Howard instead of the few dollars he envisioned he couldn't stop kicking himself. He missed her terribly and missed Cassandra too. They had become an inseparable threesome and now he was alone in his thoughts.

Rosa poured her brother a cup of coffee. "Nick, go see her, I'm sure she is feeling as lonely as you are. I know Lucinda loves you. For goodness sake, the whole town knows you love each other. If you don't do something about this, I'm going to ask Sheriff Mendenhall to lock you two up in adjoining cells and have you duke it out. Now don't be so stubborn. You are the one who created this mess now go fix it."

Nick knew when his sister got this way she meant business and he wouldn't be surprised if she did call the sheriff. Maybe he would just take a leisurely stroll by the Bentley house. He hadn't seen Jamison in a while. Maybe he would check on the plans he was drawing up for the vineyard. After all, he was investing his money in the project.

Caroline glanced out the window and saw Nick walking hesitantly by the front porch. It's about time she thought to herself. Lucinda wasn't

173

showing any outward signs of misery but Caroline knew the girl well enough to know that she was suffering since her breakup with Nick.

Nick couldn't get himself to go knock on the front door. He was so ashamed of the way he acted. Instead he went to the side door where Jamison's office was. Jamison was happy to see his friend and welcomed the interruption. He had been busy sketching the winery and was running into some logistical difficulties. Nick was able to suggest alternatives and solved the problems.

Caroline knocked on the door with a pot of freshly brewed coffee.

"Good Morning Nick. So nice to see you. It's a lovely day Maybe you would like to have your coffee in the garden gentlemen and enjoy the Indian summer weather."

Jamison thought his wife was a bit obvious but Nick agreed immediately and took the tray from Caroline and placed it on the small table in the gazebo. He glanced up and saw Lucinda standing on the far end of the garden admiring the mums that were in full bloom this time of year. She turned around and couldn't hide the smile on her face. She had never been so happy to see anyone in her life. She knew she loved this man and he loved her. They both walked toward each other, Nick held out his arms and Lucinda fell into them. Between kisses Nick kept telling her how sorry he was about his foolish behavior. Lucinda knew she couldn't stay angry at him and decided not to even try. Caroline and Jamison were sitting at the table in the gazebo both smiling broadly.

Lucinda and Nick joined them just before Cassandra and Becky came running out of the house.

"Mama, Mama Kenny is crying" shouted Becky. "He said his tummy hurts" Caroline excused herself and went into the house to see to her son.

"Must have eaten too much ice cream yesterday." Jamison said.

Within a few moments, Carolyn called from the window "Kenny is very sick, I think we should get Doc right away." Nick took off on foot and ran into Tom Campbell.

Tom is Doc McMillan's son-in-law. He is married to Doctor Julie. Years ago Doc treated Tom's dying mother and saved her life. From that moment on Tom knew he wanted to be a doctor. He and Julie fell in love long before they knew it themselves and have been working side by side ever since. Tom rushed to examine Kenny. He suspected Kenny was having an appendix attack and knew time was of the essence getting him to the hospital in Greensboro before the appendix ruptured.

"The best way to get Kenny to Greensboro is in the fire truck." Nick took off on foot again to the fire station. Cody Hill was sweeping the front walk when he saw Nick running toward him.

Cody had been working at the fire station, learning the ropes since shortly after his arrival in Camden Corners. Instinct told Cody something was not right. He shouted for Joe Taylor that there was trouble. Joe came running. Nick was almost out of breath after the two mile run to the fire station. He did manage to explain the situation. Joe and Cody hooked up 6 horses to the truck and threw some mattresses on the floor of the truck in rapid fire precision. Nick hopped in the back and off they rode to the ailing boy. Tom had given Kenny some medicine that would help with the pain. Tom and Jamison gently carried Kenny down the stairs and into the truck just as it arrived. Caroline, Jamison and Tom rode in the back of the truck with Kenny anticipating the 2 hour ride to Greensboro.

Several of the townspeople had gathered wondering what all the commotion was. April Hawthorne was on her way to school. She worked part time for the doctors trying to get experience for her future nursing career. Tom asked April to let Julie know he was on his way to Greensboro. April didn't stop to think how handsome Cody looked sitting in the driver's seat of the fire truck. She was hurrying on her way to the McMillan house to deliver the message to Doctor Julie.

Lucinda did her best to calm Becky who was remembering her mother being hauled away and never coming back home. She was afraid for Kenny. Lucinda couldn't promise the boy would be alright since she knew his condition was serious.

Doctor Julie arrived to see if she could help with Becky. She was aware of Becky's inability to speak after the death of her mother. Her father, in a drunken stupor had put that fear into her head because he wanted to end her little girl chatter. Becky was clinging to Lucinda. Julie told her Kenny would have the best of care from Doctor Tom on his way to Greensboro.

"Why can't he stay here?" she cried.

"Kenny needs to be in a hospital where the doctors have everything they need to make him well again" Julie told her.

"Why can't Kenny go to a hospital here? I want to see him." Lucinda looked at Nick and they both knew just what Shane Howard's money would be used for. She couldn't think about it now but as soon as this crisis was over she would get the ball rolling to start building Camden Corners' own hospital.

The medicine Tom had given Kenny made the pain more bearable he was drifting in and out of sleep. The long trip to Greensboro in the back of the fire truck was uncomfortable for Caroline in her condition but she hadn't noticed. All she could think of was the first time she saw Kenny and Becky staring at her from behind the hydrangea bush just a few months ago. Caroline loved these two little orphan children the moment she laid eyes on them. She knew Becky would be worried about her brother. The poor little girl had finally seemed to be adjusting to her new life and now this.

They finally reached the hospital. Kenny was transported to the operating room where Tom performed surgery to remove his appendix. What seemed to the Bentleys to be an eternity later, Tom appeared and told them little Kenny would be just fine. They had made it in time, there was no rupture. Kenny would be sleeping for the next several hours.

Jamison immediately sent a wire to Camden Corners saying Kenny was recovering and would be back home in two weeks. When Lucinda read the wire to Becky, she was somewhat relieved but wanted to see her brother. Even though hospitals didn't allow young children to visit, Nick and Lucinda piled the two girls into the Hightower's carriage and set out for Greensboro the very next morning.

Kenny finally woke up shortly before noon. He didn't like the fact that he would be staying in the hospital for two weeks but he wasn't feeling well enough to argue. His main concern was his little sister. Caroline was holding his hand and assuring him that Becky was being well taken care of when the door opened and Lucinda walked in the room holding Becky's hand. Nick had used his charm on the young charge nurse as the two slipped by her. Becky thought her brother still looked pretty sick but better than the last time she saw him. Lucinda promised if they didn't stay for more than a minute that they would be able to come back again. Becky didn't argue, she waved to Kenny and blew him a kiss and out the door they went. Nick was still charming the nurse as Lucinda and Becky walked passed her unnoticed.

"I didn't realize you were such a charmer Mr. Rossi" Lucinda said sarcastically.

"Hey, anything for a good cause" Nick liked the little hint of jealousy he saw in Lucinda's eyes.

The two weeks passed quickly and Kenny was back home again. The emergency was just a memory now but Lucinda knew the outcome could have been quite different. Camden Corners needed a hospital and she was going to do everything she could to make it happen quickly. She would set up a meeting to discuss it but now she had a wedding to go to. Her friends, Emma and Lily were being married in a double ceremony to the

Crowley Brothers.

Nettie Crowley and Ethel Fulbright could hardly catch their breath. Emma and Lily were standing before them. Emma in her grandmother's wedding gown and Lily in Ethel's. Emma could almost feel her grandmother's presence in the room. They both wore rose buds from Nettie's garden in their hair. Jonas Fulbright was giving both girls away and Oscar Crowley was acting as best man for both of his sons.

Jonas knocked on the door of the small room of the chapel where the wedding was taking place. Each girl took the old man's arm. Jonas thought the buttons would pop off of his morning suit he had such pride in these two lovely ladies.

Oscar was waiting at the end of the aisle with his two handsome sons. He had waited for this day for so long and it was finally here. He loved Emma and Lily as he would his own daughters. Out of the corner of his eye he could see Nettie, her eyes glistening with tears. What a lucky man he was. He had found two wonderful women to share each phase of his life with and now his sons and daughters-in-law would be presenting him with beautiful grandchildren.

The wedding was followed by a reception at the home of Nettie and Oscar Crowley. The guests were dancing, eating and drinking champagne. Nick and Lucinda were dancing with Cassandra in Nick's arms.

"I'd like to ask you two ladies a question" Nick said with a quivering voice.

His fist was clenched and he opened it where Lucinda and Cassandra saw two beautiful rings, one a diamond and the other an amethyst. He slipped the rings on their fingers, as he said

"Will you marry me?"

Cassandra answered first as she wrapped her arms tightly around Nick's neck "Yes, we will!" she shouted. A little more skeptically she whispered "we will won't we Mama?" Lucinda saw the happiness on her daughter's face and knew Paul would definitely approve of her answer when she said, "yes Cassandra, I think we will." Rosa and Eduardo were dancing by and she heard every word.

"Eduardo, we better order more sacks of flour. I have a wedding cake to make."

Dalton's Mountain

Vicar Will had been reciting the wedding vows so often for the new brides and grooms of Camden Corners that he knew what to say without looking at the printed word. This week was no exception. The Crowley boys had been married two days ago and now sitting in his office were Lucinda McCoy and Nick Rossi. They had passed Josie McMillan and Reggie Blackburn on their way into the vicar's office.

"Seems to be the season for weddings" he said as he looked at the two smiling faces in front of him.

Will and his beloved Kate had been married themselves just a few weeks ago.

Both weddings were very simple, Josie and Reggie were married in the chapel just west of town. Josie wore her sister's gown. A small reception was given at the lake house she and Reggie were still in the process of remodeling.

The following day, Lucinda and Nick were married under the grapevine archway behind the Marino Trattoria. The reception was in the restaurant where Eduardo had prepared all of his specialties for the occasion. Rosa and the entire Marino family were overjoyed with the two additions to the family. Nick rented a small house two doors down from the Bentley house and just south of the Marinos. He was worried that Cassandra would be lonely without her friends close by. Cassandra was just so happy to have Nick in their lives. She told everyone she saw that Nick was now her new papa.

There wasn't much time for adjusting to married life for either couple. Construction on the new hospital was about to begin. Jamison Bentley had drawn up the preliminary plans with the assistance of Doc McMillan, Tom and Julie. Lucinda was more than happy to leave the details to the professionals, however she insisted on only top quality construction material and labor. She didn't believe in cutting corners to save a few dollars.

Reggie was happy to abide by her wishes. It was a pleasure to work with someone who believed in the high standards that he did. His crew was all in place and waiting for the materials to be delivered by train. Reggie assembled the usual men in his crew. He assigned Ernie Black as foreman of the project. Ernie was one of the best men in construction. He was almost as much of a perfectionist as Reggie and was the man Reggie relied on the most. This would be the biggest project either man had ever been involved in and he knew Ernie would do the job well. Ernie voiced concern about one worker who had signed on for the job. Ernie was a good judge of character and felt uncomfortable about the fellow named Dusty Blanchard. Ernie had known Dusty's paw, Al, who died a year or so ago working on a project in Greensboro. Al was a good man. The incident had been ruled accidental but Ernie had never known Al to be careless about his safety or that of the crew. Ernie hired Dusty because of who his father was but he was such a nervous kid he wasn't sure he was up to the pressure of constructing a building of this magnitude. He'd keep his eye on him, maybe the kid just needed a break.

It wasn't too long before the first shipment of lumber arrived. The men loaded it on buckboards and transported the planks of wood to the job site. Ernie came out of the makeshift office to inspect the shipment.

"This can't be our order. The quality is poor." He picked up one plank and there was a knothole almost as wide as the plank itself. Ernie called Reggie over to do his own inspection. At least half of the order had some type of flaw. Something was not right. This lumber had been ordered from the most reputable sawmill he had ever dealt with. It was just a small outfit located at the base of a mountain in Virginia. Ezekiel Dalton owned the mill. He assured Reggie the task would not be more than he could handle.

Reggie explained to Lucinda that this lumber could not be used for the hospital. He personally would travel to the Dalton Mills to speak with Zeke about the order and see what could be done about getting the superior product he had always been able to depend on. The problem was, if he let the crew go, they would most likely finding other jobs. He couldn't expect them to be waiting around without pay. Lucinda didn't blink an eye.

"No, don't let the men go. We can find something around town for them to do. You look into this matter."

"Thanks Lucinda, I think Josie would like to go with me to Dalton's Mountain. It's beautiful country around there and I know she would enjoy the adventure."

Reggie was right about Josie wanting to go with him. She loved Camden Corners but was anxious to see more of the country. She was a little nervous when they arrived in West Virginia as to what they would find. They rented a horse and buggy and started the trek through some of the most beautiful territory they had ever seen. The only thing she knew about the Daltons was that Zeke was the head of the household. He lived on his land with his wife and their two sons. Josie had them pictured with corn cob pipes and missing teeth. Mules and critters roaming in and out of their house with no windows or doors. Reggie pulled up to a charming farmhouse.

"Here we are."

They were greeted by a nice young man who introduced himself as John Dalton. "Please come in the house. You must be exhausted from your long trip. Ma has some fresh lemonade made for you."

They walked into the warm and welcoming house. Mrs. Dalton greeted her visitors. She was a tiny woman, but Josie had the feeling she could hold her own. She had the most welcoming smile and Josie noticed all of her teeth were intact. Zeke came through the door. A friendly man with a twinkle in his eye. Behind him was another young boy. Zeke introduced him as Benjamin.

Josie liked this family right away. Zeke reminded her of Oscar Crowley although she had never seen Oscar in a pair of overalls.

"Effie, these young folks must be hungry. Let's dish up some stew for them and while you're at it, I'll have some myself".

"Just about to do that old man."

Josie had to suppress a giggle the way they spoke to each other. It was done in such a loving way that it didn't sound offensive. She had called him old man and he couldn't have been more than 40. Josie wondered what she will call him when he really is an old man, Methuselah maybe. She didn't dare look at Reggie, she knew she wouldn't be able to keep from chuckling.

Josie was thoroughly enjoying the stew. She had no idea she was eating rabbit which was probably for the best. The fresh baked bread and sliced tomatoes were the best she'd ever tasted. Effie told her they lived mostly from the land up here.

"Our families have lived in these mountains for a century or two."

"There are Daltons all the way up that mountain there" said Zeke. "We don't see them much. They don't like to come down this far. They live totally off the land and take care of their own. They're not much on having visitors either so we just leave them alone for the most part."

After dessert of a fresh baked apple pie, the men went out to the sawmill. Reggie felt bad complaining about the lumber received after being treated to a meal but knew it had to be done. He showed Zeke the block of wood he carried with him.

"Where'd you get this? It's from what we call a junk tree. They grow like weeds but you have to pull them up by the roots before they take over all the land."

"Zeke, this came from the order you sent to Camden Corners."

"Reggie, we never got any order from you, I know you mentioned it and I have some wood set aside for you but when I didn't hear from you I thought the project had been delayed or abandoned."

"I don't understand Zeke, I signed off on that order myself. It was to be in three shipments to make it easier for you. Something is not right and I will get to the bottom of it. In the meantime, will you accept my handwritten order and I will wire for your money."

Josie came out to the mill to see what the operation looked like.

"Josie is one of my best crew workers Zeke. She knows her way around a hammer and nails."

Zeke loved the idea of a woman working somewhere beside the kitchen.

"My Effie hung the door of this barn" he said proudly.

"Only to hang it back up after it fell down and broke your arm".

"It only sprained it, old woman. That was the lightning that we had that day"

"Maybe the lightning helped, but it had more to do with the bolts being too short when someone hung it in the first place."

John piped in, "Those two keep Ben and me entertained. It's like watching a Punch and Judy show."

Reggie did as he said and put an order in writing. Zeke insisted there was no hurry in requisitioning the deposit but Reggie insisted and he and Josie traveled to the general store that also housed the telegraph office. He sent a wire to Lucinda explaining that the lumber received was not sent by Zeke Dalton and he would get to the heart of the matter upon his return. He asked that she speak privately with Ernie but not to let on to the crew what the hold up is.

Reggie thought it best to wait for a reply. He and Josie took a seat at the small table by the window of the store. The store owner, Ike Goolsbee poured them a cup of coffee on the house. It wasn't too often strangers visited his store and he was happy for the company.

While the threesome chatted, a young girl entered the store. She heard them mention the Daltons and a smile came on her face.

"I'm going to marry John Dalton some day and we will have so many children that old farmhouse will be bursting at the seams."

Ike introduced the girl who couldn't have been more than 13 to the visitors.

"This is Olivia Benson, I think if anyone is capable of snaring young John Dalton it will be Miss Olivia here."

Josie didn't want to burst the child's bubble but she thought back to the

181

boy she thought she'd marry when she was 13 and shuddered now at the thought.

Before long there was a message on the telegraph machine telling Reggie the deposit was on its way. Ernie was in the office with Lucinda and Jamison and he had some ideas about solving the mystery of where the inferior wood came from.

Josie and Reggie thanked Ike for his hospitality and returned to the Daltons to bid good bye and assure Zeke that they were back in business.

Effie wouldn't hear of the two young people riding all the way back to the train station that evening. She insisted they stay the night with them. There was plenty of room and they would be able to get a fresh start in the morning.

The next morning Josie tearfully hugged her new friend Effie Dalton goodbye. It was the start of a friendship that lasted through the years. Five years after their first meeting Effie wrote that Olivia Benson was her new daughter-in-law. She and John had been married and moved into the Dalton home. Every year or two after a new arrival was announced until the old Dalton farmhouse was bursting at the seams

Just as Olivia said it would be.

The Journal

On the way home from Virginia, Reggie was very quiet. Josie didn't notice because she was lost in her own thoughts. She had felt a little queasy when she woke up this morning and the horse back ride to the train station hadn't helped. She knew Reggie was worried about the lumber order and how the inferior lumber had shown up at the job site in Camden Corners. Josie excused herself to visit the ladies room where she promptly lost the wonderful breakfast Effie Dalton had prepared before they left Dalton's Mountain. She rinsed her mouth out as best she could.

"Are you feeling alright Miss?" Josie heard someone say.

"I'm going to be fine" replied Josie "I must have picked up a virus on my visit to Virginia. Thank you for asking."

"Oh dear, I have seen the signs before and I think you may have something a little more than a virus. Are you sure you aren't expecting?"

"Expecting? Certainly not, we have only been married for a few weeks. It's much too soon to be experiencing morning sickness."

"I have five children and had morning sickness for the full nine months with each and every one of them. It does happen. If I were a betting woman, I would guess you will be feeling better by this afternoon.

In the meantime, I have some soda crackers that might do the trick. I make sure I don't leave home without a fresh supply."

She winked at Josie as she handed her several crackers. It was then Josie noticed the woman definitely had an expanding waistline.

"Thank you for the crackers and good luck with number six."

"They tell me it's going to be number six and seven this time." The stranger grinned widely and was out the door.

By the time Josie returned to her seat she had nibbled on three of the saltines and was feeling much better. She wondered if she should mention her conversation with the woman in the ladies room and decided against it. Reggie was so preoccupied she wanted his full attention before she talked of the possibility of a new baby.

Ernie Black was anxious for Reggie's return. He didn't have a clue as to what happened to the order that was suppose to go to Zeke Dalton for the lumber. He went over it in his mind. He had taken the order with him to the post office and remembered having a conversation with Jackson Parker, the postmaster. Somewhere between his office and the post office the order had been changed and had been sent to an outfit just over the border that had a reputation for cheap, shoddy workmanship. Did he stop somewhere along the way? He tried but couldn't remember.

The train pulled into the station and Ernie was there to meet it. Josie told Reggie to go along, she would walk over to the McMillan house and say hello to her mother. She would find a way home and see him later. She wanted talk to her mother about her suspicions.

Dusty Blanchard was working on the tracks on the north side of the train depot. It was one of the jobs the crew had been reassigned to while they waited for the Dalton lumber to arrive. He noticed Reggie as he and his wife stepped off the train and were greeted by Ernie Black. Dusty swore they were looking directly at him but maybe it was simply his imagination due to his guilty conscience.

Dusty's life had taken a dramatic turn eighteen months ago. He had just graduated from Greensboro High and had taken a job with the construction company his pa worked with. He was proud to be working with Al Blanchard. Al was respected by the entire crew and the owners of the company alike. Seemingly overnight, Al's attitude began to change. He was curt with the crew and with Dusty. He walked around with a scowl on his face most of the day. Even his ma noticed the change in Al. Two months later Al fell to his death from the third floor of the new bank building being constructed on Main.

Dusty stayed on with the crew but the job was never the same. He had a hard time believing his father would have ever been so careless as to slip on the scaffolding as it appeared that he did. Al Blanchard always stressed the importance of safety. Dusty's ma retreated into herself after her husband's death.

After a few months, Leo Carlisle knocked on Connie Blanchard's front door. Leo was a charmer and Connie was charmed. He claimed to have come by to offer his condolences for her loss.

As he walked into the parlor, he looked around the room and said "What a lovely home you have Mrs. Blanchard. May I call you Connie? Al spoke of you so often I feel as though I know you."

Connie was surprised that this gentleman was such a close friend to Al since she had never heard his name before.

"Would you care for a cup of tea Mr. Carlisle?"

"Connie dear, please call me Leo. Yes, I would love to have some tea. Don't bother with the sugar, there is enough sweetness in the room already."

Connie giggled. Al never said things like that to her. She felt like a school girl and after months of mourning, it felt good to be able to laugh again.

It didn't take Leo long to ingratiate himself into the Blanchard home. Dusty didn't find him nearly as charming as his mother did. He remembered seeing him around the job site. He knew he wasn't part of the crew but he would appear at various times. Dusty remembered seeing him behind the counter of a coffee and doughnut stand he'd set up by the side of the road near the site where the workers would take their morning breaks.

Leo had taken up going to church with Connie and Dusty. One Sunday, on the way back to the Blanchard home, Leo suggested they go through Al's clothes and give them to the poor.

"The Al I knew was generous to a fault and I know he would want his things to go to a good cause."

Connie hadn't been able to face that task but with dear Leo at her side she thought she was ready. Dusty wasn't sure he wanted Leo going through his pa's things and made sure he got to his dresser before Leo did.

Dusty opened the top drawer. He knew right away that it wasn't going to be easy to sort through all these things of his pa's. He found the pen knife he'd had since he was a boy. A pair of cuff links he remembered seeing pa wear every Sunday. A journal filled with entries in Pa's handwriting. Dusty had to blink away some tears and put the journal in his pocket to read when he was by himself.

Just then Leo came up behind him. He hadn't seen Dusty put the journal into his pocket but he started rummaging through the drawer himself. Dusty picked up some papers that looked like receipts. Leo grabbed them out of his hand and without saying a word stuffed them in his pocket and continued searching through the drawer. After he was satisfied he had seen everything in the drawer, he shut it abruptly and went on to the next. Dusty found another receipt tucked between two handkerchiefs. Something was not right. He saw his father's name on the bottom but it didn't look anything like his signature.

Suddenly Leo grabbed the receipt out of his hand.

"Unless you want the same fate for your mother as was your fathers, you will forget you saw this."

Dusty looked into Leo's eyes and saw pure evil. He knew at that moment that his father's death was not accidental and he knew who was responsible for it.

The days went on and Leo became more and more important in Connie's life. One day he mentioned at the dinner table that there was a big construction project beginning in Camden Corners.

"Dusty wouldn't it be a good idea for you to sign on to the crew there. I would be sure your mother remained safe here in Greensboro if you were to do that."

Dusty knew a threat when he heard it. He didn't want to leave his mother in the hands of Leo Carlisle but he also knew he had no choice.

As Dusty was packing his bag, he came across his father's journal. He had blanked it out of his mind. He dropped it in his bag. At the train station he gave his mother a big hug. She cried as he boarded the train and Leo whispered, "I'll be in touch." Dusty was still shaking as the train pulled away from the station.

Dusty opened the journal and began reading his father's entries. Al's concern showed through on the first few pages of the journal. He had been aware that the materials they received for the project were not up to the usual standards of any of the companies the outfit had always dealt with. Al mentioned finding receipts with his name in the signature line but not signed by him. According to the journal, Al hadn't mentioned his suspicions to any of the crew. He had started his own investigation and was close to finding the answer. He went on to mention Leo Carlisle. Leo appeared on the job site one morning. He told Al he was in the insurance business and was inquiring about the project. Al informed him the job's insurance needs were covered and his services weren't required. He mentioned the look of pure evil in the man's eyes as he said, "We'll see

185

about that."

Al wired each and every company where original material orders had been placed. No recent orders had been received by any one of them. The same procedure was followed every time an order was placed. After writing the order and checking it for errors, he would give the paperwork to one of the crew members to take to the post office to be mailed to the supply company. He did remember asking Emmett Larson to take the order for steel girders. He called Emmett into his office and asked him to remember everything he could about the time between when he was given the envelope and when he delivered it to the post office. Emmett couldn't remember anything unusual but after a few minutes, he did recall something that was hardly worth mentioning. On his way across the street, a fellow bumped into him almost knocking him over. He dropped the envelope and the man picked it up and handed it back to him.

"Do you remember what the fellow looked like?"

"Yes sir. I have seen him around here before. He has been selling doughnuts from a stand across the street. Some of the fellows go there every morning during break. It is almost break time now and I think he might be out there sir."

Al followed Emmett out the door and across to the coffee stand. He wasn't too surprised to see Leo Carlisle grinning at him.

"Good morning Mr. Blanchard. How nice to see you at my little coffee stand this morning."

"Insurance business not going too well these days Leo?"

"On the contrary sir, on the contrary." Leo's maniacal laugh sent chills down Al's spine.

Al spoke with several other workers who had delivered orders. In each instance they recalled a similar experience getting the envelope to the post office and each one of them remembered someone who looked like Leo Carlisle was involved.

The last entry in the journal was dated the day before Al died. He was going to report his suspicions to the sheriff first thing in the morning.

Secret Weapon

After reading his pa's journal, Dusty was even more certain Al Blanchard's fall from the scaffolding of the job site in Greensboro was not an accident. He was also certain that the man responsible was Leo Carlisle. Dusty knew Leo's threats were to be taken seriously and his mother was in serious jeopardy if Dusty didn't do exactly what Leo told

186

him to do.

Dusty was surprised Ernie Black gave him a job on the hospital project. He couldn't hide his nervousness. He couldn't stop thinking about his pa's fate and what may lay ahead for Ma. He knew Ernie only hired him because of his father and shuddered to think what Leo would have done if he came home without the job on the project.

Reggie went with Ernie back to the job site. Reggie told Ernie all about his visit to the Dalton Sawmill and let him know the first part of their order would be on its way in just a day or two. Ernie asked Reggie if Josie was feeling alright.

"She looked a little pale to me"

"Josie? She's just fine. Had a great time with Effie Dalton. If she didn't love Camden Corners so much, I don't think I could keep her away from Dalton's Mountain. Sure is beautiful country down there."

In the meantime, Josie had her head over the commode in the McMillan home. Her mother was sympathetic but couldn't keep the smile off her face because it looked like she would be a grandmother very soon.

Josie joined her mother at the kitchen table.

"I wanted to ask you if you thought I might be expecting but I can tell by the look on your face that you suspect it too."

"It's probably too soon to tell but maybe you should talk to your sister. I would guess you are suffering from morning sickness. I'll bet Reggie is beside himself."

"I haven't mentioned it to Reggie. He is so preoccupied with troubles with the lumber order. I want his full attention before I let him know he might be a father in a few months."

Reggie and Ernie were in Reggie's office discussing how the order could possibly have been switched. Ernie was quiet for a moment and then spoke up.

"I was walking from the wagon across the street when a fellow bumped my arm. I remember thinking it was odd because there was plenty of room for him to walk by me without running into me. The envelope dropped to the ground and he picked it up and handed it to me. Our eyes met and I remember feeling a chill for a moment. I then walked over to the Post Office and handed the envelope to Jackson Parker. We chatted for a few minutes and I returned back here."

"Let's start with Jackson Parker." said Reggie "We'll have him look at his log and see where that envelope actually went."

They rode to the Post Office. Reggie noticed Josie and her mother were going into the doctor's office next door to the McMillan house. He didn't think anything about it since they were all in the family.

Jackson brought out the log and scanned the pages until he came to the one that named the recipient as *Dalton Mills, Box 808, Pineville, NY.*

"I'm sorry boss." Ernie said quietly "It was so careless of me not to check that envelope. I should have known something was fishy about that guy. It was all my fault. I cost Miss Lucinda a bundle of money. I will have my resignation letter on your desk first thing tomorrow morning."

"Ernie, you will do no such thing. It wasn't your fault. Why would you even look at the envelope? You had no way of knowing someone was on the lookout for you. I just wonder how this Carlisle guy knew that order was going out at that time and knew you would have it in your hand when he bumped into you. I'm afraid we may have a spy in our organization."

The crew was called back to the job the following morning. Dusty thought he saw Leo standing next to the light pole as he walked from the worker's camping grounds to the job site. He knew he had to let Mr. Blackburn know what Leo was capable of but the veiled threat against his ma was constantly on his mind. An hour later, Dusty tripped over his tool box hurting his arm and was taken to see Doctor Tom Campbell.

Tom entered the examining room just as Dusty was removing his jacket without any obvious pain.

"Sorry Doc I didn't hurt myself, I just needed to talk to you or your wife or Doc McMillan. I know you are related to Mrs. Blackburn and I have to get some information to her husband without anyone knowing."

Tom was leery of the boy but willing to listen to his explanation. Dusty showed him the journal. Tom knew of the recent mix up with the lumber and that Reggie was very worried about who was sabotaging the hospital project.

"Has this Leo Carlisle threatened you Dusty?" Tom asked after he had read a few of the incriminating pages.

"No sir, not me. He has cast some kind of spell over my mother and he has hinted that harm will come to her if I don't do as he tells me. So far he hasn't told me to do anything except sign up to work on this job."

Tom wrapped the boys arm and placed a sling around his neck.

"We will say you have a sprained arm. That way if Leo sees you he won't be suspicious. My wife and I are expected at the Blackburn house this evening for supper. I will give the journal to Reggie then. Dusty, you are a brave young man. I didn't know your pa but I'm sure he would be very proud of the way you are handling this situation."

Dusty was walking back to the job site when Leo slithered from behind a tree.

"Looks like you will be given a job in the office for a while boy. That works out very well. You will be of more help to me there than out working in the field."

Later that evening Reggie read over pages of Al Blanchard's journal. He was furious that the man was apparently murdered because of Leo Carlisle's greed.

"Ernie said the kid acted nervous. It's no wonder. From reading through the journal, it appears that Leo is either lurking around the job site of his current victim or he has intimidated someone else to do his dirty work."

Josie spoke up "Reggie, do you remember that young girl we hired to do the filing and help with some of the paperwork? Her name was Pamela. I would find her crying at her desk almost daily. She never let on what was wrong and one day she simply didn't show up for work. She said she was staying with Evelyn Keys but when I checked with Evelyn, she had never heard of the girl. Maybe I should have looked into it further."

"We need to get this information to Sheriff Mendenhall but I'm afraid Leo is watching every move we make. For Dusty's safety and his mother's we will have to be very careful."

Doc McMillan who had been sitting quietly listening to the conversation said "I'm having breakfast with the sheriff and Oscar in the morning. I'll make sure he gets the journal. Oscar will have some ideas, too."

The sheriff was indeed interested in Al Blanchard's journal and the implications. He had recently returned from a convention of area sheriffs and it seemed Mr. Leo Carlisle had been under suspicion in several cases. None of the cases had ever been resolved because witnesses were unwilling to implicate Leo in any of them.

"I'll check the whereabouts of Pamela Fuller. It sounds like she may have the proof we need to arrest Leo Carlisle. I'm sure the Sheriff in Greensboro would be interested to know that Al Blanchard's death may not have been accidental after all."

Josie really liked Dusty Blanchard. He was still very worried about his mother but he felt assured that Leo's reign of terror would be coming to an end soon. Josie had told him not to worry. The matter was being handled. They never knew who might be listening so they limited their conversation about the matter.

Dusty was sleeping soundly in his bunk that evening when he was suddenly awakened with a poke to the ribs.

"Find the order for bricks and meet me in the park near the library tomorrow at 12:00. Bring your lunch, we'll have a picnic" Dusty couldn't mistake the evil cackle of Leo Carlisle.

Dusty reported Leo's demand the following morning. Josie quickly drew up an order with false information. She knew it would be impossible to fill the order even from a disreputable company but she hoped when Leo was transferring the information to his own order forms he would not recognize the errors.

Josie was still suffering from morning sickness. Her sister had given her some medication to ease the nausea but she had left it at home this morning. Her stomach felt a little queasy but she was determined to fight it. She was sorry she had eaten so much last night but she was terribly hungry and she couldn't seem to stop herself from reaching for that second helping. She still hadn't told Reggie her news. She wanted it to be a special time for them and with the uproar with Leo and his shenanigans Reggie was still preoccupied.

There was a knock on the office door. Josie opened it to see Pamela Fuller standing there.

"Pamela, where have you been? You just disappeared and we had no idea where to find you."

"I'm sorry Miss Josie, I have been dishonest with you and you were so kind to me. I met a fellow named Leo Carlisle. I've never had a beau before and he was so very charming I'm afraid after a few kind words I developed a crush on him. He wanted me to help him with a plan to swindle your husband and take money for himself. Oh, Miss Josie, I told him I couldn't do such a thing and suddenly he turned on me. What I thought was charm became pure evil. He threatened to hurt my dear mama. I couldn't bear anything happening to her and I went along with his plan. I started working here and copied the lumber order and gave it to Leo. Leo bumped into Ernie on the street and exchanged the envelope with the bogus one. He then took the check made out to Dalton Mills and was able to cash it at the bank in Greensboro. I suspect he may have been blackmailing someone at the bank to illegally cash the checks. I felt so guilty all those times you found me crying but I couldn't tell you. I had confided in my cousin Muriel who lives in Pennsylvania. She arranged for my mother and me to board the train under false identities and come to stay with her. My mother passed away in her sleep last week. I decided to come back here and face my punishment. Now that my mother is safe with the Lord, I am no longer afraid of Mr. Leo Carlisle."

Leo had been watching Ernie Black from across the street and hadn't noticed Pamela Fuller walking into the office until it was too late to stop her.

"I should have gotten rid of the insipid woman a long time ago" he whispered to himself.

Leo practically ran to the office door, put his ear to the door and listened as Julie spoke.

"You did the right thing Pamela, I'm very sorry about your mother but we will keep you safe from Leo. You stay here while I find Reggie. We will call Sheriff Mendenhall and have Leo Carlisle arrested.

Leo backed away from the door. They weren't going to catch him. His way out of town was right here in plain sight. Josie Blackburn was a fine looking woman and his insurance policy.

Josie was walking quickly to the construction area where Reggie was talking with Ernie and a couple of the men. She felt the bile rising in her throat but had to get to Reggie before Leo got to Pamela. Suddenly she felt an arm around her waist and felt metal in her ribs. She wasn't surprised when she turned and her captor was none other than Leo Carlisle. She heard Pamela scream and Reggie shout her name. Leo was holding her tightly and was looking into her eyes when she couldn't hold back any longer. She regurgitated directly into Leo's face. He jumped back, dropped the gun and started retching himself. Leo had no qualms about killing someone in cold blood but couldn't take watching someone vomit. Especially, when it was directed at him.

The crew wrestled Leo to the ground and held him there and hosed him down while they waited for the sheriff to arrive and haul him off to jail.

Reggie held Josie closely. "You have been doing that often lately. Do you think we should get you over to Doc's so he can check you out? A stomach flu shouldn't last this long."

"It's not a stomach flu, Papa. I was waiting for a special time to tell you but I think our little baby just saved my life and I would say this is a very special time."

Reggie picked her up and swung her around until he thought better of it. Josie was looking a little green at the moment. Instead he put his arm around her and walked her back into the office where she could rest after her ordeal.

Leo confessed to Al Blanchard's murder and several other crimes insuring that he would be spending the next 99 years in prison.

Pamela was exonerated from any criminal charges and went back to

191

Pennsylvania where she met and married Arnold Swanson who charmed her in only good ways.

Dusty was welcomed with open arms upon returning to Greensboro. He became sought after whenever a new construction project began.

The New Automobile

"Are you and Hyacinth going to be staying around home today?" Harold Hightower asked Dahlia as he scooped up his infant son in one arm and his tiny daughter in the other. Harold still found it difficult to believe that these tiny little human beings were his children.

He thought he was happy as a carefree bachelor but from the moment Dahlia Bloom came into his life, he had never been the same. The day two months ago when she presented him with twins, Harry and Violet, was the happiest day of his life.

"I'm not sure, dear. We may have found someone who is interested in buying the quilt shop. Hyacinth and I just have too many responsibilities at home to worry about the shop. We are waiting to hear when the potential buyer may arrive in Camden Corners. Why do you ask Harold?"

"Oh, no reason, I would just like to spend some time with my little family. That's all."

The nanny arrived to take the babies to the nursery for their morning baths before they were ready for breakfast. Harold followed along. He couldn't get enough of his children and was in awe of every little movement they made.

Dahlia arrived in the kitchen only to find Hyacinth already there. The sisters enjoyed preparing the morning meal together. Hyacinth was just taking a pan of blueberry muffins out of the oven.

"Good morning Dahlia. I thought I'd get an early start. Howard is as nervous as a cat this morning. He was making me so nervous myself I had to come down here just to calm down."

"How odd, Harold is the same way. I wonder what those boys are up to? Harold asked me if we were planning to stay home today."

"Howard wondered if we were going into town? Now I'm getting nervous all over again."

Dahlia was preparing the eggs and ham when the fellows joined them taking dishes from the cupboard and setting the table. The Hightower men had lived by themselves for such a long time they didn't think twice about helping their wives in the kitchen.

"Hyacinth dear, Harold and I were hoping you and Dahlia would be here today to accept a delivery. I hope you weren't planning a trip into town this morning."

"What in the world is up with the two of you. I have never known either of you to act so strangely."

The boys just looked at each other and grinned. "All in good time, my love."

The morning progressed, it was always a very busy time in the Hightower household. The babies were freshly bathed, diapered and fed. Each set of twins had their own nanny. The housekeeper was busy cleaning up in the kitchen after breakfast although the sisters had always been very neat while preparing meals. Dahlia and Hyacinth were not accustomed to having chores done for them and were very thoughtful employers. Domestic workers were always happy when their services were required at the Hightower home.

Hyacinth tucked Daisy and Henry into their carriage and waited while Dahlia did the same. They enjoyed their morning walks and knew the snow would be falling very soon. Harold had already built them two sleighs for the babies' walks when the snows arrived. It was a beautiful morning. The leaves had turned to lovely yellows, oranges and reds and the sun was beaming through the branches.

Nick Rossi was already at the vineyards overlooking the grape plants. He waved to the sisters as they passed by. Lucinda was there also having taken Cassandra to school. She caught up to them and asked if she could join them on their stroll. Lucinda said hello to the babies and she was sure Daisy smiled at her.

After hearing all about the peculiar behavior of the sister's husbands, Lucinda didn't have much to say.

"You know what the big secret is, don't you?" said Hyacinth

"Oh please, Hyacinth, don't ask me. You know what a terrible liar I am. Can we talk about something else before I spoil everything?"

It was difficult for Hyacinth not to push but Dahlia calmed her sister down and repeated what Howard told her earlier. "All in good time."

"You know too! Am I the only one who doesn't know what this secret is?"

"I'm not sure but I have my suspicions. I heard the boys talking one day last week and now their conversation makes sense to me. That is all I'm saying. Let's change the subject. Lucinda what is going on in your life and how is our darling girl, Cassandra?"

"Cassandra is doing just fine. She loves school and can hardly make it through breakfast before she is dressed and waiting for me to walk with her. I know she would be fine walking alone with the other children but I feel as though I'm losing my little girl to the big old world out there. It was just the two of us for so long. Silly, isn't it?"

"Not silly at all Lucinda. Your life has changed so much over the year or so. You are bound to have some qualms about letting go." said Hyacinth.

"What you need is a new baby to occupy your time." Dahlia whispered.

The women all laughed and Lucinda was tempted to mention that she thought that time might not be too far off but she wanted to wait a bit to make sure. She hadn't told Nick about her suspicions yet because she didn't want him to be disappointed if it wasn't true.

"I almost forgot. Rosa received a wire from Mama and Papa Rossi. They are sailing from Italy as we speak. The wire was delayed and they will be here by the end of the week. Nick is so excited to see his parents again. It has been so many years. Rosa has the whole family cleaning their house from top to bottom. She says she doesn't want her mama to find a speck of dirt anywhere. I think it's nervous energy. Rosa hasn't seen her folks since she and Eduardo were married and came to the United States."

They were headed back to the house when they heard the strangest noise.

"Sounds like a sick cow." said Hyacinth.

They looked up and saw a sleek white automobile with red trim and red wheels. The man driving it was still honking it's horn. Howard and Harold came running out of the house and waved to the girls as they stood with their mouths open.

"It's beautiful" shouted Dahlia "I thought it would be a motor car but I never imagined it would look like this. There is room in it for all of us if we hold the babies on our laps."

"That terrible racket will frighten the babies" cried Hyacinth.

But she couldn't hide the smile that was beginning to form on her face.

Nick came running from the fields along with everyone else in the area.

Elmer Griffin was driving the automobile. He and Harold exchanged paperwork. Elmer handed him the keys.

"Now, you know how to drive this thing, don't you Harold?"

"Oh sure. No problem. Howard and I can handle it."

Elmer's assistant came after him in a horse and buggy. Dahlia couldn't help but wonder why they didn't drive their own automobile from Greensboro. She wondered if that was a warning sign that the horse and carriage were more reliable than this new fangled contraption.

"Harold and I flipped a coin to see who would drive it first and he won" said Howard as he and Hyacinth got in the back seat. Harold opened the passenger door for Dahlia as she sat down on the leather seat. Harold turned the key and was clueless as to how to start the car moving. He saw two pedals on the floorboard and was embarrassed that he had no idea what to do with them. He stepped on one pedal and the car lurched forward and stalled. He turned the key again, stepped on the other pedal and it made a terrible noise but didn't move.

"Harold" Dahlia whispered "This is just like our sewing machines with the two pedals one has to go down while the other is coming back up."

Harold was so embarrassed with everyone looking on he opened the door and said to the crowd.

"I'm going to let my dear wife be the first to drive the new automobile since she seems to be an expert."

"I'm sorry, Harold dear. It was just an observation, but I will give it a try."

Hyacinth was giggling in the back seat. She had never heard Harold say a harsh word to Dahlia before and knew Dahlia was keeping her temper in check too.

Dahlia slowly pressed on the left pedal then the right as she slowly lifted her left foot. The auto purred quietly. She was as surprised as anyone when the vehicle began to move forward. It didn't take long before she was traveling down the road at close to 25 miles an hour. She had no idea how she was going to turn this contraption around and get back home.

The housekeeper, Mrs. Harper was watching with the rest of the crowd as the automobile was traveling farther and farther away.

"Oh dear! Oh dear!" she cried "What will those babies do without their mothers. I've heard those horseless carriages are not safe, not safe at all."

Lucinda tried to calm Mrs. Harper. "They will be just fine. You saw how easily Miss Dahlia drove the auto. She has it under control. I'm sure of that."

Just then she heard Dahlia's normally quiet voice shout "How do you stop this thing?"

"Step on the brake!" came Hyacinth's voice as she herself pictured her babies motherless.

Dahlia found the third pedal and pushed on it with her foot.

"Gently" shouted Hyacinth a little too late.

The automobile stopped short and all three passengers lunged forward. Dahlia was pushing back on the steering wheel as she put all her might into stepping on the brake pedal.

Dahlia was shaking as she looked around to see everyone practically sitting on the floor. She began to cry and Harold, who had bumped his head but was otherwise none the worse for wear, hugged his wife. His earlier anger had disappeared.

"Harold, I don't care how you do it but turn this thing around, I want to go home."

Everyone was happy to see the automobile head back to the house. It was something special to look at but they decided maybe they should all have a few lessons before they drove the motorcar too far from home.

The Reunion

The Marino household was filled with activity as was the restaurant. For the first time since it was established the Marino Trattoria was closed for business. Eduardo and his son Eduardo, Jr. were busy scrubbing down the ovens, broiler and grill. Everyone had a job to do including the youngest who had just celebrated her 8th birthday and wanted to help. Rosa, Nick and Lucinda were washing down the walls getting them ready for a new coat of paint. The wallpaper would have to stay because there just wasn't time.

Mamma and Papa Rossi were due to arrive shortly for their first visit to the United States. Rosa hadn't seen her parents in over 18 years. Mamma and Papa had never met their grandchildren and hadn't seen their sons, Luigi and Nicola in many years.

Nick had explained to Lucinda that Papa always wanted his sons to be educated in America although Mama couldn't bear to let her children go. Papa compromised and sent three of his children to the new land and agreed to allow the three youngest to stay in Tuscany. Papa learned English and insisted that language be used at home to prepare his sons to live outside of Italy. The entire Rossi family spoke English fluently.

Finally, the restaurant was spotless. Maria and Daniella had just put a candle in the center of the last table when there was a knock on the door.

"I wonder who that is," said Rosa "Can't they see we are closed? I don't want any of those construction workers tracking mud onto my nice shiny floor."

She walked to the door and opened it with a scowl on her face.

"Surprise" shouted her brother, Luigi

Mamma and Papa were standing in the doorway. Mamma had tears streaming down her face as she folded her daughter in her arms.

"My precious Rosa, you are as beautiful as the day we sent you off on that ship"

Papa wasn't trying to hold back his tears as he wrapped his arms around his son, Nicola. Everyone was hugging and laughing and crying. Papa gave Lucinda a big bear hug and welcomed her to the family. Mamma couldn't stop the tears from flowing as she held her new daughter in her arms. She knew instinctively that her son Nicola was a happy man and that Lucinda was the reason. One by one they met the grandchildren they had never known. Even the boys had tears in their eyes although they were trying to hide it.

After a while, Papa said, "Let me get this right. Nicola is now Nick, Eduardo, Jr. is now Eddie, Antonio is called Tony. Giorgio what do they call you now?"

Giorgio replied "Giorgio"

Everyone laughed.

The bright shiny kitchen was put to use again as the ovens and grills were turned on and the food was brought out from the iceboxes. The cooking had begun and the whole family was helping or hindering the process. Eduardo didn't mind. He was happy to see his Rosa so happy.

"We didn't expect you until tomorrow. We wanted to meet you at the train station." said Rosa

"That was my fault," Papa said

"Papa doesn't hear so well anymore" Mamma whispered.

"I thought they told me the 10th but they must have said the 9th. Anyway, a nice lady helped us call Luigi on a telephone and he came down to meet us. Why don't you get a telephone Eduardo? Then I could talk to my daughter."

"We hope to get some wires here in Camden Corners someday soon, Papa. Can't use a telephone unless we can get connected through wires."

"Where is my newest granddaughter, Cassandra? Daniella and Maria have written about her so often in their letters, I must meet her." said Mamma.

"She is playing with her friend Iris Taylor. I'll go get her now. As much as she wanted to help prepare for her new Mamma and Papa's arrival, we thought it might be best if she were otherwise occupied." Replied Lucinda as she donned her hat and coat.

A while later, Cassandra walked through the doors with a big smile on her face. She walked over to her new grandparents and gave Mamma a hug.

She looked at Papa with his white beard and said, "You look just like Mr. Pringle."

Nick laughed. "Old Chris will have some competition playing Santa Claus this year."

"La mia bellissima bambina," said Mamma through her tears

"I'm not a baby," replied Cassandra. "I'm 6 years old, I'm a big girl."

"No, you are not a baby Cassandra but you are beautiful and you and your Mama have made my bambino, Nick a very happy man."

Cassandra giggled. "My new Papa Nick isn't a baby either. Did you know my Mama is going to have a bambino?"

Silence fell over the room and everyone, even the youngest looked at Lucinda. Nick's mouth was open but he couldn't speak.

Lucinda's face turned scarlet as she realized her daughter had heard her talking with Diana Taylor a few minutes ago. She had voiced her suspicions to her.

Lucinda looked at Nick and said. "I wanted to wait another few days to be sure but I think I might be carrying our child. Somehow I didn't think I would have an audience when I told you." She looked at her innocent little daughter and couldn't help but smile.

Nick pulled up a chair and insisted Lucinda sit down and rest.

"Oh for heaven sake, Nick. I'm perfectly fine. Now give me a hug and tell me how happy you are."

Nick hugged her tightly.

The party went on until the children and the elder Rossi's were exhausted. Lucinda stayed to help Rosa with the last of the cleanup. Nick, Luigi and Eduardo were having a final glass of wine while the women were in the kitchen.

"Nick, do you see much of the Mackenzie's?" asked Luigi.

"Some of them. Anyone in particular?" replied Nick as he and Eduardo exchanged knowing winks.

"You got me. I was wondering if Amanda ever visited from New York City. The last I heard she was engaged to some high society guy."

"Couldn't tell you what happened there but I do know she's been living here in Camden Corners for several months. I saw her just yesterday. She was helping Maddie at the candy shop."

"Wonder if Mamma would like a nice box of chocolates? Maybe I'll stop by there tomorrow and see what kind of sweet treats I can find."

The men all laughed.

Mamma and Papa slept well after their long trip but were up very early the next morning. Rosa and Eduardo were already in the kitchen preparing breakfast for the family.

"Eduardo, do you know of any houses in the neighborhood that are for sale? Something suitable for Mamma and me?"

Rosa wouldn't let Eduardo answer the question. She piped in "Houses for sale? Why on earth would you want to buy a house in Camden Corners?"

"I sold the winery and all the Rossi land. I'm getting too old to manage it and none of my boys wanted it so I sold it."

Rosa couldn't believe her ears. "Papa, that land has been in the Rossi family for generations. How could you have sold it?"

"Daughter, no one wanted it. None of your brothers except maybe Nicola and his life is here in America now. Come Eduardo, come take a walk with your father-in-law."

"Mamma, tell me what happened. I can't believe Papa sold his land." Rosa asked when the men left.

"Do you remember Salvatore Russo? He had the plantation adjoining your papa's land. They were the best of friends and the best of rivals. Through the years they fought about anything and everything. It was a strange relationship but it made them both happy. They had grown up together and their fathers had been friends and rivals before them. The day I met your papa, Sal was with him. Sal and Maria were like family. Sal and Maria had one boy and five girls so they had it all planned that each of Sal's children would marry one of papa's children."

Rosa shivered thinking of marrying Sal, Jr. He may have become a halfway decent man but she remembered the adolescent who liked to eat bugs and yank her pigtails.

Mama continued her story with tears in her eyes. "Sal and your papa were walking the vineyards one day last spring when Sal collapsed. The doctor said he had a heart attack and died out there in the hot sun. Your Papa lost his dearest friend. Papa changed after that. He was so sad and so lost without Sal I was beginning to worry that I would lose him too. Sal's son took over running the vineyard and tried to help out your papa too. Then one day, Papa came down for breakfast and asked how I would like to visit my Rosa and her family. Of course I said yes. We had never been away from the vineyard in our entire married life. The next thing I knew he invited Sal's boy over for a cup of coffee and asked if he would like to buy him out. The house and all. He jumped at the chance and here we are."

"Mamma, I had no idea. I'm so sorry you lost your home."

"Rosa dear, it was just a house. It wasn't even much of a home anymore. You and your brothers hadn't lived there in so long. Roberto, Marco and Dino all left the valley and have good lives. You all have made wonderful lives for yourselves without the land and the grapes. It was time to move on. Anything that was important to me is traveling by ship to America. Papa wants us to live our final days close to you and your two brothers. I hope you will be happy to have us here with you."

"Oh Mamma, I couldn't be happier. I have missed you so through the years. I know we have written but it hasn't been the same having my sweet Mamma right here holding my hand."

Eduardo remembered the Schmidt house on the corner of Oak and Vine. He and Papa walked to the house. It was only a block away from the Trattoria. Eduardo was happy that the Rossi's were planning to stay in America. His parents had passed on several years ago and Eduardo always had great affection for his in-laws. He knew it would make Rosa happy too.

"Ah yes," said Papa when he saw the house, "I think my Anna will like her new home."

Eduardo and Papa walked further down Vine and turned back to Main Street. The shops were just beginning to open. Chris Pringle with his dog Rudy was sweeping the walk in front of his Christmas shop.

Papa noticed the beard right away and the resemblance to the American Santa Claus. "How do you do, Mr. Pringle?" I am Lou Rossi, Rosa Marino's papa. My new granddaughter Cassandra Rossi tells me I look just like you."

Both men laughed in such a ho ho ho way that Eduardo thought for a moment that he was at the North Pole.

"So your name is Lou? I always thought it was Luigi like your son."

"Yes, but I decided to Americanize it like my son and grandsons did to theirs. I rather like the name Lou, don't you Eduardo?"

"Yes, Lou. It's a very nice name."

The Best of Friends

Luigi Rossi woke up with a start. The sun was shining brightly through the window of the room he'd slept in when he was growing up and living with his sister and her family. He didn't remember when he'd had a more restful night. Probably when I was living here, he thought to himself. He could hear muffled voices coming from the kitchen. He splashed water on his face, brushed his teeth and walked down the hallway stopping at the doorway.

He looked around the room. There was Eddie. He was the spitting image of his father in looks and actions. He was a very serious young man and extremely kind and caring. Tony was the curious one. He had taken to the camera Luigi had given to him when he first began working at Weston Camera Company. Tony was a natural photographer even at his very young age. His photographs helped catch a con artist last winter. Luigi loved telling that story to his coworkers. Giorgio followed Tony every where he went. He was the chatterbox of the family. The girls, Daniella and Maria looked like his sister Rosa with their long dark hair and sparkling blue eyes. What beauties they were already.

His brother, Nick was sitting at the table with his new bride, Lucinda and their daughter Cassandra. Luigi was happy Nick and Lucinda had found each other. They were a perfect match. He had adopted Cassandra shortly after the marriage and she even looked a little like the Marino family. Luigi found himself envying his younger brother. He was so busy working and securing his future with Weston's he hadn't had time for any kind of a meaningful relationship. There was never a shortage of young women and he'd been involved with a number of them but none that he could picture sitting at the Marino family table.

He thought Mamma looked wonderful. Much younger than her age although she wasn't old by any means. Papa on the other hand had a sadness about him. Mamma told him about the loss of his good friend, Mr. Russo and how he had given up the land that had been in the family for years. He winced when he thought about the fact that none of his sons were interested in taking over the land. Nick loved working with grapes but his life was here in Camden Corners. Luigi couldn't imagine his brother living anywhere else.

"Luigi, what are you standing there for? Come have some breakfast," his sister said when she noticed him in the doorway.

Rosa worried about Luigi. She had been more of a mother to her two brothers than a sister. They were both quite young when they arrived in the United States. She had seen to it that they attended school and church, did their homework, and behaved themselves at all times. Luigi was a natural scholar, he never had a failing grade and graduated at the top of his class. Nick, on the other hand struggled to get through his final exams. If it hadn't been for Rosa working with him every night he probably wouldn't have graduated. He was never interested in learning unless it had to do with grapes. He wasn't unintelligent, he just didn't like to learn what they were teaching in school. He always did well in mathematics and science, but wasn't interested in history and related subjects. Nick was happy in his life. He was doing what he had always wanted to do and he had Lucinda and Cassandra right there beside him. If what Lucinda thought was true, they would be having a little brother or sister for Cassandra one of these days. Eduardo mentioned last night that Luigi was asking about Amanda Mackenzie. Rosa thought to herself, those two were such a nice couple in high school. I wonder if Amanda is busy today?

"Sorry Rosa, I was just admiring my family. What a handsome group of folks we are." Everyone laughed but Mamma agreed with him and smiled.

"Luigi, come sit by me," said Mamma. Your sister was telling me about a fine young girl you were friends with in high school. I do remember you writing about a girl named Amanda. I thought it was such a pretty name. Daniella tells me she is back in town after a broken engagement. Do you think she may still be interested in you?"

"Mamma, it was a high school crush. So much has happened in both our lives since then. We aren't the same people anymore. Besides, I'm sure she doesn't even remember me."

"That's not true, Uncle Luigi," Daniella said. "Why just last week Amanda asked me how you were doing and if you were courting anyone. She smiled when I told her I didn't think so."

"That settles it Luigi," said Rosa. "You march yourself down to the Mackenzie house as soon as you finish your eggs. You and Amanda have wasted enough time. Now don't be stubborn."

Luigi laughed at the women in his family who would like nothing better than to marry him off. He had to be honest with himself. He wouldn't mind that one bit. After breakfast Eduardo covered for him while he slipped out the back door. He remembered the way to the Mackenzie's house without even thinking about it. He had made the walk so many times. Amanda was his first love and if he were honest, his only love. He would have to find out more about this engagement of hers. Maybe she was pining away for the guy.

As he tapped on the door knocker he hoped he wouldn't embarrass himself. Just then the door was thrown open and a very angry looking fellow was leaving the house. He recognized Amanda as she followed him to the front walk and told him to calm down before he drove away in the horse and carriage that was waiting for him.

"He is going to kill himself," an exasperated Amanda said to no one in particular. She turned around and saw Luigi standing before her.

"Luigi, I can't believe it's you. When did you get into town? How long will you be here? Oh Luigi you are certainly a sight for sore eyes. Come inside, please." She took hold of his arm and guided him through the door.

"I don't want to bother you Amanda. It looks like you were involved in something and I interrupted you."

"Don't be silly. That was Nathaniel Lancaster, III. We were engaged for about 30 seconds and now he thinks he can win my heart with his shenanigans. I hope that is the last I see of him."

"You must have some feeling for him if you accepted his proposal of marriage."

"It's a long story but I know how honorable you are so I will tell you. I'm ashamed to say that I was mesmerized by his charm and good looks. Nathaniel's grandfather, Nathaniel Lancaster, I is the founder of Lancaster Trust."

Luigi was very familiar with Lancaster Trust and knew how influential the family was all along the eastern seaboard.

"I met Nathaniel at the wedding reception of a mutual friend in New York City when I was living there. As I said before, he was charming and I developed a crush on him almost immediately. We courted for about three months before he asked me to be his wife. I imagined my life would be filled with magic being married to a man of such wealth and influence. My friends all tried to dissuade me from even considering the marriage proposal but I was determined.

Our lives were a constant flurry of parties and activities that I had never experienced before. I didn't realize at the time but his friends were cold and indifferent to me. When we dined with his parents, which was often, his father tolerated my being with Nathaniel and was pleasant but his mother would peer over the top of her spectacles with disapproving looks. Still, I went along with it and hardly noticed. I had begged

Nathaniel to accompany me home to Camden Corners to meet my family. He finally agreed and we arrived on the train one afternoon. You know what a big boisterous family we have. I think the moment I walked through the door I knew the visit was not going to go well.

Papa began quizzing Nathaniel about how he made his living and how he planned to support me. Nathaniel had never been asked questions like that before and told Papa in no uncertain terms that it was none of his business. Of course, Papa believed it was his business and refused to approve the marriage. Mama managed to calm Papa down enough to sit at the dinner table with the rest of the family. Mama had prepared her famous pot roast and gravy. Nathaniel was unaccustomed to that type of food and could not force himself to even taste the meal. That, of course, made Papa even angrier. That was just about the time I looked at Nathaniel and whatever charm I thought he had totally disappeared. I don't know why I thought a marriage between us would work. The man had absolutely no ambition and was willing to live off his family's money for the rest of his days.

Nathaniel left that evening insisting I go back to New York with him. I knew I couldn't possibly marry him and told him I was breaking off our engagement. I handed him the ring he had given to me and had such a sense of relief.

I stayed with my family for a few more days then returned to New York. I realized I had lost my perspective. I was living the kind of life I had read about in novels and that was not the way I wanted it. I gave my notice at work and came back to Camden Corners to see if I could discover myself again.

Nathaniel is unaccustomed to not getting his way. He hasn't told any of his friends or his family that we are no longer together. He has been dropping by every week or so trying to convince me to go back to New York with him. Every time he comes it is obvious he has been drinking all the the way from New York.

So there you have it. My story and not a pretty one. I'm very ashamed that I fell for such a shallow man."

What Amanda didn't tell him is that she made a trip to Wilmington just before she became involved with Nathaniel. She had never gotten over her feelings for her high school sweetheart and Rosa had told her Luigi was not involved with anyone. She had the address of Luigi's apartment and as she was walking toward the entrance she saw him with a tall gorgeous blond. They were laughing as he opened the door for her and they disappeared into the building. She felt like a fool and high tailed it back to New York. If she had followed Luigi into the building she would have seen Luigi and the blond part at her apartment door where she was greeted by her husband who happened to be Luigi's best friend and Luigi walking by himself into his lonely living quarters.

"I'm happy you aren't marrying that fellow because now I can ask you to come to Rosa's tonight for dinner. My Mamma and papa are here from Tuscany and I'd love to introduce you to them."

"Oh Luigi, I'm so happy for Rosa. I know how much she has wanted your folks to visit for all these years. I would love to meet them."

"I'll pick you up at 5:00, that will give them plenty of time to look you over. Seems my nieces have given Mamma ideas about you and me. The whole family would like to see me married off so ignore them when they start in on you. We are still the best of friends, I hope."

"The best of friends." Amanda replied trying to keep her disappointment in check. She didn't want Luigi to know she wanted much more than friendship with him.

Without thinking, Luigi wrapped his arms around her kissing her as friends rarely do. He smiled as he walked back toward the restaurant to let Mamma and Rosa know he had invited a friend for dinner. A very special friend.

Mack Mackenzie was pouring coffee for a customer after refusing him another drink due to his obvious inebriation when Nick walked in with a white haired gentleman. Mack guessed immediately that this was the senior Luigi Rossi. The men shook hands

"Call me Lou." said the older gentleman. "I'm in America now."

"Luigi is in Camden Corners too. He is visiting your sister, Amanda as we speak. I don't think he has ever gotten over his feelings for her." said Nick

"I could have told you Amanda feels the same way. She was engaged to some rich guy from New York. That didn't last long. The poor sap had no idea that Luigi has been the only one for her ever since fifth grade."

Nathaniel Lancaster, III was hovering in the corner adding whiskey from the flask he carried in his pocket to the strong coffee the bartender was forcing on him. He was seething. He remembered seeing some chap standing near the door of the Mackenzie house when Amanda told him to get out. No wonder she broke off the engagement. She is involved with that guy. We'll see about that he said as he slithered out the front door and climbed unsteadily on his rented carriage and headed back down the road to have a little talk with Miss Amanda Mackenzie. He felt for the revolver he carried in his pocket.

"We'll just see about that!" he shouted

Kidnapped

Amanda was anxious for the afternoon to pass when it would be time for Luigi to come to pick her up for dinner at Rosa's. She wondered where everyone was. It was rare that the Mackenzie house was quiet with such a big family. She knew Mama was probably at the Burke house baking cookies. She and her good friend Nadine Burke enjoyed baking together. Between them they had so many mouths to feed that it took several batches of cookies just to make sure each child had their fair share. It gave the friends time to chat and enjoy each others company. The younger children were all in school and the older ones were most likely helping out at the Pub.

There was a knock at the door. Amanda opened it thinking it might be Luigi since he had left just a short while ago after giving her a kiss that made even her toes tingle. She opened the door and there stood Nathaniel Lancaster, III looking like a wild man.

"Nathaniel, what in heaven's name are you doing back here? We have said all there is to say between us. It's over, go back home."

"Amanda, you and I are betrothed. Nobody leaves Nathaniel Lancaster, III. I have come to take you to New York with me where we will be married and live happily ever after. Now pack your bag and come with me."

"Nathaniel, I am not going anywhere with you. Leave now or I will call the sheriff. I should have done that a long time ago."

"I know why you left me Amanda. That guy Luigi stole you from me. What kind of a name is Luigi anyway. Sounds like a waiter at The Ritz."

"And just what is wrong with being a waiter? My family runs a pub if you have forgotten. Not that it's any of your business, Luigi is an engineer and he is my friend. For the last time, get out."

It was at that moment that Nathaniel started waving his gun in the air. Amanda wasn't afraid of Nathaniel but she was afraid the fool would pull the trigger in his drunken state and shoot her or himself.

"Do as I told you. Go pack a bag. We are leaving."

Amanda started up the stairs trying to figure out what she should do. She knew she had to get Nathaniel out of the house before the children came home from school. Nathaniel followed her to her room. She grabbed a bag and threw one or two items in it trying to make it look like she was following his directions. She opened the top drawer of her dresser and saw her collection of hankies neatly folded in there. Ever since Amanda was a very young girl she had loved pretty hankies. Every birthday and Christmas she would receive a new one with lace or her initial or a flower design on it. She had kept these hankies all through the years. She grabbed a handful of them and stuffed them into the pocket of her skirt without Nathaniel noticing.

"Nathaniel, I'll have to leave a note for my mama and papa. They will come looking for me if I just disappear without telling them."

"Alright, but no funny business. Make sure you tell them how much you love me."

Amanda sat down at her desk and pulled out a sheet of paper and a pen. She slowly filled the pen with ink as she thought about what she would write. She knew they would read her message carefully.

> *Hope you will understand , Nathaniel and I are*
> *Eloping. I realized that I have always and will always*
> *Love him because he makes me happy.*
> *Please forgive me for leaving this way.*

Amanda hoped Nathaniel wouldn't see her obvious hint in the note. She needn't have worried, Nathaniel wasn't able to focus on anything. She took hold of her bag and led the way down the stairs and into the carriage. She could feel the barrel of the gun pressing into her back as she walked. She reached into her pocket and pulled out a hankie. She pretended to wipe her face with it and casually let it drop to the ground. Nathaniel told her to drive the carriage and she was happy for that since she wasn't sure he would be able to keep the horses on the road. They traveled through town and she could feel him pressing the gun a little harder as they rode by several of her friends who were waving and calling her name. She dropped hankies all along the way praying that Nathaniel wouldn't notice. A few miles out of town they came upon an abandoned cabin and barn.

"Nathaniel, maybe we should stop here and let the horses rest before continuing our journey. We have been traveling quite a way, you know."

They hadn't gone all that far but Amanda took a chance that in Nathaniel's state he wouldn't be aware of how much time had passed since they left her house.

At the Mackenzie house, Fiona returned with a basketful of cookies just as the children were returning from school. There was a knock on the door and there stood Luigi Rossi. Fiona gave the young man a hug. Luigi was always one of her favorites. She had hoped he and Amanda would find their way back to each other one day and was thrilled to see him standing in their doorway.

"Luigi, I'm so happy to see you. Rosa was bubbling the other day when she talked about you and your folks coming for a visit. How are they? I'm so anxious to meet them."

"The folks are fine. The big surprise for Rosa and the family is that Papa sold his property in Tuscany and it looks like they are here in this country to stay. I'm here to escort Amanda to Rosa's for a family dinner. I'm early so if she isn't ready I can come back."

"I didn't know Amanda was home. It was so quiet when I came into the house a little while ago. Let me go up and check her room."

Two minutes later Fiona came running down the stairs.

"He's taken her. He's taken Amanda" she cried

Luigi read the note and could see the word HELP spelled out.

"Don't worry Mrs. Mackenzie. We will find her."

Luigi called the children and told them to run for the sheriff and stop by the pub to get their father and Mac. He ran to the stable behind the Mackenzie house and mounted one of the horses without stopping long enough to put a saddle on it.

"Luigi," called Fiona. "Amanda has dropped her handkerchiefs along the way, she must have taken a handful with her. She is leaving a trail to follow."

Luigi could see the trail as he rode out of town.

The children scattered in their quest to alert the sheriff, their father and brother. Within just a short while all the men in Camden Corners were following the dropped handkerchiefs out of town. Nathaniel Lancaster, III didn't stand a chance.

Meanwhile, Nathaniel was sprawled on the couch dozing off. He'd tied Amanda up before he closed his eyes just in case she changed her mind about leaving with him. He just needed a tiny little nap and then they would be on their way. The gun was still in his hand and pointed in Amanda's direction. Amanda was loosening the ropes around her wrists. Because of his state of inebriation he hadn't noticed that the knots weren't tied tightly.

Luigi reached the cabin and saw the horses and carriage parked outside the door. He quietly dismounted the horse and went to the cabin window. He could see Amanda struggling to loosen the ropes tied around her wrists. He also saw the gun pointed at her with the sleeping Nathaniel still holding it. He was afraid if Nathaniel were startled, he might instinctively pull the trigger. He tried the door and luckily it had been left open. He quietly opened it and walked slowly toward Amanda. He could see the relief in her eyes as she gazed at him. He bent down and very carefully picked her up in his arms and carried her toward the door. Just as they reached the doorway, they heard Nathaniel shout.

"Hold it right there. Where do you think you are taking my wife?"

A gunshot rang out and a bullet shattered the glass in the window to the right of the door. The sound startled Nathaniel he dropped the gun as he passed out on the floor of the cabin.

The sheriff and most of the town arrived as Luigi was carrying Amanda to safety and gently removing the ropes from her wrists and ankles.

"I thought we had a date today and here you are playing cops and robbers with your old flame."

Sheriff Mendenhall loaded Nathaniel into his buckboard and drove him to the jailhouse.

"Amanda, you go home and rest tonight. I'm sure your friend here will be sleeping it off through the night. Come back in the morning and I'll get your statement."

"Thanks sheriff, I'm really fine and I have a dinner date with my good friend Luigi and his family."

Mamma and Papa Rossi were just exactly as Amanda had pictured them all these years. Mamma gave her a welcoming hug and Papa his usual bear hug that meant he approved of Luigi's choice.

The Marino youngsters sat by Amanda's side wanting to know every detail of the kidnapping. They were impressed when Luigi told them about the note with the word **HELP** spelled out and how she had dropped her hankies all the way to the cabin where she was being held. Luigi added a bit more drama to the story and his nieces and nephews hung on every word.

"That's enough of that talk." said Rosa. "Let's eat our dinner and talk about something pleasant." She squeezed Amanda's hand as Eduardo said the blessing with a special mention of Amanda and her safe return.

After a delightful dinner and and evening of playing board games, Luigi thought it best to get Amanda home. They walked hand in hand to her house where he stopped suddenly.

"Amanda, I still love you. I always have. Today, when you were in danger I didn't know what I would do if something happened to you. I know we said we would just be friends but I don't think that is possible. Mr. Weston has been talking about starting up a branch of his factory in this area. Just being with you and my family these last couple of days has made me realize that although work is important, it isn't the only thing in life. Tell me, do I have a chance with you?"

"Luigi, I do have feelings for you but it wasn't that long ago that I saw you entering your apartment in Wilmington with a beautiful blond woman. Is she still a part of your life?"

Luigi stared at her, he had no idea what she was talking about, She explained that she had gone to Wilmington to see him after Rosa mentioned he wasn't involved with anyone.

Luigi began to chuckle. "It must have been Pamela Farrell, she is the wife of my friend Leo Farrell. You remember Leo. He and his family moved to Wilmington 15 years ago or more. He did marry a very attractive blond. They live in the apartment across the hall from me. She works at Lawson's Department store and occasionally we run into each other on the way home. Believe me, she and Leo only have eyes for each other which is a good thing since she is expecting their first child any day now."

"Oh Luigi, I have been so silly. I was so unhappy when I saw you with another woman I returned to New York and that is when I met Nathaniel. If only I had spoken to you I could have saved myself a lot of heartache and also saved myself from Nathaniel."

"Let's not waste any more time." said Luigi as he held her close and kissed her again and again.

A Fresh Start for Nathaniel

Amanda woke up feeling a bit sore from her ordeal with Nathaniel the day before. In her mind she was reliving the afternoon and could still feel Nathaniel's gun being pressed into her ribs. She couldn't imagine what had attracted her to Nathaniel in the first place although she knew she was under the impression that Luigi was involved with someone else. She had loved him since they were children and her dreams were shattered the day she saw him with a beautiful blond. Luigi was merely opening the door for his friend and neighbor's wife.

Amanda promised Sheriff Mendenhall that she would be at the jailhouse first thing this morning to give her statement regarding the happenings yesterday. She wasn't looking forward to seeing Nathaniel again. She wanted to put the incident out of her mind and concentrate on Luigi and his confession of love for her.

"Amanda dear," her mother called as she tapped on her door. "There is a gentleman here to see you. He says his name is Nathaniel Lancaster and he's Nathaniel's grandfather."

"I'll be down as soon as I can Mama."

Amanda jumped out of bed and splashed water on her face to wake herself up. She had never met Nathaniel's grandfather. She had heard of him, of course. He was a very powerful man in New York. She had heard the stories of how he had built a fortune from practically nothing and had influence throughout the state. Whenever Nathaniel spoke of his grandfather he actually trembled. Amanda wasn't intimidated easily. She dressed quickly and walked down the stairs to greet her visitor.

The older gentleman took her hand and apologized for the ordeal his grandson had put her through. Unable to locate Nathaniel's parents, Sheriff Mendenhall had notified the elder Mr. Lancaster of his grandson's troubles.

"Miss Mackenzie, I realize my grandson put you in an enormous amount of danger with his antics yesterday. I'm not making excuses for him but I'd like you to know the difficult life he has lead. I am what they call a self made man. My father was a preacher in a small town similar to Camden Corners. My mother gave birth to twelve children. I was the oldest of the clan. There was love in my house but not much money. I found myself being envious of the folks who lived on the other side of the tracks and at a young age decided I would do anything to become rich. I won't go into the details of how I started out making money but suffice it to say, I'm not terribly proud of the way I did it. I married a woman I did not love only because her father was wealthy. She gave birth to my only child, Nathaniel's father. I didn't have time for Nathaniel, Jr. I was too busy making more money than I would ever be able to spend. His mother had always been a very spoiled woman who craved any luxury money could buy and she raised our son to be the same way. He married a woman just like his mother and Nathaniel was their only child.

I have had little to do with my son or grandson since little Nate was a toddler. For the first few years of our estrangement, I'm ashamed to say I didn't notice they were not in my life. Nathaniel only came to see me when he was in need of money. Being indifferent had become my way of life I made sure the family had all the money they needed to live their empty shallow lives.

The sheriff contacted my office last evening when he could not locate Nathaniel's parents. My first inclination was to send money to you in the form of a bribe. I am a very influential man and if I want information in the wee hours of the morning I don't have any trouble hiring people to find that information

"Miss Mackenzie, you and your family and even your hometown have turned out to be a breath of fresh air. My grandson was very fortunate to have you in his life and was stupid enough to let you slip away. I'm going to ask you to drop the charges against him. I'm afraid his father is a lost cause but I do believe I can make a difference in young Nate's life. I'd like to believe it's never too late to change and I'd like the opportunity to transform myself into a grandfather worthy of the title."

Amanda sat back in her chair. She understood why this man had made millions. He certainly was a genius when it came to the power of persuasion. She knew Nathaniel hadn't intentionally put her in danger. He wasn't an evil person, just a misguided one. She had met his parents and knew them to be cold and unfeeling. She began to feel sorry for Nathaniel. Maybe his grandfather could make him a different person.

"Mr. Lancaster, I do hope you are being sincere with me. I will consider what you have told me and let you know my decision. First, I shall have my breakfast and then visit Nathaniel in the jailhouse. Won't you please share breakfast with my family this morning? My mother is a wonderful cook and I do believe I smell her blueberry muffins baking in the oven."

Nathaniel, Sr. hadn't had a blueberry muffin since he was a lad and found himself accepting the invitation. As he was sitting at the table of this happy and loving family, he was discovering his investigators were worth the money he was paying them. He also found himself wondering if maybe there was hope for the relationship between his grandson and this lovely young girl. His question was answered when there was a knock on the door and he was introduced to Luigi Rossi. There was no mistaking the look of love on the faces of Amanda and Luigi as they greeted each other.

The younger Nathaniel was awakening with a terrible headache. Slowly the memory of yesterday was coming back to him. He had behaved poorly in his life but yesterday takes the cake. He was so ashamed. He realized he was sitting in a jail cell and would be there for many years to come. He had held a gun on Amanda and kidnapped her. He could have killed her. He deserved everything that was about to happen to him. Just then he looked up and saw Amanda on the other side of the bars.

"Good morning Nathaniel."

"Amanda, I am so sorry. Are you alright, I hope I didn't hurt you. I'm so sorry."

"No, I'm not hurt. How is your head this morning?"

"Not good but it's keeping me from remembering what a darn fool I made of myself."

"I can't disagree with that. Nathaniel, your grandfather came to see me. He would like me to drop the charges against you. How do you feel about that?"

"My grandfather is here? I haven't seen him in years. I can't believe that old man wants you to drop the charges. He must be worried about his flesh and blood ending up in jail. Amanda, you have every right to press charges against me. I put your life in danger and I deserve to be punished for that. If anything had happened to you I would never have forgiven myself. Tell the old goat to go back to his mansion and forget about me. I will plead guilty and any publicity will be short lived."

"Nathaniel, your grandfather seems to think he can make a difference in your life. He has been estranged from your family for many years. I can't imagine what it was like for you growing up without family around. There were times when I was a young girl when I fantasized about being an only child. There were always so many of us and we were usually surrounded by Burkes too. I think that is the reason I escaped to New York City. It's a long story Nathaniel but I have to admit I took advantage of you. I loved a boy for as long as I could remember but thought he was lost to me. That was just before you came into my life and I convinced myself I wanted the life you could give me. I did not treat you kindly and I'm sorry about that. What you did yesterday was wrong. I know you are aware of that and I'm sure the whiskey had as much to do with it as anything. You haven't asked for my opinion but you know I will give it to you anyway. I think you should give your grandfather a chance. Unless he has me completely fooled, I do believe he is being sincere. I could see the love in his eyes as he spoke of you. I will not be pressing charges against you. I will tell Sheriff Mendenhall that it was all a misunderstanding because I believe you have learned a lesson. Shall I ask your grandfather to step in while I go to speak with the sheriff?"

Nathaniel and his grandfather embraced as the older gentleman entered the cell.

"Grandfather, I made a spectacle of myself and endangered someone who didn't deserve that treatment. I am sorry for the embarrassment I caused you."

"I can't disagree with you son. What you did was foolish. You are not the only one to blame for your behavior though. It started many years ago with me and my indifference to your father and then you. I had the foolish idea that money was the only way to happiness but looking back I realize I haven't been a happy man since before I started gazing across the railroad tracks when I was 12 years old. I would like you to indulge an old man and come to live with me and help run my business."

Sheriff Mendenhall rounded the corner.

"You are free to go young man. I hope you realize how fortunate you are to have a friend like Amanda Mackenzie. You could have been locked up for a number of years."

The two Lancasters walked out of the jailhouse into the fresh crisp autumn afternoon. Amanda and Luigi were waiting on the steps. The men shook hands and Amanda hugged them.

"I want to hear from you. I have a good feeling that you have begun a relationship that will bring happiness to you both."

"Thank you for the second chance Amanda." said Nathaniel. "I won't make a mess of it, I promise."

"And I'll see to it that he doesn't" The senior Nathaniel replied with a wink.

Through the years Amanda did hear from both gentleman. Nathaniel started in the mail room of Lancaster Industries the very next morning. He was determined to make his grandfather proud and he did. He worked in almost every department in the company getting to know people from all walks of life. He met Betty Turner in the purchasing department and fell truly in love for the first time in his life. Betty reminded Grandfather of Amanda and he thoroughly approved. Betty and Nate, as he was known after that fateful day, made Nathaniel a great grandfather five times over and named their oldest daughter Amanda. There was never a lack of attention for the children in the Lancaster household. Nate's mother and father tolerated his new life but couldn't imagine why a son of theirs would want to work for a living. Nate never allowed his work to interfere with his family life. It was difficult for his grandfather to learn to relax and enjoy his great grandchildren but he did get the hang of it and they all loved him.

Luigi and Amanda announced their intentions to marry before Thanksgiving. Luigi would be returning to Wilmington but hoped it wouldn't be long before he would be back in Camden Corners permanently. Everyone was happy about the upcoming marriage and that Luigi and Amanda would be living in Camden Corners.

Mr. Weston was pleased that his favorite employee had found happiness with his longtime sweetheart. He knew Luigi was lonely for his family and his home. For some time he intended to open a branch of his camera business in another location and the small community of Camden

Corners would do just fine. He purchased a parcel of land just east of Camden Corners and construction began on the new facility. Luigi and Amanda were married one week before Thanksgiving. With the Rossi, Mackenzie and Burke clans all together plus practically everyone in town attending, there was standing room only in the small chapel of the hills.

Camden Corners Chronicle

Thanksgiving Day was a joyful time for all the residents of Camden Corners. Families enjoyed each others company while preparing and feasting on their turkey dinners with all the trimmings.

Cody Hill was taking advantage of his time off from the university and spending every moment possible with April Hawthorne. Cody had been blessed the day Professor Tanner became his benefactor and rescued him from the mountain life. The professor could see Cody was an intelligent young lad and was able to catch up to the other students in record time. The other children laughed at his hillbilly ways but Cody quickly fit in and because of his winning personality became one of the more popular students in his class. Cody met April Hawthorne shortly after his arrival in Camden Corners and they had been sweethearts ever since. April would be following Cody to the University the following September to study nursing.

Cody never forgot his beginnings or the hardships he and his extended family endured in the mountains. He would forever be grateful to the professor for rescuing him from that life. He thought about taking some food to the mountains but he knew it wouldn't be practical or welcomed. April suggested that they would be able to find needy families closer to home. She knew the town of Brenton had been hit with several hail storms over the summer. She had heard that those folks had their crops almost totally wiped out.

"Cody, Brenton is only about an hour away. Maybe we could arrange a group of our friends to help them out. It wouldn't take too long to get there if we left in the morning and we would all be home in time to celebrate with our own families."

Cody thought that was a wonderful idea. In the next couple of days the twosome gathered their friends together to make a plan. The parents were so proud of their children for thinking of others and all contributed to the meals. The day before Thanksgiving was a busy time in Camden Corners. All the ovens were roasting turkeys, potatoes, corn and squash and baking an extra pie or two. Thanksgiving morning all the children, young and old were wrapping and boxing Thanksgiving dinners and placing them in buckboards and carriages.

The senior citizens who weren't preparing their own feasts that day were invited to join the group and proudly rode along with the young people. Anna and Lou Rossi had never celebrated the American Thanksgiving before and were enjoying being with their grandchildren on the trip to Brenton. Sheriff Mendenhall had alerted the sheriff of Brenton that Thanksgiving would be coming to town. The townspeople were filled with anticipation as the many carriages and buckboards rolled in bringing everything from soup to nuts. There wasn't an empty plate in Brenton that Thanksgiving Day and there wasn't an empty heart in all of Camden Corners.

Josie Blackburn, whose morning sickness had disappeared by late November, was able to enjoy her own Thanksgiving dinner that day. Although she and her sister didn't have any children going to Brenton, she thought it was a wonderful idea. That evening, Josie sat down and wrote an article about the generosity of the Camden Corners young people and about Cody and April who had the idea in the first place. She mailed it to the Greensboro News. She hadn't expected it would be on the front page of the paper but when she received her copy a few days later, she was aggravated to see only a very small portion of her article was squeezed between an ad for tooth powder and an announcement of a lost dog being returned to its owner.

"Reggie, Camden Corners needs its own newspaper"

"I think you are right my dear and if anyone can pull that off it's you."

"Emma Crowley worked for the newspaper when she lived in Greensboro. I'm going to talk to her about it this morning."

After breakfast she walked to Looking Back Antique Shop to see Emma.

"Josie, I think that is a wonderful idea. I did work for the paper but I only secured ads. Mr. Wilson didn't believe a woman was capable of anything more important than that. As a matter of fact I purchased an old printing press a year or so ago. I have been meaning to ask Randy Burke to take a look at it. Randy works often with Jonas on restoration and he does have a knack for fixing anything mechanical. Let's go take a look."

The women walked to the storage building just behind the shop. The building was filled with treasures found at flea markets and auctions. Because everything was so well organized, Emma was able to walk right to the printing press. It was much larger than Josie anticipated.

"I'm not sure where I would find room to put it." she said. "I didn't think about space and I will be operating on a shoestring. It did seem like a good idea but maybe I'd better rethink my plan."

"Don't give up, I'm sure we can figure out something. You are right, Camden Corners needs a newspaper. Randy will be here this morning, I'm going to have him look at the press and we will go from there.

Word spread fast that Josie was thinking of starting a newspaper. The Hightower twins had not had any offers to buy their quilt shop and insisted Josie use it for the paper. The apartment upstairs would work out perfectly for the newspaper office with the printer on the main floor. Randy worked on the press and it was rolling again or would be when the first copy of the Camden Corners Chronicle was being printed.

Reggie had one of his more talented workman carve a sign to go above the door. ***Camden Corners Chronicle, Josephine Blackburn, Editor.*** Several of the local businesses bought advertising space. Josie had written several articles about local activities and friendly news about the residents. She wrote her first editorial reminding the citizens of Camden Corners to be careful about disposing of their cigar butts near where children are playing.

"I'll be a little more political as time goes on" she said to Reggie. "I don't want to offend anyone on the first day the paper goes out."

Randy Burke was excited about print setting. After repairing the machine, he rode to the Greensboro News office to learn all he could about printing. It was a complicated process but he was shown the basics and was able to set up the Chronicle's printer.

Josie was busy working in the office when she heard Randy walking up the stairs. He was talking with a gentleman and stopped at Josie's door.

Josie asked the man to come in. He introduced himself as Percy Van Buren.

"I would like to see a sample of your newspaper as I plan to advertise continuously."

Josie didn't feel comfortable about this man. He had a dishonest face and Josie could usually tell when someone was lying. Her instincts told her Mr. Percy VanBuren was not to be trusted.

"I'm sorry Mr. Van Buren. Our publication is not ready for distribution. If you would like to leave your advertisement with me I will be happy to include it in our next edition."

"Madam, I will not place an advertisement in an unknown product. You must have a sample of the paper."

"Mr. VanBuren, as I told you, our newspaper is not ready for distribution. I will gladly mail you a copy when it is."

217

Mr. VanBuren left her office without leaving his advertisement.

"I wonder what he was up to?" Josie said to Randy. "That man gave me the willies."

"I know what you mean," said Randy. "I tried to tell him to wait downstairs until I announced him but he kept following me until we were at your door. I'm sorry Josie, I'll be more insistent next time."

"That's fine Randy, it's not your job to police the area. Hopefully, we won't see him again."

"The Chronicle has been put to bed." Josie said to Reggie as he walked through the door of their home. "I have been waiting to say that for days," she laughed.

"I'm really proud of you Josie. You make up your mind to do something and you do it. Seems it was only a short while ago that you were unhappy about the Greensboro News editing your article and now you are running a newspaper."

"It will be distributed first thing in the morning. Billy and Butch Duesenberry will pick up the papers in front of the shop at 4:30 am. The vicar said he didn't mind getting them up so early and Kate hasn't been sleeping very soundly with the baby kicking her during the night. I can't wait to start feeling our baby move"

Reggie gently patted her tummy. He couldn't wait either. He knew he had to be the luckiest man on earth being married to Josie and expecting their child. He shuddered when he thought of how at one time he had his heart set on marrying Elena Malone.

At 4:28 am the following morning Billy and Butch stood in front of the old quilt shop. They each picked up a stack of papers. It was very dark and they couldn't see the print but knew they could see what it looked like when they took their family's copy home after they finished their rounds.

The boys arrived home 46 minutes later. Butch handed Will the paper as they sat down to eat the breakfast Kate had waiting for them.

Will donned his spectacles and let out a yelp. The boys stopped eating and Kate rushed to his side. The headline read. ***Looking Back Antiques selling cheap reproductions.*** The story went on to say that Emma Patterson and Lily Kramer were swindling people out of their hard earned money. Furniture repaired by Jonas Fulbright was falling apart due to shoddy workmanship. The article warned the unsuspecting public to stay away from the second rate shop. The byline read ***Josie Blackburn, Concerned Citizen and Editor.***

At the Crowley house, Emma excitedly picked up the paper. Her chin dropped as she looked at the headline. Just then Lily knocked on the door. Emma opened it, they looked at each other and said in unison

"Harvey Wilson!"

Harvey had been a thorn in Emma's side for as long as she could remember. She worked for him at his newspaper in Greensboro until her grandfather died. Harvey took advantage of Amos Patterson and his deteriorating mental state. He forced Emma to give up the General Store Amos had built with his own hands, and when he learned Emma and Lily were making a success of their antique business he tried to swindle them out of that too. Harvey went too far and lost his businesses except for the Greensboro News. He knew someday he would be able to get his revenge on those two and that day had come. He hired Mr. Percy Van Buren to impersonate a prospective advertiser in the Camden Corners paper. While Percy was at the newspaper office he swiped a copy of the paper. It didn't take Percy and Harvey long to copy the paper with the new headline on the front page.

Arthur Preston had worked at Greensboro News for years. He'd tolerated Harvey Wilson and his questionable ways because he loved the newspaper business and he loved Greensboro. This latest dirty trick of Harvey's was the last straw though. He would have to make it right for his old friends Emma and Lily. Arthur gathered the original copies of the Chronicle from the trash barrel where Percy had dumped them and drove to Camden Corners prepared to redistribute them himself.

The townspeople were appalled that such things were said about the antique shop and its owners. They knew Josie Blackburn had nothing to do with it and anyone who knew Emma and the troubles she had with Harvey Wilson in the past were convinced that mean, vindictive man was behind it.

Arthur told Richard and Robert Crowley that he would be more than willing to testify against his boss. He was sure he had enough knowledge of dirty dealings to put the man away for years to come.

Arthur stopped by the newspaper office. He was impressed with what young Randy Burke had accomplished. He offered any assistance that may be needed in the future admitting that he may not be employed after his boss finds out he has turned on him.

The Duesenberry boys distributed the original paper that very afternoon.

Shortly after noon that day, Emma noticed the bell indicating there was a customer entering the shop was ringing continually. She came out from the back room to see people milling around the shop. Lily was busy pulling orders. Nettie and Ethel were helping customers and even Jonas was lending a hand with the crowd. Seems that in trying to cause harm to Emma and Lily's business, Harvey Wilson's deed was the best advertisement the girls could hope for. Percy not only made sure everyone in Camden Corners received a copy of the altered paper, he placed them in shops all around Greensboro and surrounding areas.

People who knew of Looking Back Antique Shop wanted to see the alleged shoddy workmanship with their own eyes. Those who hadn't been there before were curious and wanted to see for themselves what the shop had to offer.

For the next few weeks, Lily and Emma had more customers than they had ever had in the shop and sold more merchandise than ever before.

They were exhausted the day Harvey was called into court to face charges against him. Every one from Greensboro who was now living in Camden Corners made the trip that day.

Richard Crowley addressed the court. "Your honor, after careful consideration, my clients, Josephine Blackburn, Emma Crowley and Lily Crowley do not wish to press charges against Mr. Wilson. My client and wife, Emma Patterson Crowley requests the record reflect that Mr. Wilson's actions were beneficial to Looking Back Antiques in that the sales records following the unfortunate misprinting of the Camden Corners Chronicle were phenomenal and she and her partner, Lily Kramer Crowley appreciate Mr. Wilson's assistance."

The scowl on Harvey's face was enough justice for all parties concerned.

The friends from Camden Corners gathered at one of their old favorite restaurants. Melvin Tanner announced he had been told by one of the newspaper board members that Mr. Harvey Wilson was asked to step down as president of the Greensboro News.

As the friends raised their glasses in a toast to the success of the Camden Corners Chronicle, Harvey Wilson was sitting alone in his mansion without a friend in the world.

An Unusual Engagement

It's December and the Christmas activities in Camden Corners are in full swing. Luke and Molly Shannon put on another memorable Christmas Program at the Rialto Theater. Becky Bentley had a featured part in the production. Becky had a wonderful singing voice and now that she was speaking and singing again it was obvious she was a very talented

220

little girl. Becky was unable to speak after several tragic events happened in her young life.

The children decorated the giant spruce tree in the town square as the townsfolk gathered to sing Christmas carols and Santa handed out packages for the children to take home. Chris Pringle made the perfect Santa accompanied by Mrs. Santa or Priscilla Pringle as the town knew her. Luke continued his tradition of donating toys to the children. He couldn't bear the thought of a child not having at least one gift for Christmas. Thanks to Nettie Crowley and her friends, he was no longer burdened with the full expense of the toys. That was a good thing because he and Molly were expecting their own child in the spring.

The children were practicing for the Christmas pageant at St. Peter's Church on Christmas Eve. Everyone was busy shopping for that special gift and baking their favorite Christmas treats.

Reggie Blackburn had his hands full in his construction business. So far the weather had been good. His crew had just finished the outside walls and roof of the winery and were working rapidly to complete the exterior of the hospital before the snow began to fall. They were succeeding in their quest but Reggie was not about to let his crew work long hours without working right along side of them. Josie missed her husband but didn't expect any less of him. His dedication to a job well done was one of the many reasons she loved him.

Josie had recently established the Camden Corners Chronicle. Randy Burke was her right hand man. Randy didn't know any more about publishing a newspaper than Josie did but together they were learning. Arthur Preston, the new editor of the Greensboro News was a big help to them. Arthur liked Josie and Randy and wanted to see them succeed. He felt a certain responsibility for the actions of his former boss, Harvey Wilson, who tried his best to sabotage the first edition of the paper.

Josie had written an editorial about a special family she had met recently in Virginia. Zeke and Effie Dalton lived at the base of Dalton's Mountain with their two sons, John and Ben. Josie hadn't known what to expect when Reggie decided to pay Zeke a visit. She had heard horror stories about how mountain people lived and was a bit nervous about meeting them. She couldn't have been more wrong. Zeke and Effie lived in a lovely old farmhouse that had been built by Zeke's kin years before. Zeke prided himself on the exceptional lumber he sold. They lived very frugally. Effie put up vegetables from her garden and fruits from the trees and bushes on the land. Zeke and the boys hunted and fished all year long. Effie and Josie hit it off immediately. Although the visit was not a lengthy one, Josie left Dalton's Mountain knowing a friendship had developed between them that would last a lifetime. At the end of the column, she asked her readers to submit their own stories of people who had come into their lives and made a difference. As many as possible would be published throughout the month.

Polly Cooper finished reading Josie's column. She was touched by her words and immediately sat down to write about her own saviors, Nettie and Oscar Crowley. Polly had been taken advantage of by a young man who was under the mistaken impression that Polly's father, Marlin Cooper was a wealthy man who would give up his land for his daughter. James Philpot arranged a bogus marriage between them and then tried to weasel money out of the old man. What James didn't know was that next to Harvey Wilson, Marlin Cooper was the meanest man in town. James admitted that his marriage to Polly was a sham but not before she was expecting a baby. Marlin marched his daughter off to an aunt with the intention of sending the baby to an orphanage as soon as it was born. Polly managed to escape her aunts house and found her way to Camden Corners where she knew her favorite teacher, Nettie Dawson had moved. Nettie took her and baby Faith into her home and heart. Shortly after that Nettie and Oscar were married and the four of them became a family.

Randy Burke fell in love with Polly and Faith the minute he laid eyes on them. They had been inseparable since their first meeting but Polly, who had been emotionally mistreated by both her father and her so called husband, was reluctant to commit to Randy. Randy was a patient man and was willing to give her all the time she needed.

Polly wrote her story and turned it over to Josie. Josie thought it was the most beautiful tale she had ever heard. She could feel the love pouring out on the paper and knew it had to be published in the next edition.

Several days later Marlin Cooper walked into Shaky's Bar & Grill. He liked Shaky's because nobody bothered him there. He would sit in the corner booth, grab a day old paper and drink himself into a stupor until it was time to go home to his long suffering wife and children. Marlin picked up the paper.

"What's this rag?" he said out loud to no one in particular as he read the heading Camden Corners Chronicle.

His eyes went directly to the name at the bottom of an article; *Polly Cooper, Camden Corners Resident.*

Marlin could feel his blood pressure rise as he swigged one double bourbon after another. The other patrons of the bar could hear him talking to himself but decided to just let him be. Marlin was known to get violent

222

when he drank.

"I thought I'd heard the last of that harlot. The ungrateful twit left the loving home of my dear sister to go off with her little brat to that snoopy school teacher. That woman gave me trouble when Polly was in school. She kept telling me the kid was too smart not to go to college. College? I didn't even want her to go to high school but at least it got her out of the house part of the day. She was a real pain always telling her mother she should leave and take the other kids with her. No respect. She didn't give me no respect. Well, we'll just see who she respects now. I wonder how much money I could get for that little brat of hers. Sure she's older now but some people like older kids."

Marlin got up from the table with the Chronicle in hand. He walked out without saying goodbye to anyone. Nobody was sorry to see him go. Schultz, the bartender wished there was some way he could keep the man out of the bar. He gave him the creeps.

Marlin went directly to the train station and bought a ticket to Camden Corners. He slept on the train and woke up thirsty. Before finding a bar he would find this fancy Crowley house and drag his kid home where she belonged.

Even after several days, Nettie Crowley would still tear up when she thought of the beautiful piece Polly had written about her life in Camden Corners. Nettie knew Polly was grateful to her but Nettie loved Polly and Faith and considered them her own family.

She had just finished setting the table for a quiet dinner at home. Faith had recently mastered walking and was scampering all over the dining room. Oscar entered and picked the little girl up to swing her around. She giggled as he tickled her belly.

Faith was born in the back bedroom of her great aunt's house. Polly had been treated with disdain by her aunt the whole time she was there. Polly knew she had to get away from the house with Faith and wrapped her newborn in a thin blanket before boarding the train to Camden Corners. After reaching Camden Corners she found a small chapel where she stopped and rested. Her prayers were answered when Nettie entered the chapel that fateful day just over a year ago.

Polly and Randy arrived at the Crowley home together. Polly was taking classes to become a teacher like her benefactor. Faith squealed when she saw her mother and Randy. Polly put little Faith in her high chair and they all settled down to eat their dinner when the doorbell started ringing and there was pounding on the door.

"I know you're in there you little tramp. Open this door or I'll kick it

223

down."

Polly thought her heart would stop beating. She knew that voice. She would never forget it.

"It's my father," she cried.

Oscar quietly got up from his chair and went to the door.

"May I help you sir?" he said

"Yeah, give me my daughter and her kid and I'll be on my way."

Oscar reluctantly allowed the man to enter his home. He could smell the stale booze on him and knew he was still drunk. There was no telling what the man would do and he'd heard Nettie repeat some things she'd heard about him in Greensboro. Now be believed those stories were correct.

Before Marlin could make his way into the house, Polly picked up Faith and handed her over to the housekeeper.

"Trudy, please take Faith out the back door and to Emma and Richard's house. Tell Richard what is going on here. They will know what to do."

Randy stood by Polly's side when this crazed man who was her father walked into the room.

"There you are. Pretty proud of yourself aren't you? Living here in this fancy house. Where's the kid?"

"Hello to you to, Father. I can see you are still the charming man I remember so fondly." Polly said sarcastically.

"Got a mouth on ya still, don't ya. I'll get rid of that once I get you home now get that kid of yours and let's go."

Randy fumbled in his pocket and took Polly's left hand as he slipped a ring on her finger. Polly's eyes opened wide. The ring wasn't a total surprise to her but why on earth would Randy pick this time to give it to her?

Randy stood tall, stepped forward and extended his hand to Marlin.

"How do you do sir? I'm Randy Burke and I'm engaged to your daughter. I hope you will give us your blessing"

"Engaged! Why would you want to marry the girl? She is soiled goods, you know."

Oscar put his hand on Randy's arm because he could feel the boy was going to explode if he didn't calm down.

"I love your daughter, sir. She is a wonderful young woman and you and your wife can be very proud of the life she is making for herself and her daughter. It will be an honor to be married to Polly."

"You people are all crazy. I don't know what you like about her. She won't show you any respect. You just wait and see. Right now I want to see the brat."

"She is not here and since you have no claim to me I suggest you leave right now. Go back to your happy little home. I know you won't but I wish you would tell my mother and brothers and sisters that I love them. If there was some way I could save them from you I would."

Just then Richard and Robert entered the house with Sheriff Mendenhall.

"Mr. Cooper, come with me. I'm arresting you for public intoxication. Maybe tomorrow you will feel the urge to apologize to these fine people." The sheriff put the handcuffs on Marlin and walked him out of the house.

"You'll pay for this Polly. I'll be back." He dropped the copy of the paper with Polly's words staring back at her.

"I never imagined he would ever see this" she cried. "I'm so sorry he came into your house, Oscar. I didn't think he could get any worse than he was a year ago but I was wrong. Oh Randy, I wish I could get my mother and the other children away from him. I just don't know how."

Trudy came back and started clearing the table of still full plates. Everyone had lost their appetite. Oscar proceeded to pour everyone a brandy including Trudy who was still shaking from fear.

Emma and Lily came in through the back door with Faith who was oblivious to all that was going on. Lily was the first to notice the ring on Polly's hand.

"What have we here?"

Polly looked down at her finger and for the first time she saw the beautiful ring Randy had slipped on her finger.

"Guess it's time to ask if you will marry me? How could you possibly turn me down with all these people waiting for your answer."

"Randy, this isn't the first mess you have gotten me out of. Are you sure you want a wife who always seems to be more trouble than she's worth?"

"I'll take you any way I can get you. Now, are you going to marry me?"

"Yes!"

Everyone started clapping and singing and sipping a little more brandy. Faith was still in Emma's arms and was clapping along with everyone else. She was smiling and giggling and suddenly reached her arms out to Randy and said

"Da da"

A Growing Town

After seeing Marlin Cooper board the train the next morning, Sheriff Mendenhall stopped by the Crowley home to assure Polly that he thought she'd seen the last of her father. Marlin was full of chatter that morning but he never once mentioned Polly.

"Unfortunately, I have seen my share of drunkards and they usually simmer down when they know they have been beaten at their own game of intimidation."

"I'm just sorry one of my kin acted in such a loathsome way," said Polly.

Nettie put her arm around the girl she considered a daughter. "You have nothing to apologize for my dear girl. I knew when you were my prize student several years ago that you were special. Your family, for whatever reason, has decided their place is in Greensboro with your father. You have given them every opportunity to escape that environment. They know our door is always open."

"Thank you Nettie, I don't know what I would do without you. Now, we have a wedding to plan and I would love your help. Thank you too, Sheriff. I'm glad to hear my father has left town. I hope you will be able to join us on New Year's Eve. Randy and I are going to be married that day so we can begin 1904 as a family."

The sheriff nodded at the two women as he donned his hat and walked back to his office with a much lighter step. He was always happy when trouble was averted and everything ended happily.

There was another knock on the door. Nettie opened it to see her new friend, Anna Rossi standing there.

"I hope you don't mind my stopping by like this Nettie, I was taking a walk when I saw the sheriff leave and wanted to make sure everything was alright here."

"Everything is just fine Anna. The sheriff was just following up on an incident that turned out to be nothing after all. Come in please, you can help Polly and me do some wedding planning."

"Polly dear, I'm so happy to hear you are finally planning a wedding. That Burke boy is a real catch if you ask me. My Rosa thinks the world of the Burkes. Don't tell her I told you this but she has a Burke girl all picked out for her Eddie. I think she is working her way down the entire family."

226

The women all laughed. Nettie and Polly knew Rosa well and didn't doubt for a minute that it was true.

"I'll do what I can to help with the matchmaking when I'm a Burke too."

Polly excused herself to check on Faith who was in the kitchen watching Trudy bake sugar cookies.

Nettie knew Lou Rossi was having a hard time adjusting to his retirement. He had given up his family's vineyard in Tuscany to move across the ocean. He lost his best friend and fellow vintner in Tuscany and the pleasure he once took in his vineyards was there no more. Out of all his six children, only Nick ever showed any interest in the wine business and he had lived in America for too long to ever go back to Italy.

"Luigi and Nicola have been working together. I mean Lou and Nick. I can't get use to saying these Americanized names. Anyway, I think the sparkle is coming back into Lou's eyes. He can't wait to get out of bed in the morning and go to the vineyard to check on the plantings. I just hope he doesn't get in Nick's way. Nick has been doing everything on his own for so long I wonder how he is handling his father's constant presence."

"I wouldn't worry about Nick, Anna. He is a very good man. I often heard him quote his father when he talked about growing grapes here in our area. I'm sure Nick and Lou will get along just fine. Everyone is anxious for the winery to be completed. We are really coming up in the world here in Camden Corners. Before long we will be as big as Greensboro. I do hope we can keep the friendly atmosphere. There isn't one person in town I don't know and I like it that way."

Nick and Lou were hovering over the grape plantings when the wind started to pick up.

"Let's go inside the winery. The shipment of oak barrels came in yesterday. I'd like you to look them over for any flaws."

Nick put his arm around his father and the two Rossis walked through the doors of the winery. The workers were finishing up the wine cellar where the barrels would be placed waiting for the harvest the following September. Lou was impressed with the workmanship. In Tuscany the same barrels had been in service since he was a boy. His father and grandfather had insisted that their wine had an aged flavor thanks to their reuse. Lou never put that to the test but was interested to see if these new barrels would make a difference.

Lou was very proud of his son. He hadn't lived in Tuscany or around a winery in many years but he had absorbed much more than Lou realized when he did live there. He knew his son would make a fine vintner and was pleased to be with him every step of the way.

Nick was happy his father was there to give him moral support. He spent many sleepless nights wondering if he was proceeding correctly. The Hightower brothers had invested an enormous amount of money into this project. They had wanted to go first class with the winery building and Jamison Bentley came through for them. The building itself was going to be lavish. It would have a wine tasting room that would fit two hundred people at one time, a lounge area and a panoramic porch that was large enough for another hundred. The second floor is the ballroom with a platform big enough to hold a full orchestra. On the third and fourth floor there would be suites where out of town guests would be accommodated for the night or as long as they wished to visit Camden Corners. The success of the winery and all of its amenities rested on the success or failure of the grapes growing out in the field. Anna didn't have to worry about Lou being a pest to his son, Nick thought he was a godsend.

"Hello gentlemen" Reggie Blackburn called out as he and Jamison Bentley walked through the doors. "As you can see we've had to slow down on the winery for the time being. The crew is working full time at the hospital site completing the exterior before the weather delays us any further. Leo Carlisle and his shenanigans set us back on our timetable a couple of months and we are just catching up."

"Lou, have you heard about Josie's heroics the day Leo was caught?" The men all laughed but they knew it had been a serious matter when Leo Carlisle held Josie at gunpoint. Josie was struck with a bout of morning sickness and couldn't hold it back any longer when she regurgitated into the face of her captor causing him to drop his weapon.

"Jamison, your design here in the winery is impressive. It's bound to be a landmark in Camden Corners," said Lou.

"To be honest Lou, it didn't start out this way. The Hightowers had their own ideas and had me add more and more on until this was the result. I do think it will be a fine looking building when the work is completed. The setting is lovely too, the vineyards look wonderful now. Just imagine how grand they will look when they reach maturity. The proximately to the lake and all the space beyond will just add to the beauty."

"I was looking at that land son. Don't you think that should be cultivated for plantings."

"Now that you are here Papa, I think that's a possibility. I didn't want to bite off more than I could chew for the first year."

"We'd better get over to the hospital site. I think the crew is ready to finish up the roof today and start installing the windows. If the weather will hold off just a few more days I think we will be alright.   We'll see you later at the lake house, I hope. The ladies have plans for all of us to go out caroling tonight. I told Josie I'd rather just hang around the wassail bowl but she gave me one of those looks."

Lucinda was waiting at the hospital site when the men arrived. She was pleased that everything seemed to be going smoothly. Reggie was surprised at how much progress had been made since he left earlier that morning.

"Did you get your whip to the crew this morning Lucinda?"

"I didn't need to, the drop in temperature is speeding them up. They want to get inside the building. You just missed Doc McMillan. He stopped by to see how things were going. He seemed pleased that eventually we will be able to make additions to the building. Doc has heard from several of his colleagues who may be interested in joining the staff here. That means more work for the two of you with the housing needs that will be arising. It won't be long before we are open for business and we need to think of recruiting. Doc is expecting a young doctor this afternoon. He is coming in from Buffalo. He just completed his residency there and is looking for a place to begin his practice. Doc said he would bring him along to the caroling party tonight."

"Hey, the more the merrier. Hope he likes to sing. It will help drown me out. I can't believe I let Josie talk me into this thing."

Doc was waiting at the station just as the train was arriving. A good looking young man stepped off the train.

"Dr. Murphy?"

"Yes sir, and you must be Doctor McMillan. It is a pleasure to meet you sir and I do thank you for this opportunity. Please call me Grady."

"Good to meet you, Grady. Everybody calls me Doc. I probably wouldn't answer if anyone used my given name anyway. I have arranged for a room in the Wharton House. I think you will find it comfortable. I'll walk you there and introduce you to Mrs. Wharton. We will pass the medical office on the way and you can stop by after you are settled in."

Doc and Grady didn't notice the two young ladies following him off the train.

"Audrey Lynch, you didn't tell me you were chasing after Dr. Murphy. I should have known there wasn't any job waiting for us here. I can't believe I fell for your deception again. I have a mind to wait in the station until the next train leaves for Buffalo in the morning."

"Elizabeth, don't be such an old crosspatch. This is an adventure. Maybe there isn't a job waiting for us today but they will be opening a hospital next year and they will need nurses. You and I can get a feel of the town and decide if we want to move to Camden Corners."

"You mean if you haven't gotten over your silly crush on Dr. Grady Murphy by then. You know he doesn't have any interest in you. For heaven sake Audrey, the man doesn't even know you are alive."

"He will Elizabeth. He'll know me very well. I'm starving, let's see what they have at O'Sullivan's Pub over there. We can inquire about a place to stay for the night."

"Alright, I'm hungry myself but I'm not staying here overnight and that's settled. As soon as we eat, we will make arrangements to go back to Buffalo."

"Oh look, it's snowing. It would be pretty except that wind is blowing so fiercely."

The girls walked into the pub where Fiona was just clearing off the last of the lunch crowd tables.

"Hello young ladies, Please have a seat. I'll fetch a menu for you. Looks like you have arrived in town just ahead of the big storm that's headed our way."

"Thank you ma'am, we are from Buffalo and have seen our share of storms. I'm sure we will be able to handle it."

Audrey and Elizabeth both had the pub's specialty, corned beef sandwiches. They even had a piece of Fiona's pumpkin pie. The pie was delicious and reminded Elizabeth of her granny.

"Do you know of a boarding house in town Mrs. Mackenzie?" Audrey inquired as Elizabeth frowned at her. Maybe staying overnight wasn't such a bad idea. Elizabeth was tired and the weather looked pretty nasty out the window.

"Mrs. Wharton's but she was in here earlier and said she was booked solid for the whole week."

She thought of the Watson House but since Caroline and Jamison married and adopted Kenny and Becky plus Jamison's two boys visiting often, they didn't have the room anymore.

"I'll tell you what girls. Why don't you come home with me. We have a house brimming with children of all ages but you will have your own bedroom and you should be comfortable for the night. Just looking out the window I don't think the train will be going anywhere very soon."

Caroling in the Snow

Gordon Mackenzie was worried his wife, Fiona would have trouble getting through the snowdrifts on her way home from the pub. He hitched the horses to the sleigh and set out to meet her. Along the way he saw a young man walking against the wind.

"Hey there young fellow, would you like a lift?"

"Don't mind if I do, sir. I'm on my way to visit Doc McMillan, his office is just down the street but I seem to be fighting a losing battle trudging my way through these snowdrifts."

"Climb on in, I'll just stop here at the pub for my wife. Here she comes now. It looks like she has some company."

Grady moved over and looked up into the eyes of Elizabeth Lawrence. She looked familiar but he was always so distracted lately he couldn't place her and couldn't imagine that he knew anyone who lived in Camden Corners.

Introductions were made. Gordon drove slowly to Doc's office. Fiona noticed Audrey couldn't keep her eyes off of Grady Murphy and Grady couldn't seem to look away from Elizabeth who was watching the sky and wondering if she would ever be able to board the train to get back home to Buffalo.

"Dr. Murphy, we haven't met formally before but we have worked together at Buffalo General Hospital. Elizabeth and I are nurses there."

"You must be here to visit the new hospital in town. We are very proud of our facility. Camden Corners has long needed a hospital of its own," said Fiona. "It won't be completed until the spring at the earliest, are you all going to be working with Doc until then?"

Elizabeth chimed in, "No, Mrs. Mackenzie, we aren't here for work although it does seem like a lovely town. My friend, Audrey was jumping the gun a bit wondering what Camden Corners was like. As far as I know there is no need for our nursing skills just yet."

Grady spoke up. "Miss Lawrence, I do recall seeing you at Buffalo General. I believe it was in the children's ward."

"That is where I have been assigned Doctor. You may also remember Audrey. She has been there even longer than I have."

"I don't think we have ever met before miss." His eyes drifted back to Elizabeth who seemed to be oblivious to his attention.

They reached Doc's office and Gordon stopped the carriage to let Grady off. He thanked Gordon for the ride and smiled at Elizabeth as he fought the snow drifts up to the front door.

"Oh Elizabeth" sighed Audrey. "Did you see how he is being coy with me. He pretended he didn't know me. The silly man. He's going to play hard to get with me."

Fiona and Gordon glanced at each other skeptically. It was obvious the good doctor only had eyes for Elizabeth.

Jack Mackenzie met them near the barn. He helped his father take care of the horses while his mother and her guests went into the house.

"You go ahead mother, I'll bring the suitcases in after I help Papa with the horses." He glanced at the two visitors and liked what he saw.

Jack was the most serious of all the Mackenzie children. He was a talented artist and seemed to lose himself in his painting. He worked in New York for a couple of years and established himself as an artist there. He missed his home and family though and moved back much to the delight of Fiona and Gordon. He recently opened an art gallery in Camden Corners and invited other artists in the area to display their works. Jack was amazed at what young Tony Marino was able to capture with his camera and proudly displayed his creations also. His sister, Carrie helped him in the gallery and took pains framing each and every work of art. The gallery was a huge success and had an enviable reputation as far away as Connecticut. Even with his success Fiona worried that he had forgotten how to have fun. All through high school Jack never lacked for female companionship. He was a bit on the wild side back then. Although he never spoke of it, Fiona believed his heart had been broken while he was living in New York. She was happy to see the sparkle in his eyes when he saw the two pretty girls walk by him and into the house.

"I certainly hope he doesn't fall for Audrey. She seems to have eyes only for her young doctor friend." she whispered to Gordon as they were getting out of the carriage.

"The young doctor has eyes only for Miss Elizabeth so maybe she will need Jack around to pick up the pieces." Gordon said quietly. Gordon was as worried about their son as Fiona was.

Fiona showed the girls to Amanda's old room where they unpacked the few clothes they had brought with them and changed into some dry footwear.

"Jack is very nice looking, don't you think Elizabeth?"

"Audrey, you are suppose to be head over heels in love with Dr. Murphy. Why are you looking at Jack Mackenzie? Yes, I guess he's good looking, I'm still angry with you for dragging us all the way here for no reason at all."

"What do you have waiting for you in Buffalo that's so important Elizabeth? Your father has moved to Pennsylvania with his new wife. Your brother is in New York City and you don't even have a cat to go home to."

"I'm glad my father has found happiness with Janice and you know it. Why do you make me sound like a pathetic orphan? You know my father begged me to move to Pittsburgh with them and I'm always welcome at my brother's home."

"I know but they have their own lives. You work all day and go home to an empty room in a boarding house at night. Wouldn't you like to have an adventure of your own?"

"Like a wild goose chase after your doctor friend?"

Fiona knocked on the door. "Come downstairs girls and meet the rest of the family. We will be having a quick supper and then piling into the carriage for some caroling. We won't let a little thing like a blizzard keep us from entertaining the neighbors with our glorious singing."

Audrey thought it was a wonderful idea. Elizabeth wondered if it would be rude of her to stay here under that toasty looking quilt and read the novel she had begun on the train. She decided it would be and joined in with a smile on her face.

Jack liked Elizabeth right away. She had a sensible head on her shoulders especially compared to her friend Audrey. Audrey was pretty enough but she was silly and scatterbrained. The Mackenzie's stopped by the Burke house. They also had their own carriage and the two large families covered in blankets and quilts were on their way to the Blackburn house for a little liquid refreshment before venturing back out for their caroling.

Elizabeth was happy she decided to come along. She didn't remember ever having such a good time. She and Audrey were welcomed by everyone. Dr. Murphy came along with the McMillans and was appearing to be much more relaxed than he had been earlier in the day. Audrey was staring at him with longing in her eyes. Jack noticed the doctor was looking in her direction but could only see Elizabeth.

"I think our new doctor friend is trying to get your attention Elizabeth."

"Oh no, he is interested in Audrey. She has set her sights on him and once Audrey makes up her mind to snag a gentleman, he doesn't have a chance."

"That figures. She does seem to have her head in the clouds, doesn't she?"

233

"Jack, are you interested in Audrey?"

"No, of course not. I like a girl more down to earth."

Lucinda walked by and mentioned that she would like to talk to Jack about art work for the hospital when he had some time.

"Go ahead, I've been monopolizing Jack's time long enough. I think I'll check on my friend Audrey." Elizabeth walked Audrey's way and noticed a scowl on her face.

"Elizabeth, Grady keeps staring at you not me. I think he is attracted to you. After traveling all this way he doesn't even know I exist."

"Don't be silly, Audrey. Every man in this room has noticed you. Jack Mackenzie can't stop talking about you. Why not go over there and make his evening."

Audrey's eyes lit up. She looked over at Jack and her heart skipped a beat. He really is very nice looking. Grady Murphy was all but forgotten.

Fiona and Gordon smiled at each other. "If anyone can bring Jack out of his shell it's Audrey" said Fiona.

The young people all went out caroling in spite of the weather. Everyone else stayed behind to have a little more cider and eggnog. Reggie was happy to play host. After working outside all day he was very comfortable in the warm cottage.

The snow had let up and it was just falling lightly as the carolers made their way through the town. Mack and Maddie Mackenzie saw a noticeable difference in Jack. It seems Nurse Audrey was just what the doctor ordered.

"He's practically giggling." Mack said to Maddie and Carrie.

"It's about time he got back to the living" Carrie said with a smile.

"I think our new physician and nurse will be playing doctor themselves before too long." Maddie said with a chuckle as she glanced at Grady and Elizabeth. Mack was embarrassed but Carrie laughed.

Elizabeth found herself standing next to her friend Audrey and whispered in her ear. "Isn't Camden Corners a wonderful place? I'm so glad you brought me here." Audrey just smiled.

The evening came to an end. Elizabeth and Grady bid each other a good evening with the promise of meeting the next day.

Grady slipped into his room with thoughts of Elizabeth as he readied himself for the big feather bed. It had been quite a day. Grady was nervous about his meeting with Doc but he needn't have been. Doc was a warm, kind man just like his mentor, Dr. Gilbert said he would be. Grady had met his share of egotistical physicians at Buffalo General. He knew he would feel comfortable in a small town setting and already he was sure

Camden Corners would be the place for him. He had spoken briefly with Elizabeth about her plans for the future. She indicated she might be thinking of a change herself.

Within the next couple of days Audrey and Elizabeth both had promises of positions in the new hospital when it opened. In the meantime, Doc Julie hired them both to help out in the office.

"Dad, a nurse can do many of the things you, Tom and I have been doing for the patients and it will allow us more time to help them. Now that there are four doctors in the practice, we can't expect mother and April to do even more work than they do already. April will be leaving for nursing school before we know it and then it will only be mother." Julie said

"Yes, and you would like them both to stay in Camden Corners. I may be getting on in years but I know when romance is blossoming. I can see our Dr. Murphy is smitten with Elizabeth Lawrence and your old friend Jack Mackenzie has found a new lease on life with the spunky Miss Audrey. I think it's a wonderful idea. Let's hire both of them."

It was decided all three would return to Camden Corners shortly after the new year. It would give the hospital time to fill the soon to be vacant nursing positions. Elizabeth and Audrey also wanted to be there for the children who sadly had to spend their Christmas in the hospital. They, along with the other nurses and doctors always made the day very special for their little patients.

Shortly after the train pulled out of the station heading north, Jack Mackenzie was at the counter purchasing a ticket to Buffalo for the following weekend.

Christmas Magic

It was the week of Christmas and the town of Camden Corners was a bustle of activity. The sun had come out a few days after the early December blizzard and the snowdrifts were disappearing each day although there was a fresh coating of snow covering the ground.

School was out for the holiday and the children were taking full advantage of the snow. Billy and Butch Duesenberry were looking forward to their first Christmas in Camden Corners. They had always been aware of the holiday. People were always a bit more generous at that time of year and the boys had found panhandling to be very profitable in December. They were very happy they didn't have to rely on strangers' generosity anymore. Kate and Will were delighted their home was filled with laughter and activity that the two growing boys provided. Will believed he was the luckiest man in the world. Kate was everything he had ever dreamed of. In less than a year's time he was a married man with two sons and a baby on the way. He had to pinch himself every once in a while to make sure it was true.

Will was looking forward to the annual Christmas pageant. The Ladies Auxiliary had always taken charge of the event in the past with Will's blessing. It was an event everyone in town looked forward to every year. The tradition had gone on for so many years that some of the early Marys and Josephs were watching their grandchildren in those roles now.

This evening is their last rehearsal before the Christmas Eve presentation. Cassandra Rossi is Mary this year. Kenny Bentley is playing Joseph. Becky Bentley is a singing angel. This is a variation of the usual performance because Becky's sweet voice is so heavenly. Will's son, Butch also is playing a solo on his clarinet. He is a natural with a musical instrument.

Iris Taylor is one of the wise men. She had been practicing the word frankincense all morning. She thought it would be easier if she had been the wiseman carrying the gift of gold to the baby Jesus but she accepted her part and her lines without complaint. Iris was rehearsing while her new baby sister was watching from her cradle. Little Jennie Taylor had been born in September. She will be playing the part of the baby Jesus in the pageant. Joey was running around being a boy but Iris didn't seem to mind.

Diana and Joe Taylor were watching their children from the doorway. The day Iris came into town less than two years ago changed their lives completely. They had been married for five years and were afraid they were not going to ever have a baby. Shortly after they became parents to Iris, little Joey was on the way and before too long Diana discovered she was expecting another and Jennie was the result. Diana and Joe had so much to be grateful for this year.

Kenny Bentley wasn't sure he liked the idea of wearing a beard in the pageant tomorrow night.

"This thing itches. Couldn't we pretend Joseph went to the barber shop that day?"

Caroline Bentley laughed. "Have you ever seen a barber's pole in a picture of the desert Kenny?"

Caroline was reflecting on the previous year too. She was all by herself in this big house just a few months ago when her daughter, Grace married her long time beau, Ted Evans. Shortly after Lucinda and

Cassandra came to live in the boarding house she was reunited with Jamison Bentley. Caroline and Jamison knew they were meant to be together and planned a future. Suddenly, two young orphans were in their lives and they became a family. The surprises weren't over when soon after their marriage, Caroline discovered she was expecting a baby. She didn't believe it was possible since her daughter, Grace was making her a grandmother for the first time.

"Grandmother's don't have babies," she insisted to Doc McMillan.

Once the shock wore off, she and Jamison were delighted at the prospect of a new baby of their own.

Lucinda and Cassandra moved out of the boarding house after Lucinda's marriage to Nick Rossi but the house was still full especially when Jamison's two sons came for a visit.

Caroline knew Kenny would be wearing the beard whether it itched or not. He was a pleasant child who had faced more tragedy than any young boy should have to. His mother died after a long illness and his father eventually drank himself to death after he lost his wife. Kenny took full responsibility for his young sister, Becky. Becky was mute because of fear her father had instilled in her. After a few months of living around people who loved and cared for her she came out of her shell and began speaking again. That was when it was discovered that she had such a lovely singing voice.

Caroline didn't think she could ever be happier than she was right now and then felt Jamison's strong arms wrapped around her waist.

Cassandra Rossi picked up the necklace her papa, Paul McCoy, had given her shortly before he was gunned down on the streets of New York City. Cassandra was only 2 years old when her papa was taken away so suddenly. She was having a hard time remembering him. Her life had changed dramatically in the last year. As it turned out, Mr. Howard who lived next door to Cassandra's mama and her in New York was her great grandfather. He left her mama a lot of money when he died. She and Mama moved here to Camden Corners and met her new papa, Nick Rossi. Cassandra loved Papa Nick with all her heart but cherished the necklace with the pink heart. She only wore it for special occasions but she liked to put it around her neck. She wanted Papa Paul to know she loved him and would never forget him and the necklace had become a symbol of that love to her.

"Cassandra" her mother called from the stairwell. "Kenny and Becky are here for you. They want you to come with them to the park to build a snowman."

Cassandra, forgetting she was wearing her necklace, raced down the stairs to get her coat and boots on and took off with her friends where they met other children in the park.

After an hour or so of being out in the cold, Cassandra and her friends were back inside the house sipping hot chocolate and nibbling Christmas cookies.

Lucinda noticed her daughter had a chain around her neck. "Cassandra where did you get that chain, is it from your necklace?"

Cassandra put her hands to her throat. She felt for the pink heart and it wasn't there.

"Oh Mama, I forgot I had my necklace on and the heart is gone" she couldn't hold the tears back. The only remembrance of her papa was the necklace and now she had lost it.

Nick had just arrived home and said he would help her look for it. The children put their coats and boots back on and they all went out the door to the park.

Nick and Lucinda knew it would be like finding a needle in a haystack. The snow had been falling since the children had come in from the cold. The heart would most likely be covered with snow by now. They searched until the children were almost stiff with the cold. Lucinda took them home but Nick kept looking until the daylight disappeared. Nick knew how much that necklace meant to Cassandra. He knew losing the heart was like losing her father all over again. He came back home and told Cassandra they would look for it every day and when spring came and all the snow disappeared they would surely find it. Nick knew the chances of finding it were slim but he couldn't let his daughter know that.

Nick spent the better part of the following morning in the park looking for the heart. Lucinda and Cassandra looked with him. It was too cold for a little girl to be out for too long at one time. It was Christmas Eve and Cassandra had to get ready to go to the church for the Christmas Eve service and pageant.

All the children did a wonderful job with their performances. Becky Bentley sang her little heart out. Nick noticed Cassandra touching her neck a time or two. She had planned to wear her precious necklace under her costume while playing her part as Mary that evening.

After the ceremony ended, the parishioners gathered in the basement meeting room for coffee and sweet treats provided by the Ladies Auxiliary.

Everyone wished their friends and neighbors a Merry Christmas and bid good evening as they all went to their homes. The children were anticipating the arrival of Santa Claus and wanted to be sure they were in bed and asleep so that he wouldn't pass them by.

Butch and Billy were a little old to be waiting for Santa but this was the first time in their young lives that they were part of the celebration and joined in and enjoyed the fantasy.

Caroline and Jamison encouraged Kenny and Becky to talk about their mama and Papa. Caroline knew the children loved their new parents but wanted to keep the few memories they had of their birth parents alive. They would always miss their mama and even with his faults, their papa too but they were so happy in Camden Corners with Caroline and Jamison and knew their mama would be happy for them too.

Iris' life was filled with love and laughter. Her little brother and sister adored her and she felt the same way about them. She also loved her Mama Mavis' friend, Cody. He was very special to her. Not only because he knew her mama but he saved her life at the Founder's Day picnic last summer. Iris rarely thought about her father, Earl Short anymore. She felt as though she had lived with Joe and Diana Taylor forever. She liked it that way and she knew she was loved.

Cassandra walked home with her parents. She decided she wasn't going to be sad anymore because of losing the heart. Papa Nick told her she would always have her Papa Paul in her own heart. His love could never be lost. She was deep in thought about how much she loved Papa Nick when she heard him shout.

"Cassandra, look!"

She glanced at the snow pile where Nick was standing and saw a sparkle that made her want to cover her eyes. She walked over to it and and saw her pink heart resting on top of the snow. Her heart had been there all along. Or had it? Through her excitement, Cassandra thought she heard the sound of jingle bells as she reached down and touched her pink heart. She looked up at Nick who was beaming and her own heart felt like it was going to pop out of her chest. Cassandra knew she was a very lucky girl to have two papas who loved her.

After they got home Cassandra said her prayers, mama and papa tucked her into bed.

"Merry Christmas, Cassandra," said her mother

"Merry Christmas, Mama and Papa."

They left the room arm in arm as Cassandra closed her eyes.

"Merry Christmas Papa, thank you for my pink heart and thank you for my Papa Nick."

It was a Very Good Year

Polly Cooper was giddy with excitement, tomorrow she would be Mrs. Randolph Burke. She picked up Faith and held her tight. She tried not to think about what could have happened if her father had sent Faith to an orphanage as he planned. Polly gave birth to Faith and escaped her Aunt's house coming directly to Camden Corners where her life had been transformed thanks to Nettie Crowley and Randy Burke.

Faith was a happy toddler who gave kisses and hugs to everyone she knew. They would miss living with Nettie and Oscar. Polly was studying to be a teacher. Randy thought she would make an excellent teacher and encouraged her to continue her studies after they were married. She planned to do that but her first priority was going to be wife and mother. She knew she would never be like her mama who was browbeaten by her husband. Nettie told her not to be too judgmental towards her mother. She didn't know the background of her relationship with Polly's father but Nettie knew first hand what a nasty man Marlin Cooper could be. She didn't know Alice well but she suspected she may have been intimidated into marrying the man.

Polly chased away those unhappy thoughts and danced around the room with the giggling little girl. "We're getting married tomorrow Faith."

Nettie knocked on the door. "Sounds like there are two happy ladies in here" she said.

"Oh Nettie, I am so happy I have to pinch myself but we are going to miss you so."

Nettie's eyes filled up. "You will be living close by and I'm grateful for that but it won't be the same. This is the way it should be though and I couldn't be happier for my two girls. Randy Burke was made to order for you and you for him."

Polly hugged Nettie who was like a mother to her. "Guess we'd better get going Faith. We have to get to the church to decorate for our wedding reception." she turned to Nettie "I think half the town will be there this morning. The Burkes have a big family and wherever there's a Burke there is always a Mackenzie close by."

Nettie offered to watch over Faith while Polly went to the church to arrange the decorations. She was surprised when she arrived there and most of the work was done. It looked beautiful with all the shimmering lights and silver and gold decorations.

"Polly dear, I hope you don't mind that we did all this" said her soon to be mother-in-law, Nadine. We didn't mean to take over but we started and there are so many of us before we knew it we were done."

"Mind? I love it." Polly hugged her and went around the room embracing everyone in the room. She was going to like her new family very much. Being the oldest in her family it was Polly who had to do all the planning for any occasion. Her mother was always too busy or too tired to even hang a streamer on the door when it was one of the children's birthdays. Polly had to chase those feelings away. As much as she would like to have her brothers and sisters at the wedding it wasn't going to happen and she had to stop thinking about it.

Randy Burke was becoming an expert with the printing press. He and Josie were able to put out the Chronicle three times a week now. Josie was a natural journalist. She was able to make the ordinary seem unusual and the unusual seem extraordinary. She was up on all the the current events and made sure her readers were well informed. She was able to voice her opinion in her editorials without infuriating anyone. The size of the paper was expanding into two pages thanks to all the advertisement. The businesses around town were anxious to have their ads in the paper and business in Camden Corners was booming.

Arthur Preston of the Greensboro News would drop by occasionally to see if Randy needed any help. Randy had been a quick study and was almost as adept at running the machine as Arthur was. Arthur enjoyed visiting the Chronicle office. Today he was listening to Randy talk about his upcoming wedding. Arthur remembered Polly from Greensboro. She was a lovely young woman which was hard to believe considering the family who raised her. The last he heard Marlin Cooper was in jail for assaulting the bartender at a sleazy tavern just outside of town. Mrs. Cooper spent her days waiting to see her husband and leaving her children to fend for themselves. The children all went to school and were always clean although their clothes were ill fitting and tattered. Arthur's wife suspected the other children at school teased them and it was the older children that made sure the younger ones were clean. There wasn't much they could do about their torn clothing but it was always clean too. Arthur innocently asked if the Coopers would be at the wedding. Kenny told him of the estrangement.

Arthur returned to Greensboro. He and his wife Gladys thought they should do something to rectify the situation. They knew Polly well enough to know she would want to have some of her family at her wedding. Arthur knew the two oldest boys as they delivered papers for the News. Gladys knew all the children as she volunteered in the school cafeteria three days a week. They had a plan. With Mrs. Cooper gone

241

most of the day she wouldn't have to know about their plans until after they had everything in motion.

That very afternoon, Arthur and Gladys rode to the house in the country that the Cooper family called home. The oldest girl, Gretchen opened the door.

"Hello Gretchen, Mr. Preston and I have come to let you know that your sister Polly is getting married tomorrow. Would you and your brothers and sisters like to go to the wedding with us. I'm sure it would make Polly very happy if you were there for her."

Gretchen's eyes were like saucers. "Polly is getting married? Papa said she was soiled and nobody would ever marry her."

"Your Papa was mistaken" Gladys said with a shudder "Polly is marrying a wonderful young man named Randy Burke. He loves your sister and little Faith very much and they love him too. Would you like to go to the wedding?"

"Papa says we can never see Polly again." By then the other children were also standing at the doorway.

Ginny, the youngest girl called out. "I want to see Polly get married. Can we Gretchen, please?"

The other children joined in.

"Papa isn't here, he doesn't have to know."

"Yes, let's go Gretchen. We haven't seen Polly in ever so long."

"I want to see Polly's baby."

Gretchen knew she was making a mistake but she missed her sister too and was about to say they could go but then looked down at her torn dress.

"We can't go in these clothes. It would embarrass Polly if we showed up in these old torn dresses and shirts. Ginny doesn't even have a pair of shoes that don't have holes in the bottom from being worn by each of us girls. Thanks Mrs. Preston but we won't be able to go"

"Nonsense. If it's only clothes and shoes we can fix that this afternoon. What time does your mama come home today?" Gladys was having to think fast because she knew Mrs. Cooper would never let the children go to the wedding.

"Mama won't be home until Papa gets out of jail on Tuesday. She said he wanted her to stay at the jailhouse with him."

"Why?" Gladys found herself asking.

"Because he loves her so much he wants her to be near him even though he can't see her."

Gladys couldn't understand where the woman's head was but now was not the time to figure it out. These children looked hungry and cold. She knew it would be a little crowded at their house tonight but she insisted they come home with her.   She had a big pot of soup on the stove that should fill them up and then they were all going to go shopping.   She knew Arthur would be in agreement without even asking.

The big day was finally here. New Year's Eve. Polly and Randy would start the new year as husband and wife. Polly wasn't nervous as she slipped into the beautiful pale yellow dress she would wear as she repeated her vows with the only man she had ever truly loved. Randy couldn't understand why she couldn't wear white like other brides but he liked the color yellow better anyway. Faith's little dress was made of the same pale yellow material as her mother's. Nettie, Emma, Lily and Ethel were all there to help her. For something old Nettie gave her a pendant to wear around her neck. Nettie's mother had worn the pendant on her own wedding day and Nettie also wore it the day she married Oscar. Emma gave her a blue hankie to carry. Lily let her borrow her small bible and Ethel placed a new hair clip in her hair.

All of Polly's friends had made her feel like a member of a family again. She was so grateful to them for making her almost forget her real family in Greensboro.

Randy was peeking into the crowd of people from the side of the altar when he saw Arthur and Gladys Preston being escorted down the aisle followed by several well dressed children. Randy knew right away who the children were. The tallest girl looked exactly like his soon to be wife. The children were all decked out in lovely new clothes and shoes. The littlest with a big bow in her hair. Everyone was sitting quietly when the organ music started and the procession of lovely bridesmaids started down the aisle.

Randy couldn't take his eyes off his beautiful bride. She was walking with Oscar Crowley and was smiling at him as she walked toward him. Just before she reached the altar she heard a little voice say "Hello Polly"

She turned around and saw her brothers and sisters sitting in the front pew and looking so beautiful and handsome. She went over to them and hugged each and every one.

"It's so good to see you but I think I'd better not keep these folks waiting any longer. They came here to see a wedding.

Vicar Will pronounced the couple husband and wife and introduced Mr. & Mrs. Randy Burke to the guests.

The new Mrs. Burke spent the next 30 minutes introducing her Greensboro family to her Camden Corners family. She was grateful to

Gladys and Arthur Preston for what they had done for the children. She knew her father had not provided them with the clothes they were wearing.

Arthur and Gladys spoke briefly with Oscar about the circumstances they found the youngsters in. They wondered if there was a legal way they could take custody of the children. Oscar thought it was quite possible that Mrs. Cooper's mental state might be in question. He promised he would look into the matter.

The Cooper children had the most wonderful time at the reception. They were able to play with the other children there. Something they were never allowed to do at home. They all loved their little niece and their new brother-in-law. Ginny thought he was very handsome. Gretchen caught the eye of Danny Mackenzie. He asked if he could take her to a movie next week. She reluctantly turned him down. She knew her father would never let her go out with a boy. He told all his daughters that only evil comes from boys. "Just look at your sister," he would say. Gretchen supposed he was talking about Faith but how could that dear little girl be evil. She was beginning to wonder if maybe her father might be the evil one.

The party was in full swing. Even the youngest were still awake waiting to see the new year in. All the older men synchronized their pocket watches and everyone started counting down
FIVE-FOUR-THREE-TWO-ONE
HAPPY NEW YEAR.

There was much optimism in the crowd that evening. Polly and Randy's lives together were just beginning. It wouldn't surprise anyone if by this time next year Faith had a little sister or brother.

Life was never going to be the same in the Cooper house outside of Greensboro. Gretchen changed her mind and accepted Danny Mackenzie's invitation to the movies and she didn't care whether her paw liked it or not.

Arthur Preston was already planning to give up his study to make it into a bedroom for the Cooper boys.

Oscar Crowley was discussing the custody of the Cooper children with his sons.

Several of ladies who were expecting babies were gathered in one little corner of the room discussing layettes and nursery colors. Julie Campbell joined them with a smile on her face. Her sister Josie was thrilled at the prospect of having a little niece or nephew.

Reggie and his father were giving their opinion of the wine that was being served at the reception until Lucinda and Anna interrupted them for a dance.

Nettie was holding a sleeping Faith as she looked around the room and wondered what lay ahead for the folks of Camden Corners in the new year. It would be a year filled with anticipation. The winery should be open for business soon and the first grapes will be ready for harvesting in the fall. The hospital will be up and running bringing many newcomers to Camden Corners. The Weston Camera Company is schedule to begin operation soon. What new surprises lay in store for her adopted little town? She hoped the good would outweigh the bad, the smiles would be plentiful and the frowns infrequent. She loved watching the happy expressions on the Cooper children's faces and knew their future was going to be brighter because they had won the hearts of the good folks of Camden Corners. Nettie looked up and saw Oscar smiling at her.

"Yes my dear, it's going to be another very good year."

The Cabin on Cedar Lake

Sipping her tea on an unseasonably warm January day, Nettie Crowley was deep in thought. What an eventful year it had been. Oscar's two sons were married in a double ceremony to Nettie's dear friends, Emma Patterson and Lily Kramer. Her darling Polly was married just last week to Randy Burke. Nettie knew it was time Polly married and started her own life with her daughter, Faith and Randy but it was so quiet in the house now. Oscar was with his cronies making final plans for their trip to Cedar Lake.

Last September Nettie and Oscar purchased a large cabin. Cedar Lake was a beautiful spot and they thought it would be a wonderful place to have the whole family gather on weekends during the warm summer months. They planned to begin renovations in the spring. There was a large kitchen and sitting room downstairs with two bedrooms on the second floor. The bedrooms were large enough to separate into smaller rooms where there would be plenty of room for each family to have their own area.

Jonas Fulbright, Lou Rossi, Melvin Tanner, Chris Pringle and Oscar had made plans back in December to stay in the cabin overnight and do some ice fishing. They didn't plan on a change in the weather in January and Oscar was concerned it might just be too warm to safely fish on top of the ice.

Nettie scolded herself for her melancholy. She was grateful for the wonderful life she had in Camden Corners. It was time she got up and baked some cookies. That would shake her out of this self pitying mood. She was just about to add raisins and nut meats to the batter when Oscar dashed through the door.

"Nettie, pack your bags, we're all going to the cabin."

"What on earth are you talking about Oscar? This is a men only trip. I can't be there alone with all of you men. What would I do when you were out on the ice? I'm certainly not going to sit on a cold stool in the middle of the frozen lake for heaven sake."

"You aren't the only female who will be there. We have decided to bring the wives along in case the water isn't frozen enough for fishing."

Nettie thought it was a foolish idea but if her friends wanted to go with the men she would join in too.

After some persuasion the men convinced the ladies that they would enjoy themselves. They all packed plenty of blankets and ingredients for their favorite dishes and gathered together in the Fulbright's covered wagon and were off for the hills and Cedar Lake.

Jonas drove the horses while Oscar sat next to him to give directions. Anna Rossi was happy to be doing something spontaneous with Lou. They never were able to venture too far from home when he was caring for his vineyard. Priscilla Pringle had been feeling blue since the holidays were over. They were already planning for next Christmas but it seemed so far away that this diversion was just what the doctor ordered. Ethel was happy to be with her friends and Alma Schrum was delighted to be spending time with Melvin Tanner. He had asked her to marry him and she accepted. Melvin lived in the Wharton Boarding house with his ward, Cody Hill. Cody was staying in the dorm at college but came home often to be with April Hawthorne. It was decided after the wedding Melvin and Cody would move into the home Alma had shared with her husband for over 30 years. The house had been a lonely place for Alma until Melvin came into her life. They both had a second chance at happiness.

Chris Pringle began singing *I'm a Yankee Doodle Dandy.* It was a catchy tune and everyone joined in. They laughed and sang all the way to the cabin and felt 20 years younger than they did when they all climbed aboard the wagon that morning.

The cabin was fairly warm inside thanks to the sunlight streaming in through the window. The Crowley's first guests were impressed with the purchase. The women went directly to the kitchen to find everything they would need to prepare a big dinner for the hungry travelers. The men began building a fire in the massive fireplace. They were happy to find a generous supply of cut logs in the storage shed just outside the back door. Oscar bought the cabin from a gentleman who decided he was getting too old for winters in the north and moved with his wife to North Carolina where his daughter and her family lived. It was obvious the cabin had been meticulously taken care of through the years.

After a fine midday meal, the tired group sat on the large sofas around the blazing fire. After the long trip and experiencing full bellies, they were happy to relax in front of the fire.

Anna spoke up, "I know Melvin came to Camden Corners to be with Cody and met Alma but what brought you to Camden Corners, Nettie, Ethel and Jonas? I'm sure Greensboro wasn't happy to see any of you leave."

Ethel explained that their daughter and her family live in Camden Corners. They decided to sell their farm and move closer to her.

Nettie spoke up, "I found that I missed my dear friend Ethel and when she suggested I pack my bags and move here I was on the very next train." Looking at Oscar she said in a low voice "And I'm awfully glad I did."

Noticing the fond expressions that were exchanged between Oscar and Nettie, Anna couldn't help but say "Was it love at first sight?"

"Now Anna" it was Lou who spoke up. "I know you enjoy a love story but it really isn't any of your business."

"I'm not shy about talking about it" said Oscar who was still smiling at his wife. "In one day my life was transformed from a lonely old widower to the happiest man in the world. Miss Nettie Dawson walked into my office with her friends. One look and I was a goner. She was the loveliest, feistiest woman I had ever seen. She was like a mother bear protecting her cubs, Emma and Lily against the meanest man in Greensboro. I was smitten and I still am."

"That's all it takes is one look" piped in the professor. "I was a blubbering idiot when I first laid eyes on Alma."

"Are you sure it wasn't my oatmeal cookies that attracted you Melvin?"

"Well, that probably had something to do with it," he chuckled.

Nettie's curiosity was piqued, "Anna, how did you and Lou meet back in Italy? Was it love at first sight for you too?"

Lou laughed "Hardly. She couldn't stand me and I didn't like her too much either."

"It's true" said Anna "Our marriage had been arranged when we were less than two years old. My papa and Lou's papa were the best of friends. They owned adjoining property and both grew grapes and had their own wineries. They were thinking of future generations of grape growers and decided it would double their value if their children were married to each other. I was the youngest of six girls and Mamma became more frail after the birth of each one of us. The doctor told Papa not to expect any more children after I was born. He wanted a son and heir but he loved Mamma enough to follow the doctor's orders. Papa's biggest fear was that all of his daughters would marry feckless characters and the land would go to seed. My sisters all married very nice men but none of them wanted anything to do with the vineyard or land so my papa's fears weren't totally unjustified. Lou's papa knew how important a wife could be in a vintner's success and he didn't want some femme fatale getting her hooks into his son and distracting him from his work. Lou and I played together as children. I was told I had been promised to Lou and it seemed very normal to both of us. Then one day when I was walking down the road to school, a new boy in town walked by me. He was older than Lou and so handsome. It was the first taste of romantic feelings I'd ever experienced and I suddenly realized that I didn't have those feelings for my friend and intended Lou Rossi.

Lou joined in, "I was more interested in playing ball and getting into mischief with my pals than I was in Anna. The whole town knew of our papas' agreement and I was teased by my friends until I avoided Anna whenever possible. Eventually I discovered girls were a rather pleasant diversion but I never looked at Anna in that way. It finally occurred to our papas that Anna and I couldn't stand each other. They were disappointed but they did back down on the idea of uniting the families."

Anna spoke up. "I think our Mammas influenced that decision. It was obvious to them that Lou and I could barely be in the same room together. The first time I ever heard Mamma raise her voice was when she told Papa *"No child of mine will ever be traded for land and that is final."* It didn't take long before Lou was prancing around town with a different female on his arm every night of the week."

"Anna, I never pranced around town and as much as I would like to think it's true, I can't remember being with a female every night of the week although I'm glad to see that little spark of jealousy after all these years. What about you and your beaus? Once the fellows learned of our broken engagement they were lined up at your door."

"It wasn't much of a line. As I recall it was a very small town. I'll admit, I did have a few gentlemen callers. After the years of being promised, I was finally free to make my own choices. The trouble was, nobody measured up to Lou. After a couple of years of maturing, he had become a very handsome fellow. I would see him walking in the vineyard and my heart would skip a beat. This was the boy I played with as a child. I told him my deepest, darkest secrets and he told me his. He was my best friend and now he refused to look in my direction."

Lou smiled and said "I was trying my best not to look at Anna. She had grown into a beauty. After a rather heavy rain, I was checking the vines for damage when I glanced over in the direction of her papa's land. Anna was on her knees inspecting the underside of the vines for damage. I noticed her scooping a handful of dirt and examining it like any other girl would examine fine jewelry. At that moment I realized I had been in love with Anna all along. Papa told me when I married I should look for a wife who would love the earth as much as I did and it was obvious Anna was that girl. Something came over me and I walked over to her, lifted her up and clumsily kissed her right there in the middle of the vineyard."

Anna was giggling. "I still remember that kiss. I didn't know it was clumsy because it was the first time I'd ever been kissed in that way before. My knees grew weak and I thought I was going to swoon when suddenly I heard applause. Our Mammas, Papas, and all of my sisters were looking on as well as the farmhands. I could feel my face turning red and looked at Lou and he was as red as the grapes we were surrounded by."

"My skills at kissing must have improved because Anna agreed to marry me a week later."

"That is so romantic" said Nettie. "It's obvious the marriage has been a success. Look how happy you two are after all these years. Lou, I'm glad you came to your senses."

Even the men had listened intently to Anna and Lou tell their story and no one thought to look outside. It seemed the mild weather had taken a turn. Snow was piled up against the door and the wind had started to howl.

Oscar said "I'm glad you ladies brought an assortment of blankets, I think we may have to settle in for the night."

"Lucky we have two large bedrooms." added Nettie. "One for the ladies and one for the gentlemen."

After a light supper and a few hands of whist, the group was ready to settle down in the comfortable beds for the night.

It didn't take long for the men to begin snoring in one bedroom while the ladies were giggling and gossiping until they all dropped off to sleep as the snow continued to pile up outdoors.

Let it Snow

Oscar was the first to wake up in the cabin that cold January day. The unusually warm weather was forgotten as he piled logs on the fire. One by one the men all came down the stairs wearing their warm woolen sweaters and trousers. They were happy their womenfolk had prepared for a change in the weather and thought to pack the heavier clothes. Alma warned Melvin that he might need some warm clothes and he was happy he listened to her.

Chris made one pot of coffee and was getting ready to pump more water for a second pot when the women all came down the cedar stairs bundled to their chins in blankets. The fire was starting to warm the downstairs much to the relief of Nettie who was beginning to wonder if it was such a good idea to plan this little excursion in the middle of January.

"Good morning ladies" called out Oscar "Good thing you brought as much food as you did. It looks like we may be here for another day or two."

"Thank heaven for indoor plumbing" cried Nettie

Ethel was glad she thought of bringing fresh eggs and ham with her just in case they had to stay the night. She started cooking those while Priscilla and Alma prepared the biscuits. Nettie squeezed the oranges for juice and Anna shredded and fried the potatoes.

After the hardy breakfast everyone pitched in to clear the table and clean up the kitchen. The men ventured outside to clear the walk to and from the wood pile. The woman set up folding tables to put together a couple of jigsaw puzzles the former owners left behind.

"Ethel, tell the others the story of how you and Jonas got together." said Nettie as the fellows were walking in carrying the logs.

"Don't start without us" Chis said "We want to hear it too."

Once everyone was seated around the tables and turning puzzle pieces upright, Ethel began.

"My mother gave piano lessons to the neighborhood children. She loved playing and since her daughter was completely lacking in musical ability, she decided she would teach other children to play. I can remember the sound of the scales in my head. Thank goodness she only taught three days a week. I had seen Jonas at school of course, but he sat in the back of the room during school and was always playing ball or climbing trees with the other boys while the girls played hopscotch and jacks on the opposite side of the building.

On a Wednesday in May, Mama mentioned she was going to have a new student, his name was Jonas Fulbright and he was in my class. I groaned thinking how often Mama had the new students practice the scales. Since it was a nice spring day, I would just go outside and maybe finish my school work later that evening. Jonas knocked on the door and I answered it. He had a scowl on his face. He grumbled hello. Mama knew right away that piano lessons were not what this boy wanted. She was sure it was his mama's idea and not his. Further down the street I could hear the other boys taunting Jonas saying the piano was for girls. I found myself feeling sorry for this boy who so obviously wanted to be anywhere but in my family's parlor learning to play the piano. I marched down the street and in the harshest voice I could muster told the boys to be quiet. There were more famous men who played the piano than there were ladies. Beethoven, Chopin, Mozart were all I could think of at that moment. My disapproval fell on deaf ears and the boys just continued to make fun of Jonas until they heard the music coming from our parlor. We all walked toward the house and couldn't believe our ears. Jonas was playing *America the Beautiful.* I could hear mother asking where he had learned to play like that. He told her there was a piano at his grandmother's house and she showed him how to play but he couldn't learn the notes. He just liked to play the piano. He didn't want to learn how. Mama said he was playing by ear and that was a special talent but he would be able to play more music if he would learn to read the notes. It was always hard for anyone to say no to Mama and Jonas was no exception.

The boys didn't tease Jonas so much after that. In fact they use to hang around our parlor window on Wednesday afternoons waiting for Jonas to play a song or two. Jonas eventually did learn to read music but he still depends on his ears for most of his playing.

Except for those Wednesday afternoons Jonas pretty much ignored me. I was developing a crush on him and was rather impatient waiting for him to look in my direction. I remember Mama telling me that it sometimes took a little longer for boys to be attracted to young ladies. I also remember the day that Jonas finally took notice of a female. It was the day the mayor's niece rode into town in the fanciest carriage I had ever seen. Miss Hattie Mae Worthington stepped from that carriage with her red hair flowing. She looked like a princess. I glanced at Jonas and his chums and they were all staring at this beauty with their mouths hanging open. My daydreams of walking hand in hand with Jonas were shattered. I looked down at my scuffed shoes and my hand me down dress that even

I had outgrown. I put my hand to my mousy brown pigtails and knew I looked as frumpy as I felt."

Jonas chuckled "Yes, that Hattie Mae was a fine looking young lady. I don't think my mouth was hanging open though Ethel and if it was it was because of the fancy carriage she arrived in." He winked at his cronies. "You have to realize, this was Greensboro in the 1840s. I was just a farm boy who spent most of his summer days milking cows and tending crops. We didn't have many visitors to Greensboro and none that looked like Miss Hattie Mae Worthington. Ethel tells you I ignored her that summer. That wasn't true. I thought she was a pretty little thing but I couldn't get myself to talk to her. I was much more comfortable playing the piano and she didn't know it but I hated those lessons every Wednesday and only agreed to sit through them because I knew Ethel would be sitting at the parlor window. Hattie Mae's grandpappy asked me to accompany her on the piano at a fancy dinner he was giving for some of the other mayors in the county. He arranged for his tailor to make me a suit as the one I wore to church on Sunday *wasn't up to snuff* as he put it. Ethel's mama taught me enough about reading notes that I was able to learn the songs with the sheet music Hattie Mae brought with her. I hadn't practiced with Hattie Mae until the afternoon of the dinner. I was in for quite the surprise. Hattie Mae's voice was like a wounded cat caught in a prickly pine tree. Even the mayor was holding his hands over his ears. Hattie Mae was a very beautiful young lady until her grandfather told her she couldn't sing at the dinner that evening. I had never seen a female with such strength. She started picking up glasses that had just been placed on the tables and throwing them against the wall. She was screaming at the top of her lungs until two of the mayor's aides carried her out of the room kicking and bellowing. The dinner went on as planned except I was the only musical accompaniment. It was my first and last public appearance. From that moment on I only played for pleasure."

Alma said "We all know you eventually revealed your true feelings to each other because otherwise you wouldn't be here with us now. How did that all happen?"

Ethel spoke up, "Thanks to Nettie we finally were forced to open our hearts to each other. It was the first week of school. We were all sitting around the lunch table when Nettie asked Jonas if he had asked me to go to the harvest dance with him. I was so embarrassed I was tempted to hide under the table. Jonas looked dumfounded and finally said he didn't know if I would go with him if he did ask. Nettie said she was pretty sure I would. Come to think of it, I'm not sure he ever did ask me but we did go to the dance together. After that he came to the house after his chores every morning to walk me to school. I don't know when we got over being shy with each other but eventually we did."

Nettie said "I wonder what ever happened to Hattie Mae? I don't remember ever seeing her again in Greensboro."

Melvin spoke up. "I believe she married one of the professors at the university. I do remember going to a soiree given by this fellow and his wife Hattie Mae. She was the entertainment and your description of her singing was accurate. I remember Professor Danforth smiled through the performance. I later learned the man is hard of hearing and he'd turned his hearing device off. After that experience, anytime I received an invitation to any gathering at the Danforth residence, I always regretfully declined."

"Now it's your turn Priscilla and Chris. Tell us the story of your meeting and marriage."

Priscilla answered "There really isn't much to tell. Christopher was the only child of Nicholas and Belle Pringle and my folks were Noel and Eve Claus. As you can imagine by the sound of their names, our families loved Christmas and that love was passed down to us. I don't remember a time when I didn't love Chris. He was always so jolly no matter what was happening around him. We never thought twice about getting married it seemed the natural thing to do."

"Priscilla is correct. There was never anyone else for me either. Our only regret is that we were never blessed with children of our own."

Alma said "Oh you two are loved by all of the children of Camden Corners. I know they love visiting your Christmas shop even in the heat of the summer. Our boys, Butch and Billy cherish the ornaments you made for them this year, Priscilla. This was their first Christmas with a family and those ornaments made it even more special for them. I know Butch keeps his on the nightstand by his bed. I have seen Billy admiring his ornament when he thinks no one is looking."

Nettie said "I know what you mean about not being blessed with children of your own. I was lucky enough to teach school for many years and my students were always very special to me. I loved it when they had grown and brought their own children into my classroom. Of course, there is Polly. Even though she had only been with us for a short time she quickly became a daughter to me."

"How are Polly's brothers and sisters, have you heard Nettie? It was so good to see them sitting so proudly at Polly's wedding. The Prestons did a wonderful thing by making sure Polly's family was represented on such an important day for her."

"Yes, they are doing very well living with Arthur and Gladys. Arthur has already begun building an addition to the house to allow for extra bedrooms for their expanded family. Oscar was there just the other day checking on Alice Cooper and the children. Alice is still insisting Marlin needs her to be near him. She never even asks about her children. I know she has been told they are not in the old house any longer but she doesn't seem to care. I'm afraid she will never be the same. Marlin was taken to the hospital last week. The doctors aren't sure what is wrong with him but he is a very sick man. I think the hospital has taken pity on Alice and she is allowed to sit with Marlin for a few hours a day. It's a rather tricky situation. Nobody wants to take the children away from Alice but she is incapable of caring for them now and they are living a normal life with the Prestons. While I was there, Danny Mackenzie was calling on Gretchen."

The men ventured outside and thought the roads looked clear enough to travel. They thought it might be best to start for Camden Corners in case the weather took a turn for the worse.

Everything was packed up, the fire in the fire place was out and everything shut down until the next visit.

The Crowley's and their friends were sorry to see their visit to the cabin come to an end. Everyone had enjoyed their get together. There was a knock on the door. Oscar opened it and saw Greensboro's Sheriff Eb Daniels standing there.

"Eb, what are you doing in these parts?"

"I'm sorry Oscar. I'm doing my duty as sheriff of Greensboro. At times I really don't like this job and this is one of those times. Oscar Crowley, you are under arrest for the murder of Marlin Cooper."

Murder in Greensboro

Everyone gasped when Sheriff Daniels stood at the door of the Clear Lake cabin and announced Oscar Crowley was under arrest for the murder of Marlin Cooper.

"I'm going with you," cried Nettie

"Sorry ma'am. This is official business and you will not be allowed to ride with Mr. Crowley. You may follow us to the police station and wait to see him until after we complete our investigation."

"Nettie, darling. Go back home with Jonas. Tell Richard and Robert what is happening and have one of them meet me in Greensboro. There has been a huge misunderstanding. I want you to go home and wait for me. I'm sure I will be there before dinner tonight. Jonas please take Nettie back to Camden Corners."

Off the sheriff went with his prisoner in tow. Nettie and her friends were watching in disbelief as Oscar was hauled away like a common criminal.

Jonas said "Let's get back to Camden Corners right away. The best way we can help Oscar is to let his sons know what is going on."

The ride back to town was a somber one. Not anything like the trip to the cabin just the previous morning when they were laughing and singing. Nettie couldn't understand why that sheriff would even consider her Oscar could do such a thing.

They finally arrived in Camden Corners and went directly to the law office. Robert was standing at the doorway.

"We know father was arrested. Richard is already on his way there. I was waiting for Nettie to return. We knew she would want to go with me to Greensboro. Polly is at your place, Nettie. She is packing an overnight bag for you. Emma is taking care of Faith for a few days. Polly will be joining us also.

"Of course she will. In my state of mind I have only been thinking of Oscar. I haven't even considered the fact that Polly's father is dead. I'm sure she has mixed feelings about him but he was her father. Robert, why on earth would they think Oscar of all people would have anything to do with a murder? It's absurd."

"I don't know what led them to Father. The sheriff showed up at your house early this morning he handed the housekeeper a search warrant. She didn't know what to do and rushed to our house very distraught. The sheriff found a bloody knife tucked in the seat of Father's carriage. Robert and I are sure someone planted it there when Father was in Greensboro the other day. Unfortunately, he was spotted at the hospital talking with Mrs. Cooper. He didn't mention going into the room to see Marlin and I can't imagine that he did. The sheriff referred to an anonymous tip. Nothing adds up here. We know Oscar Crowley is incapable of murder. We will get to the bottom of this Nettie, I promise you."

Polly was anxious to arrive in Greensboro. The trip seemed to take longer than usual and the snow packed roads didn't help. Nettie held her hand trying to calm her but Nettie was upset herself.

"Paw was a mean husband and horrible father Nettie, but he was my father. I can't help but wonder what in his life made him the way he was. I have a hard time believing a man can be born evil. I won't be shedding a tear for him but I am concerned about Mama. I know she has all but abandoned the children and now with Paw gone I don't know how she will cope with the loss. The Prestons have been a godsend to our family. I can't imagine what would have happened to the children without money to buy food or clothing. I feel so guilty about living in such a happy home with you and Oscar while my siblings were suffering so."

"Polly, don't be so harsh toward yourself. You were told not to come home or to try to see the children. There was nothing you could do for them. Gladys Preston told me your little sister, Ginny has started calling her mama. The other children are all happy and healthy. We will make sure your mama is taken care of. She may need some rest you know. There is a small home just outside of Greensboro that helps people who are distraught. Oscar visited the home when he was in Greensboro the other day. He was very impressed with the caregivers there. I know he'd planned to discuss it with you. It may be where your mama needs to be for a while."

When they arrived in Greensboro, Polly went directly to the Preston house. The children were happy to see their big sister again. They were adjusting well to the news of Paw's death but were worried about their mother. Gladys told her Alice was still sitting in the waiting room of the hospital. She didn't seem to understand that her husband was dead. The nurses were willing to let her stay until Polly arrived in town but something had to be done soon. Polly was the oldest and therefore had the authority to have her mother placed in the home Oscar had been to a few days ago. Arthur accompanied Polly and Gretchen to the hospital. Their mother was still sitting on the sofa in the waiting room.

"Mama" Polly said tearfully, "It's Polly."

There was no response. The frail woman was staring into space. Polly and Gretchen agreed that she would not be able to go back to the family home. Alice was taken out of the hospital and escorted to the rehabilitation home as both girls held each other and cried for their mama.

Polly left her sister and Arthur promising to return to the Preston house in time for supper. She needed to be with Nettie as she waited to hear word of Oscar.

Richard finally came out of the interrogation room. "There isn't much to tell. Father is doing well. He is more worried about you Nettie than he is about his situation. He will mostly likely be staying the night in a jail cell. I think the district attorney has a vendetta against Father because of a case he tried here a few years ago. He made a fool of him and he is still carrying a grudge."

Robert spoke up, "They aren't going to let you see Father tonight. He insists we register you and Polly at the hotel on Main Street for the night. We will escort you to the Preston house where you are expected for supper and Arthur will make sure you arrive safely at the hotel later this evening. Richard and I have a bit of investigating to do. We will meet you at the hotel and fill you in on what we find."

Reluctantly, Nettie agreed to the plan. She didn't want Oscar worrying about her so she did as he asked.

The children were relieved their mama was going to be well taken care of. Polly spoke privately with the older children. Their house would have to be sold to pay for their mother's room and care. Oscar Crowley had set up a trust fund for Alice but Polly refused to allow him to shoulder the expense of caring for her mother. The children were all in agreement. The house had been filled with nothing but unpleasant memories for several years. They were happy they would be able to stay with the Prestons.

Oscar told his sons everything he could remember about his time in Greensboro. His first stop was to the Preston house. He was assured the children were happy living with Gladys and Arthur. One by one the children all arrived home from school. They had all put on weight since Polly's wedding just a couple of weeks ago. It was obvious they were being well taken care of. While Oscar was there Danny Mackenzie came calling for Gretchen. It was unmistakable the boy was smitten and Gretchen couldn't keep the smile off her face. Oscar was happy for her. She couldn't ask for a nicer family to be a part of. Gladys said she was was worried about Alice. She had been to see her just yesterday. The woman just sits in the waiting room until the nurse tells her it's time to visit with Marlin. She doesn't seem to be aware of her surroundings. Gladys mentioned the home in town. I would much rather see her in a place like that rather than an asylum. I have spoken with the director and she said they have had people like Alice and with time they have been able to come back to the living. Oscar's next stop was to the hospital. He sat with Alice for a while but she didn't respond to him. There were many people in and out of the area but he did remember seeing a disheveled looking gentlemen entering Marlin's room. The man didn't stay for long and had his head turned but Oscar recalled seeing that face somewhere before. He'd left his carriage in front of the hospital. He remembered the valet telling him a gentleman was getting very close to his carriage and he approached the man and asked if he could help him. He told him no, he was just admiring the carriage. When he described him, Oscar thought it sounded very much like the fellow he had seen coming out of Marlin's room. He left to tour the home that had been recommended for Alice and spoke with the director and caregivers. He met Cody Hill who had just finished his classes at the university for an early supper and then left for home.

The sheriff was much more cooperative than the district attorney. He told the Crowleys a messenger had dropped off an envelope with a torn piece of paper in it with the words. *Oscar Crowley is a killer. Look in his carriage.* We had to investigate because it was a known fact that your father was in the hospital just before Marlin Cooper was found stabbed to death. Sheriff Daniels thought the whole thing seemed fishy but the DA insisted we go after Oscar.

The Crowleys examined the paper and determined it had probably come from butcher paper that was used to cover tables in some of the less than desirable watering holes. They knew Marlin had frequented Shaky's Bar and headed there to see if they could find any evidence of the torn paper.

The lights were dim in the dingy little bar. The Crowley brothers realized they were out of place in their natty suits and overcoats. All heads turned when the two men walked through the doors.

"What can I get ya?" the bartender grumbled.

"A couple of beers and a little information" Richard said "Our old man is in jail accused of murdering Marlin Cooper. Anybody in here know anything about that?"

A squirrely little man started toward the back door. Robert went after him and caught him by the collar of his frayed jacket.

"Come on pal. Let me buy you a drink. Come sit down with my brother and me. We want to ask you a few questions."

"Hey, stop disturbing the customers. If your father did off Marlin Cooper he should be given a medal. Benjy, tell these blokes to leave you alone."

Benjy felt his knees go weak. A drink sounded awfully good and with these guys buyin' he was gonna get himself a double shot of the best bourbon in the joint.

"Don't know nothin' about no murder but I'll take that drink."

After Benjy downed the drink in one swallow Richard said "Tasted pretty good huh Benjy? How would you like another?"

Benjy nodded his head and thought he must have died and gone to heaven.

"We'll get you another one Benjy as soon as you tell us what you know about Marlin Cooper and how he died."

Benjy thought for a minute. It really wasn't his fault Marlin was dead. It was self defense after all. His mouth was watering for another shot, this time he'd order a triple.

"I'll tell ya what happened. Marlin is a pal of mine. We were in the pokey together. They said I was a vagrant just because I was sleepin' in the alley. I'm no vagrant. I have a home. I was just too tired to walk there that night. Marlin was madder than a pistol when he was in that jail cell. He said he was goin' to go to some little town down the road and wring the neck of somebody named Polly. Then he said he'd do the same thing to Oscar Crowley. I remembered a fellow named Oscar Crowley. He was a friend of Judge Martin. I like the judge. He always put two bits in my hat when I was just sitting and resting by the court house. I used to see him with Oscar Crowley too. I knew Mr. Crowley because of the time I had a really awful belly ache. Mr. Crowley stopped when he saw me and asked if he could help. Everybody else just passed me by. Mr. Crowley took me to the hospital and they fixed me up good. This pretty little nurse told me Mr. Crowley paid the doctor to help me feel better. Now I'm feelin' kinda low 'cause of what I did. He didn't deserve to be blamed for Marlin bein' dead.

When I got outta the pokey a few days later I went to see Marlin. I thought he was my friend but boy was I wrong there. He gave me a knife that he had swiped from somewhere. It wasn't a very big knife so I guess he could hide it pretty easy. He said the nurse told him Oscar Crowley was out in the visitor's room with his wife. He said he was tired of the woman 'cause she was always cryin' about somethin'. He told me to go out there and stick the knife into his wife's heart and then yell that Mr. Crowley killed her. Oh yeah I was suppose to hide the knife in the sofa. I told Marlin I ain't never killed nobody before and I didn't want to do it. He started yellin' at me and called me all kinds a names and then he started laughin' at me sayin' I was a yellow bellied coward. I just wanted him to stop. My paw always called me a coward just before he took his belt to me. I had that knife in my hand and before I knew what was happening, I had shoved that knife deep into Marlin Cooper's belly. I'll never forget the look on his face when he realized I wasn't a coward after all.

259

I walked out of the hospital and saw a swell lookin' carriage there. The doorman asked what I was doin' near Mr. Crowley's carriage. It was like I wasn't good enough to stand by a fancy carriage. When he turned his head I stuck the knife in between the seats. When I got here to Shaky's, I started wonderin' if maybe somebody saw me in Marlin's room. That was when I wrote that note about Mr. Crowley bein' a murderer."

Robert brought the anticipated shot of bourbon to Benjy. "It's a triple, just like you wanted Benjy." It would be the last drop of bourbon Benjy would enjoy for a long, long time.

After telling the sheriff his story, Oscar was released immediately. On his way out of the jail, he told Benjy he would arrange to have one of his friends represent him. Oscar knew what kind of a man Marlin Cooper could be and that he was capable of angering someone to the point of murder. He knew he would be sentenced to a prison term but a good defense lawyer should be able to shorten the term. He also was hopeful Benjy would be able to get some help with his drinking problem. He really wasn't a bad guy.

Arthur Preston walked Nettie and Polly through the doors of the hotel. They looked up to see Oscar waiting for them with his arms wide open.

Polly listened silently as Oscar repeated Benjy's confession to the murder of her father, Marlin Cooper. Tears were streaming down her cheeks at the thought of her father's intent to kill her mother. She knew he was an evil man but this was too much even for him.

"I can't believe Paw would go so far as to have my mama killed."

Oscar put his arm around her. "Polly dear, it's true your paw was not a kind man by any stretch of the imagination but from what the doctors told Robert and Richard he was also a very sick man. There was nothing that could be done for him to make him well. The medicine he was given to relieve the pain most likely affected his reasoning. Since he considered me the enemy and heard that I was with your mama he thought of her as the enemy too."

Polly cried in Nettie's arms. She cried for her father who she hoped had found the peace in death that he never had in life. She cried for her mother who lost her spirit but with the help she would be getting had a chance to find it again. She cried for her siblings who lost one set of parents but had a chance for a full and happy life thanks to the Prestons. She then thought of her new husband Randy and her precious Faith and the love she felt from these two wonderful people who sat beside her. The tears stopped and she was able to smile again.

The next morning after a brief stop at the Preston household to say goodbye to the children, the group headed towards Camden Corners. It would be so good to be home.

Oscar's incarceration had been the talk of the town and everyone was relieved when he arrived back home

Josie Blackburn's editorial was a demand for the firing of the district attorney. She talked about the vendetta he had against Oscar and how he'd forced the sheriff to arrest an innocent man. *Anyone who knew Oscar Crowley knew he would never commit murder and even if he did he wouldn't be dumb enough to hide the murder weapon in his own carriage.* Arthur Preston reprinted Josie's editorial in the Greensboro News and the following week it was announced that the mayor had appointed a new district attorney.

So Good to be Home

The townspeople were out in full force welcoming Oscar home. Everyone knew Oscar was an innocent man. Faith squealed with delight when she saw Polly. Randy held his wife close. He was sorry he couldn't shield her from all the pain of the last few days but looking into her eyes he knew she would be fine.

Jack Mackenzie was pacing on the platform of the train depot. He didn't notice the cold north wind blowing the snow against the train tracks as he waited for Audrey Lynch to arrive from Buffalo. He met Audrey just before Christmas but he felt as though they had known each other all their lives. He knew she had followed another man to Camden Corners but Jack knew her crush on Doctor Grady Murphy was in the past.

Jack's mother, Fiona had invited Audrey and her friend, Elizabeth Lawrence to share a room in the Mackenzie house when there was a sudden storm and the train would be delayed in its return to Buffalo. It was love at first sight for Jack. His heart had been broken when a romance in New York City had ended and Jack never intended to be that vulnerable again. Then he met Audrey and everything changed. Jack had been a fun loving young man until the ill fated affair that left him soured on love and shattered his trust in the opposite sex. It was a time of his life he was trying to forget and with Audrey's help he was winning that battle.

Audrey and Jack had been separated more than they had been together but that was about to change within the next few minutes. Nurse Audrey and her friend Elizabeth were moving to Camden Corners to work in the McMillan medical offices and eventually in the Camden Corners Hospital.

The hospital would be up and running in just a few short months. Grady Murphy who had just completed his residency at Buffalo General was joining the medical practice and would be the first new physician to be affiliated with the hospital when it opened its doors.

Audrey's crush on the young doctor was what encouraged her to follow him to Camden Corners last December. She mislead her good friend Elizabeth into thinking nursing positions were available immediately in the hospital. Audrey was certain Dr. Murphy was playing hard to get with her but in truth he only had eyes for Elizabeth. When Audrey stopped looking in Dr. Murphy's direction, she noticed the handsome face of Jack Mackenzie.

Jack and Audrey became an item. Jack's family and friends could see a difference in him the moment the lively Audrey came into his life. Jack was an artist and had opened a gallery in town. As well as his own work, he encouraged artists from surrounding towns to display their works in the showroom. He had developed quite a positive reputation in the art community. He was often questioned by outsiders why he didn't relocate to New York City where his work would be in demand. Jack only told them his life was in Camden Corners and that is where he belonged.

The train arrived right on time and Audrey flew into Jack's arms. He shook hands with Grady and gave Elizabeth a hug. Grady was staying at the Wharton House while Audrey and Elizabeth would be returning to the Mackenzie's and Jack's sister Amanda's old room. Fiona and Gordon greeted the girls at the door. They were delighted their son had found someone who could bring the sparkle back into his eyes.

Everyone settled into their new lives. Grady fit in nicely in the McMillan medical offices. Doc Julie was beginning to experience the early stages of pregnancy and was happy to slow down her pace as Grady pitched in. Audrey and Elizabeth were an added relief especially with the seasonal ailments of the good folks of Camden Corners.

Audrey had gotten in the habit of visiting Jack at the gallery during her lunch break. They would share a sandwich from O'Sullivan's and just enjoy being together for an hour during the day. Jack hadn't officially proposed, he was waiting for Valentine's Day for that but in their hearts they knew they had found their future in each other. Audrey walked into the studio. Carrie, another Mackenzie sister was just finishing framing Jack's latest work. Audrey loved this painting. It was bright and cheerful. So different from his previous works.

"Audrey, because of you my brother has become a different man. You can see it in his work." Carrie set the painting on an easel and turned it so it had just the right lighting. "Jack is at the Pub. Mack needed some help moving a new freezer into place but he should be back in just a few minutes. He told me not to let you leave. I'd say the boy's in love"

"I am too, Carrie. Jack is the best thing that has ever happened to me. I know I'm still a scatterbrain in many ways but Elizabeth says I've calmed down some. Jack has grounded me somehow if that makes sense."

"Don't change too much Audrey, we love scatterbrains in the Mackenzie house. Speaking of which, I promised Mama I'd be at the Pub to help her with the chicken pot pies. They are on the menu this evening which means we will be having a big crowd for the dinner rush. You and Jack should stop by later."

The two friends hugged and said good bye just before a very sophisticated woman entered the shop. Audrey felt like an old frump in her nurses uniform and clunky white shoes.

She walked toward the woman to tell her the owner would be returning shortly when the customer said "I'm looking for Jack Mackenzie."

"He should be returning soon. You may look around while you're waiting."

"Oh I know his work very well" she said dripping with sarcasm.

Audrey felt very uncomfortable and frumpier every minute. She realized she should probably keep quiet at that point but she couldn't help herself. "How do you know Jack?"

"We go way back, dear. I can see you have never been out of this provincial little town. My name is Daphne Saint Marie. I set Jack up in a studio in New York City a couple of years ago. He was my protege until a silly misunderstanding drove him back to this place." The look on her face suggested she didn't see anything redeeming about Camden Corners.

Audrey didn't like Daphne Saint whatever, but she might be a paying customer and Audrey didn't want to say something that might ruin a sale.

"I'm sure Jack will be back momentarily. Please make yourself comfortable Miss Saint Peter."

"It's Saint Marie young lady but before long it will be Mackenzie. Will that be easy enough for you to remember?"

Audrey was sure her heart had fallen to her feet. Could this possibly be the woman who broke Jack's heart in New York? Does he still love her and why did he ever love her in the first place? She could barely speak as she walked into the back room and out the back door. At that point the tears started to flow. She made it back to the office and dissolved into Mary McMillan's arms. Mary had two daughters and knew what a broken heart looked like. She just let Audrey cry it out while she held her tightly.

Jack opened the door of the gallery anxious to see Audrey and spotted Daphne immediately. "What are you doing here Daphne? Slumming today?"

"Darling Jack, you silly boy, I'm here to whisk you off to New York and away from this horrible little town."

"This horrible little town is my home and I have no intention of going anywhere with you. I can't see that we have anything else to discuss so feel free to leave the same way you came in."

"Darling, I know you are a tiny bit miffed at me but the good news is that my husband is dead. We can finally be together my love."

"Golly Daphne congratulations on your dead husband. Now go find yourself another naïve jerk. I don't want you anymore."

"But darling, you need me. What do you have in this place, people like that plain little nurse that was in here a short while ago? I know you better than that. Only I can make you happy darling."

"Was Audrey here? Where is she? What did you say to her Daphne? It's time for you to leave."

Jack escorted her to the door and gave her a little shove locking the door behind her. He turned the open sign to closed and slipped out the back door forgetting to lock it. He went directly to McMillans and found her there. Her eyes were red rimmed and he knew she had been crying.

"I'm not sure we have anything to say to each other Jack. I met your intended today. I can't begin to compete with someone with her sophistication."

Jack put his fingers to her lips. "In the first place, you are my intended. At least I hope you are. I was waiting for Valentine's Day to ask you to be my wife but today will do too. I did have a crush on Daphne but that was a long time ago. I was young and foolish and I thought I wanted to live a life that wasn't me. Daphne took me under her wing. I thought I was in love and I thought she was in love with me. I was so trusting I didn't realize she was using me as her latest diversion. She was married to a much older man who was also a very rich man.

"But she broke your heart. There must be some feelings left for her."

"Yes, she broke my heart two years ago. I realized she wasn't for me very quickly. It wasn't a broken heart that upset me it was the way I was duped. I swore back then that I would never let any woman do that to me again. She made a complete and total fool of me. I was use to strong women, I've been around them all my life, but never any that were dishonest. I learned Daphne was married when her husband strolled into the gallery. He was looking for her latest play thing. I packed my few things, put my paintings under my arm and was on the next train back to Camden Corners.

"The day I first saw you I fell in love. I realized I had been wallowing in self pity. Not because of Daphne but because my pride was hurt. When you opened your heart to me I knew you would never hurt me as I hurt you by not telling you about Daphne. If I had spoken up earlier, you wouldn't have been upset today."

Mary McMillan stepped into the room. "Hello Jack. Audrey has worked hard enough today and we aren't that busy this afternoon. Why don't you two enjoy the afternoon together."

The young couple walked hand in hand to the gallery. When they approached the front door it was standing wide open. Jack remembered locking it behind Daphne. They entered the shop and discovered the walls were bare, the easels were empty. Not one painting, sketch or photograph was left in the entire shop.

"Daphne!" Jack uttered under his breath. "Audrey, I am going to New York City. I can't imagine why she took all of the artwork but I won't let her get away with it. Not so much for me but Tony Marino's photographs were here as well as other artists works."

"I'm going with you. You don't think I'm going to let that witch get her clutches into you again do you?"

After a quick stop in the Pub and a visit to Doc McMillan, Jack and Audrey were on the 4:45 to New York City.

Daphne had just arrived in New York City. She was waiting for a carriage to take her and her newly acquired artwork to the studio she'd set up for Jack. She expected he would be following her on the next train. What she didn't expect was that he wouldn't be alone.

Daphne's Plan

The box lunches didn't compare to the chicken pot pies that were being offered at O'Sullivan's Pub this evening but Jack didn't notice. He was irritated that he was on his way to New York City to retrieve the artwork Daphne Saint Marie had stolen from him earlier in the day. Audrey was sitting by his side. She tried to calm him down but he was furious.

"We will go directly to the police station when we arrive in the city.

Jimmy O'Rourke is on the force. He and I were roommates. He's a good man. Come to think of it he warned me about Daphne. I should have listened to him back then."

"Don't be so hard on yourself, Jack. We all make foolish mistakes at one time in our lives. Remember we would never have met if I hadn't followed Grady Murphy to Camden Corners because of my silly crush on him."

"That's true and because of you, Elizabeth and Grady are now together. I can't say I like the thought of you mooning over another man but if it brought you to Camden Corners and me, I'm glad of it."

The train pulled into the station. Jack had lived in New York long enough to know his way around. Audrey was mesmerized. She had never seen so many people and buildings in her life. She was caught up in the excitement and began to wish she and Jack weren't on a mission to recover artwork. Audrey knew the Hightowers had a motor car and she had seen quite a few in Buffalo but it was amazing how many automobiles and horse drawn carriages were together on the streets. Jack felt more comfortable in a carriage and that is what they rode to the police station.

The officer on the front desk called Jimmy to the reception area.

"Jack Mackenzie, I can't believe it's you" Jack and Jimmy had kept in touch but this was the first time they'd seen each other since the day Jack packed up and left New York vowing never to return.

The men embraced and Jack introduced Audrey to his old friend. Jimmy was glad to see Jack had moved on.

"Am I ever happy to meet you Audrey. I can tell just by looking at my friend Jack that you have brought out the best in him. I'm off duty in just a few minutes. Come home with me. Eileen will be thrilled to see you again."

Jimmy lived in the neighborhood so they walked to the brownstone and surprised Eileen who was balancing a baby on her hip.

"Jack, what a wonderful surprise. Come in, please."

Audrey and Eileen hit it off immediately. Jack told Jimmy about the stolen artwork and Daphne's visit.

"Eileen can tell you about Daphne and the scandal after her husband died. She gets all her information from the gossip columns."

"Yes, and Jimmy loves to hear all the gossip. Daphne's husband died about a year ago. He left most of his money to charity and only an art studio to Daphne. She tried to fight the will but she didn't have enough money for a lawyer and nobody would take her case because the will was ironclad. It came out that her name was really Doris Schultz. She is from

266

a small town in Kansas where she lived on a dairy farm. She changed her name and latched onto Grover Fulton. Daphne was one of Grover's five wives. He divorced them as soon as he felt they were past their prime. Daphne was young and naïve when she and Grover married. She didn't realize she was signing away all rights to his money."

"I say she got what she deserved" said Jimmy.

"Well now Daphne or Doris has my property and I want it back."

"Let's go," said Audrey. "I don't feel quite so intimidated by her now that I know her name is Doris Schultz instead of Daphne Saint Marie"

Daphne was putting the last painting on the wall when the studio door opened and in walked Jack, that insipid girl from Camden Corners and a uniformed police officer. This was not in the plan thought Daphne.

"Darling, I thought you would be following me to New York. Haven't you missed the city, my love? I know what is best for you and having your wonderful work displayed in my studio is so much better than that silly little town of yours."

"Hi Doris, nice to see you again" said Audrey.

Daphne was surprised her true identity had been discovered by this child. Her whole demeanor changed in that moment.

"Look honey, you may have your hooks in Jack now but I know what a man likes in a woman and you can never compete with me. Now you and the officer can be on your way. Jack and I have unfinished business."

"You are right Daphne, we have unfinished business. My entire business is in your studio without my permission. Officer O'Rourke is here to help me retrieve it. I would suggest you move your carcass out of the way while we pack everything up. By the way, don't call my fiancee *honey* again."

Daphne shrugged her shoulders. "Artists like you are a dime a dozen. My studio will be filled with expensive art in no time. Now get this junk out of my sight." She stormed off into the back room wondering how she was going to pay the light bill next month. Maybe it was time she found another occupation. She had a few good years left in her. There are plenty of older gentlemen who are in need of companionship.

Jack, Audrey and Jimmy wrapped each piece of art carefully and carried it one by one to Jimmy's waiting carriage. With that problem taken care of, Jimmy was anxious to celebrate a visit by his old friend with a night on the town. Eileen dropped the baby off with her mother. It had been a while since she and Jimmy had taken in all the sights of Manhattan. She had always liked Jack and was happy to know his relationship with Doris Schultz was finally over. Audrey was the perfect match for her husband's good friend.

Audrey was delighted with the hustle and bustle of New York. They stayed on for a couple of days and there was still plenty to see but they did have to get back to reality.

Jimmy and Eileen saw them off at the train station promising to return for another visit very soon. Audrey was looking out the window when she noticed a tall regal looking woman walking arm in arm with an older gentleman at least five inches shorter than she was. He had a stogie dangling from his mouth and sparkling diamond rings on his fingers.

"Looks like Daphne Saint Marie is back in action" she said to Jack who simply shook his head.

Everyone in Camden Corners was happy to see the travelers return with all of the art work intact. Carrie helped hang the paintings in their places.

Audrey stopped at the medical offices to thank everyone for being understanding about her leaving.

"It hasn't been that busy" Elizabeth told her friend.

"Are you feeling alright Elizabeth? You look a little pale"

"Oh I'll be fine. I haven't been sleeping well the last few nights. I think I just missed my roommate."

As the day wore on, Audrey worried about Elizabeth. She wasn't herself. Grady was busy treating one of the Burke boys who had been enjoying a toboggan ride with his friends until his steering went bad and they landed smack into a pine tree. There weren't any broken bones but Grady was making sure none of the boys had head injuries. He noticed Elizabeth was a little quiet but didn't think anything was wrong until Audrey came rushing into the room.

"Elizabeth just fainted. I helped her to the examining room and she is awake but she is burning with fever."

Grady ran into the room. He could tell just by glancing that she was a very sick young woman. Doctor Tom took over the care of the toboggan riders as Grady wrapped Elizabeth in as many blankets as he could find and drove her in his carriage to the Mackenzie house where he put her to bed. Audrey went with them. Grady insisted Audrey wear a mask while she cared for Elizabeth. Grady knew Elizabeth's illness was extremely serious. He had seen an outbreak of influenza during his residency in Buffalo. He erased from his mind the young woman who died from the disease while under his care. He knew the best place for Elizabeth to be was in the hospital but he didn't think she would survive the long trip to Greensboro. Doc McMillan agreed. The new Camden Corners hospital couldn't be completed soon enough. After swallowing medication, Elizabeth was able to sleep. Grady and Audrey stayed by her side. The bedroom was closed off to the rest of the family. Audrey and Grady took turns sleeping on Audrey's bed. Jack made sure food and drinks were brought into the bedroom for the caregivers. Their carefree days in New York were just a distant memory. Jack knew if anything happened to Elizabeth, Audrey would be devastated.

Everyone in town was anxious for Elizabeth. She had only been a resident of Camden Corners for a short while but she, Grady and Audrey were well loved already.

Vicar Will opened the church for a special service offering prayers for Elizabeth and also for the containment of the flu virus. Everyone was taking extra precautions to wash their hands often and see one of the Docs if they experienced any symptoms at all.

After looking through the log, Mary McMillan saw that a young man who was passing through town had been to see Grady. He was suffering from a cough and fever. Grady had treated and released him. His nurse was Elizabeth. Grady was beside himself with guilt that he didn't recognize the symptoms as influenza. If only he had treated Elizabeth earlier she wouldn't be suffering as she was.

"Grady, you can't know everything there is to know about medicine just because you have an M.D. after your name. Even we seasoned physicians miss clues. Medicine is very complicated. It wasn't obvious this young man was as sick as he was." said Doc trying to comfort him.

"Why did Elizabeth have to be the one to come down with this disease? Why couldn't it have been me?"

"We never know why some people are more susceptible to contracting an illness. Her isolation has helped to curtail the spread of the disease through town and that was your doing. How is Audrey? Is she showing any symptoms?"

"No, I'm checking her carefully because I know she won't let on if she is feeling poorly because she is set on seeing Elizabeth through this."

Four days later Elizabeth opened her eyes. "Am I late for work? What are you doing in my bedroom Grady?"

He and Audrey laughed and cried. Everything was going to be alright. Audrey thought about that day just last week when Daphne Saint Marie entered Jack's gallery. How silly she had been to be envious of that superficial woman. This was what life was all about. Living in a town like Camden Corners where people cared about their neighbors. Where families grew and loved and riches were not the ultimate goal. Where two friends could be happy and planning futures with two handsome men. Valentine's Day wasn't too far off. We'd better start making plans. I wonder how Dr. and the soon to be Mrs. Murphy feel about a double wedding. She looked toward the bed and saw a sparkling diamond on Elizabeth's left hand.

Yes! Life is good.

The Valentine Dance

Camden Corners was abuzz with the news there would be a Valentine Dance held in the newly finished ballroom of the Hightower Winery. Special dance classes were being held for those who needed a refresher course in dancing or had never mastered the art in the first place. Even those with two left feet were getting into the spirit of the holiday.

Everyone involved in the building of the Hightower Winery was proud of the final results. The décor in the tasting and meeting rooms in the lower level was exceptional. The ballroom was reminiscent of the finest dance halls in any large city.

The Hightowers engaged the services of a catering company from New York City for the event enabling the local restauranteurs to attend the party as guests. They also brought in a band they had heard in New York when they were there finalizing their Uncle Shane's estate several months before.

At first the Hightower brothers thought they would sponsor the dance for adults only. Their wives thought it would be a better idea if the whole town was invited to the dance no matter what their age.

"Our town is growing thanks to Uncle Shane and his hard earned money. Why not let the children be a part of the growth since we hope they will be part of the town's future and build their lives here." said Dahlia

Jennie Burke was tossing a ball back and forth to her brother Ben on the school playground. As usual, Jennie's clothes were disheveled. She was wearing her snowsuit pants and jacket. Her long braids were hidden under her brother Jack's old stocking caps. Her face was smeared with mud.

"That's a pretty good arm you got there kid"

Jennie turned around and looked into the most beautiful blue eyes she had ever seen.

The boy with the beautiful eyes said "Bet you could pitch for the New York Highlanders. That's my favorite team."

Jennie, who was never at a loss for words just stared at the boy.

Ben shouted "Hey Jennie, toss me the ball, I'm going over to Billy's. Tell Mama I'll be home before supper."

"Sorry miss, I thought you were a fella. Are you gonna be at the dance tonight? We are new in town so maybe I'll see ya there."

Jennie could only nod her head. She couldn't get any words to come out of her mouth. She walked back home in a daze.

Meanwhile, Nadine was preparing a light supper for her family before the big dance tonight. Maddie was visiting with her mother with some happy news.

"Mama, I guess I should have known but you know how busy we were in the shop during the holidays and then that whole mess with Polly's family and Oscar being arrested for murder, it just didn't occur to me that I could be expecting. You know Jack has been helping Mack with his drawing, he is becoming quite good at it too. Well, Mack drew a sketch of me and my face was fuller than it had ever been. It was only then did I realize I had been feeling tired lately. Everyone has morning sickness but I didn't, not even once. Doc Julie told me some women never do have it although she isn't one of them. Julie had to excuse herself two times while I was there. She doesn't know how much longer she can keep up her patient load. Anyway, she confirmed it. Mack and I will have our own baby in August."

"Maddie, that's wonderful news. I know you have been wanting to start a family. Mack must be thrilled."

"He's passing out cigars to everyone. I told him that was suppose to be done after the baby's arrival and he just says he'll pass them out then too."

Fiona arrived and threw her arms around Nadine. "We are going to be Grandmas together Nadine. Our dreams have come true." She hugged her daughter-in-law and patted her tummy.

Jennie walked in the back door staring into space.

"Jennie, are you alright? You have a very odd look on your face"

"I'm wonderful Mama." She proceeded to take her heavy snowsuit off.

"Jennie, I know you didn't want to go to the dance tonight. I discussed it with your papa and he has agreed that you can stay home, we won't force you to go."

"Oh no Mama, I want to go to the dance. I wonder if Bethany will let me borrow that pretty pink dress she wore at Christmas."

Jennie walked up the stairs to the room she shared with her sister

Lucy and her adopted sister Bethany. She sat down at the dressing table and looked at herself in the mirror. Lucy didn't think Jennie ever looked in a mirror. She never wanted to dress up in frilly clothes as Lucy did. She would rather play ball with her brothers than dolls with her sisters. She was a funny, happy girl and everyone just accepted that Jennie was being herself and they loved all her little tomboy ways.

Without warning, Jennie let out a yelp, yanked at her pigtails and started to sob.

"Mama, come quick, something terrible has happened to Jennie."

The three women ran up the stairs two at a time. "What's happened?" shouted Nadine.

Jennie was still seated at the dressing table. "He thought I was a boy. He's right, I do look like a boy and even Bethany's pink dress won't make me look pretty like all the other girls."

"Who thought you were a boy Jennie?" Everyone in town knew Jennie didn't dress in frilly dresses or brush pretty curls into her hair.

"I don't know who he was but he had beautiful eyes and my tummy did flip flops when I saw him."

Lucy shouted out, "Jennie's in love!" She was just a year younger than her sister but she herself had been in love at least three times in the last year.

"That's enough Lucy. Why don't you go downstairs and check on your little brother." Fiona walked with her while Nadine and Maddie stayed with Jennie.

Nadine dried her daughter's tears. She knew behind all that smeared dirt on her face there was a very pretty young lady. Maddie helped untangle her braids and helped her sister wash her hair. She curled her pretty auburn hair with rags and pins. Bethany was more than happy to lend her sister her pink party dress.

Jennie was afraid her brothers would tease her if they saw her in her rags and pins and decided to stay in her room until just before they all left for the dance.

Papa talked to all the boys and told them not to tease their sister about the way she looks. "What's wrong with the way she looks? All my friends like her and want her on their team. They wouldn't ever make fun of her. Besides, she would sock them if they did."

Maddie hurried home to change for the dance herself and she and Mack came back so Maddie could oversee her sister's transformation.

Jennie watched in the mirror as Maddie brushed her hair. She had never seen so many curls. Maddie applied just a touch of blush to her cheeks and a pale pink lipstick. Bethany's dress fit her perfectly. It was time for her to walk down the stairs. The whole family was waiting for her as she stepped into the parlor. There was total silence in the room. Jennie was about to dissolve into tears when her papa turned on the phonograph and asked his daughter for a dance. Liam told his little girl how beautiful she looked. Her brothers and sisters all started talking at once. They had a hard time recognizing this lovely young lady before them.

"We'd better hurry if we are going to make it to the dance on time." Everyone hurried into the waiting carriage and headed for the Mackenzie house so the families could go together as they always did.

Dr. Clayton Springer and his wife Margie were getting dressed for the dance. Clay was hoping he had made the right decision in moving his family to Camden Corners. It meant taking the children away from their familiar surroundings and their playmates. All three seemed to be taking it in stride and the youngest, Abigail already had two best friends in Camden Corners. Pete came home laughing about a girl he had mistaken for a boy. He told his father she had a better pitching arm than any of his chums back in New York. Samantha was always rather quiet. She enjoyed helping her mother with the cooking and loved reading. She was an excellent student and there weren't any signs that she was slipping in that area. He shook off his doubts and watched as his wife brushed her hair. She was the love of his life. Margie had a calming effect on Clay and just watching her face in the mirror quieted his unease.

"I'm very excited about the dance tonight Clay. I think we made the right decision in moving to Camden Corners. The children seem happy and it is such a beautiful little town. The people all care about one another. Mary McMillan and I went to the antique shop on Main and I met some of the loveliest ladies. Oh, by the way, I bought a pretty little lamp for Samantha's room. I think she likes it. It has an interesting history behind it. When I told Lily Crowley, one of the young owners of the shop, about Samantha's interest in antiques, she suggested she might like to work at the shop one or two afternoons a week. It seems everyone involved in the shop is a history buff. She even suggested Samantha might like to attend an auction with her friends Ethel and Jonas one day this summer. Samantha is thrilled with the idea and is planning to visit the shop after school on Monday."

Clay was certain Margie could read his mind. She knew just when reassurance was required and always seemed to have the exact words he needed to hear.

"I'm a lucky man," Clay said as he kissed his wife on the forehead

"Why, because you have a wife who enjoys spending your money on antique lamps?" Margie laughed.

The night air was very brisk as people began arriving at the winery. This was the first time most of the townsfolk had seen the winery. All of the carpentry work had been completed but it wouldn't be in operation until the fall when the first wine harvest began. Nick Rossi was happy to show off the winery to everyone and his papa, Lou was right at his side.

Upstairs in the ballroom, people were milling around enjoying a glass of champagne or fruit punch while they greeted their friends and neighbors.

The McMillans welcomed the Springer family and began introductions as they circled the room.

"It looks like Lucinda Rossi is busy behind the scenes," said Doc "I'll introduce you to her later. Lucinda is responsible for the Camden Corners hospital being built. She is an extraordinary young woman. She and her daughter are also from New York City. She married Nick Rossi after she and Cassandra moved here just over a year ago."

Peter looked around the room. He recognized some of the fellows from school and excused himself to join them at one of the tables set up with appetizers. The girls were at the other table and he noticed a pretty girl with very curly hair. He thought she was staring at him. She did look vaguely familiar but he couldn't place her.

Lucy noticed her sister staring longingly in the new boy's direction. "That's him, isn't it Jennie, the boy who you saw today? My goodness, he really is cute. He's looking over here Jennie. Go say something to him."

"I can't, I can't move my legs. Oh Lucy, I'm such a klutz. These shoes are so tight I just want to kick them off and walk around in my stocking feet. Doesn't he have the most beautiful eyes you have ever seen?"

Lucy didn't know how she was going to do it but she was determined her sister would have at least one dance with that boy, sore feet or not.

Harold Hightower stood at the microphone announcing it was time everyone took their seat. Shortly after that Will Duesenberry gave the blessing.

Harold walked back to the microphone and asked everyone to begin eating their dinner. He wanted to announce that Camden Corner's Hospital would be fully functional within the week. He introduced two new doctors in town, Grady Murphy and Clayton Springer. The men stood at their seats while the audience showed their appreciation in applause.

Harold then said, "I would like to introduce the young lady who saw a need for a hospital in Camden Corners and fully funded the cost to build it with some left over for its operation. Mrs. Lucinda McCoy Rossi."

Lucinda was walking into the room just as the building shook with the sound of applause. Harold called her to the microphone. She slowly walked to the front of the room.

At the McMillan table, Clayton Springer looked on with astonishment. "I know that woman. She brought her very ill daughter to the clinic and she is definitely not who she pretended to be."

Everyone turned to look at Clayton. It was obvious he was not as impressed with the hospital benefactor as the rest of the room was.

The Party Goes On

Margie Springer reached out her hand hoping to calm her husband. She had known Clayton Springer since they were in sixth grade together and she could tell when his temper was getting the best of him. She couldn't imagine what he meant about knowing the pretty young woman who stood at the podium in front of the applauding crowd.

Clay was seething as he listened to Lucinda praise a man called Shane Howard. He had no idea who she was referring to. His only thought was how she had made a fool of him. He couldn't understand why she would masquerade as she did and the fact that she would put her sick child in danger infuriated him. Was she testing him to see if he was up to her standards as a physician? Was this just a trick to get him to agree to uproot his family and move to Camden Corners? Most importantly why did she choose him to humiliate? His mind was whirling and then he heard her mention his name.

"I would personally like to welcome our newest physician and his family to Camden Corners. I'd like to tell you of my encounter with Dr. Springer when Cassandra and I were still living in New York City.

As you know, Cassandra and I were struggling to make ends meet in our little apartment in New York. It was a cold January day just over a year ago when Cassandra woke up with a fever. I was grateful that there was a free clinic in town and I knew they would be able to help Cassandra but it was three trolly car rides away and Cassandra was such a sick little girl I didn't want to take a chance that the cold would be the worst thing for her at that time. There was a small medical office three doors down from our apartment building. I bundled Cassandra up in blankets, held her as close to me as I could to protect her from the howling wind. I was so relieved when I made it to the doors of the office. The nurse was very pleasant and told me to have a seat. I tried to explain that I only had some change in my pocket but that I would visit the pawn shop as soon as I was able. I had a pearl ring that was found with my mother after the accident. One of the attendants at the orphanage gave it to me as a keepsake. She told me to hide it and I kept it inside a hankie all the years I was in the orphanage. I never thought of selling it even when I was down to my last few pennies for the week. Cassandra's health was more important than any ring and I knew that was what I had to do to pay the doctor's bill.

I could hear the nurse explain my situation to Dr. Pike. He glanced my way and I heard him tell the nurse that they didn't accept charity cases and to send us to the free clinic. At that point, a man with the kindest of faces walked through the doors. I think he heard what Dr. Pike said and came over to Cassandra. He sat down next to us and then asked that we come into his office. I told him I didn't have very much money and he told me about his children at home and that if they were sick he would want someone to help them too. He gave Cassandra some medicine and she was so much better the next day. I asked Mrs. Coleridge, our neighbor to watch Cassandra while I took my ring to the pawn shop. I stopped in the medical office and asked to see Dr. Springer. He was making a house call at the time so I left the money with the nurse. That very afternoon there was a knock on the door. It was Dr. Springer. He said he was checking on his favorite little patient and then handed me my pearl ring. His nurse had told him that I had mentioned pawning my ring and this wonderful man searched the pawn shops until he found it and brought it back to me. You can understand why I mentioned Dr. Springer as a possible addition to our hospital. I'm just happy he agreed to join the hospital and our community.

Margie could feel the tension slipping away as Lucinda told her story. She didn't doubt for one minute that Clay would do as he did. She always knew he was an exceptional man.

After the applause settled down, Clay asked "Maybe it isn't my business but in one year's time how was that poverty stricken young lady able to build a hospital?"

Doc laughed "To make a long story short...."

Mary interrupted him "It's a lovely story and I will tell it. You will leave out all the details Doc." Mary began at the beginning and ended with the happiness Lucinda found in Camden Corners with Nick Rossi. Clay listened intently to every word. He was ashamed of his previous distrust of Lucinda. She could have lived a life of luxury with money left to her but instead donated it to the building of a hospital. Any doubts he had about moving his family to Camden Corners were dispelled that evening. Clay and Margie were born and raised in a big city but they were both small town people at heart and Camden Corners won both their hearts that evening.

Young Peter Springer found himself glancing in the direction of the pretty young girl seated at at the table directly across from him. She would look his way and turn her head as soon as their eyes met. He hadn't met too many people just yet. Mostly the boys from his classes at school. This girl looked familiar but he couldn't place her and then he spotted another boy sitting at the table. He was playing ball with the kid with the great pitching arm he saw earlier that day. It turned out that kid was a girl. He suddenly realized this was that girl, the one with the curls all over her head.

Peter never thought much about the opposite sex until his sixteenth birthday just three months ago. He remembered noticing the red haired girl in his history class in New York. One day she was just another girl and what seemed to be overnight she was transformed into a beauty. He wondered what she would do if he tried to hold her hand but he never would find out since his pa moved them to this little town. Pete wasn't sure he was going to like it in Camden Corners. It was always so quiet. His little sister, Abigail had already made friends and had forgotten all about New York. Samantha seemed to be happy wherever she was as long as she had a book in her hands. He heard Mama tell her about some antique shop and how the owner said she could work there a couple days a week. Samantha was excited about that and couldn't wait to start. Maybe he should think about getting a job after school. He thought of the art gallery on Main Street and wondered if they needed someone to sweep and empty trash. He wouldn't even ask for pay. He liked looking at the artwork and he liked to draw and paint. He stopped in the gallery earlier in the day and met the owner, Jack Mackenzie. He liked Mr. Mackenzie, he always thought painters were a little unbalanced like Vincent van Gogh, but Mr. Mackenzie seemed like a normal guy. He told him he could come into the shop anytime he wanted to. He even told him to bring over some of his work and he'd take a look at it. Pete wasn't sure he was ready to have an artist look at his work. He'd have to think about that.

The dancing started and Pete saw his classmate, Marty dancing with that girl. They seemed to be having fun. Pete wasn't much of a dancer but he could see other fellas cutting in on the dance floor and wondered if he should do the same.

"Come on, Samantha, let's dance." He took her hand and Samantha didn't have much choice but to follow her brother to the dance floor. She didn't mind because she loved to dance. Even as a little girl she would dance around the house pretending she was a ballerina.

"Samantha, I want to cut in on that kid over there. Would you help me trade dancing partners?"

"Pete! I can't do that, what if he turns me down and I'm standing on the dance floor all alone, I would be mortified."

Pete didn't listen to her and danced over to Marty and Jennie and tapped Marty on the shoulder. Marty turned around and saw Samantha standing there with a petrified look on her face. He could almost read her mind and asked if she would care to dance with him. She nodded her head in relief.

Pete held Jennie in his arms. She thought her knees were going to buckle. What was wrong with her and why was she acting this way?

"Hello, my name is Pete. I'm the dumb guy who thought you were a boy. You sure don't look like a boy tonight."

Jennie found her voice. "I'm Jennie"

Jennie's brother Ben tapped Pete's shoulder. He didn't want to give Jennie up but didn't have a choice when he started to pull away, Jennie pulled him closer.

"Get out of here Ben or I'll sock you. Go dance with somebody else."

Pete couldn't help but laugh. This was the girl he saw with the great pitching arm. She was going to be a lot of fun to be around. She turned back to him with a demure smile on her face.

"So Pete, how do you like living in Camden Corners?"

"I think I'm going to like it here just fine Jennie"

Samantha was enjoying her dance with Marty Mackenzie. He was an exceptional dancer and they glided across the floor. She didn't want the dance or the evening to end.

"Samantha, where did you learn to dance like this? You could be in a musical. The high school always puts on a show in the spring. Mr. Lane was talking about doing the Wizard of Oz. If you can sing as well as you dance you should try out. I'm going to try for the straw man myself."

"That would be fun Marty but I'm not sure I would be able to perform in front of all those people"

"Nonsense, we are all your friends or will be by then. Anyway, look around you now. All eyes are on the two of us."

Samantha looked up and sure enough, everyone was standing next to the dance floor and watching them dance. They all started clapping and instead of feeling shy, Samantha found herself enjoying the attention.

Margie turned to Clay. "I don't think you have to worry about our children here in Camden Corners, I do believe they are fitting in very well." She pointed to a table on the far side of the room where Pete and Jennie were talking and laughing. Margie chuckled as she saw Pete take hold of Jennie's hand. She noticed Jennie didn't pull her hand away.

According to Grace Evans' calculations, she should have given birth two weeks ago. Doc Julie told her not to worry, babies have their own schedules and her little one would be here soon. She had felt rather like a cow that evening while she dressed for the dance.

"Maybe I should stay home" she told Ted "I'm so big and fat I'm not sure I'll be able to waddle up to the second floor of the winery."

"It will be fun Grace, and if we don't show up, your mother will worry about you. You know how she has been looking forward to this evening."

Grace was enjoying herself more than she expected. She was very calm and almost forgot she had been with child for over nine months. She was in Ted's arms as they glided over the dance floor.

Suddenly she had the strangest feeling and then a suspicious pain.

"Maybe you'd better take me home, Ted."

Ted scooped her up and carried her to the carriage with her mother, Caroline and Doc Julie following behind.

The band began playing "Rock A Bye Baby" with everyone wishing the new parents good luck as they exited the building.

A Belated Valentine

Fredrick George Evans entered the world just after midnight and narrowly missed being a valentine baby. Little Freddie was named after his two grandfathers. Ted was in awe of this tiny little creature Grace held in her arms. He wondered why he put off getting married for so many years. He had never been happier than he was at this moment.

Caroline Bentley was proud of her daughter. She handled delivery very well. Caroline hadn't given birth to a baby since the day Grace was born. She was now a grandmother and would be a new mother herself in just a few short months.

Jamison brought their children, Kenny and Becky into the room. Kenny was glad there was another boy in the family but wondered how long it would be before he was big enough to toss a baseball. Becky was fascinated with her little nephew. He was so small, almost as small as her favorite doll, Bess. Jamison and Caroline adopted Kenny and Becky shortly after their arrival in Camden Corners. Caroline found it hard to believe that less than one year ago she had been living alone in her big house and now it was filled with her new husband, Jamison and their two children. Jamison's sons visited often along with Grace and Ted and now little Freddie was a part of the growing family.

Jamison was relieved the new hospital was scheduled to open before Caroline was due to deliver their baby. Caroline wasn't as young as most of the new mothers in Camden Corners. Without her knowing, he had spoken with Doc about the danger involved. Doc reassured him that Caroline was healthy and there wasn't any reason to fear for her safety. Doc didn't tell him Caroline had already been in to see him for the same reason.

Reggie Blackburn was touring each and every floor of the hospital. The finishing touches were being completed. Equipment and supplies were being delivered daily now. There wasn't a train that rolled in that didn't have a box or package for the hospital. The doctors were meeting that very afternoon to supervise the placement of beds in the rooms. There were two large wards and several small rooms on each floor. Different areas of the hospital were assigned for different tasks. Anyone with a broken bone or sprain would be directed to that section. Someone coming in with stomach cramps would be sent to another section. Reggie felt confident the doctors would be pleased with the results since they had all participated in one way or another with the design. All except Dr. Springer, but he seemed like a reasonable man.

Reggie took a special interest in the nursery and delivery rooms. Josie hadn't decided whether she would be giving birth at home or in the hospital. He suspected that she would opt to be in their bed when their child was born. Most women seemed to prefer to stay home but there hadn't been an option before. At least the rooms were available if they were needed. Everything about the hospital had been well thought out. Jamison was the best architect he had ever worked with. He seemed to read people's minds and came up with exactly what they had envisioned. Reggie's last stop was the chapel. He often visited this quiet room to gather his thoughts after a hard day. It was such a beautiful room. Lucinda, with the help of Jack Mackenzie, was able to have a stained glass window commissioned. The sun reflected on it near the end of the day and the colors seemed to flicker on the ceiling. This room was nearly complete which was a good thing because in just three days Grady

Murphy and Elizabeth Lawrence were going to be married here.

Caroline stayed with her daughter and made a light supper for the new parents to enjoy with their baby. Jamison headed over to the hospital after making sure the children were safe at home with the housekeeper who loved having them underfoot. Jamison was pleased with the way everything looked. Lucinda was very clear in what she wanted in the building and she never hesitated to ask for input from the doctors and folks from other hospitals around the state. Lucinda arrived at the same time Jamison did and they toured the facility together.

Dr. Springer was the first to arrive. The men shook hands and Clay gave Lucinda a hug. Julie and Tom arrived with Doc. The doctors were very pleased with the facility. They all agreed where everything should be placed and the crew started filling the rooms.

Lucinda told Julie as much as she would like to have her baby at home she thought it would be a vote of confidence to give birth in the new hospital. Julie agreed she would be doing the same when her baby was due. "Maybe we will start a trend."

While her soon to be husband joined the group at the hospital, Elizabeth Lawrence and her good friend Audrey Lynch were busy stitching the last row of pearls on their dresses for Elizabeth and Grady Murphy's wedding.

"Father and Janice will be arriving in the morning from Pittsburgh for the wedding" said Elizabeth "I'm so happy Father will be here to give me away. Janice is bringing along the veil she wore when she and Father were married. Oh Audrey, I can't believe I will be Mrs. Grady Murphy in just a few days."

"I'm happy you will have your family here to help you celebrate. Did Grady hear from his father?" Audrey asked.

"He didn't expect to. Grady says the famous Dr. Ellington Murphy is much to busy taking care of his wealthy patients to attend something so mundane as his only son's wedding," answered Elizabeth.

"It is sad to see a father and son who are so entirely different. Grady chose to be a doctor to help people and his father seems to have decided on his profession to help himself to people's money."

"Grady told me his father says rich folks are just as easy to treat as poor ones and the rewards are greater at the end of the day. I'm sure he would have preferred Grady married one of his high society patients rather than a lowly nurse from Buffalo. To be honest, Audrey, I'm relieved Dr. Murphy won't be at the wedding."

Three days later, holding her proud father's arm, Elizabeth Lawrence walked down the aisle of the hospital chapel and became Mrs. Grady Murphy. She hadn't noticed the older gentleman looking at her from the corner of the room. She'll do, he thought to himself. I'd prefer Grady hadn't married beneath his station, but I do believe I will be able to mold her quite easily. I've got to get my boy out of this provincial town before he becomes too attached to it. Little did Dr. Ellington Murphy know his son had already become attached to Camden Corners and wasn't about to go anywhere.

"I now pronounce you man and wife. You may kiss the bride," Vicar Will Duesenberry proclaimed with a smile. This was one of the happiest parts of his job and he had become an expert at it since there always seemed to be a wedding to look forward to in Camden Corners.

Grady followed orders and happily kissed his bride. He and Elizabeth turned to face their admiring friends and neighbors and that was when Grady spotted his father staring at him from the back of the chapel. His heart sank. He hadn't heard from this overbearing man in months and now, on the happiest day of Grady's life, he chose to make an appearance.

Grady nodded in the man's direction but there was no sign of affection in his face. He would have to deal with Dr. Murphy eventually but for the present moment he was happy to accept all the handshakes and hugs he was receiving as he and his new bride walked arm in arm out of the hospital chapel.

Elizabeth could feel the sudden tension in Grady as they turned from Vicar Will. She caught the sign of recognition in Grady's face when he glanced at the gentleman at the rear of the chapel.

Grady hadn't said much about his family. Only that his mother died when he was still a toddler. He didn't have any other living relatives with the exception of his father. She knew the relationship had never been close.

Grady was hoping his father wouldn't show up at the reception which was being held in the winery ballroom. However, he knew where champagne was flowing his father wouldn't be far behind.

Grady introduced Elizabeth to his father. He smiled at his new daughter-in-law but seemed much more interested in the two ladies entering the room at that moment.

"I'll tell you right now young lady, I'm not going to rest until Grady comes back to his home in New York and practices his profession where he belongs, in the office next to mine."

"I will travel wherever my husband desires Dr. Murphy, but I do believe Grady is very happy here in Camden Corners." replied Elizabeth.

She was having a difficult time believing this cold, detached man could have raised a wonderful and caring person like Grady.

"We will talk about the move later. Now go dance or cut the cake or something, don't worry about me, I'll just mingle with your guests."

Grady knew they had been dismissed. He almost felt sorry for the man. His father made an embarrassing amount of money catering to the rich ladies but never found time to enjoy his wealth. He was always on the look out for a needy rich woman to fawn over. It seemed he had found one even here in Camden Corners.

Millicent Merryweather Stout entered the room with her visiting cousin Maybeth Merryweather DuBois. Millicent lived comfortably in Camden Corners but she wasn't what one would consider a wealthy woman. Maybeth on the other hand had inherited her father's fortune the year she turned 25. She married Francois DuBois just before her 30th birthday. He died a year later leaving her his fortune also.

Ellingsworth Murphy recognized wealth when he saw it and introduced himself to the cousins.

Millicent had met Grady Murphy several times since he moved to Camden Corners. She found him to be a very unpretentious young man. That was more than she could say for his father. Maybeth, however, was completely mesmerized by Dr. Ellingsworth Murphy.

Dripping with charm, the doctor asked "May I get you ladies a glass of champagne?"

Millicent would gladly have taken a glass but her cousin was president of her hometown branch of the Women's Christian Temperance Union and abhorred alcohol in any form. The only way Millicent could get her cousin to attend the wedding reception at a winery today was to tell her the wine was not produced yet and when it was it would only be used for holy communion.

Maybeth clutched her chest and was about to tell the doctor he could sit elsewhere if he was planning to imbibe in the devil's brew.

Ellingsworth could see he was losing the battle and corrected himself immediately. "I'm so sorry ladies, that was a slip of the tongue. Of course I meant to say fruit punch. I myself never indulge in anything with alcohol in it."

Millicent wasn't fooled for a second but Maybeth seemed to be clinging to every word that flowed out of the doctor's mouth. Millicent marveled at the way he seemed to know exactly what to say to her vulnerable cousin. She knew Maybeth was lonely and thought a little harmless flirtation would be good for her. Maybeth seemed content to sit with Doctor Murphy but Millicent had had enough and excused herself to join the others.

Maybeth couldn't believe her good fortune. Dr. Murphy came along just at the right time. She was having such trouble with her lumbago. Dr. Murphy reached in his bag and brought out a vial of medicine. He told her it would help her ills and he was right. Within a short time Maybeth was twirling on the dance floor with the doctor.

Millicent couldn't believe her eyes. She hadn't seen her cousin ever act in this way. She pulled Doc McMillan aside and said she was worried about Maybeth's heart condition. Doc was wondering what got into Maybeth or more specifically what Dr. Murphy may have laced her punch with. Doc had heard tales of Dr. Ellingsworth Murphy's unusual treatment of elderly rich women. He had a reputation of being reckless with his care. The ladies were always more than willing to pay him generously for his services.

Maybeth could feel her heart racing but she couldn't seem to slow down her dancing. She felt the room spinning and then nothing as she collapsed on the floor. Doctor Grady Murphy rushed to her side. His father watched helplessly as Grady hovered over Maybeth willing her to breath. She finally came to and was very lucky to be alive. With the assistance of some of the men at the party, Millicent took her cousin home but not without a stern message to Dr. Ellingsworth Murphy not to ever come near her cousin again.

This Apple Fell Far From the Tree

Ellingsworth Murphy had to admit his son, Grady knew just what to do with that old bag, Maybeth. She was starting to get on his nerves. Maybe he'd slipped her a little too much Laudanum. He was getting a little careless with his measurements lately. He was tired of waiting for the drug to take effect on these old women. Most of them imbibed in a good amount of sherry throughout the day and he figured they needed that extra little push to make them pliable enough to be manipulated easily. His latest victim was not accustomed to alcohol in any form and the drug must have affected her more quickly than his previous experiences.

Maybeth was being hauled out of the room when he looked up and saw that country bumpkin Doc McMillan looking down at him.

"Doctor Murphy, I don't know what you gave Mrs. DuBois but I would guess if I called the sheriff over here he would find Laudanum in your pocket. I will not further ruin your son's wedding reception by causing a scene. I would strongly suggest you bid farewell to your son and find your way out of town before I change my mind. You are a disgrace to the medical profession sir."

"I will gladly leave this hick town Doctor. Whatever that old bat ingested, it was all her doing. I was trying to keep her company as she was being ignored by that cousin of hers. I'm sure I saw her empty her flask of spirits into her punch glass so don't go blaming me for the old drunk's behavior."

Doc's face was turning red as Grady approached. "Your train is at the station, Father. I'll walk you over to it. Thank you for coming to the wedding. I'm sorry you couldn't stay longer. Let's go" Grady grabbed his father's arm and guided him out the door. He was back in time to cut the cake with his bride.

As much as Grady tried to hide it, Elizabeth could see the worry lines on Grady's forehead. She loved this man so much and couldn't understand how he could be so unlike the man who was responsible for his birth. Her question was answered when she looked at Grady's beaming face. He had spotted an older couple standing in the doorway. He grabbed Elizabeth's hand and rushed to the man and woman embracing them both in a big bear hug.

"Miss Addie, Mr. Leo. I can't believe you are here."

"Oh Grady darlin', we came as soon as we could get here. We couldn't miss seeing our boy as a married man and meeting his beautiful wife," Addie said as she threw her arms around Elizabeth.

"I'm so pleased to meet both of you. Grady has spoken of you so often." It was true, Grady had spoken of the older couple who had cared for him as long as he could remember. His father was so rarely at home and Addie and Leo were the only family Grady had ever known. He had talked about them moving to Camden Corners after he was settled in town but they were set in their ways and didn't think they wanted to leave New York City. Addie was a cook and Leo a handyman for a family on Fifth Avenue. They had their own small room in the basement of the house and were content as long as they had each other and knew that Grady was happy in his new life.

Grady introduced the Schmidts to the other guests. Before long Addie and Alma Tanner were discussing how to best roast a chicken and Leo was accepting an invitation from Oscar and Chris Pringle to try out ice fishing on Camden Lake. Elizabeth noticed the worry lines had disappeared on her new husband's forehead. She marveled at the difference between his father and these two people who obviously meant the world to him.

Maybeth woke up the next morning with a terrible headache and vague thoughts of what transpired the evening before. She was mortified. What in the world had gotten into her. The last she remembered, that handsome Dr. Murphy had told her about a miracle medicine he had that would help her lumbago. It must have worked because her back wasn't bothering her in the least. If it weren't for a groggy head, she would feel just fine.

"Good morning Maybeth" said her cousin as she entered the bedroom carrying a pot of tea and some buttered biscuits. "How are you feeling this morning, dear? You gave us all quite a scare."

"What on earth happened to me? I remember enjoying myself immensely with Dr. Murphy and then nothing until I looked up and saw young Dr. Murphy hovering over me."

"Cousin, I'm afraid you were given something called Laudanum"

"What in the world is Laudanum?"

"I'm afraid it is a combination of opium and alcohol." Millicent whispered quietly.

"Alcohol! On no, how on earth will I ever face anyone after I have ingested alcohol? I must resign my position with the Women's Christian Temperance Union immediately. Oh Millicent, what am I to do?"

"Now cousin, it wasn't exactly your fault, you were duped by the elder Dr. Murphy. I didn't like that man the minute I met him."

The maid tapped on the door. "Excuse me ma'am, Dr. Grady Murphy is here to see Mrs. DuBois."

Millicent welcomed Grady. "You are on your honeymoon Grady, you shouldn't be here today of all days."

"Elizabeth understands, she is waiting in the carriage for me. I wanted to make sure Mrs. DuBois was recovered from her bout last evening. How are you feeling this morning?" Grady asked as he listened to her heart.

"I'll be just fine if I can ever forgive myself for imbibing in spirits. I'm so terribly ashamed Doctor Murphy."

"You have nothing to be ashamed of, now tell me, how did my father persuade you to sip the Laudanum?"

"He said it would help my Lumbago. Oh my goodness Doctor, my back feels perfectly fine. Better than it has in years. Maybe he did have the cure for my pain after all."

"Now Mrs. DuBois, it wasn't the Laudanum that cured your back pain, I would venture a guess that it was the dancing you did. Your body has reacted positively to exercise. You will have to be sure to do more of

286

it in the future and your back will give you much less trouble."

"I believe you are right Dr. Murphy. Now you go to your bride. I want to hear from Millicent very soon that you and Elizabeth have started your family."

Grady chuckled as he left the ladies to join Elizabeth and start working on that task.

"What a wonderful young man Dr. Murphy is. He has given me cause to think, cousin. I do believe I will take my leave and return home. I am resigning my position in the WCTU. I still don't believe alcohol should be used on a regular basis but I did so enjoy myself for a time last evening. I never mentioned this but Mayor Russell has asked me to join him at the annual policeman's ball. I'm thinking I might just accept his invitation. I know he enjoys a glass of port from time to time. I can't see any reason not to join him."

"Maybeth, that is a wonderful idea. I will miss you terribly but I'm sure the mayor will enjoy your company. I want to hear all about the ball and the mayor."

One month later Millicent received an invitation in the mail. His Honor Mayor Lindsey P. Russell and Mrs. Maybeth Merryweather DuBois cordially invite you to attend their nuptials on the Fifteenth day of April in the year of our Lord Nineteen Hundred Four. Millicent silently thanked that rascal Dr. Ellingsworth Murphy. He had no idea what he started when he slipped Maybeth her first taste of alcohol.

Addie and Leo Schmidt woke up in their comfortable bed in Mrs. Wharton's boarding house.

"Leo, I do like it here in Camden Corners. I never thought I'd be happy in a small town but the people have been so friendly and kind I hate to think of leaving this afternoon. It has been so pleasant being with our dear Grady and Elizabeth for this short visit. I don't want it to come to an end."

"I feel the same way Addie. I have been awake for the last hour trying to think of a way we would be able to stay here instead of going back to New York but I don't see how we can leave our employment for another two or three years."

There was a soft knock on the door. "Mr. and Mrs. Schmidt, are you awake?" Leo recognized the voice of Mrs. Wharton. "I don't like to disturb you but a telegram was just delivered from New York City and I thought it best to get it to you right away. I'll just slip it under the door."

Leo got up out of the warm bed and picked up the telegram. He knew it couldn't be good news and braced himself before he opened it and read that his employers had decided to keep their temporary replacements on permanently and the Schmidt's services were no longer required.

"Addie, I do believe our wish has come true. We will be staying here in Camden Corners. I'm not sure where we will live but the Lord has always come through for us and I suspect He will again. We'd best get dressed and have a talk with Mrs. Wharton. We won't be able to stay here any longer. We will have to be careful with the little money we have."

The couple talked with Mrs. Wharton. She was sympathetic and asked the Schmidts to stay on at the boarding house. "I don't expect any boarders at this time of year. Leo, you can help me with chores around the house and Addie, I would love your help in the kitchen." The Schmidts knew Mrs. Wharton wasn't in need of any extra help and appreciated her kind offer. Maybe they could forget their pride for a few days until they could think of another solution. They both hugged Mrs. Wharton who sincerely didn't want this lovely couple to leave Camden Corners.

Word spread fast through the community that the Schmidts were out of work. The privacy of Mrs. Wharton's boarders was not high on her list. Millicent Merryweather Stout had met the couple at Grady and Elizabeth's wedding before her cousin's medical emergency. She liked them immediately. The couple who had been employed by Millicent had recently retired and moved to Greensboro to live with their son and his family. The night of the wedding she was tempted to ask the Schmidts if they would ever consider moving to Camden Corners and if they did, she would be interested in employing them. She donned her heavy coat and hat and set out for the Wharton House.

Mrs. Wharton knew if she told the right people, the Schmidts wouldn't be unemployed for long and as she expected, Millicent Stout would be first in line for their services. Before the end of the day Addie and Leo Schmidt had moved their meager belongings into the second floor of the Merryweather Stout mansion. Millicent wouldn't hear of them residing in the damp basement. She had plenty of room on the upper floor of the big sprawling house. Addie and Leo pinched themselves. Not only did they have a big beautiful bedroom with a huge bed and fireplace, they had their own bathroom and sitting room. Millicent would become much more than an employer to the couple. She would become their friends. "Wait until Grady hears of our new positions and that we are the newest members of the Camden Corners community.

Millicent's Dilemma

Millicent Merryweather Stout had never been happier. Her new domestic helpers, Addie and Leo Schmidt brought a ray of sunshine into the old mansion she had called home since the day she was born many years ago. Grady and Elizabeth Murphy were frequent guests along with half the residents of Camden Corners. Millicent enjoyed the visitors. She had been a bit standoffish in the past. The Merryweathers were brought up to believe they were higher in station than the rest of the town and never socialized with their neighbors other than civic affairs. Addie and Leo were delighted with their new home. Leo kept busy with many projects around the mansion while Addie cooked and baked up a storm. She was worried that Millicent was painfully thin. She was determined to fatten her up.

Mr. Harvey from the bank arrived one afternoon. Addie welcomed him into the parlor but Millicent said she had a headache and wouldn't be able to receive him. Addie was suspicious since Millicent had been joking with Leo just moments before Mr. Harvey arrived. He thanked Addie and left in despair. His next stop was at the Crowley Law Firm. He was hoping to catch Oscar in his office and was glad when he indeed was there.

"Oscar, I have been hoping to avoid this conversation but I have no where else to turn. Millicent Merryweather Stout is on the verge of bankruptcy. That mausoleum she lives in has eaten up all the money left to her by her father and her husband. I have tried talking with her about it several times and she either ignores me or refuses to see me. Oscar, I am at my wits end. I know how much she respects you and I was hoping you would be willing to reason with her about this matter. I'm afraid we will be forced to take legal action if we cannot come to an agreement."

"I've often wondered how she was able to keep up with that old place. Cyrus Merryweather was in over his head when he built the house years ago. I know the Stout fellow poured money into the property when he was still alive. He mentioned one time that Millicent refused to consider moving out of there. I'll go with you to talk to her. Maybe we can convince her it is time to sell but I doubt it. Would you mind if I stopped by the antique shop and asked Nettie to come with us. She has a way with people and it might help to have a woman there to soften the blow."

Nettie was distraught to hear her friend may be forced to leave the only home she had ever lived in and was happy to accompany her husband and Mr. Harvey.

Millicent knew she had no choice but to listen to Oscar and Mr. Harvey tell her she couldn't afford to live in her home any longer. As much as she tried to ignore her predicament, she had expected this day to come eventually.

After greeting the Crowleys and meeting Mr. Harvey, Addie and Leo excused themselves to leave the guests alone with Millicent.

"No, please stay. This is your home too and I want you to be aware of what is happening. Please, Addie, Leo, sit down while these fine people tell me I have to leave my home."

Mr. Harvey explained in detail how much it was costing Millicent to keep the house running and how little was left of her inheritance.

"Millicent, it pains me to tell you this but you simply do not have enough money to keep this house going."

Nettie spoke up. "Millicent, tell me, do you ever use the main floor of your house? I know whenever I have visited you I have always come through the back door and up the stairs to the second floor. You seem to have plenty of room on this level including a very nice roomy kitchen."

"Oh yes, there are several guest rooms that we never use. Even when I was a girl we rarely spent any time on the main floor. Mama and Papa would open the ballroom several times a year but I don't give fancy parties. Mr. Stout was unlike Papa in so many ways and never cared for large gatherings. He much preferred to entertain company here on the second floor."

Oscar could tell by the look on his wife's face that she was the perfect person to have along. Nettie Crowley could always come up with a solution to any problem it seemed.

"Nettie dear, I can tell you are forming a plan in your head. Why don't you share your idea with us."

"I'll have to check with Emma and Lily, but they have been talking about opening another location for their goods. They are running out of display area in the shop. I wonder, if you would be willing to rent out the first floor for that purpose."

"You mean having a shop on the first floor where people would actually come in and purchase goods?"

"It was just an idea, Millicent." Nettie said afraid she had offended her friend.

"And a wonderful idea, Nettie. Oh Addie, wouldn't it be delightful to have people coming and going each day? When can we talk to the girls to see if they would be willing to go along with the plan?"

"Mr. Harvey, just how much money do I have left? I will need it to set up the business. Now if you will excuse me, I have some planning to do. Oscar would you be willing to help me with that end of things. Nettie, I would like it if you would come to the third floor with me. I think I have a few things that would be appropriate to sell in the shop. Oh dear, I'm getting ahead of myself. Maybe we should speak to the Crowley girls first."

Addie had never seen Millicent this excited. She was getting into the swing also. She and Leo would be able to scrub and shine the old ballroom. She had only been down there one time but she remembered there were heavy dark curtains on the windows. She would wash them all by hand and pull them back to let the sunshine in. The enormous kitchen could be renovated slightly to make it into a cozy dining area serving breakfast and lunch. Addie's mind was twirling. She felt ten years younger than she did just this morning.

Emma and Lily were receptive to the idea immediately. "Nettie, this is like a dream come true. That old house is the perfect place for an antique shop. What would we ever do without you?"

The young ladies left Ethel and Jonas Fulbright in charge of the shop as they made their way to Millicent's home. Millicent was on the wrap around porch waiting for them as they approached the house.

"Lily, this porch would be perfect in the summer to serve lemonade and cookies in the afternoon. I think we would be able to get a dozen small tables and chairs out here." Lily nodded in agreement.

They walked into the large foyer picturing at least fifteen pieces fitting in it nicely. Next was the ballroom. The girls had never seen anything quite this beautiful before. The draperies had been pulled back to let the sunshine in. Lily imagined the drapes had been closed for years and that helped preserve the old mahogany floors and even the wallpaper. Off the ballroom were several smaller rooms that had been used as dressing rooms, a library and study. Emma counted ten fireplaces in all. The kitchen was enormous with several wood burning stoves. The equipment was in top shape but may have to be replaced for efficiency.

The girls were delighted with the Merryweather location and would have their husbands draw up the paperwork. They were also pleased that Millicent was interested in lending her hand with the shop. She and the group rode the elevator to the third floor. Addie had never been to that floor and Millicent couldn't remember the last time she was here herself. They stepped off the elevator and everyone gasped. Never had Emma seen so many treasures in one place and she had seen a lot. There was row after row of fine old furniture, lamps, vases and figurines in the main room.

"Mama liked to shop and Papa could never deny her anything. What she couldn't fit in our home she would store up here until she needed it. I don't remember her ever using any of these things."

"Millicent," Emma said honestly "You could sell some of these things to pay your taxes on the house and still have money left over. You wouldn't have to turn your house into an antique shop."

Emma felt disappointment but couldn't let things progress any further until she made Millicent understand by selling these treasures she would be able to keep up with expenses on her own.

"Oh but Emma, I want to open a shop downstairs. This old house has been full of life since Addie and Leo came to live here. I never did like knowing that big space downstairs was empty when it's main purpose was to welcome joyful party goers. Mama enjoyed her shopping expeditions so much I'm just sure she would be happy to have others enjoy picking out their favorite pieces from her collection up here. Honestly, I had no idea there was quite this much."

Work began on turning the first floor of the Merryweather mansion into Looking Back Antiques II. It became known simply as Merryweather's before too long. A visit to the original Looking Back Antique Shop always ended with a stop at Merryweather's. Some of the village teenaged boys were hired to haul the many items from the third floor to the first. With just a few alterations, the shop was ready to open for business. The kitchen and dining room required major remodeling but that was something Leo and Jonas thought they would be able to handle on their own. Before they knew it they had helpers from all over town. The men and even some of the ladies were glad to help out. It gave them an opportunity to see the inside of the Merryweather mansion. For years they could only imagine what it was like inside. Cyrus Merryweather didn't spare any expense when he had the dwelling built. They were to discover the inlays in the tiles were not merely gold in color, they were solid gold.

The newest treasures being stored in the third floor rooms had been purchased before Millicent's mother passed away over 50 years ago. Most had been new at the time but had been kept in the closed up rooms without ever being used. They were all in excellent condition but not true antiques. These pieces were moved to one of the many rooms off the main showroom. Each room had it's own theme, a young girl's room, a young boy's room, a sewing room, a dining room, parlor, guest room. Once a piece was purchased there were many more to take it's place. As with the original antique shop, the prices were very reasonable which was one reason for its enormous success.

After many days and nights of labor, the doors of Looking Back Antiques II were opened to curious lookers and anxious buyers. Browsing was encouraged in both shops even though no purchases were made. Millicent was happy to greet each and every customer. She began to really know the people in town. For years she had been known only as the rich woman who chaired the Ladies Auxiliary and seemed to make all the decisions concerning the social activities of the community. Millicent insisted she wasn't too old to learn new ways and her best teacher was Addie Schmidt. Addie had a knack for remembering everyone she met and also knew each of their children and even their dog's names. She loved people and it showed. Millicent was learning to listen and even though she had to write down names for future reference she was beginning to show a sincere interest in her neighbor's lives.

Millicent and Addie were admiring the just completed dining room of Merryweather's. They had tables and chairs all in place and were selecting vases for the center of each when the bell rang indicating a customer.

Millicent greeted the young man who looked vaguely familiar to her.

"Good morning and welcome to Merryweather's. I am Millicent Merryweather, I don't believe you are from this area? Is there anything in particular you are looking for?"

"Yes, Aunt Millicent" replied the young man. "I'm looking for my father, Neville Merryweather."

Addie appeared from the dining room just in time to see her friend collapse onto the ruby red Queen Anne Fireside chair.

The Merryweathers

From the moment the Merryweather family arrived in Camden Corners over one hundred years ago, they had been treated like royalty.

The truth was, Merryweather Wentworth had absconded with his employer's bank receipts and rode his horse until it gave out. He walked until he came to the the small village of Larkspur. Merryweather had always abhorred his name. His mother had given it to him after the disappointment of giving birth to her seventh male child. He made the decision to change his name to Wentworth Merryweather and no one ever questioned it. Wentworth Merryweather was an extremely handsome fellow who had the ability to charm anyone who came in contact with him.

He cleaned off the dirt and dust in the river just outside of town. He grabbed a pair of overalls hanging on a line in a nearby shack. They weren't a perfect fit but they would do. He didn't want to look too affluent when he strolled into town. Wentworth found the town's saloon and walked through its door. Larkspur was accustomed to strangers since it was located on the road leading west from New York City. This stranger was like none the rickety old saloon had seen. He dressed like a farmer but he didn't have the look of a farmer. Pollyanna Pride, the innkeeper took an instant shine to the stranger. She hoped he would stay in town for a while but Wentworth had other ideas. He joined a poker game already in progress. The card players were happy to take money from this hick kid and Wentworth proceeded to lose the first few hands. After a while, Wentworth told the men he was down to his last few dollars and he'd like to raise the stakes to help him win it back. Before the other fellows knew what hit them, Wentworth had taken every last cent from them and was out the door. Pollyanna chuckled in the background as she watched Wentworth ride off on Rawley Wilson's horse. He came to the next town, stopped in a fine looking men's shop and slipped out the back door with two new suits, four shirts, six neckties, two pairs of shoes and eight pairs of socks before the proprietor noticed the items and the customer were missing. Wentworth's next stop was Greensboro where he swindled people and stole anything he could get his hands on. He never lost track of Pollyanna though and found his way back to Larkspur to visit the fair Miss Pride.

After a few years and an accumulation of ill gotten gains, Wentworth set out for Camden Corners. He knew he would have a better chance being a big fish in a little pond and Camden Corners was just the right spot for him. First, he needed a wife and the mayor's daughter, Sue Ellen, would do just fine. She was a pretty girl with impeccable manners and best of all, she was shy and quiet. She adored Wentworth and was thrilled when he asked for her hand in marriage. The mayor and his wife were happy to give their blessing to the marriage but disappointed to learn the couple would be relocating to another town.

The dowry given to Wentworth was adequate and with the money he had scammed out of the folks of Greensboro, he would have enough to purchase a large home in Camden Corners. Since the town was just beginning to grow, Wentworth had to wait several months before he would be able to take his bride to their new home. He hadn't planned on staying around Sue Ellen's family. He found it difficult to make excuses to leave town to be with Pollyanna without the mayor or one of his cronies catching him. His frustration grew through the months of waiting and then Sue Ellen announced she was with child and had no intention of leaving her family at this time.

The Merryweather house was completed and as Wentworth planned, it was the largest in town. He purposely had the builders put an addition on the house that would be the maid's quarters. The people of Camden Corners were happy to welcome Wentworth to their small village. They were impressed with the fact that the Merryweathers had a live in maid. It was too bad Mrs. Merryweather was forced to stay in Greensboro until the birth of her child but the Wentworth maid, Pollyanna Pride, seemed to be fitting into the community very well. She was well liked by the women and admired by the gentlemen in town.

Everything was going along smoothly in the Merryweather household. Wentworth visited his wife in Greensboro whenever he had the opportunity. Unfortunately he wasn't able to visit as often as Sue Ellen would have liked because he was so very busy working to provide a life of ease for his family. Sue Ellen didn't know what line of work he was in and didn't even think to ask. She was happy she would be mistress of the largest house in Camden Corners. She wondered about the maid but didn't care as long as someone else would be cleaning. She would have to speak to Wentworth about hiring a cook and butler too.

Right on time, little Cyrus Merryweather came into the world. He was the spitting image of his father and even as a young boy knew how to charm everyone around him.

For the next eighteen years, the Merryweathers enjoyed a content life in Camden Corners. Pollyanna remained the dutiful servant although Sue Ellen wasn't exactly sure what the woman did since Wentworth hired housekeepers to do the cleaning and cooks to prepare the meals.

Shortly after Cyrus' 18th birthday, he and Sue Ellen visited her parents in Greensboro. When they returned, Wentworth was nowhere to be found and Pollyanna Pride had disappeared along with him. The authorities later informed Sue Ellen that her husband had been found shot to death in a small town out west.

Sue Ellen was saddened by her husband's death but her life didn't change. She still continued to buy her many frilly dresses and jewels and preside as mistress of the largest home in Camden Corners.

She and Cyrus never spoke of his father again. The maid's quarters were left empty until the house was sold. Cyrus decided he needed to build a mansion for for himself and his new bride.

Back in present time, Millicent was trying to catch her breath as she raised herself from the chair she had just collapsed in. The young man standing before her was the spitting image of her brother, Neville.

"I'm sorry ma'am. I shouldn't have blurted it out that way. I'm afraid I'm not thinking too clearly since I just recently discovered that the man who I believed to be my father was not my father after all."

Millicent wanted to protest and send this fellow on his way but she couldn't deny he was somehow related to her brother and therefore to herself.

"Let me fetch you a cup of tea, Millicent." said Addie who had witnessed her friend's reaction to this boy's words.

"I think I could use it with maybe a little bit of brandy added."

"Of course. Young man may I get you something to drink?" Addie said.

"No thank you ma'am. If you could just tell me where I can find Neville Merryweather, I will be on my way. I don't wish to disturb you any further."

"Please, dear boy. Come upstairs to the living quarters. I want to know what makes you think my brother is your father. I'll admit, you look just like him so there must be a connection. My brother is a fine upstanding married man. Respected in his community and the father of two daughters. He would never..." Millicent couldn't finish her sentence.

The young man followed Millicent and Addie up the stairs to Millicent's parlor. Millicent insisted Addie be a witness to the meeting. She was sure there was some mistake and Addie would help her make sense of the boy's accusations. Or, maybe protect her from him. He didn't look like a serial killer but one could never be too careful.

"Sit down young man, now first, tell me your name and why you think my brother is your father."

"My name is James Robinson. My mother is the former Helene Simpson. My understanding is she and your brother met when he attended school in Plattsburg. Mother grew up in that town. They fell in love but your brother's family wouldn't allow them to marry because my mother's kin were not included in the Social Register of Philadelphia."

"Well, there you are. My brother was in Plattsburg years before you were born and I'm sure he has never been back there. You couldn't possibly be his son."

"That wasn't the only time they met. Just about 20 years ago, your brother was attending a business meeting in Albany. My mother's family had relocated there several years before. Mother had not married after her relationship with Neville ended. They ran into each other and what began as an innocent encounter resulted in my birth nine months later."

"I don't understand, if your mother wasn't married at the time, who is this man who you call your father?"

"Chester Robinson was a very kind and loving man. He passed away about six months ago. Before he died he told me he wanted me to know the truth about my roots. I know he loved me as though I was his own flesh and blood. He knew my mother would never face the shame she had always felt after her tryst with your brother. Mother never stopped loving Neville and from what Chester told me, he had never forgotten her. They met and one thing led to another. I must give Neville credit for telling Mother he was engaged to be married. I don't remember Mother ever imbibing in spirits, but according to Chester, she and Neville toasted his upcoming nuptials with champagne. I'm sure you can imagine that one thing led to another" James said with a reddening face.

"Oh dear, Neville does have his flaws, but I can't imagine he would leave a young woman in that kind of a predicament and continue on with his life as though nothing happened."

"He did contact Mother after that but she was so ashamed of what she had done and she knew she would never be accepted into the Merryweather family. She refused his letters until finally he gave up and stopped writing. Mother confided in Chester and he insisted on marrying her and claiming me as his son. Luckily, I was a very small baby and no one suspected I wasn't Chester Robinson's biological son or that I was conceived out of wedlock."

Millicent remembered her brother mentioning a young woman named Helene. She also remembered her father was vehemently opposed to the pairing. She even remembered Neville remarking how regretful he was for not fighting to be with the woman he loved so many years ago.

"I do believe you are telling me the truth James. Your father lives in Greensboro. You have two sisters. Melanie and Melinda. They are lovely young women. I know them well enough to know they will welcome you into the family. However, Neville's wife, Prudence is a different story. I'm not sure how to approach this but if you are in agreement, I would like to telegraph my brother and ask him to come to Camden Corners to meet with you here. You are welcome to stay in one of the guest rooms until his arrival."

"I would like that very much. I would also like to get to know my Aunt Millicent a little better. You have been kinder to me than I deserve after barging into your home as I did. I'm still in a bit of shock knowing I have a family I've never met."

Millicent gave her nephew a hug and showed him to one of the guest rooms before she donned her coat and hat and summoned her carriage to take her to the post office to send a telegram to her brother.

Neville Merryweather was finishing up some paperwork on his desk when his secretary knocked on the door with a telegram in her hand.

Neville was on the next train to Camden Corners the words of the telegram still in his head. *Remember that son you always wanted? He has finally arrived and is occupying my guest room. His mother is the former Helene Simpson and he is the spitting image of you.*

Hello, Son

James Robinson sat fidgeting on the sofa in Millicent's parlor. Addie was attempting to occupy him with chatter about the town of Camden Corners. Addie was nervous too. Her friend, Millicent was meeting the train that was carrying Neville Merryweather to meet his son for the very first time. Neville was in for the shock of his life when he received a telegram from his sister informing him his encounter with Helene had resulted in the birth of a child over twenty years ago. Although James would have preferred to join his aunt at the train station, he understood it would be better if the meeting took place in the privacy of the Merryweather home.

Neville hadn't told his family why he was visiting Camden Corners. He didn't know how he was going to tell Prudence that he had another child. He was worried too about the reaction of his daughters. What would they think of their father's behavior. Granted he had never known about the boy. He also was angry that Helene had found it necessary to keep this information from him. He still loved Helene after all these years. She was never far from his mind. He thought back to the time when they met and fell in love.

Neville was sent to Plattsburg University near the beginning of his senior year in college. From the beginning of his first year in Yale, he struggled to pass his classes since he spent most of his time with his fraternity brothers carousing at the local pubs. Neville had inherited the charm of his father and grandfather before him. He was able to persuade his professors to give him the benefit of the the doubt and pass him along each year. He was successful until he met up with Professor Helmut Kline. Professor Kline had his fill of offspring of the rich who sailed through college and were ill prepared to face the real world outside of the hallowed halls of his beloved University. Neville made the mistake of paying one of his classmates to complete an assignment. Professor Kline discovered the deception and Neville was expelled that very day.

It was only through a hefty donation to the university in Plattsburg by Cyrus Merryweather that Neville was allowed to finish his education there. He had only been attending the school for three days when he happened to pass by a small sandwich shop. He realized he had skimped on breakfast and he was feeling quite hungry. He entered the shop and sat at the counter when a lovely young girl handed him a menu. She smiled at him and he smiled back. Later when he thought about their first encounter, he was sure he had fallen in love that very moment.

Helene Simpson was in her third year at Plattsburg. She was studying to be a librarian and had taken a job at the coffee shop to help with the cost of her education. Helene was a good student. She couldn't imagine anyone not giving their best efforts in their studies. Helene was the first in her family to attend college and she knew the sacrifice her parents had made in order for her to further her education.

Helene was like no other girl Neville had ever met. She was a beauty but more than that she seemed to have a head on her shoulders and knew there were more important things in life than the next party or frivolous flirtation. Helene was attracted to Neville but knew he was in a different social class than she was. As improbable as their friendship was it developed until they became inseparable. Helene was a good influence on Neville. He began studying as he had never done before. He graduated with excellent grades that spring.

Neville was anticipating his parents' arrival in Plattsburg for the graduation ceremony and was anxious for them to meet Helene. He had planned to propose to her the night of his graduation. Cyrus Merryweather was appalled that a son of his would even consider marrying below his station.

"Why the girl's father is a shopkeeper. What are you thinking, Neville?"

It had never occurred to Neville that his father wouldn't approve of Helene. She had made him happier than he had ever been since the day he'd met her at the diner.

Helene had misgivings about their relationship. She was well aware of the difference in their upbringing. Her parents were loving, kind people who did their best to provide for their family but were not in the the same league as the Merryweathers. As much as it broke her heart, she told Neville he should return home with his parents and forget about her

299

Neville was never the same after he left Plattsburg. He didn't think he would ever forgive himself for running away from the girl he loved.

Several years later his father arranged his marriage to Prudence. He never loved her but it was expected that he would marry and produce sons to carry on the Merryweather name. How ironic, Neville thought as the train pulled into the station, my only son is not carrying the Merryweather name after all.

Neville was surprised to see a sign in front of his old homestead reading open for business. He would have to question Millicent about it but for now he had other things on his mind.

One look at James Robinson and he knew he was indeed his son. He could see himself and his father in the young man's face. He could also see a trace of Helene and his heart ached at the thought of her.

It was an awkward moment. The father and son had no idea what to say to each other. Neville wanted to embrace his boy but was afraid he would be rejected.

Finally, he blurted out "How is your mother?"

What a ridiculous thing to say, he thought. How would she be after losing her husband and having her son questioning his paternity.

"Mother is doing well, sir. She sends her regards."

"Her regards? What was she thinking? Why didn't she send her regards twenty years ago when she knew she was having my baby?"

Millicent put her arm on Neville's shoulder to calm him.

"I'm sorry, James. None of this is your fault. I just don't understand why I never knew about you."

James handed his father an envelope. "Mother wanted me to give this to you. It's her attempt to explain."

Neville took the envelope from his son's hand.

"I think we could all use a little brandy" Millicent said as an uncomfortable Leo excused himself to pour a glass for everyone including himself and Addie.

Neville put Helene's letter in his jacket pocket. He wanted to read it when he was alone. He could smell her delicate perfume lingering on the envelope and thought of their time together so many years ago.

James was interested in his sisters. He wanted very much to meet them but would understand if Neville didn't want to share the news of his existence with his legitimate daughters. Neville immediately reassured his son that he was now part of the Merryweather family and would never be hidden away again. Neville wasn't too sure what Prudence would have to say about that but he didn't care. He lost years with his son and he would make up for that loss in any way possible.

After a few hours, Neville finally realized what he had seen when he walked through the front door of his old home.

"What in the name of Sam Hill have you done to our house, Millicent?"

"Neville, I thought you wouldn't notice. Don't get upset but I simply don't have the money to keep this old place running. It was either turn it into something useful or let it go on the auction block."

"Why didn't you come to me if you needed money? You know I would be glad to help you with the expenses."

"Don't you see Neville, I needed to find a purpose in life. For years I have been living up on this hill and never really belonged to the community of Camden Corners. Oh, I know I have lived here all my life, but we Merryweathers always stood apart from everyone else. Papa flaunted his money and taught us to expect to be treated as though we were something special. Well, for the first time in my life I do feel special. Not because I'm above the rest of the town but because I'm working along side them. I have friends, Neville and I'm enjoying my life."

"Millicent, I'm proud of you. We both should have learned that lesson years ago. I ruined my own life because of snobbishness and almost ruined my daughter's chance for happiness because of it too."

"How are Melanie and Michael?" Millicent asked

"They are doing well. Melanie spends more time with the Cassidy family than she does with her own and I don't blame her. Our household isn't a happy one. Prudence takes to her bed at least three times a week. She has been pouting since Hermione retired."

"Hermione had been in Neville's household since the day he and Prudence were married. She is the reason Melanie and Melinda turned out as well as they did. She practically raised them single handedly." said Millicent

"Now Millicent, don't start on Prudence. My sister never did have anything good to say about my wife." Neville explained

Millicent was tempted to list the many flaws of Prudence but decided now was not the time.

Addie and Leo excused themselves to the kitchen to create a special meal for the guests. Millicent headed upstairs with Neville to prepare one of the guest rooms for his stay. James needed to get his thoughts together.

"I hope you won't mind, Mr. Merryweather," said James. "I think I will take a walk around the village to clear my head. I'd like to see more of Camden Corners I honestly didn't notice my surroundings when I was looking for this house."

"Of course I don't mind James. As much as I would like to hear you call me Father, I understand your reluctance to do so but I wish you would call me Neville."

James smiled at this man who he knew would be important in his future. He liked Neville Merryweather. He could understand why his mother had fallen for the guy. He felt sadness that they had never been a family but was also grateful for Chester Robinson's love and caring through the years.

James walked leisurely through Camden Corners. He had heard of small town hospitality but had never experienced it first hand. He was surprised at the number of people who called hello to him.

Diana Taylor was setting out a plate of cookies for the children. "Would you like a sugar cookie young man? They are still warm from the oven."

Rudy, the Pringle's dog wagged his tale and licked James' hand when he petted the top of his head. He walked by the antique shop and wondered if Aunt Millicent was in competition with them. At that moment, Nettie Crowley walked down the stairs.

"Hello young man. Are you visiting our town today? Oh my, you must be a relative of Millicent Merryweather, there is definitely a family resemblance. I didn't realize she had a nephew."

James wasn't quite sure what to say to this very observant woman. "I'm just passing through ma'am. I do like your town and the people seem very nice." James said trying to change the subject. Nettie took the hint and scolded herself for prying. She had a tendency to make everyone's business her own.

"Enjoy your stay in Camden Corners young man. Make sure you visit the candy shop across the street before you leave. Maddie Mackenzie makes the best double chocolate toffee fudge you have ever tasted."

"I'll do that ma'am, thank you." He tipped his hat to her and continued his walk. Mother would love this town he thought to himself. I think she would fit right in here.

Alone in the guest room, Neville opened the letter. His heart skipped a beat as he began to read.

Lost Love

Neville Merryweather sat in the chair by the window of the guest room of the house he grew up in. He had just finished reading the letter written to him by Helene Simpson Robinson, the mother of the son he never knew he had. How things would have been different if only she had told him the truth so many years ago. He had to admit, twenty years ago he wouldn't have defied his father. Neville was a weak man. He always had been and he was always afraid if he went against his father's wishes he would be stripped of all fringe benefits that came with being a Merryweather. As much as it pained him, he was grateful to Chester Robinson for raising James as his own. James would never carry the Merryweather name. It was a false family name to begin with. Neville would be the last of the Merryweathers and that was just as well. Neville reread Helene's letter.

Dear Neville,

I know this unexpected visit from our son will be a shock to you. I am sorry for the pain you are going through as you realize I kept the truth from you all these years. Believe me when I tell you that I have regretted that decision every day of my life.

Please be assured, Chester Robinson was the best father a boy could hope for. Chester loved James with all his heart and was committed to him from the beginning.

Neville, I don't know if I can ever make you understand why I kept this secret from you. What we did was a mistake. I loved you very much and I know you loved me but we were very different people. You needed a wife and mother to your children who would be by your side in the social situations that were always so important to you. I was not that woman. I was not born to that life and I'm not sure I would have been able to learn all the social graces that came naturally to you and your friends.

The announcement of your nuptials appeared in the newspaper just about the time I discovered I was in the family way. Even though I returned all your letters unopened, I was still heartbroken to learn of the marriage. Chester Robinson, a very dear friend of mine was the only person who knew of my dilemma. He offered to marry me and claim our child as his own.

Neville, I was in such a state. I wasn't sure what I was going to do. I didn't love Chester but didn't feel I had any choice. I felt I was being punished for my sinful behavior and I would have to pay the consequences.

As it turned out, Chester and I were married that very afternoon. Mama and Papa had always liked Chester and welcomed him into the family immediately. James was born 8 months later. He was a very tiny baby and everyone just assumed he had come early.

In time, I learned to love Chester. He was a kind and caring husband and adored James. As James grew older, Chester talked about telling him the truth about his parentage. I was against it from the start. Chester had been the only father James had ever known and I wanted to keep it that way for everyone's sake. I knew if James found out about you he would want to find you and my shameful secret would be revealed. Chester didn't concur but agreed to keep the secret.

Around this time a year ago, Chester fell ill. In time, he realized he was never going to get better. He had never betrayed me in all of our years together but in his deteriorating state, he told James the truth about you. I tried to convince James that it was the delirium that made Chester say those words but he didn't believe me. Your son had suspected something was amiss when he realized he looked nothing like the man he thought was his father.

After Chester's death, I begged James not to pursue the matter. He agreed but it kept eating away at him. He had a need to meet his birth father. I should have written to you to warn you but I was afraid of causing unrest in your home. I remembered you had come from Camden Corners and I assumed your sister still lived there. Again, I wasn't certain how well James would be received. I do hope you will treat him well. I can assure you he is not looking for any monetary benefits. He simply wants to meet his father. Sincerely, Helene Simpson Robinson

Neville read the letter over and over again. He knew Helene was right. She never would have been happy living in his world. It had taken him years to realize he wasn't happy living in that world himself. The best time of his life was the few months he and Helene were together when he attended school in Plattsburg.

Neville knew what he had to do. After a short rest and a filling meal, he announced he would be leaving that afternoon for home.

"I want to get this out in the open and I need to start by telling Prudence that James is my son and I want very much to be part of his life. That is if you feel the same way James."

"Yes, Mr. Merryweather, err Neville. I would very much like to get to know you better. I don't wish to cause you or your family any distress though."

"Prudence lives in constant distress" Millicent said quietly.

Neville glared at her but was in agreement.

"I'm not going to be dishonest with you son, Prudence will not be happy about this situation but she will have to accept it. I do think your sisters will be pleased to know they have a brother. The next train leaves in 20 minutes. I will return as soon as I can. Millicent, I hope you will keep my room open for me. I would like to spend some time with James upon my return."

When Neville arrived home he entered the parlor where Prudence was sipping a glass of sherry. Neville was hoping the sherry would have a calming effect on her when he told her his news. Prudence accepted the news better than Neville anticipated. She excused herself to go to her room and that was when she dissolved into a heap on the floor. Prudence Wingate Merryweather was dead drunk.

Neville wasn't sure Prudence had even heard his confession. He carried her to her room and deposited her on her bed where her personal maid took over.

Melinda, the younger Merryweather daughter came bouncing in through the front door.

"Hello Papa, we thought you were on a business trip."

"I came home sooner than expected. Is your sister with you? I have something I'd like to speak to you both about."

"Melissa and Michael are smooching under the sycamore tree. Those two are revolting. Always kissing and hugging. I'm never going to get engaged if that is what you have to do."

Neville laughed. "I think you will change your mind about that one of these days."

Melissa walked in the door. "Hello Father, what's wrong? You look so serious."

"I have something to tell you both, it's good news but it will be a surprise to you. I hope you think it's a good surprise because I'd like you to be happy about it."

The girls listened intently as Neville explained the situation and how they had a brother they didn't know about all these years. Melissa thought it was the most romantic story she had ever heard. She cried for her father and his lost love. Melinda didn't quite understand how her father had a baby with another lady but she was happy she now had a big brother. They wanted to pack that very minute and leave for Camden Corners on the next train.

Neville told the maid to inform Mrs. Merryweather that the three of them were leaving to visit his sister for a few days. In Prudence's current state, he didn't think she would object.

Melissa asked if Michael could go along with them. After all, he would be part of the family soon. Neville agreed and the foursome boarded the train two hours later.

James was amazed that his father had been to Greensboro and back and brought his sisters with him. They were such pretty girls. It was difficult for him to keep his emotions under control. How nice it would have been to have watched these two young girls grow up. He and Michael Cassidy were instant friends. The girls both hugged him and welcomed them into their family. Millicent and Neville stood with their arms around each other watching the young people become acquainted.

"How did Prudence take the news?" Millicent whispered.

"I'm not really sure she even knows. My high society wife was as drunk as a skunk when I told her about James."

"Oh my, Prudence always manages to surprise me." laughed Millicent.

The sun was beginning to set as Neville relaxed in the parlor watching his three children talking and laughing as though they had known each other all their lives. He still was in a disbelief that this fine young man was his son. He wouldn't trade his daughters for anything in the world but he had longed for a son to complete the family. Prudence wouldn't hear of it. She cursed him both times she found herself in the family way and refused to even consider having another child. If it meant they would never again share a bed, so be it.

Addie had gone all out with the evening meal. She was thrilled to have two hungry young men to cook for. Millicent and her nieces helped set the table. Millicent had never learned to set a table or do any of the mundane chores before. She found she was enjoying giving a helping hand and was even known to wash a dish or two.

When the men were called to the table, James walked into the dining room smiling broadly, he picked up his wine glass.

"I'd like to make a toast to Aunt Millie for her hospitality and arranging for me to meet my family."

The group stared at James with their mouths open wide when he referred to his aunt as Millie. They then glanced in Millicent's direction.

"Thank you James dear. No one has ever called me Millie before. I like it. It sounds so much friendlier than Millicent. Don't you think Addie? Yes, I would like to be called Millie from now on."

From that moment on Millicent Merryweather Stout was known simply as Millie Stout. Her new name suited her well because she was no longer the rich lady who lived in a mansion on a hill. She was everyone's friend and neighbor.

"Oh Aunt Millie" said Melinda as the two were saying goodnight. "I don't want this day to ever end. It has been so wonderful meeting our brother. Father says we have to leave tomorrow morning. I wish we could just move to Camden Corners but mother would never leave all her snooty friends."

"I know dear but you have a life in Greensboro too. I know you love Michael's family. They would miss you both if you moved out of town. I'm hoping James will stay on for a while and it is a short train ride from Greensboro."

The next morning the visitors returned to Greensboro with a promise of a return the following weekend. They would bring their skis and take advantage of the late winter snowfall in the hills of Camden Corners.

"Are you sure Aunt Millie? You have been so kind to me I don't want to burden you and Addie."

"Don't be silly my boy. It has been a pleasure having a young person around this old house. You are welcome to stay as long as you wish. Now, you and Cody go off and meet April and her friend and have a good time."

Cody Hill was waiting for James. Word had gotten around town that there was a new fellow in town, like any newcomer he wouldn't be a stranger for long.

Back in Albany, Helene Robinson was holding the telegram that arrived an hour ago. James was going to be staying in Camden Corners for a while. He wanted to get to know his new family better. Helene was happy he hadn't been rejected but suddenly felt very alone and lonely.

We Meet Again

Helene Robinson understood why her son wanted to get to know his father and half sisters. She didn't blame him, she was too busy chastising herself for keeping this secret from him all these years. Chester had been right all along. James needed to know the truth. Helene couldn't face having him know of her behavior so many years ago. He didn't seem to think twice that his mother behaved like a harlot. Thinking back on the night James was conceived, she realized over indulgence in champagne was only an excuse. What happened with Neville Merryweather was not an accident, it was intentional.

"Maybe it's time you forgave yourself, Helene." said her good friend Margaret with whom Helene had confided in several months before. "Chester loved you and married you knowing you were carrying another man's child. He never thought any less of you because of one mistake. You gave him the greatest gift of all. A child who adored him."

307

"Maybe you're right, Margaret. I just can't help thinking I'm being punished because James seems to be happy living in Camden Corners and being with his other family. His last letter said he had been hired at a local photographic factory. It sounds like he is planning a very long visit there."

"He also asked you to come to visit him. His Aunt Millie even sent you a note asking you to join your son. What in the world is keeping you here? I've already told you I'd keep an eye on your house and water your plants. Could it be you are afraid to see Neville Merryweather again?"

"You know me so well, Margaret. I know I'm older and wiser than I was 20 years ago but what if I fall into that same old trap? He's a married man. From what James has hinted it isn't a happy marriage but that might make it even more difficult to keep my emotions in check."

"What if he is bald with warts all over his face and weighs 300 pounds? Maybe you are worrying for nothing." Margaret laughed.

"You're right, Margaret. He can't be as beautiful as he was back when I knew him. I probably will laugh when I see that overweight, bald headed, wart faced man again."

Before Helene could change her mind she went to the telegraph office and telegraphed her son. She also sent a telegram to Millie Stout thanking her for her invitation to be her guest. She wouldn't dream of imposing on Mrs. Stout and would ask her son to arrange for lodging in a local boarding house.

When the telegrams arrived, Millie told her nephew not to even think about arranging for his mother to stay at Mrs. Wharton's. She wouldn't hear of it.

"We have lovely rooms in this house and I want to get to know the only woman who ever made my brother happy. As far as I'm concerned she is much more a part of this family than that insipid Prudence."

"I'm happy you feel that way Aunt Millie because I know you two will be great friends. My mother will love this old house and all the antiques. She and my....ah Chester liked to visit estate sales and such before he became so ill."

"James, I want you to feel comfortable calling Chester Robinson your father. He was your father in every sense of the word. Neville understands that too and we are both grateful to him for the part he had in making you the fine young man you are today."

"Thanks Aunt Millie," James said as he gave his aunt a big bear hug.

One week later, Helene Robinson walked off the train and into the arms of her son. Waiting with him was an attractive older lady with a happy grin on her face.

"Welcome to Camden Corners, Helene. I am so happy to meet you."

The two women embraced as if they'd known each other all their lives.

"I can't thank you enough for your hospitality toward James. I'm sure his visit was the last thing you expected. I hope we haven't disrupted your life too awfully much."

"Disrupted my life? Nothing could be further from the truth. Young people fill my parlor with laughter every day of the week. Even my nieces are happy to visit their old Aunt Millie more often these days. James has brought nothing but joy to that old house on the hill. Which reminds me, I won't hear of you staying anywhere but in my home."

Helene appreciated why James was happy in Camden Corners. It was such a picturesque town. People walking down the street shouted hello to them as their carriage rode by on their way to the house on the hill. Helene couldn't believe Neville had grown up in this mansion. She knew he came from wealth but had no idea how rich his family was.

"Don't let this big house fool you Helene, I was in hock up to my cheekbones until Nettie Crowley gave me the idea of opening the antique shop on the first floor. You'll meet Nettie soon. I thought it would be nice if the two of us became acquainted before I shared you with the rest of Camden Corners."

Addie had prepared a nice supper for the guest. She and Leo thought the two women should be left alone to talk and made the excuse they were visiting the Pringles for the evening.

Helene felt she had known Millie all her life.

"Millie, you have made me feel so welcome. I believe you and Neville share the same charming ways."

"Yes, Helene, Neville can be very charming. He takes after our father and grandfather in that way and also in other ways. Being accepted into society was a priority for our grandfather, he married our grandmother for that reason alone. I'm sorry to say, from what I knew of Grandmother Merryweather, she was a rather shallow person herself. She never bothered with Neville and me when we were children and I would guess she was the same with our father. With all his charm, Cyrus Merryweather was a cold man. Neville always craved his approval and even after his death tried to emulate him. It didn't help that he married a superficial woman like Prudence. Neville has mellowed over the years. He hit the roof when Melanie's beau followed her to Camden Corners a year ago. It was only after remembering his lost love that he acquiesced and allowed them to be together. Now he thinks of Michael as his own son."

"I have to admit Millie, I'm a little worried about meeting Neville again. I think a small part of me has never gotten over my feelings for him. I hope it won't be too awkward for you. I know he visits James occasionally."

"I know for a fact that Neville still has feelings for you. He has carried that torch for so long. If only he had the gumption to fight Father so many years ago you two would have been married to each other. I know Prudence doesn't deserve loyalty, but I doubt very much he will ever leave her."

"I don't want him to. I am hoping we can be friends though. For the sake of our son."

"I'd like that very much," came a voice that Helene would never forget. She turned around and looked into the eyes of the man she had loved since she was a young girl.

"Neville, how nice to see you. I didn't expect we would meet again so soon after my arrival."

James spoke up. "You can blame me Mother. I knew you and Neville would both be anxious about seeing each other again so I thought it best we get this first meeting over with."

"You raised a very bright young man here, Helene." said Neville as he embraced her.

The awkwardness disappeared quickly and Helene and Neville were just two old friends enjoying an evening together with family.

Neville left on the morning train with the promise of returning for a longer visit in just a few days. James had to report to his new job but knew his mother was in good hands with Aunt Millie.

Millie didn't waste anytime. She left Addie in charge of the antique shop and had Leo drive them in the carriage to the Emma and Lily's shop to start their tour of the town. After a delightful morning meeting the residents of Camden Corners, Helene was falling in love with the little town. She was already dreading leaving. She and Millie walked by the Camden Corners Library.

"I studied to be a librarian." said Helene. "I stopped working when I married Chester. I've been thinking of seeing if they need any help in our local library."

Millie's ears perked up. "Sarah Harcourt is the head librarian here. She has become a writer and she and Max are expecting a baby. I know she has been talking about giving up her job at the library. Why don't we drop in to see her. Maybe the answer to her dilemma has just come to town."

"Millie, I couldn't possibly move to Camden Corners. My life is in Albany. I have friends there and obligations."

"You have family here. Let's just talk to Sarah. There is no harm in that."

An hour later Helene Robinson was the new head librarian at Camden Corners Lending Library. Helene didn't know what hit her. She didn't know if it was her decision or Millie's. Her new friend could be awfully persuasive.

James took some time off from his new job to help his mother pack up their home in Albany. Along with his other good qualities, Chester had provided well for his family. The house had sold quickly. Helene was sorry to leave the home she had lived in since James was a baby but she had a new life to look forward to. She said a tearful goodbye to her friend Margaret who had promised to come for a visit during the summer.

James held his mother's hand as the train pulled away from the station. With tears in her eyes she bid farewell to Albany and all the memories she would carry with her to her new life in Camden Corners.

At that moment in Greensboro, Neville Merryweather was ducking his head to save himself from the perfume bottle that was headed toward his nose.

"I know you are carrying on with that woman. You spend more time in Camden Corners than you do here. What does that harlot have that I don't have?"

"Now Prudence, why don't you just go back to bed. You know I have been faithful to you since the day we were married. I visit Camden Corners to see my son. I would have him come to visit me here if you would just open your heart to him. He is a very nice young man. I think you would like him."

"Like him? I loathe him. He and his trashy mother. Now get out of here," Prudence shouted as she picked up another bottle off her dresser.

Neville left the room and ran into Melanie.

"Why don't you just leave her Father. You don't deserve to be treated like this. You don't owe Mother anything. I'm sure you could find happiness with Helene and you know how Melinda and I feel about her. Just in the short time we have known her we have grown to love her and you know you still do."

"I won't leave your mother, Melanie. She is my wife and that is all there is to it. Besides, she gave me two beautiful daughters and I will be forever grateful. I'm glad for Helene's friendship but that is all it is or ever will be."

"Never say never Father."

As Neville walked down the hallway, he heard another bottle hit his wife's bedroom door. No Melanie, I never will say never. He thought to himself as he looked at his pocket watch. She should be leaving Albany about now. I'd better hurry if I'm going to catch that train to Camden Corners. His step felt lighter as he walked away from his wife's room.

Made in the USA
Charleston, SC
12 April 2012